D0242668

# The House in the Olive Grove

## EMMA COWELL

avon.

Published by AVON
A division of HarperCollins*Publishers* Ltd
1 London Bridge Street
London SE1 9GF

www.harpercollins.co.uk

HarperCollins*Publishers*
Macken House
39/40 Mayor Street Upper
Dublin 1
D01 C9W8
Ireland

A Paperback Original 2023
1
First published in Great Britain by HarperCollins*Publishers* 2023

Copyright © Emma Cowell 2023

Emma Cowell asserts the moral right to be identified as the author of this work.

A catalogue copy of this book is available from the British Library.

ISBN: 978-0-00-851587-4

This novel is entirely a work of fiction. The names, characters and incidents portrayed in it are the work of the author's imagination. Any resemblance to actual persons, living or dead, events or localities is entirely coincidental.

Typeset in Sabon LT Std by Palimpsest Book Production Limited,
Falkirk, Stirlingshire

Printed and Bound in the UK using 100% Renewable Electricity
at CPI Group (UK) Ltd

All rights reserved. No part of this text may be reproduced, transmitted, down-loaded, decompiled, reverse engineered, or stored in or introduced into any information storage and retrieval system, in any form or by any means, whether electronic or mechanical, without the express written permission of the publishers.

MIX
Paper | Supporting
responsible forestry
FSC
www.fsc.org
FSC™ C007454

This book is produced from independently certified FSC™ paper to ensure responsible forest management.

For more information visit: www.harpercollins.co.uk/green

# Praise for Emma Cowell

'The brilliant Emma Cowell creates worlds of warmth, laughter, healing and hope in her delicious novels. *The House in the Olive Grove* is a glorious story that celebrates the power of love'
**Adriana Trigiani**

'I adored *The House in the Olive Grove*. It is a hymn to friendship and love, and is utterly perfect'
**Liz Fenwick**

'A Grecian journey with a culinary twist, female solidarity, friendship, and romance. What more does one need for a perfect summer read?'
**Nadia Marks**

'Exploring the power of friendship and love through delicious writing and Greek food, *The House in the Olive Grove* is evocative, compelling and moving. A glorious story'
**Kate Frost**

'An enchanting treat of a book.
Sunshine and friendship, broken hearts and secrets. Cowell's exquisite writing is as delicious as the food she describes. Five honey-smothered stars from me'
**Jenni Keer**

'A compelling and tender story, beautifully told by an exciting new voice'
**Santa Montefiore**

'Beautifully written. Emma Cowell writes with warm assurance and brings the Greek setting to life'
**Sue Moorcroft**

'Such an emotive tale of love and loss'
**Rosanna Ley**

'A delicious slice of Greek life. A beautiful love story'
**Jo Thomas**

'A beauty'
**Peter Andre**

'A sweeping epic Grecian romance about grief, healing, and the unpredictable ways they can drive our stories, *One Last Letter From Greece* is a Jojo Moyes-esque saga that I inhaled'
**Laura Jane Williams**

'Breathtaking world-building, stunning imagery and genuine emotion cooked into every page. I adored it'
**Helen Fields**

'[An] unputdownable mystery, wrapped up in a heart-wrenching tale of love and loss . . . A great read for the beach as well as a grey day'
**Tessa Harris**

'When you look up from your train seat/sofa/garden sunbed this summer, you'll be genuinely confused you're not in a taverna knocking back an ouzo'
**Caroline Corcoran**

**Emma Cowell** lives in Cornwall with her husband, Tony, and their fur baby, a Russian Blue called Papoushka Gerald Cowell. A former actress and BBC presenter, Emma is currently Head of Philanthropy for national charity Together for Short Lives. Outside of work, Emma is a keen angler and held a Cornish record for over ten years until her crown was toppled. She is yet to get over it but tries to keep calm by practising yoga. Also a keen linguist, Emma is attempting to learn Greek to maintain her love affair with the country where she has set her first two novels. She is yet to achieve a level of proficiency outside of tavernas and bakeries. *The House in the Olive Grove* is Emma's second novel.

For more info, visit www.emmacowell.com. You can follow Emma on Instagram @emmalloydcowell or Twitter @emmalloydcowell.

By the same author:

*One Last Letter from Greece*

*For my Tony*

# Prologue

## *Maria*

**New York, ten years ago**

When I was a child, everyone thought I was a witch. I stuck out for the wrong reasons and it's why I longed to leave Greece as soon as I could. There, it felt like I faced life alone . . . most of the time. I created a fantasy world of my own making amongst the wild flowers, bees and sun-kissed meadows. Now, as an adult in New York, I've once again fashioned a space that's entirely mine. But it's real, it's my kitchen.

I grab my keys from the hall console, shouting a goodbye to my husband upstairs. There is no reply. Lucky him, languishing in the luxury of sleep.

As I turn to head out, the hallway slowly fills with gossamer strands of silver. They hover and shimmer in the sunlight until they eventually take the shape of *Yiayiá*, my beloved grandmother. Her tiny frame appears in the doorway, blocking my way, but her usual cheerful expression is grave. Her beady eyes fix on to mine, urging me to understand something I can't interpret. Her gaze causes my neck to prickle, followed by a series of jumbled snapshots pinging across the backs of my eyes: a stove, a pan, the acrid stench of sizzling oil.

I frown as the vision evaporates, along with *Yiayiá*.

I've been able to see the dead for as long as I can remember. The gift of premonition – extrasensory perception, or witchcraft, call it what you will. A gentle mist descends with a tingle, running the length of my spine. But today feels different.

As I move through the space where the apparition appeared and out of the front door, I shiver. I should warn my team to be careful in the kitchen today. It seems someone might get hurt.

The sharp autumn chill sucks the breath from my lungs as I jog down Hudson and Bank. Running to work is my meditation. Jumping through the steam floating up from the grates in the sidewalk, I feel invincible. Adrenaline pumps through my veins as the subway rumbles underfoot. I note the change in the light, hinting at a new season. The leaves on the trees shine russet and gold.

I reach Maria's Kitchen, my beautiful restaurant in Soho, and mutter my daily words of thanks as I stare up at the cobalt sign.

As I step into the kitchen, the familiar shivers creep up my back once more, and my *yiayiá*'s voice inside my head echoes a warning to beware. Puzzled, I stare around the empty space. All is as it should be. I shrug and feel a tingle of excitement about the day. I count my blessings. I am lucky. I have love and I am living my dream. Nothing can stop me.

I head over to the stove and reach for a pan.

* * *

## Alessandra

**Rome, one year ago**

Closing the clasp on the finished necklace, Alessandra returns the pliers to her workbench. She holds it up to the light. The green malachite glints, some stones richer in colour than others. It is weighty, pleasing, and she knows she won't sell it. She will wear it later today; it deserves an expedition. The cool rocks take on her body temperature as she fastens it around her neck.

As she walks across the grass from her little workshop into the house, the early morning air sends a chill through her cotton nightgown. Alessandra couldn't sleep last night and chose espresso and creativity instead, labouring over the necklace through the early hours until dawn. She is rarely able to settle when there's a man in her bed who isn't her husband.

Later that morning, as she stands in front of the mirror brushing her long hair, which she dyes a rich golden blonde, she tries to seek out the root of her malaise. Her graceful body retains its tone and dancer's physique, though it has been decades since she last performed. Her limbs still respond to a diligent exercise regime with an athlete's muscle

3

memory, remaining willowy and strong. But something has changed – she doesn't understand her body anymore.

The stranger is gone from her bed, awkward and red-faced. Unable to navigate the yielding of midnight passion to morning mundanity, he disappeared with an embarrassed '*Ciao*' when she returned from her workshop. Perhaps he only just realised she may be in her sixties, the heady haze of last night's jazz club masking age and rational judgement. For him, at least. Alessandra shrugs. She does not care; she didn't even ask his name.

She chooses her outfit carefully – one of her husband Phillipo's favourites. It will complement her new creation hanging around her neck; the opposing purple-coloured dress will encourage the green stones to gleam. Phillipo will be home soon. She smiles at the thought.

The plop of letters on the doormat brings her out of her musings and she glides to collect the post. Her heartbeat quickens as she sees the stamp on the top of an envelope addressed to her. Shredding the seal, she unfolds the paper with trembling hands and devours the words with her eyes. She hugs it to her heart, trying to absorb the meaning, then rereads the text to ensure she didn't dream it. Leaning back on the wall, she knows she must tell Phillipo. They've never hidden anything from each other, no matter how painful the news is to share. This is an unexpected journey neither of them could have predicted they would go on.

Their first unwelcome adventure, and it will change everything.

\*   \*   \*

# Kayla

## London, one week ago

The slick concrete pavement glistens with oil and grime. Umbrellas unfurl, as if the street were a giant flowerbed revealing its multicoloured petals. Shoulders hunched, footsteps splashing in muddy puddles as shadows huddle in doorways.

Kayla sees them driving towards her, discussing the cross words she'd exchanged with them some ten minutes ago. Oblivious to any peril, they near the traffic lights, because why would they think the worst? But why wouldn't they? Kayla's father indicates left. In the distance, she sees the other car making its illegal move. Weaving wildly along the bus lane, spraying water. Frozen to the spot, Kayla is unable to tear her eyes away as a blur of blue hurtles past.

As the car nears the junction, the world suddenly stops, suspended in motion. She can't work out how to prevent what she knows will follow. She is powerless as the scene restarts, wincing as she hears a sickening crunch, the loudest smash that alters everything, metal on metal, screeching and scraping. Cars crumple like screwed-up balls of paper. Kayla's mouth opens to scream, but another voice replaces hers.

'Mummy, Mummy, help me! There's a lion biting my toes!'

Untangling from the bedsheets, Kayla automatically looks at the empty space her husband Daniel used to occupy, before dashing to their daughter's room, blood rushing in her ears as she hears desperate cries.

'Rosie, you scared me,' she gasps. Clutching her chest, she tries to calm down from her own dream. 'There aren't any lions, and I can see all of your toes, little one.'

Wrapping Rosie in her arms, Kayla smooths sticky tendrils of titian curls from her daughter's forehead, willing her own thudding adrenaline to dispel. The reoccurring nightmare for five-year-old Rosie is a new phenomenon, the imaginary toe-gnawing lions making an almost daily appearance, and they were all suffering from sleep deprivation. 'They' in reality meant Kayla. Daniel sleeps like the dead, whether consigned to the spare room or not. Cradling Rosie's little body and rocking her gently, Kayla hopes her daughter returns to a dream-free sleep. She wishes the same for herself, but it rarely happens. The imagined horror of how her parents' deaths played out plagues most of her nights. Bad dreams are something she and her daughter have in common, along with their glossy red hair.

She gently tucks Rosie back in and kisses her brow. Kayla tiptoes out of the room, suppressing the urge to sit with Rosie until daylight.

In the hallway, Daniel's coat is flung over the bannisters. Kayla didn't hear him come in last night, such are his working hours. His all-consuming job, leading a murder squad in West London, is in stark contrast to Kayla's world of celebrity food writing, television shows and glamorous forced jollity. She doesn't know how he compartmentalises the daily horror he deals with, but he rarely opens up about the mental toll it must take. And therein lies their problem – they don't talk anymore, existing like acquaintances or roommates rather than lovers. He speaks to her assistant more than he talks to her.

Kayla picks up his jacket. Being a mother along with her demanding career has tipped life's balance, and the marriage part seems to have suffered, possibly beyond repair. Although Kayla harbours hope they can rebuild what is crumbling.

She takes Daniel's coat downstairs to hang in the nook under the stairs. As she's about to close the cupboard door, a whiff of a perfume she can't place permeates the air. Her heart starts to thud. Grabbing Daniel's jacket from the hanger, she holds it to her nose, trying to absorb the scented clue and attach it to something familiar. But she can't. Frantically emptying his pockets, rooting around for receipts, she finds evidence of a dinner last night. But he told her he was working. She scans the receipt in her trembling hand. The bill is for two from an upmarket restaurant in Mayfair. Overpriced and overly pretentious. He was out to impress.

Walking slowly back up the stairs, she feels tears prick her eyes harder with each step, and her breath is short and sharp. The painful realisation that it may finally be over washes through her body. She trudges across the landing, places her shaking hand on the spare bedroom doorframe and peers in through the gap. Surely he wouldn't start something else before he'd finished their marriage, out of respect for her and Rosie. Kayla watches her sleeping husband and her head feels light with nausea.

Because all Kayla can smell in the spare bedroom is a stranger's perfume.

# Chapter 1

## *Maria*

**Present day, April**

The view still surprises me, even after a decade of being back in Greece. An ever-changing seascape that is comfortingly constant. As my eyes trace the horizon, I absorb the colours and shapes as if they were created solely for me. The gentle lapping of the sea, soft rustling olive trees and a seemingly never-ending cerulean sky. An everyday picture postcard, a fantasy, my home.

Sunshine had woken me at dawn, beams creeping across the floor, gently tumbling onto my bed. The opposite of how my life was in Manhattan, where I would be jarred into waking by the garbage truck squeaking and grinding outside my townhouse at 4 a.m. But in my motherland, it feels like slipping into a forgotten, albeit damaged skin. I know who I am here, not lost in the anonymity of a city.

As I idly pull weeds from my terrace pots, my eye reluctantly leaves the spectacular view. Slate planters overflow with delicate grey and vibrant green succulents; fleshy tentacles reach for sun, leaves like oversized ballerina skirts. Enjoying the peace, I inhale the crisp salty air, allowing molecules of taste and smell to invade my senses, letting them lead the way forward.

The first session of the year in my cooking school looms next week, heralding the start of the marathon towards fall. The nature of relying on tourism, as Petalidi does, is that April will soon become summer, unnoticed, the endless list of chores lengthening hand in hand with spreading sunset shadows. Holidaymakers descend, and you cannot take a breath until the evenings begin to chill and searing heat gives way to a cooler tranquillity.

Time has sped by in my beachside haven since my return to Petalidi ten years ago. It was a surprisingly easy decision to leave America; so many things had come to an end. My marriage dissolved and my career stalled, both casualties of my accident. With no children to depend on me, I could simultaneously close the door on my restaurant and New York, and turn the key.

Standing at my vanity, I tuck a picture of my parents back into the edge of the mirror. It had fallen down. I look at their smiling faces frozen in time. My father's death jolted me into an awareness of my own mortality, and I cling to my memories with him like a comfort blanket. When he died, I mourned the end of my childhood even though I was in my forties, grieving for all that was lost, a painful cluster of goodbyes rushing up to surprise me. I was unprepared for the depth of bereavement and all his passing represented. He was the one who encouraged me to leave Petalidi and follow my dreams to America. Which I did, achieving more than I could've hoped for in the twenty-five years I lived there. I thought I had it all, until I didn't.

Now, at fifty-three, it is finally about me. For the first time in so long, I know I am exactly where I am supposed to be. It's everyone else in this village that's the problem. But this is where I live. I won't be driven away from my birthplace for being different. It was always the case even when I was a child and, I suspect, always will be.

As I pull my long, sun-kissed brown hair into a ponytail, the sight of my exposed neck reminds me of my survival. The indelible blemish is an everlasting souvenir of that terrible day. It marks me out. I could have had a crisis, retreated into my broken shell, consumed with self-loathing for my lost beauty. My appearance became so offensive to my ex-husband that he rejected me. Instead, I am trying to embrace ageing with all its new jagged lines. I am unique. The shape of my scar resembles a clumsy map of the Americas. My very own atlas. Blotches that plot Alaska down through Brazil. I am distorted, permanently scarred, but I am me. Changed, but perhaps a better version of myself – despite appearances.

In my office downstairs, I double-check the dietary requirements for my inbound cooking guests: Kayla Moss, the celebrity food writer and television personality, and Alessandra Rossi, a jewellery maker from Rome. Both are arriving during the build-up to Easter, the most magical time in Greece. I know of Kayla from the gossip magazines and I stream her TV shows. A good write-up from her

11

could substantially boost business. I'm intrigued to see what she's like. Having a celebrity in Petalidi will cause a stir when word gets out, which inevitably it will. Occasionally, life in a tiny place can become insular, like living in a goldfish bowl. At least Kayla will give the busybodies someone else to pick apart, instead of me. A few famous faces have come to my cooking school – minor royals, actors and influencers who helped me put our little village on the map, in turn leading people to flock to find healing through cooking with me.

Beside my office papers are cards and notes from former students thanking me for how their life has changed after coming to Petalidi. I permit myself a smile. Making such a difference to others is the most rewarding part of my cooking school. Some when they arrive are lost, at a crossroads, floundering in aimless indecision; others are escaping something or someone, seeking perspective from this magical corner of Greece. Nobody, it seems, comes only to cook. Creating my food somehow inspires an answer to their predicaments, to emerge from their deepest subconscious. Just as a *Saint Fanourios* cake rises in the oven as it bakes.

'*Kaliméra, Mamá!*' I say as I knock on the door to my mother's annexe with coffee. My mom, Eleni, lives in a self-contained 'wing', separate to the main house, enough to give her independence and me an attempt at my own space.

'*Kaliméra, ángelé mou,*' she replies, referring to me as her angel, even though I am aware she thinks the devil has branded me. An opinion held by most who live here. Occasionally I catch *Mamá* making the sign of the cross whilst eyeing my scarred neck. A punishment she believes is mine for 'messing with spirits' – my childhood gift of foresight, which has now deserted me. My husband leaving me somehow put paid to that and my abilities all but evaporated. Since I was a child, I could see those who had died but hadn't yet moved to the next realm as clearly as I could see the living, which sent a wave of horror around Petalidi. I couldn't understand why it seemed to terrify others. The spirits meant no harm; they simply wished to watch over their loved ones until it was time for them to rest. But now, that part of my gift has gone – an additional reminder of what went wrong in New York.

Growing up, I was the odd one out. I couldn't wait to leave as soon as I was of age, and the irony is, I couldn't wait to come back when the moment presented itself. I had changed, but sadly the attitudes of those who still live in Petalidi had not. In the village they call me '*Mélissa*', as in 'honeybee'. It is not meant to be a kind nickname, but a mockery of my passion. The bees I keep are my most trusted companions. *They* don't judge or discriminate.

As I place a circle of freshly made baklava on my mother's coffee table, I recall the prayer I'd muttered while making the delicate filo pastry, dousing it with honey from my hives: *'Please let my mother support my choices and let me live my life.'*

Whether a plea to God or to my dead father, I hope someone hears me.

My mother's lap is laden with greenery as she makes decorations for the week-long Greek Orthodox Easter celebrations. Entwining flowers of various colours and sizes, along with fragrant herbs, nettles and wild garlic to ward off evil spirits. Figs and pomegranates will be woven into each display, and she will say, as she does each year, '*for fertility and prosperity*,' eyeing my stomach with sadness.

I open the patio doors to let in the warm spring air. I've come to terms with my barren status; my mother mourns it on my behalf.

'You know, you let life slip through your fingers, Maria. You will be left a spinster,' my *mamá* warns, wagging a crooked finger. 'And why you cannot work in the tavernas here, I do not understand. Maria, you are more American than Greek making all this work, but for what? If you were married, you could keep the house for your husband, not only for yourself and for me.'

I sigh as my mother hits her daily stride.

'And when will a wedding come again, *ángelé mou*? I wait and I wait and yet there is no sign of this day. In your position you cannot be choosy, especially since . . .' Her flinty eyes look up from the wreath on her lap and scantly trace my neck, Maine through Boston.

This Orthodox urge to marry everyone off, place folks in a neatly filed box of wed, widowed or without, exhausts me. It's like going to war with *Mamá* each day about something. Whether it's a sauce she could've made better than me, fruitless mourning over her lack of grand-children or my continued divorced single status, there is always a thing. I long for the day of acceptance from her, but it's unlikely to come. But I know she loves me . . . in her own way.

I bend and kiss my mother's cheek and in return receive three *ftou-ftou-ftous* in my hair to ward off the evil ghouls

*Mamá* believes are present, threatening and lurking. I wouldn't know, being unable to see spirits of any kind now. The sunlight kisses the dusty white-grey of my mother's hair, which contrasts with her sombre widow's weeds of everlasting mourning. I wonder if the cycle of grief is ever completed, before another wave of sadness crashes in, like the sea inevitably thunders onto the shore. I glance to the shrine on the sideboard. Candles flicker beside photographs of my dead father. The reminder of lost love hangs in the air like a ghostly shadow.

Stepping outside into the hot sunshine, I am unable to resist the magnetic draw of the water as I consider my mother's pressing about marriage. Deep in thought, I walk through the olive grove and orchard, mentally retracing my choices that led me to this moment in my life. I don't need a man to validate my existence. If someone came along, perhaps I could let them into my heart, to share in my success . . . Did I need love? No. Did I want it? *That* was different. Although I gave up on love long ago, how I wish to feel another's touch, for fingers to trace my flawed skin from my jaw downwards, lingering tantalisingly in the ocean, yearning for them to travel to Antarctica.

The fragrant lemons on my trees are ripe and I pick some, breathing in their pungent scent. My skin prickles with excitement and as a light gust of wind engulfs me, the sound from my bees becomes louder. I know exactly what to do with the lemons: grate the zest into cookies I will bake later this morning. Whenever I hold an ingredient, be it fruit or vegetable, fish or fowl, they give me ideas, as if I'm being told how to use them. Or, upon meeting someone, I know the precise flavours they will respond to.

It is how my gift now manifests. I no longer see the future or the dead, as if my husband leaving me pulled away my original ability and left me with only this skill. As my heart drained of love, so – in turn – the spirits left me.

But now, I find I can heal with my food, somehow mend hurt and repair broken emotions, instinctively identifying the flavour to unlock another's heart. Pupils come to Petalidi to cook, but underneath, they're searching for enlightenment, closure or resolution. Through my food, they uncover what they were looking for. It is beautiful, magical and it is mine.

I walk across the lawn to harvest a little honey from my bees, lifting two empty jars from my apron pockets. These insects are my passion, comfortingly humming as they tirelessly work to make golden nectar, the precious currency of the gods. I watch as the liquid oozes into the containers from the tap mechanism on one of the hives, each drop filled with sweet, sticky goodness, infused with a unique flavour: thyme, oregano and lavender. Nature's pristine witchcraft at work.

I start as I see a pile of stones in the shape of a cross. This is today's warning sign from someone in the village meant to scare me. Sometimes they're made from twigs and fabric, sea glass or string, occasionally depicting the *mati* – the evil eye. But it is not meant for protection. It is a signal that I am being watched, that I am not wanted. They hide in anonymity and pick on me because I am unusual. This started several weeks ago, and I admit I am afraid. I kick the rocks apart and scoop them up, taking them back to the beach below my garden, my pulse increasing at the idea of being targeted in this way.

Out at sea, the Mani headland marks the perimeter of the bay. Stone towers puncture the landscape, a reminder of feuding neighbours in days gone by, competitively building higher and higher to gain the upper hand. The echo of brutal moments from history nestles within the landscape, the cruelty of mankind charges the air with a fierce purpose, and still it resonates today. Someone in this village wishes me ill.

My phone sounds. It's a message from 'them', my cowardly tormentor, as if I've been seen dismantling the pebble crucifix:

> **You don't belong here. You are from the devil. Leave, or else.**

I sigh in despair and, against my will, I feel my legs tremble. I wish I knew who hated me enough to torture me this way, but there are several candidates. The messages began with occasional warnings to accompany the curious creations beside my beehives, but these past weeks, the piles outside the hives appear with greater frequency. I thought I'd endured enough pain, which in turn led me back home to Greece to create my cooking school dream. But it seems there is yet more for me to learn.

And yet, the smallest corner of my soul wishes I could understand why, so late in my life, I must be faced with such additional torment.

*And the honeybee navigates its own pathway, visiting each hedgerow before alighting upon its chosen subject. Flora and fauna, fragrant herbs to fuel and feed its tireless task. Zooming along the shoreline in search of the sweetest treat, flying dangerously close to the water, it works in tandem with the wind, undeterred as it buzzes along, humming a song in a tribute to the elements. It notices everything and everyone. Nobody escapes its five eyes.*

# Chapter 2

## Maria

Next morning, I walk along the promenade below my garden that runs the length of the stony beach, to the centre of the village. The scent of my freshly baked lemon cookies precedes me as the wind gusts at my hair and dress from behind. The mountains across the bay shimmer with hovering heat, trapped in limbo, the humidity intensifying as the day unfolds.

I'm headed for the Easter committee meeting, where roles will be assigned for the feasting weekend. I know the biscuits I'm carrying will inspire disquiet amongst the more orthodox villagers who are still taking part in the Lenten restrictions, but my very presence causes feathers to be ruffled anyway, so I may as well cook up extra consternation.

'*Yiá sas*, Father Kyriakidis,' I say, greeting the aged village priest who has known me all my life. He baptised me and doesn't show visible signs of regret in admitting me to his flock. So far.

The church of *Agios Nikolaos* sparkles in the sunshine. The tall white bell tower glints, making its terracotta roofs gleam the deepest orange. The large green surrounding the church is busy with locals preparing for the festivities at the end of the week, attaching Greek flags to the columns, playfully winding bunting around tree trunks.

'Ah, *yiá sou*, Maria, hello. It is only Easter and yet it is like the summer has arrived.'

'I know, this heat is crazy. Thank God for air conditioning!'

The priest smiles wryly at me. 'I thank God for many things, but air conditioning hasn't been in my prayers today.'

He teases me with a good nature, one of the handful of people in this place who accept me. You'd think if the priest can talk to me without sprouting horns and cloven hooves it would be acceptable for the rest to ease their superstitions.

'Well, if you get a moment, send one upstairs from me to say thanks! The air con is saving me. And you know I need to be saved,' I say as I look around the green and note the knowing glances from the elderly women who think I'm a witch. 'Anyhow, I've brought cookies to sweeten up the misery-makers. They do have dairy in them, though I know it's Lent. Am I going straight to hell?'

'Maria, you are deliberately provocative, almost as if you wish to be singled out.' Father Kyriakidis' white beard twitches in amusement as we find solace in the shade beneath the church columns.

'You see, that's where you're wrong, Father. I know some will disapprove, but I guarantee not everyone is as devout as they say. They're not refraining during Lent as they claim. I've smelt the char of meat on the evening wind. You believe they're just eating shrimp *saganaki* and octopus as Lent dictates? I don't think so!'

'Maria, in all the years I've known you, you've challenged the boundaries of belief, in what you say you see and what you know. I do not judge or disbelieve you, but others . . . Why do you not make your life easier?'

I consider his suggestion. Life is *not* easy; I learnt the hard way. He's one of the few people who understood I could see spirits when I was little. He let me tell my stories and received them good-naturedly, nodding at my accounts of visitations. I was able to inexplicably name and physically describe dead relatives from decades before. Many put it down to the fact that I spent so much time in the churchyard, suggesting I'd memorised family trees and could recite them at will. Others accused me of being a child gossip, eavesdropping and gathering information wherever I went.

It's been so long since I last saw an apparition. I miss seeing the wispy figures. It always struck me as strange that my ability disappeared hand in hand with my husband's desertion, as my heart emptied of love. But now, my bees and the sensual delight of my homeland give me messages of inspiration, the intuitive gift of flavour remains, and I feel no reason to prove or disprove myself any longer, nor to answer to anybody. They don't know my visions are gone, but it wouldn't alter their stance. I am tarnished in every sense, enough for someone to take

23

the trouble of leaving a warning outside my beehives each day. Today's was an evil eye made of leaves and twigs followed by a message on my phone that simply read:

Time to go, Maria.
Nobody wants you here.

I don't report it; there seems no point. And what could the police do? It would only make additional trouble and risk ostracising myself further from the community by drawing more attention my way. But I am frightened, I concede. It highlights how alone I am. Even my former childhood best friend shuns me. Athena and I were inseparable until she discovered she was the pretty popular girl, the one everyone wanted to be, who had unwittingly befriended the local freak. She suddenly stopped speaking to me when we were eleven and I became even more of a social outcast. Her ex-husband Leonidas, also one of our peers who I used to be close with, apparently returned to the village a month or so ago, according to my mother. I haven't seen him for decades, not since . . . I cringe at the memory.

We all had a crush on Leonidas at school, and I used to sign my name with his surname, Balafoutis, trying it out for fun. He was dashingly handsome, so tall and strong for his age, managing to skip the chubby phase most of us grappled with. I remember marvelling at his skin tone – he would tan nut-brown from one glimpse of the sun – and his natural charisma was compelling. I tried repeatedly to recreate his perfect tan in the identical shade of biscuit but was unable to capture it. We'd exchange glances across our textbooks, but I couldn't find the courage to speak to him in public. I assumed he stayed away because he didn't want to risk social ruin. But away from the cool kids' eyes, we would sit together after school in my father's fields amongst the wild flowers and goats; we were inseparable.

We lived in our own secret bubble. His parents' house was just along the promenade from mine when we were growing up. He was beside me when I fell in love with bees. We'd watch them for hours in the meadow as they suckled on pollen, making up names for them, inventing stories and giggling with childhood innocence. I recall telling him I would keep bees one day. I saw the vision then as clearly as if I were watching a film. He was fascinated by the idea at the time and bought me a book about apiary – the art of beekeeping – for my birthday. I wonder if he even remembers. Unlikely. His memories of me will be tainted by what happened between us. I haven't returned to that beach since. There are too many ghosts walking the sand – emotional ones, that is.

Leonidas is bound to have heard the cruel jibes about me in the village, since he returned, so he must know I finally have the insects we talked about as children, though I suspect I do not matter to him anymore. Apart from Father Kyriakidis, he was the only other person who didn't make me feel crazy and believed my visions. But the prettiest girl, Athena, captured his heart in the end, until they divorced a few years ago. They have a fourteen-year-old daughter, Zoe, who regards me with the same suspicion her mother does. It's a shame; it pinches both their pretty faces.

I return to the present and become aware of Father Kyriakidis looking at me, waiting for a response.

25

'Father, I am here to help and take part in our village celebration. My life is easy, and it is full. I can't help what others may think or say. Now, are you sure you don't want a cookie? I know they're your favourite . . .'

He laughs, shaking his head as he opens the door to the church. The heady scent of incense overpowers the aroma of my home baking.

Maybe I should take the hint from God: me and my biscuits aren't welcome in church today.

*　*　*

After all the Easter jobs have a name against them, the meeting is adjourned. I can feel eyes on my back as I say goodbye. My politeness is challenged by their small-minded rudeness. The usual suspects, led by Athena, making ungodly remarks in the name of religion at me. They aren't subtle in their digs – the level is more applicable to kindergarten than to grown women – but I endeavour to take the high road and not rise to it. My task in the festivities is to bake the traditional Easter cookies, as always, and I am damn sure (forgive me, Father) that they will be the best biscuits anyone has ever had.

As I walk back along the seafront, I resolve to never let those bullies defeat me, to only pity them. They haven't evolved since childhood, living in their small world, treating me like an outsider in a place that's my home. I was already tarnished with the devil's mark in their eyes long before my accident; the little atlas on my neck only confirms their fears about me. I got used to my scar, so why can't they? They, like my mother, attach a dark meaning to my wound, suspecting it's a curse for my 'blasphemous' visions. They're afraid to eat what I cook, but cannot resist, probably paying penance with emotional flagellation for succumbing to temptation. Instead, I kill them with kindness and food.

I tend to my bees as I do each day at sunset. Their sound soothes me, transports me into their busy little world. My platter of cookies is beside me on the lawn. Most have been eaten, and I was responsible for two of the casualties. The others were snaffled unseen from the plate, much to my amusement.

I gently open the first hive and see the queen has laid eggs where she should, away from the honeycomb. They know me and continue their work as I carefully scrape away cobwebs. The honey stores are sufficient for the bees to take nourishment and for me to use in my cooking. Springtime is busiest for my hives. I must ensure they're in good repair, but this early heatwave means the provision of shade is imperative. The overhang on one of the structures has cracked, warped by the winter storms, and it's buckled in this heat. I'll visit the hardware store for new wood in the morning. The bees will roast alive if this weather continues. It would ruin years of nurture if I lost any of these nests. Already one is without a queen and the brutal selection process is underway. I will not disturb that hive further until order is re-established.

*Sweet honeybees, gather your spirit to fly,*
*I am blessed to assist you and grateful am I,*
*For the harvest of honey, sweet as can be,*
*And all I do ask is you stay with me.*

I recite my made-up childhood poem like an incantation as I sweep away the bodies of dead woodlice, maintaining a clean working environment, just as I would have scrubbed down my kitchen after a busy dinner service. It seems to bring a calm to the hive. There is no need to use smoke to sedate the bees; they recognise my voice as I talk to them every day. My confidantes and winged companions.

I consider my cooking pupils, Kayla and Alessandra, and tell the bees about them. I close my eyes and feel the shivers run up my spine as I see Kayla's image in my mind, marrying her with vanilla; followed by Alessandra's, and I am given cinnamon. I smile in confirmation of my flavour choices and nod at my bees. These flavours will inform the week's menu for my students.

The scent from my biscuits suddenly wafts over my face. The hum from my hive grows and an invisible finger traces my neck. The zingy lemon zest mixes in the air with sweetness of honeycomb. The tang of sour dairy pricks at my tongue and a forgotten memory rises as ingredients assemble into a logical order. My father drifts across my mind, passing me a spoon at the breakfast table, urging me to taste yoghurt he'd made from his goat's milk, drizzling golden honey over the pillowy white contents of a bowl.

I immediately know what I should bake for my Easter Sunday offering. It won't only be the biscuits I bring. To break the Lenten fast at the feast on the big day, my contribution will be extra special.

The evening church bells chime, sending cats fleeing amongst the olive trees as the recipe slowly emerges, just as an alchemist concocts a potion. A lemon-honey cake, made with yoghurt, topped with a citrus syrup and flaked almonds. I sit back on my heels, silently thanking the wind and my bees. I begin to imagine the scent and my taste buds tickle, pre-empting their response. It will be a cake like no other.

# Chapter 3

## *Kayla*

Leaving England in the dead of night has its advantages. Kayla is able to sneak out of the bedroom to lovingly kiss Rosie goodbye, careful not to disturb her and to avoid Daniel. She lands in Greece at lunchtime.

Petalidi is a collision of breathtaking colours, a glittering turquoise sea that meets eternal powder-blue sky, and the warm air smells like it is spiced. Kayla is early for check-in at Maria's Kitchen, so decides to kill time by seeking out local delicacies in the name of research. Anything to stop her mind replaying the terrible argument she'd had with Daniel yesterday when she accused him of having an affair. But against her own wishes, she relives it again.

Yesterday, she had cooked lunch for their ghastly neighbours, Eve and Stephen Houseby. Kayla had watched Daniel as he'd fiddled with his phone during their meal, obsessing about who he was messaging, all whilst she played the perfect hostess and fended off oily Stephen Houseby's leering looks. The Housebys had become a constant pest in her life, and she regretted ever inviting them into her world. But she didn't wish to be seen as the aloof celebrity living next door. So, when they moved in, she had extended her hospitality by arranging playdates with Rosie and their daughter, Milan, who became forced arranged friends by nature of their age. It was a companionship encouraged enthusiastically by Eve Houseby, who seemed desperate to capture the tiniest piece of Kayla's stardust by association.

After lunch, when their neighbours had returned to their home, Kayla put Rosie to bed, and then confronted Daniel.

'Is there something you want to tell me, Danny?' she'd asked, knowing there would be no going back from this moment, depending on his response. She would be unable to trust him again, and their marriage would finally be finished.

'Umm . . . no. We're fine, aren't we?' he'd replied, putting his phone under a cushion on the sofa beside him, fuelling Kayla's bubbling anger. 'You're just tense 'cause you're going to Greece tomorrow.'

'I know what's been going on. You might think I'm too busy to notice what's happening underneath my nose, but I'm not, and I have. All I need is for you to tell me it's over – with us or with her.'

She had sat down to face him and watched as her husband mentally scrolled through his two options: lie or tell a truth she wasn't sure she had wanted to hear. The silence had been like a slow death. Any sort of noise would be preferable to the gaping space in the air.

'I've . . . I've found things difficult for a while with us. With you, and dealing with your ups and downs . . .'

'That's not what I asked, is it? I didn't ask for a list of reasons not to be with me; I want to know if you're leaving us,' Kayla had hissed, trying to keep her voice down, not wishing to wake Rosie. 'How long's it been going on? Do I know her?'

'I don't know what to say, Kay. I'm sorry.' He'd run his hand through his thick hair. 'A few months . . . maybe six. No, you don't know her.'

It had been like taking a bullet to the gut. Kayla hadn't expected him to reveal his affair so easily. In fact, she'd hoped he'd deny it, putting it down to a paranoid delusion on her part. Living in a fantasy was easier than reality – it was what she did for work, after all. Creating a glossy celebrity façade to mask the real her and hide her terrible secret.

'How could you do this to us? *How could you?* And you sit here watching me make lunch for our dreadful neighbours, messaging your bit on the side, while I play happy families. You've made an idiot out of me and the life *I've* created for us. I will not play second fiddle in my marriage.'

'Oh, of course, it's all about *you*, isn't it? Your books, your TV shows and the next series of wretched *Home-Grown Chef*. Do you know what I talk about every day? You! All I do is answer questions about my famous wife. I even have to book in our conversations via a bloody assistant! And when I get home, you don't ask about my day and, what's worse, you don't care. It is exhausting. I am so tired . . . tired of you . . . of it all.'

'Oh, but you accept the paycheque I work so hard for. *That's* good enough for you but apparently, *I'm* not. You can't have it all, Danny.'

That was when Kayla had begun to cry, as she felt the last bastions of all that kept her grounded and secure start to crumble. She had run to the bathroom to be sick, sitting on the cool marble floor, sobbing for all that was lost. The dream family she'd longed for was fading away, the one she'd never got to have when she was younger, because of her parents' deaths. She'd wanted to make it perfect for Rosie, to provide the backdrop for an idyllic childhood. But she'd failed. *Daniel* had failed them both.

Kayla shudders now. The memories are becoming too much, and back in her Greek present she forces them away. She looks around the simple stone grill house on the beach, more like someone's home than a restaurant. The hypnotic waves gently splash on the large stones, lulling her into relaxation as she tries to shake off thoughts of her deceitful husband. She also couldn't ignore the overwhelming feeling she should be at home with her child. Rosie was what kept her going, motivated her to work so hard. Had her drive and ambition pushed Daniel into another woman's bed? Her career and food are either her nemesis or the perfect distraction, and she is yet to decide which category this work assignment falls into.

She inhales as much of the salty sea air as she can into her lungs, quelling the beginnings of tears as an image of Daniel in the arms of a faceless woman pops into her mind. A handsome waiter interrupts her masochistic meditation with her lunch order, placing several plates down with a smiling flourish. He locks eyes with her, giving

Kayla an unexpected flutter in her heart. She tucks her red hair behind one ear, and pulls her cream cashmere cardigan tighter around her, embarrassed by her physical reaction to him. She hasn't felt anything resembling an attraction to anyone since she first met Daniel, and immediately she feels guilty.

'*Kalí órexi!*' he says and leaves her to it, wishing her 'bon appétit' in Greek. She watches him leave, admiring his swagger, his complete awareness of how attractive he is. How glorious it must be, sighs Kayla to herself, to be so comfortable in your skin. Tearing her gaze away from him, Kayla's jaw drops at the amount of food. The Greek salad, *tzatziki* and sardines are enough to feed four, if not six. She feels hot and discards her woollen layer, aware the waiter is watching her. She thought she'd ordered light, but one thing is becoming clear: this will be a foodie adventure like no other.

\* \* \*

Wheeling her suitcase along the promenade, Kayla follows the sign for the famed Maria's Kitchen. After only ten minutes in the afternoon heat, her shoulders are tingling with sunburn and she is dripping with sweat. She didn't expect it to be this hot. Kayla sees a petite brunette with a basket over her arm, picking fruit from a tree. A series of small wooden structures sit on the lawn, and bees buzz around the little roofs. The woman turns, smiling, and gives a warm welcome.

'*Yiá sou!* Hi, Kayla, right? I'm Maria. *Kalós irthes*, welcome to my home.'

Her accent is American, but her skin and features are unmistakably native, thinks Kayla as she takes in her host's appearance: shining brown hair streaked with sunshine highlights and skin the colour of dark golden shortbread. Apart from a lengthy burnt trail up her neck, which almost glows pink. Kayla averts her eyes and plasters on an extra-wide smile to compensate for having noticed. It is rude to stare at another's afflictions.

'So lovely to meet you, Maria,' she says as she drops her bag to the ground and releases her suitcase handle. 'Wow, your house is amazing!'

Maria laughs and joins Kayla admiring the expanse of water.

'Thank you. The view never gets old,' replies Maria, beaming with a genuine pride. 'Let's get you out of this heat before you broil to a crisp.'

She guides Kayla towards the house, which has a large overhang that affords much-needed shade. Gnarly vines twist their way around the pergola. Maria pours from a large jug that clunks with ice cubes as mint and cucumber cascade into the glass.

'Home-made lemonade – the lemons are straight from my trees. Enjoy! *Yiá mas!*'

They cheers, chinking glasses, and Kayla feels her shoulders drop a little from their default tense position. There's something about the colours in the landscape and an almost magical energy in the air that makes her want to relax, which in turn makes her anxious because it feels so alien. She sighs heavily inside, recognising her patterns and triggers, trying to fight her way through her tedious vicious mental circle.

'So, I guess you took the early flight. It's a killer, right?' says Maria. 'And we're having this crazy heatwave. It's never this hot through spring until at least May or June. You won't need that cardigan, believe me. Anyway, please use this place as your own; come and go as you want. We start cooking tomorrow morning, so you have today to enjoy Petalidi.'

'I will, thank you,' Kayla replies after a refreshing gulp of sweet yet bitter lemonade. 'I have some writing to do for my articles, but maybe I'll explore later.'

'Let me show you your digs,' Maria says, taking Kayla's suitcase handle and gesturing that she should follow with her other bag. 'This all used to be my father's farm, and when my folks got too old to maintain it and Dad got sick, I moved from the States to look after them. I was already separated from my husband, so it worked out. I'm a good Greek girl at heart after all – apart from my divorce. It's just Mom and me now. She lives in the annexe, but no doubt you'll meet her. She'll make herself known – you can be sure. These outbuildings used to house my late father's goats and now they're my teaching kitchen and dining room.'

Maria chatters unfiltered and unprompted as they walk through the extensive plot. A courtyard separates the cooking school from Maria's main house, which is made of simple stone. Further up the path through regimented lines of olive trees is an orchard and well-stocked vegetable and herb garden. Kayla catches the scent of jasmine on the wind, sweet dill and pungent Greek basil. Through the rustling foliage, she sees four simple villas. It feels to her like a miniature village in its own right.

'Did you renovate all this?' Kayla asks, impressed at the scale of the operation.

'I did. It was a labour of love – literally.'

Kayla watches Maria look around at the buildings. Her scarred neck gleams in the sunshine, and Kayla feels impolite to have noticed it again. It is beautiful in its imperfection. Her journalist instinct is itching to bombard her with questions, but that would be unforgivably rude.

Maria unlocks one of the front doors and gestures for Kayla to lead the way in.

'So, this is you. Please let me know if there is anything you need. You can join me for drinks at sunset if you like on the patio. Also, another pupil, Alessandra, is arriving today from Rome. You can meet her too. It'll be just the three of us – a great number.'

She turns and leaves, and Kayla steps into the cool air conditioning of her villa. The house is beautifully decorated, the perfect balance between modern, clean lines and traditional touches. The wooden beams and exposed brick walls remind Kayla of a Cotswolds coach house. It feels like the start of a journey that is all hers, and Kayla feels a frisson of excitement.

She'd been looking forward to meeting Maria, having already known of her even before she'd started her research for her articles on Greek cuisine. Maria is a legend in foodie circles, a leader in her field who'd dominated the New York gastronomy scene, winning every accolade. But she'd ditched it all to build a cooking school with a reputation for transforming people's lives. Hailed as some kind of food guru, dispensing wisdom and deliciousness from this tiny village in Greece. Kayla feels like she's found her way here at exactly the right time in her life, although the cynic in her knows her problems can't be whisked away with a forkful of moussaka.

She unpacks her laptop and journal on the desk beside the door and sits to make a note of everything she's eaten today. She looks around her little Greek villa and feels the basic simplicity of it like a warm embrace. Her eyes alight on the corner kitchen nestled across the room. A contrast to her oversized stainless steel 'chef's kitchen' at home. She imagines herself standing at that stove, the setting for countless photoshoots over the years, one of which is the cover of her latest book exploring the joys and provenance of seasonal eating.

Writing is how Kayla's celebrity had started. Her weekly national newspaper column became several publishing deals, followed by stints as a judge on a prime-time cooking show and then more books, all bestsellers. Kayla snorts at the irony as she pictures her smiling face beaming outwards on the front cover of her new cookbook, conveying the approachable yet aspirational perfection of her domestic life. Which is now a lie. Daniel has seen to that. But she'd already been lying about something else for years. The only difference was, nobody had found out. Yet.

She unpacks and changes into comfy clothes, or 'sloppy joes' as Rosie calls them. It always made Kayla smile, as Rosie has a slight lisp. It makes Kayla love her even more. She steps outside into the searing heat, enjoying the sudden surge of independence in her chest as she considers her place in the world.

If Daniel is willing to throw away their marriage, then there's little she can do to change that. It's a confusing notion, as ordinarily she would have panicked, cancelled her trip and grilled him for more answers, torturing herself in the process. Perhaps she's in denial or in shock . . . or both. Instead, as she sips at her tangy lemonade, she notices a weight gradually lifting from her heart. Like reaching a decision she is reluctant to make. Tasting the sour lemons, mint leaf and a rush of mild sweetness at the back of her tongue, it leaves her feeling anonymous, unjudged, like she can simply be, existing quietly in Petalidi with no drama.

It is strange. As if she's meeting herself for the first time.

# Chapter 4

## *Maria*

Whichever spirits sent my mother out to dinner tonight, leaving me in peace to welcome my guests, has my heart-felt gratitude. I sink into a chair at the patio table and say a silent thank you.

The wind has dropped away and silence descends as the sun tinges the mirror-flat sea bubble-gum pink. The peace is all-encompassing; even my bees embody the calm. Only the odd one darts from the hive, attracted by the earthy air flavoured with sun-scorched oregano. It will return with droplets of water to ensure the inside of their home is kept cool.

'Brilliant little bees,' I say out loud to them.

My phone shatters the quiet with a shrill bleep. I know what it'll be before I unlock the screen. I have my anonymous tormentor saved under the name 'COWARD' in my contacts. It's the moniker they deserve, hiding behind bullying namelessness, but I still feel a lurch of apprehension when I tap to open the message.

> **You should be more careful.**
> **I see everything.**

I instinctively look around me, then put my phone on the terrace table, trying to pay little heed to the threat even as I feel my pulse quicken. I stand from my chair as the person who I assume to be Alessandra Rossi, my other pupil, wafts up the pathway, moving with a dancer's grace and poise. She greets me with two kisses and a loud, '*Ciao!*'

Alessandra is incredibly tall, so much so that I feel miniature in comparison. She is dressed in denim dungarees and her vest top underneath displays tanned arms that boast spectacular muscle tone for someone who is perhaps sixty. I notice the chunky green stone necklace around her smooth neck. The largest rock hangs from the chain to the top of her singlet amongst her blonde wavy hair. It is strikingly beautiful and she catches my admiring gaze.

'It is the most wonderful stone, *sì*? I made this myself but it's very special. It absorbs the heat of the body. Feel.'

Without warning, she grabs my hand and presses it to her chest. The necklace is hot, as if it possessed an invisible inductor. The sudden intimacy of touching a stranger's sternum is uncomfortably surprising.

'It's beautiful,' I say retrieving my hand. 'Do you have more of your jewellery with you?' I start walking to the guest houses and Alessandra follows.

'Of course! And I look forward to *your* work,' she says.

'I feel your energy already. I have a sense for people's auras, you know. I met this man once in Marrakesh who asked me to feel his energy core. And he put my finger into his belly button in the middle of the souk! Quite remarkable, the pulsing from his body . . . wonderful!'

The idea of probing someone's body parts in a street in Morocco is bizarre and makes me want to giggle out loud. Alessandra's expansive gestures continue to punctuate our walk. I already feel an intriguing connection to her infectious energy, wondering what she'll say next. She pauses to remark on shrubs, trees and the stunning vista, changing her rucksack to her other shoulder. It rattles like a maraca as she slings it around.

'I'll leave you to get settled,' I say. 'If you want, come to the main house for a glass of wine. The sunset is beautiful and it's only just getting started. There's another guest, Kayla, who arrived earlier, and I can recommend places for dinner in the village if you want.'

I point along the shore, and Petalidi ripples in the oppressive heat haze.

'*Perfetto!*' exclaims Alessandra. '*Grazie*, Maria. I will see you for drinks soon. *Ciao!*'

She breezes away and I can't help but smile. So many fascinating people have landed at Maria's Kitchen over the years, and already, Alessandra is up there with the best of them. Aside from cooking, I take joy in hearing so many varied stories, versions of love and life experiences over the food we create together, like a ritual or communion of sorts. The beginning of the course is as thrilling as the actual act of cooking. It's astonishing how social barriers quickly disperse when you share the preparation of food.

As if with each paper-thin wispy sheet of pastry, a layer of inhibition falls away.

Although, I think, as I hear Alessandra's tuneless singing through the windows as she unpacks, I'm not sure how much reserve she has to begin with. She appears to have a considerable head start compared to most.

\* \* \*

The sun has passed over the expanse of Petalidi bay, pausing at the far end of the cove. I introduce my guests and Alessandra immediately grabs Kayla, enthusiastically kissing her with the unabashed intimacy of a Mediterranean. I feel a moment of concern for the welfare of Kayla's tummy button, but so far, Kayla seems intrigued to greet this bundle of energy from Rome.

'*Yiá mas!*' We clink wine glasses with a Greek cheers and pick at the mezze I've made to welcome them.

'So, when do we cook?' asks Alessandra in her almost perfect English.

'We'll gather at ten tomorrow, after your breakfast. This coming weekend is Greek Easter and there's an open invitation for you both to join in with the festivities. It's like nothing you'll have ever seen. I'll teach you traditional dishes for the celebrations, for us to eat of course, but also to prepare for the village feast. Whether you're religious or not, Easter here is a unique experience.' I take a piece of home-made sourdough, spread with *fava* – a creamy yellow split bean puree dip – topped with ruby-red diced onions and garnished with slices of tangy capers.

'I look forward to this very much! And Kayla, where is it you are from?' asks Alessandra.

'From London, just south of it. I do have a bit of an accent.' Kayla laughs, biting her nail as a flush creeps across her cheek, emphasised by the golden light. I take in her appearance. It's impossible not to admire Kayla's fragile beauty. She's much thinner in real life than on screen, with a beautiful smattering of freckles over the bridge of her nose and high cheekbones. Her Celtic colouring is as striking as it appears in magazines and Kayla's naturally bright red hair is captivating. She has a natural shyness, amplified by her complexion when she blushes, which is as charming as it is endearing. It isn't her fame that impresses me, though, it's her rags-to-riches story, creating a nook for herself to stand out in the crowded celebrity chef market. And she has done it with an approachable grace and elegance.

As if Alessandra tunes in to my thoughts, she declares, 'But surely, Kayla, you are Irish, or something different? This red hair like a Botticelli goddess's colours!'

Alessandra seems unaware that Kayla appears to be uncomfortable talking about herself. It is curious to watch, given how famous she is, having graced the cover of hundreds of fashion magazines, lauded for her sense of style. Surely, she is used to being both scrutinised and complimented. She fiddles with her fingers as she responds.

'My . . . my husband, Daniel, is Irish, but I don't have any immediate connections there, although I know I look it.'

She sips her water, avoiding all eye contact, and picks

up a piece of mezze cautiously, inspecting it before putting it on a plate in front of her, leaving it untouched.

'There is a wonderful antique market in London, yes?' asks Alessandra. 'I remember buying some *favolosa* glasses for reading in the Notting Hill. Made of tortoiseshell from the 1920s, but my husband tells me I look like a mad-woman in them! I do not care and wear them anyhow. Kayla, how do you meet your husband?'

I fear I may have to intervene in Alessandra's relent-less questioning. Kayla looks pained, smiling sadly at a memory.

'We met in a park, one of those random encounters that stuck. We were together nearly twelve years. Are together,' she corrects herself swiftly and picks up another olive, adding it to her plate.

As a comfortable silence falls, I think back to the other conversations on this subject I've been part of over the years. I'm always struck by the circumstances in which people find love. It is a common topic of discussion around the cooking stations or supper table. Adversity, crisis or simply out of the blue in the most unexpected way, love will find you, whether you want it or not. I know if my husband hadn't left me because of my accident and my scar, I may not be living in Petalidi and wouldn't have created my second chance at life. If things had been different with Leonidas all those years ago, perhaps none of this would have happened either. I hope Leonidas has found a peace with how we left things.

The sounds of dusk call me back to the moment as the cicadas begin to chirrup. The lapping waves and buzzing of my bees fills the air as birds begin their nightly roost, heading for cover in clusters of trees. Alessandra suddenly says, 'I meet my husband when he was naked.'

Our heads snap around in shock, and Kayla and I burst into giggles. We'd need to expect the unexpected with this wayward and eccentric guest.

Alessandra laughs, popping an olive in her mouth. 'I got to see what I'm in for. Is very efficient.'

'Dare I ask why he had no clothes on?' Kayla ventures, taking a small sip of rosé, her mezze still uneaten.

'It was a life drawing class, and he was the model,' Alessandra replies, clearly enjoying her captive audience. 'Staring at him and all his beautiful body parts for hours was enough to convince me that I would like to stare at him for the rest of my life. He is photographer and artist. In those days I was training to be a dancer, but now I make the jewellery. I am too old for dancing. It's for young creatures like you, Kayla. We have a creative *casa*, Phillipo and I, married for forty years.'

There is a collective sigh at the unusual romance of her tale and we allow the sounds of nature preparing for night time to wash through the silence. 'This only lasts because we sleep with other people.' She shrugs and drinks from her wine glass. 'Love comes in different guises and is not the same for everyone, yes?'

I thought I'd heard it all, but Alessandra is a walking surprise. I see Kayla's mouth harden into a thin line and she knits her hands. Alessandra has shattered the romantic rose-tinted illusion from moments before. I feel Kayla's energy shift to further discomfort, and she quickly excuses herself from the table, saying she needs to visit the restroom. I watch one of my bees trail her through the orchard.

I can't imagine how such an arrangement would work within a marriage. But perhaps I am so out of practice in the dance of love, my mind has closed to even the most unlikely possibility. The highs and lows, elation and despair that are part of any affair. Even to feel the dark stab of jealousy would be better than nothing, or the urgent overwhelming need to be close to someone you desire. I haven't felt like that for longer than I care to remember.

*And as she is chosen, the path of ascension is secured with murder and violence. She will wreak havoc on her sisters and unsuspecting drones. Coaxing them with seduction, humming sweet songs, then dispose of them when she has had her fill. Death will come quick. Even the meekest of us has the ability to kill in the name of love.*

# Chapter 5

## Kayla

The next morning, the smell of cinnamon whirls around the kitchen as Kayla watches Maria add a teaspoon of the spice to the pan. She and Alessandra follow suit, stirring the sweetness into the frying onions and garlic. Their first lesson is to learn to make *Imam Bayildi*: baked aubergines stuffed with a fragrant tomato sauce.

'This is very interesting to put cinnamon in savoury. In Italy, we use occasionally with pork but mainly in cake, sometimes breads,' Alessandra says adding the chopped tomatoes to her own saucepan, as Maria does.

'There's a fair amount in Greek cooking, and it works beautifully in this dish, as you'll find out when we eat it.'

'How long have you had Maria's Kitchen?' asks Kayla, trying to get part of an interview recorded during the class. She ensures her phone is far enough away from the sizzling sauce but near enough to capture conversation.

'I read it is ten years,' interrupts Alessandra.

'I know, but I want to hear it from her,' snaps Kayla, her tone harsher than she intended, but Alessandra's interjections are grating. Kayla can't understand why the Italian irritates her so. Last night, she'd found Alessandra amusing at first, until she revealed her casual marriage agreement. The thought is putting her off her food, more so than usual, as an image of Daniel writhing underneath another woman flashes before her eyes. Kayla feels horrified, unable to imagine accepting adultery as part of a relationship. It seems unnatural to manipulate love and treat it with such disregard. Kayla took that, and most things, very seriously. Following the rules and the recipe of life to the letter. Much good it had done her.

'Yes, that's right – it's been a decade now. It was like a second chance, so I had to make it count. This place is my baby.' Maria looks around the room fondly. 'When I came home after New York, I had a shot at making a dream come true. I never knew when and where I would create a cooking school, although I'd always wanted it. I was so caught up in my work in the States. But after my accident and my divorce, it was like it was all meant to be. As painful as it was at the time. I knew in my heart I could help people with my food in a more meaningful way; I just didn't know how back then. But it's grown beyond my wildest imaginings, and it gives me immense joy. Here it is about the simple things in life.'

'Why did you leave New York? It's the most wonderful city,' says Alessandra, and Kayla surrenders with a sigh. She'd wanted to ask about the accident, but thanks to Alessandra she'd missed the perfect opening. The interview can wait; they have all week. She urges herself to shift away from tension, not wishing to create a bad impression, despite what she thinks about Alessandra's arrangement with her husband. Her cooking counterpart is tenacious and will probably wheedle out the answers to the questions she would have asked Maria, anyway. But Kayla is grateful not to be the current subject of Alessandra's inquisition.

'Don't get me wrong, I loved America. But here I get woken up by sunshine and the sound of waves rather than traffic and beeping horns.'

'Nobody gives up New York because of traffic . . .' Alessandra laughs, and from Maria's slightly strained smile, Kayla can tell there's more to her story than she'd have them believe.

'True, but first I need you guys to scoop out the flesh from the roasted eggplants and add it to the tomatoes and onions. Then lay the empty skins back in the baking tray so we can stuff them with the sauce when it's ready.'

Kayla silently applauds Maria's expert deflection of Alessandra's nosiness and carries out her instructions, hearing the growl of her appetite spring to attention. It's a welcome change, she thinks, to treat food with the enjoyment it deserves rather than as work. Although since her gigantic lunch at the taverna yesterday, she hasn't eaten much. She busies herself chopping parsley, waiting for Maria to elaborate.

'So, here's the brief version of my story: my parents were getting old, and I guess New York had also gotten old for me. My marriage was done, and I'd stopped feeling satisfied with my life.' Kayla nods in agreement, recognising the sentiments Maria is describing. 'That wasn't only about my ex and the reasons for our separation, it was about me. I had my own restaurant, was financially secure, but there was suddenly something missing, like none of it was enough. I don't have kids so everything had to feel exceptional to make up for not having them. When the opportunity arose, I moved back to Greece and built this place from scratch. My husband leaving me turned out to be a blessing in disguise. As painful as it was, I can't regret it. It was meant to be.'

Maria sprinkles parsley into the sauce and combines it, stirring vigorously with her wooden spoon as the others replicate her actions. 'I was here when my father died, months with him I wouldn't have had, and I now look after my mother, as challenging as that is some days. I was given the gift of time by a bunch of unforeseen and, I guess, brutal circumstances. Leaving America is the best decision I ever made.'

Maria smiles as she spoons the contents of the pan into each of the aubergine halves. 'So, any questions . . . about the food *or* about my life . . . ?'

As they place their baking dishes side by side into the oversized country range, a gentle, jovial atmosphere descends over the kitchen.

'I have a question,' Kayla says, taking a sip of water as they clear down their workstations. 'Is it enough? You said you needed your life to be enough to make up for what was missing. Is it?'

Maria falls silent as they walk outside and sit at the table set for lunch. Kayla worries briefly the question has offended her teacher and anxiously gnaws at her thumbnail. As she's about to apologise, she sees Maria

54

is smiling, gazing wistfully over the sparkling sea. Kayla follows her eyes and sees the Mani headland looming through a mist across the bay, its outline almost ghostly in the shimmering heat.

'It truly is enough. I'm where I'm meant to be, doing what I'm supposed to. As much as it drives my mother nuts, I am, unapologetically, authentically me.'

Kayla slumps back into her chair, considering the notion that it's possible not to have it all, but to have what is sufficient to find gratification. But Kayla feels such a long way off from anything resembling satisfaction. Yet, since her marriage is over, perhaps she too could get another version of life, like Maria did. It gives her a glimmer of hope that all is not lost, as hard as it is to feel hopeful most days. She considers Alessandra, who seems to be effortlessly inhabiting her own space, unabashedly unapologetic for her unconventional life, as much as it morally jars with Kayla's own ideas about love.

Kayla stares at the sea, watching it deepen to a temporary inky hue under the patches of billowing white clouds. Struck by the sharpness of the light, Kayla wishes for a similar clarity. Her first taste of Greece has shown her life could be about the modest but important things: food, family and love. But as she watches the sunshine dance across the water, she wonders why, for her, nothing is ever enough. Feeling like she can always be more, do better, especially for Rosie. Because if she stops striving, she might never reach perfection and it would all have been for nothing . . . And failure for Kayla is never an option.

\*　\*　\*

Lunch passes in a sunny blur of tempting tastes and smells, the fruits of the morning's labour thoroughly enjoyed by all. The rich taste of aubergines lingers on Kayla's tongue, their smoky sweetness without a trace of bitterness. The servings had been huge, but she managed to eat a few mouthfuls.

This afternoon's task is to make the special Greek Easter cookies: *paschaliná koulourákia*. Maria says she needs as many trays as possible for the forthcoming festivities. Folding and twisting vanilla dough to create the staple of the annual celebrations is a rewardingly repetitive but instructive task, teaching them a new skill. Kayla is meticulous about uniformity, Alessandra less so with a range of varying sizes and plaits – another source of testiness for Kayla, who finds herself itching to redo the Italian's efforts. A small batch will be baked for the women to enjoy at their leisure, Maria explains, and the rest can be frozen for her to cook later on in the week.

Kayla sniffs deeply. There's a heartening quality to the smell of batter, she thinks. It's as if the flavours speak to her, deep inside, like a spell is being woven around her. As she has the thought, she watches a bee flit around the kitchen, hovering over her head. It is strangely comforting.

Throughout the day, Kayla notices her carefully crafted guard slowly slipping, as they discuss the challenges of fame over the dough on the floured work surfaces. Their dynamic has shape-shifted, with Kayla finding a place of trust in Maria. She rarely confides in anyone, not even Daniel – a source of frustration for him she has unwittingly allowed to fester. But each time Kayla looks at Alessandra, she is reminded of Daniel's treachery, and she can barely meet her eye.

'I think your television show is on in Italy, but I do not watch much. I have never seen your work before although I do recognise you from magazine covers.'

Though she tries to smile at Alessandra, Kayla cringes at the idea of her face in close-up. Whenever she did a shoot, she felt vulnerable, exposed, like there was nowhere to hide.

'What would you say is the worst part of being known to millions of people?' Alessandra asks, intricately twisting and clumsily shaping her biscuits between queries.

Kayla pauses her own labours for a moment to consider her response, having an unusual urge to reply with complete honesty, quashing the need to protect her thoughts out of fear of being judged.

'The constant criticism of my talent – or lack of it, depending which side of the fence you're on. And strangers sharing their opinions about what I say and do, but also what I look like. As if it has anything to do with food or cooking, but apparently it does and it seems to matter a whole lot to people. That's the worst bit of being famous. And I know it sounds bizarre, but I spend most of my time feeling like a terrible imposter. I never craved to be known. It just went hand in hand with it and it sort of . . . snowballed.' She laughs nervously as her brow furls.

'But you're so talented,' Maria says. 'I love the way you show the contestants how to do dishes; you're like a mentor and so supportive. And you're always right.'

Kayla shakes her head in disagreement, blushing slightly. 'But imagine everything you dislike about yourself, your darkest thoughts, being written about like they're facts by someone you don't know and who inexplicably despises you. After a while you start to believe it, even if it's not true. It's hard to feel positive when I look in the mirror some days. It's the worst thing to be judged or rejected just for being who I am.'

Kayla balks as she finishes her sentence, realising what she's said, too ashamed to look at Maria and the terrible scar that snakes up her neck. But Alessandra saves her embarrassment, as she begins to gasp for breath, clutching at her chest, as if her lungs are unable to absorb oxygen.

'This feeling I know. Only once. My daughter . . . she and I . . . She said . . . very terrible things . . . we did not . . . She—'

Suddenly, Alessandra breaks off, panting with effort, and her knees buckle. She grabs on to the counter and covers her mouth with a floury hand, leaving a streak of chalky dust on her face. Kayla stands inert, stunned by the outburst as Maria rushes to steady Alessandra, who is gripping the worktop so hard her knuckles turn pale.

'Forgive me, I am not well.' She continues trying to catch her breath, unable to fix her eyes as if the room is blurring around her. 'I feel . . .'

Maria quickly eases Alessandra into a chair as Kayla fetches a glass of water. With a trembling hand, Alessandra drinks. A tear escapes and tracks slowly down her cheek, mixing with the white flour mark.

'Do you want me to call the doctor?' asks Maria.

'No!' Alessandra shouts, wiping her brow to collect herself, before speaking more quietly. 'No, I will be fine. Just this heat is making me feel faint.'

Maria takes a bottle from the top shelf of the kitchen dresser and pours a generous measure into a tumbler.

'Then a shot of *my* medicine – *Metaxa:* smelling salts for the soul.'

She smiles as she replaces the glass of water in Alessandra's hands with the Greek brandy, encouraging her to drink, saying, 'Water is bacteria; Metaxa is wisdom!'

Alessandra obliges and the colour immediately returns to her face.

'Is *bene*, good, very strong. Please, I will be fine. Continue.' She waves her free hand extravagantly gesturing to the bowls of cookie dough waiting to be coaxed into shape.

'Are you sure? You don't want to lie down?' Kayla asks, feeling guilty for thinking badly of her.

'I will sit here a while. If I lie down, I may not get up again.' She laughs but has recovered enough for them to continue.

'Come by the window – you'll get the sea air.'

Maria gingerly helps Alessandra to a comfy chair where a light breeze gently lifts the white muslin curtains.

Kayla and Maria continue to bake as a silence descends. After a few minutes, Kayla cranes her neck to check on Alessandra, who has fallen asleep, her head lolling back onto a cushion.

'I didn't realise she had a daughter; she hasn't mentioned her before. Did she to you?' asks Kayla, hushing her voice.

'Not a word. It's sad she got so upset,' replies Maria, placing a full baking tray into the oven.

'I know – upset enough to have a funny turn, as well. I wonder if her daughter knows about her "understanding" with her husband.'

'Not sure I want to go there after what just happened. Day one of lessons and we're almost a woman down.'

'Maria . . . I hope I'm not speaking out of turn,' begins Kayla with a bravery that surprises her, 'but, what I said earlier about my appearance and being criticised for it, I hope I didn't offend you . . . because of . . .' Kayla manages to meet Maria's eyes, hoping she understands.

Maria looks her in the eye with a frank smile. 'Here's the thing you need to know about me, Kayla: I'm rarely offended by anyone or anything. I have a mother who can lift me up as fast as she pulls me down. And there are some people in the village who, let's say, would prefer I wasn't here. But this . . .' Maria turns her neck to expose her injury, running her finger along it '. . . is my battle wound from New York. Literally scarred from my love of cooking. I slipped holding a pan of hot oil during lunch service but it's also my badge of honour from the end of my marriage. My ex couldn't deal with it, so I wear it like a medal of self-acceptance – a reminder, if you like, that nobody will ever be able to love wholly, until you can love who *you* are, inside and out. It wasn't easy, believe me, but I got there. I'm different. And that's OK. It's allowed.'

'He couldn't deal with it?' asks Kayla, shocked by the assertion.

Maria takes another tray of biscuits to the oven. Immediately the scent of vanilla wraps itself around Kayla again, and she notices bees circling the central ceiling fan.

'He couldn't cope with how I changed, physically. It sounds pretty shallow, and I guess it was. With every skin graft I had on my neck, he retreated until he could barely stand to look at me, like I'd been spoilt for him.' She shrugs as she takes a tray of cookies to the walk-in freezer.

'I think you're amazing,' says Kayla, horrified at the

brutality of Maria's accident, and marvelling at her courage. 'I'm sorry your ex didn't think so.'

Maria shrugs and laughs. 'Hey, it's his loss. But *que sera* . . . if the accident hadn't happened, I wouldn't be here cooking with you and ole sleepyhead over there. It led me to my dreams, and how can I regret that? My scar is like a birthmark, but my second birth, I guess. It's the greatest gift to accept your lot.'

'What do you mean?' Kayla asks, amazed at how open and straightforward Maria is. Kayla can barely speak about the tragedy of her parents' accident in her own mind, let alone out loud. It's why it still haunts her dreams over twenty years later.

'You should give yourself props, you know? Now, it's on *me* not to speak out of turn, but you're pretty down on yourself for someone who's forged such an amazing career. I'm fangirling a bit, but you're allowed to celebrate yourself. If you don't do it, who will?'

Kayla takes a deep, steadying breath. She's travelled thousands of miles to a stranger's house only to be seen more clearly by her than anyone she has ever met.

'You have no idea how I long to feel like that, Maria. I'm ashamed to say this when you describe what happened to you with such bravery, but there is something in me that's too afraid to be kind to myself.'

'And yet, you complain about strangers being mean to you, when you're the worst of them all.' Maria holds her hands up in a gesture of retreat. 'Just saying.'

Kayla smiles at her straight-shooting host. 'Hey, how about I sign some of those books I see up on your shelf?'

Maria gapes at her. 'Are you kidding? I'd love that. You don't have to, just to shut me up.'

'I know, but I want to. But you can't look at the inscriptions until I leave, OK? I'll take them to my room so I can decide what to write later.'

Maria nods and removes her pile of Kayla Moss cookbooks. Although Kayla feels the weight of what she is hiding press heavier than ever, there is an indescribable sense of magic being spun in this kitchen. As if a spell has been cast on her. For the first time in so long, Kayla feels hopeful about her next steps forward. Like she can own her decisions and inform her future, taking control in a positive way. That would certainly be a considerable sea change.

# Chapter 6

## *Maria*

'I made you the same as the cooking school today. Hope it's OK, *Mamá*?'

I place the dish of *Imam Bayildi* in the centre of the table on the terrace and lightly dress a beetroot and rocket salad with balsamic vinegar. Just as I'm about to sprinkle over shavings of *kefalotiri* – a Greek sheep's milk cheese – my mother stops me.

'No cheese for me,' she says. 'It's still Lent in case you forget, so no animal products aside from shellfish. And I will not sleep – cheese causes nightmares. You won't hear me shout, you sleep so heavy.'

Criticising how I sleep is a new one from her, but I don't rise to the bait. Besides, she's deaf as a post; her slumber is always uninterrupted so she can't complain.

'Today was a great first day. They're both super interesting. Kayla is the one I told you about, the famous television star

63

and food writer. She seems to be enjoying herself. At least, I hope she is. And Alessandra is very eccentric. She used to be a dancer and now she makes jewellery, although she wasn't very well today. I might check on her later.'

'It is wonderful how much you care for others, Maria, and for me. We are all grateful, I'm sure. But when I am dead, what then? You spend all your energy, all your time fixing everyone else. When is the time for fixing *you*?'

I roll my eyes discreetly. '*Mamá*, I'm not broken. I'm happy. Can you not accept that?'

'I do not see how you can be happy; you have no one to share in your life. What is the point?'

'I've made *horta* for you, too – the greens are good for your heart,' I say, ignoring Mother's well-intentioned pestering. I leave the table to fetch the boiled leaves from the kitchen, but she continues calling after me.

'But what is good for *your* heart, Maria?'

I pass the shrine on the sideboard in the lounge and meet the eyes of my father in the image next to a gilded postcard of Jesus. I stand for a moment and smile at my *babá*, imagining how, if he were here, he'd make me laugh, joining me in exchanging exasperated glances behind my mother's back.

'Give me strength, *Babá*. Help me, please . . .'

My mind transports me back to my childhood. Watching my father tend his animals, the scent of hay, ammonia tinging the air as he filled the metal pails. The sour tang of warm goat's milk on the back of my tongue.

'What do you taste, Maria?' *Babá* would ask.

I was unable to express my feelings, nor interpret the swirl of flavours zinging around my juvenile palate back

64

then, but somehow I knew which foods would enhance the taste. *Babá* was my driving force, urging me to be who I wanted to be, not what others expected. He nurtured my creative spirit, made me determined to become something other than the conventional woman my mother longed for me to become. Clearly, she still harbours such hopes.

When I return to the dinner table with the vegetables, my mother is already eating with gusto. Her physical frailty is evident with each passing day, but her appetite matches her relentless criticism of me: both are savage. We are similar, not only in our mutual love of food but also in our headstrong characteristics. It is a known fact that we all turn into our mothers eventually. The downside is, we both know how to press the other's buttons.

Despite *Mamá*'s morbid suggestions she hasn't much longer on earth, she has lived and loved, fully and richly. As the years gallop onwards, I take pleasure in the fact she had a long and happy, albeit traditional marriage with my father. They were tactile and adored each other, always reaching for each other's hand over the dinner table, and he would often make my mother giggle. A lightness that dimmed when he died. They sparred often, but with affection, and their love warmed my heart.

Now it's almost as if *Mamá* is waiting to die, rather than continuing to live, and the thought disheartens me. Although she presses me about *my* happiness, I'm sad to think that my mother has already been as happy as she is ever going to be again. So, what's left for her? Apparently, badgering me into a marriage that isn't forthcoming. There are no prospects for a suitor, and I don't wish to endure any further heartache – I've already had a lifetime of it.

Being rejected or hurt by a man isn't something I'm prepared to risk again.

As we enjoy our food, my mother shares her newly learned gossip of the latest goings-on in the village. Someone will have told her of my scandal with the lemon cookies in church, but she doesn't mention it. I nod occasionally to keep her talking but tune out, listening to the noises of the night. The comforting buzz from my hives grows in volume and I know from their altered hum that a new queen is in residence. She has outwitted the competition, and she is chosen. I look over, smiling, congratulating the new matriarch in my mind.

*Mamá*'s voice grows louder and I force myself to rejoin the conversation. 'Leonidas has come back, this last month or so. He divorced Athena years ago, so I'm surprised you've not gone to see him.' I close my eyes, but she persists. 'You were such close friends when you were children. It would be good for you to have someone in your corner. Don't waste your chance. Again.'

'I'm sure he doesn't wish to speak to me after what happened, even though it's in the past. Besides, I'm too busy with work.'

*Mamá* tuts. 'I always thought you two would marry, but no, you ruined it and then wasted your time marrying that American who broke your heart anyway. Silly girl! You say you and Leonidas were only friends – well, love can grow from anything if you give it a chance. But off you ran to America and he was snapped up by another.' She takes another scoop of aubergine and plops it onto her plate with more force than necessary. 'You know what they call you in the village, Maria?'

I turn to my mother wearily. 'Yes, I am well aware of it. "*Mélissa*" – the "honeybee woman". So, they make fun of my hives, they think I'm a witch, they're scared to eat my food, but they love it when they do. They made up their minds to mistrust me when I was a child. Yet they secretly thank me for making Petalidi famous with my cooking school, and still I am not accepted. I resigned myself to this a long time ago, *Mamá*. I don't know why you cannot.'

'You will never attract a new man here. There is too much history. Besides, you and Leonidas are meant to be; I know it in my bones.'

As if the bees overhear, their insistent buzz becomes louder. I believe it to be a protest on my behalf.

'Never going to happen. I'm happy being on my own,' I reply, wishing an end to the conversation. She has it wrong. That ship sailed, if not sank, decades ago. His pride will have been mortally wounded by what passed between us and, besides, we've both moved on since then.

'Your bees will not nurse you in your old age, Maria.' Her voice softens. 'You'll get what you wish for and die alone like me.'

Mercifully, I see Kayla rounding the perimeter of the house, heading for the path to the beach. I wave and beckon her over, relieved to have respite from my mother.

I introduce them and *Mamá* says, '*Kalispéra*,' wishing Kayla a good evening.

'Lovely to meet you, Eleni. Your daughter is such a talented cook – she has a real gift,' says Kayla.

I tell her to speak up as my mother is very hard of hearing, so Kayla repeats herself at a louder volume.

'Yes, yes, she is very good, *kalí, kalí,* good, good, but her gifts cause nothing but trouble. She is always working, never time for much else. Tell me, how will she meet a man this way?'

I can tell that Kayla is slightly taken aback by my mother's brashness. I'm used to it, but give her an apologetic glance. 'Forgive my *mamá*'s bluntness. You see where I get it from. She doesn't believe I will be complete until I find another husband!'

'Are you married and with children?' my mother enquires of Kayla.

Kayla swiftly answers the question. 'Yes, and I have a daughter, Rosie.'

*Mamá* clutches her hands to her chest. 'Ah, children are the greatest blessing. And you are the one who is on the television, writes the books and you have a child and husband. You have it all, whereas Maria . . .'

Kayla looks at me, a horrified expression on her face, but I shrug and smile, turning to a safer topic. 'Where are you eating tonight?'

Kayla appears relieved at the change of subject. 'I thought I might go back to that grill house at the end of the beach. I had lunch there yesterday,' she says, smiling.

'Yes, you should eat there,' says my mother. 'Kostas is the owner. He is old but very experienced in grilling things.' She pauses thoughtfully. 'The seafood is OK, but the meat is better. He is old, as I say, but very experienced.'

'And the waiter, Dimitris, is very easy on the eye!' I whisper below my mother's hearing threshold.

Kayla colours, which confirms she's met Dimitris. He is considered a bit of a catch in the village, but nobody has tethered him. He enjoys the benefits of living in a tourist destination with a new influx of beauties every few weeks. I only hope Kayla sees him for what he is.

'It was lovely to meet you, Eleni,' says Kayla and she takes her leave. The calm sea barely moves, caressing the tideline with the lightest of watery kisses. I frown as a handful of bees follow Kayla along the seafront. What do they want with her? A barely formed half-thought occurs to me, chilling the nape of my neck that I cannot pinpoint, an energy of regret, sparked by Kayla seeing me with my mother. It is like trying to trap the wind in my hand, gone as soon as it arrives. A sadness is pulling at her that I cannot unpick. I was certain the vanilla cookies would be the key to opening her shell. My gift gave me that flavour when I thought of her. Perhaps tomorrow, the answers will come. These things cannot be rushed.

# Chapter 7

## *Kayla*

As Kayla heads for her dinner venue, she passes a row of houses. Balcony doors have been thrown open, to encourage what breeze there is in the humid evening inside.

There is an energy about the centre of the village, focused around the church. Children play on the green, people chat with one another on the benches framing the building, communing with an ease so alien to Kayla. She sees a priest conversing with the locals, walking from group to group, shaking hands, engaging with the little ones. Women bustle with armfuls of flowers, disappearing into the chapel. The simplicity of custom, the ritualistic preparations for Easter, seem to her like a scene from a bygone era. None of it seems real; it is deeply romantic. Even the wind is spiced with an exotic tang outside of the permanent smell of bread that someone, somewhere, always seems to be baking.

Kayla reaches the restaurant and sits at one of the empty tables. The handsome waiter, Dimitris, places a menu in front of her along with a basket containing a mouth-watering sourdough loaf, its crust sprinkled with sesame seeds. It dawns on Kayla that she cannot escape food in Greece; it is in the air, on the tables, creeping into your thoughts with each breath. As she meets Dimitris' dark brown gaze, she feels the frisson of attraction again, but nudges it away. She's far too old for him – he must be in his late twenties, at least ten years' difference. Besides, she is still married. Although Daniel seemed able to conveniently forget that fact when it suited him, so perhaps she should take a leaf out of his book.

'So, you return. Was it the food . . . or something else that brings you back?' he says languidly with an assured, seductive confidence.

Kayla manages a smile, uncertain how to play the flirting game and feeling vulnerable in her strappy green sundress. She's never been any good at it, far too self-aware. Daniel had done all the chasing when they'd first started dating and she never got the chance to find out if she was a natural seductress. She suspects she isn't.

Instead of engaging with Dimitris further, she orders a small jug of white wine, in the Greek quarter-kilo measurement, which he brings with a pot of ice to keep it cool. He begins to list the specials and a tension descends between her shoulder blades. She watches him retrieve his notepad from his jeans pocket in anticipation of her order. His muscular arms are tattooed and tanned, and his skin looks like a caramel she longs to taste. His jet-black hair is shaved tight to his head at the sides and the rest is pulled into a short ponytail at the nape of his neck. He is different, the opposite of any choice she's ever made before, which makes him even more enticing. Her eyes travel to his mouth as he lists the plates of the day.

'*Souvlaki*, pork or chicken grilled; *briam* is vegetables in the oven; *gemistes piperiés*, stuffed peppers; and *kleftiko* is lamb cooked for many hours with potatoes. The rest is grill specialties, and all is very . . . very delicious.'

She doesn't hear what he says. Instead, Kayla imagines how it would feel to experience the sheer lust of a one-night stand, pinned beneath his strong arms, hot skin on hers, being made to feel like the sensual being she longs to be. She's never indulged in such a thing. But this waiter has sparked something within her, and she flushes at her own reckless thoughts.

'If you need anything from me, I am Dimitris. Anything you need . . .' He fixes her with a weighted look and leaves her to consider the list of options. Whether or not it was only food he was offering, she feels the creeping warmth of temptation spread through her veins. She catches the scent of his cologne, woody and with a note of sweetness, and her stomach flips. It is a decision she could make that is entirely hers, of her own making, and it feels thrilling to have the power of choice: to pursue the waiter, or not.

Her phone vibrates on the table, interrupting her illicit thoughts and replacing them with instant exasperation at seeing Eve Houseby's name. Immediately declining it, she swats an insect away from her face but feels a stab on her finger, making her yelp. Tears prick at the backs of her eyes as she pinches her skin, looking for the offending barb. She hopes it isn't one of Maria's bees, as it will now die. She picks up an ice cube and presses it against the area. She can feel the weight of strangers' eyes on her, aware of heads turning.

Kayla has been enjoying the incognito nature of her visit, but as a little boy with doleful eyes lined with long lashes approaches her table, egged on by his parents to request her autograph, she graciously complies. But the last thing she wants is any unwelcome attention – apart from maybe Dimitris'. Overhearing whispers and mutterings, she notices diners nodding at her, as patrons recognise the celebrity in their midst. The boy returns gleefully to his table, and the ripple of excitement spreads. She smiles but longs to dissolve into the air.

She suddenly feels very alone. This is what her life will be like without Daniel, and she should find a way to embrace it. She briefly wishes he were here, before the reminder of his betrayal presses on her chest. She read Rosie her bedtime story on video call earlier and thankfully her little girl remains blissfully unaware of any domestic turmoil. She is staying with Daniel's parents again tonight as he is working late. Supposedly. Or is he now free to do as he pleases in their home?

Kayla feels the chill of shame in her blood, but it isn't about Daniel. She is lauded for her honesty on television, priding herself on straight talking, but off screen, she's as deceitful as her husband, only in a different way. Because what she is concealing could spell the end of her career. Since discovering Daniel's affair, work and Rosie are all that is left in her world, and she doesn't want to risk losing them too.

Kayla picks up the menu again, looking at it through her misty eyes, emotionally reacting to all the dishes, craving everything she would usually deny herself. She holds it up in front of her face to block out all the gaping looks, the covert snapping of pictures, cursing her misplaced bravery in venturing out alone.

She beckons to Dimitris with her swollen finger, pretending not to notice his smouldering look. She attempts to ignore the way his low-slung jeans accentuate his height, giving tempting glimpses of a trail of hair and where it might lead underneath the denim. She wishes she could order a platter of anonymity with a side of self-acceptance instead of all the calorific options in front of her. Perhaps she could ease her isolation after all. It would only take a flicker of her eyes to summon the waiter for something not listed on the menu. The thought emboldens her for a moment as she takes a sip of wine. Then, she returns to countless pairs of eyes scrutinising her every move and gnaws at the skin around her nail.

She won't entertain any other version of tonight. She mustn't.

# Chapter 8

## *Alessandra*

Alessandra strides towards a taverna at the furthest end of town, which seems popular this evening. The good-looking man playing guitar in the corner casts a glance her way. Perhaps, she thinks – and perhaps not. Although her indecision is out of character, as she reaches down into the corners of her heart, she realises she doesn't want to be with anyone else other than Phillipo, her husband. Strange, she thinks, as she recognises yet another part of herself that is changing.

She had thought this trip would be simply a series of lasts: her final liaisons with other men, one remaining solo adventure without Phillipo and the last time she would see anywhere outside of Rome. She had always longed to visit Greece and the unexpected bonus of experiencing the glorious creativity of the famed Maria's Kitchen seemed like a perfect combination. She has survived life on impulsive decisions and, for the most part, that instinct hasn't let her down. Apart from one time. But she can't think about that now.

The air cools her shoulders a little in contrast to the sweltering heat of the day, although she feels a chill in all weathers nowadays. She tries not to relive how faint she felt earlier, pushing it away as deep as it can go. She spots Kayla alone at a table. It would be good to have company, she thinks, even though she can tell the English girl dislikes her.

'*Ciao*, may I join you?' Alessandra doesn't wait for an answer and takes a chair.

'Feeling better, I see,' says Kayla, visibly bristling as Alessandra sits, uninvited.

'Much better, just the heat. Think nothing of it. Did you order?' asks Alessandra.

Kayla nods, begrudgingly handing her a menu and Alessandra decides quickly. She requests from Dimitris a rich beef stew along with *skordalia* – garlicky cold potatoes whipped until impossibly fluffy – and okra cooked in a richly scented tomato sauce. She notices the electricity between Kayla and the waiter and raises an eyebrow. Kayla blushes scarlet and pours Alessandra a glass of wine. The two women sit in awkward silence before Alessandra attempts conversation.

'Have you been to Greece before?' she asks, but Kayla seems unwilling to engage, responding with a curt: 'No, I haven't.'

Alessandra observes a woman on another table surreptitiously snap a photograph of Kayla on her phone. She feels pity for her reluctant dinner companion; it is no wonder she's so uptight. Alessandra gives up making small talk – silence doesn't trouble her.

'How old is your daughter?' Kayla asks, breaking the quiet that appears to bother her as much as sharing a supper with Alessandra. 'You mentioned her earlier.'

'Arianna is thirty-eight. We've not spoken for more than twenty years. I saw her in Rome by accident just before I came here.'

Alessandra remembers every detail of that day with clarity, replaying it in her mind like a scene on a loop as she tells Kayla what happened.

Piazza Navona had been heaving with tourists gawping and gasping at the statues surrounding the *fontana*. Fish spurted water from their generous mouths, carved marble sinew of Bernini's river gods sparkled sensuously in the sunshine. Phillipo and Alessandra had traversed the main square into a back street, so narrow there was barely room for a Fiat 500 to squeeze through. One of her favourite bookshops, nestled in the alleyway, doubled as a wine bar. A place for the shift and sway of new encounters, a glance across a paperback, a seductive sip from a glass, the promise of an unexpected liaison.

After lunch, she and Phillipo had walked along the Tiber, passing stalls boasting tourist trinkets, hawkers peddling fake designer handbags and wristbands proclaiming to cure all ills. The river was grey; muddy swirls circled. Statues of angels towered overhead, grubby and soiled from the pigeons cooing on their perches. *Roma* was a façade of idealised fairy tales; the weight of history and overbearing religion at every corner covertly moulding you into conventional obedience. The inescapable *duomo* roofs, impressing upon you omnipresence, overwhelmingly extravagant interiors boasting gilt to inspire guilt. But beneath the surface, there is dissatisfaction, poverty, the hidden gritty reality. Yet in the sordid undercurrent is where the truth of any city lies and where art thrives, straddling the line between perception and actuality. Phillipo and Alessandra had reached the bustling *Campo de' Fiore*, dodging visitors who loitered with indecision, obstructing their way.

Suddenly it was as if the blood had drained out of her body.

Alessandra had seen her profile at first, unmistakable. Sharing identical features with Phillipo, save for a nose piercing. Her hair was as dark as ever, but it was hanging long and lank around her shoulders, having lost its shine. Alessandra had watched the girl buy *pomodori*, stepping out of her eyeline, but she had tracked her like a spy. They moved in improvised choreography, her to one side, Alessandra to the opposite, forwards, backwards, a half turn the other way.

The girl's head had shot up and turned, as if she sensed Alessandra's observation, an instinctive connection that, despite her daughter's efforts, remained unbroken, if not completely intact.

Alessandra shakes off her memories and asks her mind to rejoin her body at the beachside restaurant. She sees Kayla look at her sadly but doesn't require her pity. A scruffy tabby cat mews by her feet. His forlorn eyes yield a successful result, securing a piece of bread from Alessandra, which he greedily devours.

Their food arrives and Alessandra feasts with indulgence, enjoying the freedom of unburdening herself, even if it is upon someone who appears to dislike her.

Alessandra doesn't care. The joy of travelling means you meet people you'll never see again. The gentle sound of the tide brushing the shore, coupled with guitar music, fills her body with the desire to dance.

She concludes the subject in between mouthfuls. 'So, I have no way to contact her. She does not respond to my emails. And one day she will have regret she cannot repair. You see, Kayla, she doesn't agree with my lifestyle, as it is clear you do not either. I protected her from it when she was younger but unfortunately, when she was seventeen, she discovered me with another man. She never forgave me and yet, curiously, she was kinder to Phillipo. It is because she saw with her own eyes what she considered *my* act of betrayal, unable to remove it from her mind. It's simple to understand, even though she wouldn't accept any explanation. So, she cut me from her life. My daughter blames me for all that is wrong in her world. She rejects me instead of dealing with her own demons and there is nothing I can do. You may think me callous, but it is the way things are. Different lids for different pots, yes?'

The guitar music grows louder and some of the diners begin to dance. They perform intricate steps they all seem to know. A man comes to the centre of the floor and spins around, jumping and hitting the ground with his hands, leaping with enthusiasm as the other dancers crouch to their knees and clap in time to the music.

Kayla leans forward and takes a breath. 'I . . .' It's as if she is searching for words that won't come. Alessandra returns to her meal, allowing Kayla space to continue. She smiles, wondering if the girl might apologise for her rudeness. If she doesn't, it won't affect Alessandra. She notices that Kayla has hardly touched her dinner and realises she hasn't seen her eat more than a couple of mouthfuls since they arrived. The haunting guitar music strains the atmosphere as Kayla pushes food around her plate before sinking back in her seat, apparently defeated by her own thoughts.

'My marriage is . . . it's over. My husband's been having an affair,' blurts Kayla in a whisper, looking around her in case of eavesdroppers.

Alessandra raises her eyebrow as she takes a slow sip of her wine, having ordered a second, larger jug, again observing the tension between the waiter and Kayla. 'And this bothers you?'

'Yes, it bothers me! I can't believe he'd lie to me, to our child. She is only five,' snaps Kayla.

'So, if he cheats . . . *you* cheat. Although if it is over, it is not adultery, so what does it matter?' Alessandra indicates towards Dimitris with a nod.

Kayla's mouth drops open in shock at the idea of revenge, despite the obvious eyes Dimitris is making. 'It matters because I care about what marriage means.'

'But your marriage is finished, yes? So, you are free. You don't have to be confined. Stop caring about what is holding you back.'

Kayla leans forward to make her point through gritted teeth. 'You clearly don't care – that's fine, you do you. I can't. It's too risky.'

'Because you are famous?' Alessandra asks casually.

'No,' Kayla spits with venom directed at herself rather than Alessandra. 'Because I'm me.'

\* \* \*

82

A warm breeze has found its way into the cove. Kayla left Alessandra to join the dancing, and the Italian was glad. She finds Kayla exhausting company; her emotions are so tightly coiled and inevitably will unravel. Alessandra feels the stirrings of sympathy. If only Kayla could understand how freeing life could be if you ceased worrying about what others think, responding only to passion and desire. Even though such impulse had been the destruction of her own relationship with Arianna, a dose of wild abandon won't do any harm. She'd watched the waiter's fingers deliberately stroking Kayla's whilst handing her the bill.

Such a shame, she thinks, to have talent and beauty yet appear utterly dissatisfied with life, unable to enjoy success. She understands Kayla's traditional outlook, that their morals clash, especially given Kayla's husband's recent infidelity. But if it is over, she should move on. Life is far too short to wish for something that will never be. She's learnt that in the cruellest of ways.

As Alessandra breaks from the exertion of dancing, she catches the eye of the guitar player again. Years pass by too fleetingly to squander time, she thinks again, and glides towards the musician through the densely scented air, impulse overriding thought. A cluster of bees bring a waft of cinnamon on the wind, which weaves its way into her nostrils.

The night has become heavier with humidity and the temperature is stifling once more. She has read of the record-breaking April heatwave in the region. There is no telling what will happen from one day to the next: sudden storms, waterspouts descending from the clouds to suckle from the sea, blazing sunshine igniting wildfires. The only guarantee is that the tide will meet the shore. And tonight, it washes noisily against the stony tideline, like a sombre drum beating Alessandra's determined footsteps along the promenade.

She couldn't bring herself to approach the musician. Something in the air made her change her mind – and she is bewildered by what is shifting within her.

# Chapter 9

## *Maria*

'*Kaliméra!* Good morning! You're up super early. Did you sleep well?' I ask as I see Kayla furiously typing on her laptop outside her villa, bashing the keyboard violently.

'Not great, no,' she replies snippily. 'I'm trying to start my articles.' A lack of sleep clearly makes her tetchy.

'Uh-oh. The idea of a review makes me nervous. Be kind!'

Kayla puts her sunglasses on, managing a smile. 'What are we cooking today?'

'A Greek classic. *Pastitsio.* The most comforting comfort food, but extra heavenly. Oh, and: *Kalo Pascha*! Happy Easter! It's Holy Thursday, which means we paint eggs and make special bread too. I'm off to the village to run errands first. Do you need anything?'

'No, thanks, just waiting to speak to Rosie, before she goes to school.'

She lights up when she talks about her daughter, but I detect a tension, though not the source of what she is trying to hide. There is something there, though, a willing for it to be uncovered.

'While I remember,' Kayla calls to me, 'there was this weird bundle of sticks and rocks in the shape of a crucifix on the lawn by your bees. And a figure made from twigs.'

My skin chills. I've forgotten to check for this morning's offering from my nameless hater.

'Is it a Greek Easter thing?' Kayla asks when I say nothing.

'Oh . . . it's . . . yes . . . a silly superstition. I'll clear it away later,' I say breezily, but Kayla frowns. Trust me to have a journalist on the premises when I have a mystery stalker to uncover. Or not. I have little inclination to unmask them. I instinctively know it'll cause more damage for me. But as I wave goodbye and head for town to buy some wood to fix my hive, I begin to wonder if that might be the right thing to do. I could confront the bully, catch them in the act. It would put a stop to it once and for all.

\* \* \*

The village bustles and a lengthy queue stretches outside the bakery for *tsoureki* bread, the traditional braided Easter loaf laced with the aniseed flavour of mastic and a cherry seed tang from mahleb. It's a considerable undertaking to make, but, in my opinion, worth the hassle. I started my dough just after sunrise. It needs to prove for four hours before a further prove when it's plaited. But I'll do that with Alessandra and Kayla when we get to class. We'll also paint hard-boiled eggs red and incorporate them into the bake.

'*Kalo Pascha!*' I say to those I encounter. Some return the greeting, others turn their backs. I see Athena before she spots me, holding court on a bench surrounded by her lackeys, drinking takeaway frappés. Although we left high school thirty-five years ago, you'd think we were still infants the way their clique operates. They're teenage mean girls in grown-up bodies and I remain baffled as to why some women thrive on being so unkind.

I was as sorry to hear of the end of Athena's marriage as I was surprised to hear about its beginning. She and Leonidas weren't romantically involved at school, but somehow ended up together. When I learnt of their engagement from my mother on the phone, I was ensconced in the kitchens of New York, learning my craft. I recall the faint pull of envy, which I quickly dismissed as a childish notion, and threw myself into work. I had my chance, but I hurt him, badly. I heard via *Mamá* that Leonidas took a job in Thessaloniki soon after I returned to Petalidi ten years ago. I hoped I'd see him when I first moved back. But he was gone within days following my arrival. Sadly, he and Athena were unable to make the long-distance work and eventually divorced. He remained in Thessaloniki for years until a few weeks ago. I wonder what brought him back here after all this time. Athena refuses to accept my condolences about her marriage. We were once the closest of friends, but such are the perils of the playground; kinships disappear as quickly as a summer rain shower. I was profoundly wounded by it at the time, but I've since been hurt worse.

These women live the life my mother would love me to emulate; crowing about how hard their husbands work – save for Athena – and fussing over their children, who run around the green, high on sugar and Easter anticipation. It is a life I could've chosen, slipped into without thinking. Apart from the motherhood part, which wasn't in my destiny. Still, I'd have easily been able to play house, nurture love, cook all day for my husband like the good Greek girl my mother wishes I was. But life had another plan for me. *I* had another plan for me.

'*Yiá sou*, Athena, *yiá sas* everyone,' I say. 'Happy Easter!'

I'm not one to shy away from bullies, neither as a teen nor as a fifty-something. But the small tremor of fear they still inspire is as amusing as it is frightening.

'Oh,' says Athena, her chestnut hair glistening in the morning light. 'We were just talking about you, *Mélissa*.'

Her cronies dissolve into giggles as a bee makes a timely dart through the group.

'Quick! One's escaped, what will you do, *Mélissa*? Maybe it has the evil eye, possessed by a demon. Or maybe it's one of your imaginary ghosts come to haunt us all!'

They laugh again as if Athena has said the funniest thing they've ever heard. She flicks her hair from her shoulder, preening and primping. She was always vain and had good reason; she was beautiful. Although her beauty has faded as it does for us all. Mine has done so in a more dramatic fashion.

'You should come to my hives for some honey. You could do with something to sweeten you up.'

I can't resist and immediately chide myself for descending to their cruel level. I should find more grace, but for the moment it has deserted me. Athena's laughter is wiped clean away as she stands from her bench, towering over my petite frame.

'At least I am not marked by the devil's hand like *you*.' She crosses herself as she glares at me. Her cronies follow suit. 'No man will ever love you. Don't you ever forget that.'

Even as I allow her words to wash over me, I can't help but notice that they sound like one of the warnings I receive on my phone. Could Athena be behind the 'COWARD' texts? I let her beady green eyes stare at me, and I return her glare in a standoff. The back of my neck prickles with a message that doesn't arrive. I feel a wave of sadness. Is it from me, or is it her unhappiness I can sense? She breaks away from my gaze as if she can feel my mind reaching for hers.

'Well, I hope you all have a happy Easter and enjoy the feast on Sunday,' I say as I turn and walk across the green to the hardware store.

I hear Athena say deliberately at my back, 'Maybe we should burn her instead of Judas on Sunday. I wouldn't eat any of her Easter biscuits if you paid me.'

As their laughter dissolves into the sticky air, I shake my head. I almost feel sorry for them, despite their blatant malice. Athena has my pity for her hidden misery, notwithstanding her animosity. It must seem hard to have watched the village misfit jet off to New York and 'make it' in a glamorous world she could only dream about. My return and subsequent success must gall her further. I know I'm making excuses for her viciousness, but it is the way I am. I don't believe people are intrinsically bad.

I cross the village green and see Athena's daughter, Zoe, standing statue-still, staring at me. She is a beautiful fourteen-year-old, I think as I nod at her, but she turns her back and hastily moves away. I sigh out loud, wondering what nonsense Athena has filled her daughter's head with.

The hardware store smells of sawdust and metal, like there's a tang of blood in the air. The bell rings with a pleasing tinkle as I enter, alerting the owner that he has a customer.

'*Kaliméra, i* Maria *eimai.*' I announce myself in advance to prevent any surprise. My appearance can startle, even though I've hidden my scar with a scarf as I usually do when I'm outside my kitchen. Only parts of the Americas peep out from underneath the fabric, but there is no escaping it.

'Ah, *Kalo Pascha, kaliméra,* Maria,' says Giorgos, the store owner, wishing me a happy Easter and a good morning.

I describe the size of the wood I need for my hive's repair and wait for the piece to be cut. I take a small jar of honey from my bag to thank Giorgos with, knowing he won't charge me for the wood. He is one of the few in the village who treat me with kindness.

The loud screech of the jigsaw machine masks the ring of the bell above the door, but I instinctively turn and find myself face to face with my childhood meadow friend.

Leonidas.

It is the first time I have seen him in decades, and my breath catches. The youngster in me immediately re-appears. My heart beats a little harder in my chest and I know if I had Kayla's skin tone, I'd be the colour of a terracotta pot. He looks unchanged since I last saw him over thirty years ago; time has been kinder to him than I. The passing of years has peppered his dark, thick hair with grey around the temples and it becomes him. His laughter lines are more pronounced. His eyes remain the colour of the darkest honey, warm and rich. I didn't realise what close attention I'd paid to his features until now. Even when he entered my mind, flooding it with shame fleetingly in New York, I thought I must have made him up. But no, he is exactly as I recall: his aquiline nose, full lips that pout when he is deep in thought and soft eyes that blacken in an instant when he is angry. I've only seen them that way once, and it was entirely my doing. The tan in his skin is heightened against the rolled-up sleeves of his white linen shirt, and he looks in good shape, so incredibly tall without a hint of a middle-aged spread. I self-consciously pull my shirt forward to cover my tummy.

'Well . . . look at who has blown in on the Easter wind,' I say, unable to help my smile. I quietly wince at my choice of words since there is very little wind today. I'm babbling.

A slow grin creeps across his handsome face and he laughs with the boyish charm he always possessed, and I feel instant relief he doesn't seem to be holding a grudge against me. I offer my hand to shake his as he steps forwards to kiss my cheek. In our contrary choices of greeting, my hand bashes his middle, and we nervously laugh aloud. He opens his arms and folds me into an embrace. I want to stay there for the rest of the day in his bear-hug, but we awkwardly pull apart.

'Little Maria Leventi.' He looks at me for what seems like an eon. 'Here you are after all this time. And what is this you have . . . is this honey from your own hives?'

I look down at my hand and notice I am still holding the jar meant for Giorgos. He takes it from me and holds it to the light. The honey glows like a golden precious treasure.

'Oh, yes . . . it is.'

'I heard you finally got your bees. You did what we talked about all those years ago, what you dreamed of.'

He returns the jar to me. I can't believe he remembers my childhood wish from our time together in my father's olive grove and fields.

'Oh, I'm sure you've heard all about it, the names I'm called in the village. As if they didn't already think I was loopy, they certainly do now.'

A sadness crosses his face, and he looks down at his shoes. 'This village can be as cruel as it is beautiful. It's why I didn't return for so many years. They make it impossible to truly be yourself, yes?'

The old friendship we once had starts to tentatively shift into the familiar exchange of honesty, yet we are in adult form, well past the teenage nonsense of indecisions and regret. For the most part.

Giorgos appears with two large pieces of wood for me. 'Here, Maria, is one for fixing now and a spare if you need it. This weather is making everyone's doors and windows warp. It is good for business but be sure to look after your bees. Ah! *Kaliméra*, Leonidas.'

I hand him my precious jar, as Leonidas returns his greeting.

Giorgos beams at my gift. 'You will make my wife very happy, which makes *my* life happy!' He thanks me heartily and I try to give him some euros, which he refuses.

'Well . . .' I begin, turning back to Leonidas. 'It was lovely to see you again. Really lovely. Welcome home, although I know you've been back for weeks, but . . . hello again.'

'You haven't changed, Maria.'

I gaze up at him, flustered. He is still unnervingly handsome, and I don't know how to respond. I leave the shop without saying anything else, letting his parting statement sink in. I instinctively know he meant it, and his intention is entirely honest, but how can that be the truth? I've changed beyond recognition. Even with silk around my neck hiding the worst of my atlas scar, it is still visible with Newfoundland peeking over the top of the fabric. Of course, he noticed. At least he didn't recoil; I know how shocking it is.

I shake my head as I head for home, unable to empty my mind of Leonidas. We knew each other so well and I used to be able to read him clearly – he was utterly transparent to me. I would see the ghosts of his relatives walking with him in the shadows, knowing he was guided and looked after. But now, I get no sense of his secrets, not even a tickle on the back of my neck alerting me to what he hides, like his heart is as closed as mine. That could be the remnants of what I inflicted on him. He was furious; I hurt him profoundly. But so much has happened since, a myriad of moments in our lives that the other knows nothing of.

I am bewildered as to why I cannot access his energy with what remains of my gift. My divination of the perfect flavours that may help someone on their way to healing has never failed before. But with Leonidas, I am given no message by the spirits who coast on the air. I know from my past students that pain and damage lurk around us all, only some are more adept at concealing it. Perhaps he has a thousand secrets buried too deeply to register.

My phone chimes and I see a message from 'COWARD':

**The clock is ticking for you.**
**Do the right thing and leave.**

I feel tears prick my eyes, making my nostrils sting. My stubborn nature refuses to be driven out of my home by this person, but I am desperate to understand why they hate me so. I don't delete the message. The chain of historical hatred reads like a sickening thread of contempt.

An energy flows through my blood as I arrive at a decision. Tonight, I will sleep outside and catch them leaving a warning beside my bees. It may end this nonsense before any real damage is done. I won't be bullied any longer, nor apologise for who I am.

*It is said the bee represents the connection between the spiritual and material realm. In the annals of time, the bee instinctively knows their part and the role they must play in the continuous cycle of life. As there is birth, there is new beginning, but so must death come to keep the scales of justice in check. One inevitably follows the other. After death once more comes life, comes resurrection.*

# Chapter 10

## *Kayla*

Alessandra breezes into the kitchen as Kayla and Maria are chopping onions, sniffling from their streaming eyes.

'*Buongiorno, Kaliméra* and good morning! Sorry I am late – I was speaking to my husband.'

Before she can stop herself, Kayla gives a disdainful sniff and shocks herself at her visceral reaction. She'd been considering the sanctity of marriage as she tried and failed to get to sleep last night. Eventually slumbering fitfully, missing Rosie and how her life used to be before she knew. This morning she exchanged brief messages with Daniel and the more distant he is, the more she can feel her frustration turning to Alessandra. She can't believe she revealed Daniel's affair to the one person who was wholly unsympathetic about it, and it galls her that Alessandra's immediate response to her news was to suggest she jump into bed with another man.

And yet, Kayla's dreams last night were haunted by Dimitris. He shouldn't be in her broken slumber, but something about his scent and skin arouses her, despite her attempt to suppress such urges. It's Alessandra's fault, she thinks, throwing the woman an angry look. She's the one who made Kayla think so explicitly about him. Kayla clears her throat to cover up her reaction, which Alessandra seems oblivious to. She can see that Maria, however, has noticed, and feels her cheeks colour.

'We have a busy day, so let's get going,' Maria says, trying to defuse the tension.

Alessandra finishes washing her hands and says, '*Sì!* I am ready,' as she strides over to Kayla, to pull her stiff body into a hug. 'How beautiful you are. Your bone structure is quite exquisite.'

Alessandra's finger is poised to trace Kayla's cheekbone, but Kayla pulls away sharply.

'Goodness, and *you* have the most exquisite misunderstanding of personal space. But that's to be expected.'

She catches Maria frowning at the pair of them. The beautiful dynamic they had yesterday, despite Alessandra's near fainting fit, has now disappeared like a shaft of sunlight swallowed up by a storm cloud. Maria claps her hands to garner everyone's attention.

'So, *pastitsio* is like a Greek lasagne – and given it's a holy day, this one will be divine! Alessandra, you do the béchamel; Kayla, you're in charge of the meat sauce . . . all the way over here. I'll do the bucatini pasta.'

Maria expertly guides Kayla to the furthest end of the kitchen and returns to Alessandra to talk her through the white sauce with added nutmeg. Kayla is trying not to allow her irritation to bubble over like the fiercely boiling saucepan of pasta. Seeing Maria jovially chatting to Alessandra is pulling at her last nerve.

She endeavours to focus on crumbling up feta as instructed by Maria to fold into the pasta once it's cooled. Followed by some egg whites she's already vigorously beaten to a fluffy pulp. The sound of Alessandra's laughter makes her grind her teeth against her aching jaw.

As a wind whips through the open windows, it brings with it a scented puff of cloves and nutmeg from the other end of the kitchen, engulfing Kayla in a wave of comforting fragrance. She closes her eyes and inhales. The sudden ringing of her phone jolts her out of temporary calm. Seeing Eve Houseby's name, she declines the call with irritation, leaving a salty feta smear on the phone screen.

'Someone you don't want to speak to?' asks Maria wryly.

Kayla sighs. 'Yet another nuisance in my life. One I don't wish to deal with in Greece. My neighbour, Eve, is a bit of a stalker.'

Maria looks equally fascinated and horrified. 'Do you want to talk about it?'

'I accidentally allowed her into my life. It's my fault. She's the type who's obsessed with celebrities and she and her husband have become a nuisance.'

Kayla tries to pinpoint the moment she began to suspect the Housebys' intentions . . .

'Look, we got one too! Snap! Haw haw!'

Eve Houseby was proudly showing off her newly acquired paperweight with glee. It was a limited-edition rare creation by a renowned contemporary artist, identical to the one Kayla had bought for her own lounge some weeks before. The Housebys must have clocked it over cocktails, then somehow hunted it down. And there had been countless other occasions since involving the same handbags or duplicate jackets Eve suddenly appeared in after admiring them on Kayla. She ought to have been flattered, but there was an undercurrent of desperation that irked her. The photographs of their lunches appeared on social media, hailed as 'cosy intimate gatherings' when picked up in the online gossip sidebars, suggesting they were the best of friends. Eve had also joined a 'Kayla Cooks' fan page on Facebook and regularly shared her 'inside track', as she called it, leading Kayla to withhold information that could be manipulated into a juicy, exclusive morsel. She is now on guard in every aspect of life, and it is suffocating. When can she ever truly be herself?

There was also something odious about Eve's husband, Stephen. He gave her the shivers. They'd be the sort of people who'd turn up on your holiday and never leave – they'd actually done it before on one of her and Daniel's weekends away. Kayla rues the day she invited them in. Eve in particular has become a magpie for her life's trinkets, boasting and bragging about their connection at the school gates. But it is too late to unpick. Their daughters are now friends and Kayla doesn't want Rosie's happiness to be a casualty of any mistakes she's made. If only Daniel applied such reasoning to his actions.

Kayla returns to the present, noticing Maria is looking at her curiously.

'I was worried the call was about Rosie. My phone usually rings with bad news. But it was only ghastly Eve.'

Maria shrugs. 'My mother – who you know doesn't mince her words – has a saying that if you keep expecting something bad to happen, the universe will reward you with what you wish.'

Maria takes a tray of appetisers out of the oven. Kayla watches her spoon small squares of honey-roasted goat's cheese onto a platter, sprinkling them with dried oregano and a drizzle of oil. She offers one to Kayla, who hesitates before slowly reaching for the plate. Maria is clearly an expert at imposing the infamous Greek hospitality. The moment Kayla bites into the warm cheese, the honey visibly works its magic, and a smile warms her expression.

'Oh, my goodness, this is incredible, Maria. Your food is changing my life – and the size of my thighs,' she adds, feeling a quiet panic seep into her bones.

Kayla lets the flavour flood her mouth with sweetness, and any annoyance at Alessandra or Eve Houseby dissipates. She feels like a bird soaring into the sky, propelled by the flavours tickling her tongue, imagining her favourite tastes, flying over honey-coated cheese clouds, buffeted by a sweet breeze before landing on warm straw, the scent of cosy herbs, buttery carrots and roasted chicken wrapping her in a comforting hug.

Although welcome, the moment is temporary and Kayla excuses herself from the lesson to go to the bathroom.

\*    \*    \*

'Hi, gorgeous girl . . . neighbour, haw, haw! Sorry to be a bother when you're away, but it's important we chat. Can you call me when you get a mo? Byeee!'

Kayla listens to the recorded sound of Eve Houseby's sing-song voice, which agitates her from across the ocean like nails on a chalkboard. Kayla deletes the message and calls Daniel. She leaves him a voicemail. They still haven't spoken properly since she arrived. Rosie has been at his parents' so they've facilitated her calls with her daughter.

She returns to the outside table where Alessandra and Maria are painting hard-boiled eggs a bright red. Their lunch is now cleared away. Despite Kayla being unable to eat much, she admits it was delicious. Alessandra's company still vexes her, but she decides to attempt cordiality for Maria's sake. She doesn't wish to upset her gracious hostess, who has become such a calming influence on her.

Alessandra finishes painting an egg with a flourish and reaches for another. 'Hey, Kayla, come and join. We're nearly done with the eggs and then we plait the bread dough around them, and bake.'

Kayla forces a smile and takes a seat. She is grateful for the shady overhang of the grapevines; the heat is amplifying her irritability, like she's about to explode.

'Why is it you do not have children, Maria?' Alessandra asks.

Unable to bite her tongue, Kayla snaps, 'Sorry, but I really don't think that's a question anyone should ever ask. It's like saying, why aren't you a boy or a girl; why are you in an open marriage? I'm not sure why you need to be so personal. Not everyone enjoys airing their dirty laundry in public.'

Alessandra is undeterred and shrugs. 'It's a valid question and I am interested, that is all. Not everyone is unable to discuss their feelings.'

The barb hits Kayla right between her ribs as Maria intervenes quickly. 'I don't mind answering, but that's just me. I'm an open book and I get that some people aren't and that's OK too,' she says softly, then turns to Alessandra. 'I couldn't have them. Children, that is.'

Her words hang in the air and Maria dips her paintbrush in colour as if it was the start of an ironic fertility ritual, given that the traditional red paint is supposed to symbolise the Mother's tears for Jesus. Alessandra reaches out her hand, resting it on top of Maria's knuckles, and gives it a tender squeeze.

'I'm so sorry for you, if it's something you wanted and couldn't have,' Alessandra says quietly.

Maria smiles with her usual warmth, placing her other hand on top of Alessandra's. 'I wanted a child more than I loved to cook. I used to tell people that motherhood wasn't for me, but it was a lie. I couldn't fall pregnant, no matter how much my ex and I tried – and when it was good between us, we tried a lot!'

Maria laughs heartily, without a trace of bitterness. Kayla can't imagine feeling such warmth for a broken marriage.

'I'm sorry too,' manages Kayla as her thoughts alight on her daughter. It hurt to be apart from Rosie, like a dull constant ache. But she is beginning to realise this time away is the necessary space she needs.

'Thank you,' says Maria, smiling at both women, 'but I'm rich in so many other ways and I'm grateful for those blessings. It fills the void, I guess.'

Kayla squirms in her seat, feeling guilty for her own incredibly blessed life. She has money and success; a beautiful, healthy daughter, so why does she still feel incomplete? It's the notion of failing at something, namely her marriage, that frustrates her and Kayla hates to have anything less than perfection.

'Here is my chink of wisdom, for what it's worth,' says Maria. 'It's a long and lonely road being a woman. We all feel like we're holding the world on our shoulders, kids or no kids. Work, family, marriage, friendships, love . . . it's the hardest thing to keep all those plates spinning. But it's even trickier to find the courage to take some of those plates away, clear the clutter from your life. Whether it's people, missed opportunities, what could've been . . . And if you do, let me tell you the relief is enormous. It's like giving yourself permission to accept what's happened and to stop fighting, to no longer wish for more or for something different. Sometimes we need to hear it's OK, you're already amazing and you can do it. That's proper sisterhood, not the pretend version you read about. We have the power to truly uplift and give each other a safe space to say, "I've failed, but I'm still awesome and I'm enough."'

Kayla considers Maria's words, her sentiments a balm for her soul.

'How did you come to terms with not being able to have children?' asks Kayla.

Maria shrugs as she watches some of the worker bees leave their hive. 'I had no choice in that part, as far as biology went, and I did grieve it for years. But it's not in the universe's plan for me and I had to accept that. It was exhausting, pointlessly regretting an impossibility.

104

And that acceptance transformed me. So, instead, I focus on what makes me happy: my bees, food and people. In that order!'

One of the bees lands on the table and Maria allows it to climb onto the end of her paintbrush, watching it devotedly.

'What about love?' Alessandra asks.

'I don't need a man to be happy. That said, never say never. It's just unlikely for me because there isn't anyone in my life . . . not really.'

Maria watches the bee climb along the wooden stick with an almost maternal love. After a while, she speaks again with a laugh. 'Maybe I haven't completely given up on love yet. We gotta have hope, right?'

'You said "not really" . . .' Kayla smiles. 'So there could be a someone . . . ?'

Kayla's words hang in the claggy air and Maria stands, encouraging the honeybee onto a lavender bush. It resists the new landing spot, flying back to where Maria was sitting. She bends once more to coax it away as Kayla says, 'That little bee wants your attention, Maria.'

Maria laughs with Kayla. 'He's trying to tell me something, I'm sure, but I don't know what.'

Kayla looks to Alessandra and sees that she is staring at the seaside entrance to the lawn, paying no mind to the toing and froing of the bee. She suddenly whistles quietly. Kayla follows Alessandra's gaze and sees a man in the garden. Alessandra exclaims in admiration, '*Mio Dio!*'

Maria's head whips around in the direction of her exclamation, and she gives a small gasp of surprise and mutters to the air, 'Leonidas.'

Leonidas is walking up the path from the beach. The afternoon sunshine frames his athletic build as he smiles broadly at Maria. He is a striking figure, tall, with a large leather satchel slung across his body. Kayla watches Maria's reaction as she unconsciously smooths her hair. The bee lifts off from the table and zooms high into the air before flying low near the visitor. Maria observes the insect with a questioning look, before her eyes lock with Leonidas'. Her bee seems to have an interest in him.

Kayla turns to Maria, eyebrows raised teasingly, and asks, 'Anyone you know, Maria . . . or "not really"?'

# Chapter 11

## *Maria*

I introduce my guests to Leonidas, and both women succumb immediately to his charms. He has a magnetic effect on everyone he meets. Their eyes twinkle at his gentle manner concealed within his masculine shell. But in a rare moment of agreement, they both decide to end our cooking class early. They excuse themselves and retreat through the olive trees, giggling like co-conspirators. At least they're joined in something, even if the joke is at my expense.

I wipe down the lunch table and take the painted eggs into my teaching kitchen, and Leonidas follows.

'What can I do for you, Leonidas? Shouldn't you be at church, praying for your soul?'

I seem to be flirting and his hazel eyes glint with mischief in the sunlight streaming through the window.

'I thought I'd come and see your empire. I'd very much like to meet your bees.'

'If you're here to laugh at me and report back to the gossips, then I wish for no part of your scheme.'

I know I am being unnecessarily spiky, but I don't want to be the subject of mockery at his hands; he is too important to my few happy recollections of growing up here. Apart from that day on Kalamaki beach. I weave an extra layer of protection around my heart, locking it firmly closed, just in case.

Leonidas holds up his hands in protest. '*Ochi*, no, Maria, I wish to see what you have made here on the fields where we used to sit. That is all.' He smiles fondly, as if picturing the memories. I am struck by the fact that he holds those times with similar affection. But we are adults now and so much has changed; we aren't the same anymore.

He watches me while I finish plaiting the bread, squishing the painted eggs within the dough, then place the loaves in the proving drawer. I wipe my hands on my apron, untie its ribbons and turn to him, my hands on my hips. I scrutinise his face but see only good intentions.

'Fine, I will show you my bees,' I say cautiously.

I take him through the cottage garden and the olive trees. He remarks on the planting with each step we take, stopping to smell the fruit and flowers as we go. I search my mind for clues as to his motivation as we walk.

'They did well converting all this for you, Maria. You know I ran a building company in Thessaloniki after I left here. For me, the pleasure comes in making something from nothing. It's why I now return to woodwork. We have both found what we love,' Leonidas says as he places his bag on the ground and crouches down in front of my hives. 'I cannot believe this was once your father's farm.' He turns his head to me. His gaze is too intense to hold, so I look away.

'I'm glad you've found your passion. You always loved making things, scouring the beaches for driftwood and sea glass, I remember. Making boats, people, little treasures, anything you could think of.'

He smiles fondly. 'I wish I had been here to help you build all this. But I couldn't be.' A cloud crosses his face, a shadow of regret and sadness.

'We missed each other . . . with . . . with the timing, I mean,' I stutter. 'When I came back to Petalidi, you left not long after. It was a shame, I wanted to see you, but I was a bit of a mess when I got here, kind of reclusive. I'd been through a lot . . .'

I don't know what I'm making an excuse for.

'He was a good man, your *babá*. I didn't know he died until long after the funeral, otherwise I would have been here for you. Athena wasn't good at letting me know important news, and by the time your mother's letter reached me, it was too late.'

'I didn't know you were in touch with my mother,' I say in surprise and resolve to mention it if only to remonstrate with her for trying to intervene in our doomed relationship that never quite got going. 'I was sorry to hear things didn't work out with Athena. It must be hard for you both to be in such a small place together, all those opinions . . . It's good you came back, though. For Zoe.'

'I had to come back, like I was drawn home. Not only because your mother encouraged me to – and she didn't mean any harm, before you start.' He fixes me with a look, ensuring I understand before continuing. 'But I didn't want to miss out on Zoe growing up, be *that* kind of father, absent, just a name on a birthday card. Maybe this is what happens when we are old: we finally realise what is important.'

'You speak for yourself. I'm not old. I'm just getting started.' I smile at him, and he returns my warmth.

'It was the right time to return after all those years away. And now I do what I always longed for: making things in my workshop, like I used to.' He sighs heavily with the weight of unseen burdens. 'Do you wonder if we can ever find that same happiness we had as children?'

My bees go quiet, as if someone has turned their volume down so they can eavesdrop. The sunshine beats down so hard on our backs, I feel a trickle of sweat fall down my scarred neck. Suddenly self-conscious, I look away. I must seem so different to him, spoilt and changed. I feel naked without a scarf to cover my mark.

'We knew nothing of the world, Leonidas, as children. We had no cares, no pain, nothing could harm us. We were accepting of life, without any judgement: a simple existence. At least it was for you; less so for me.'

'That is where you are wrong, Maria. There is always a pain we carry inside even as an innocent, only we don't realise it at the time.' He looks down at his large hands. 'There is always regret about how things should have been. My daughter, Zoe, is a wonderful child, but she is difficult. Athena is hot-headed and jealous. She played out every moment of our break-up to our daughter, read out every solicitor's letter to turn her against me. I regret being responsible for hurting her. That is time I cannot take back, so I must live with my mistakes. Zoe carries

110

pain she does not deserve, at my hands, but it was for the best in a way. It would have been worse if I'd stayed. For us all.'

He sends me another loaded look as he runs his fingers through his dark hair, and I feel my head swim as my heart swells. I quickly stand and walk over to my tool shed to fetch the wood to repair the broken hive.

'You may wish to stand back,' I say, preparing to gently prise off the warped overhang to replace it. 'The bees are likely to get angry with a stranger here.'

'Is that what I am, Maria – a stranger?' He stares at me with an unfathomable expression. In this moment, I have no idea what he wants from me. Finally, he breaks the silence that hangs between us like an early morning fog. 'Here, I've brought you something.' From his satchel, he hands me a large tissue-wrapped parcel.

As I reveal the contents, my neck prickles and the hives vibrate once more with a loud hum that I feel in the marrow of my bones. The thick piece of varnished oak wood glints in the light. It is hand carved, with three honeybees in relief. They are so beautifully formed it looks as if the insects are alive and have just landed. My fingers trace over them, enjoying their contours, the smooth shape of their bellies. I hold it against the hive, where it will replace the damaged piece of wood. He has even made screw holes so it will bolt onto the main body of the hive, creating the vital shade for the bees. It is a perfect fit, almost as if he has been here to measure the beehive. He must have asked Giorgos when I left the hardware store.

'Leonidas, I don't know what to say. It's beautiful, perfect. Thank you so much.'

'You see, I am doing what I love again. Just as you have done. You inspire me, Maria.'

He kneels beside me and it is as if the world pauses. I cannot look away from his eyes. A small swarm of the bees funnel out from the hive between us, and I long for him to lean forward and fill the space in my heart with a kiss. I am shocked by my own thought, a ridiculous notion, and quickly sit back on my heels to move away from him.

'Maria! *Pou eísai?*' My mother breaks the moment with a shrill shriek from the terrace, demanding to know where I am. 'Oh! Forgive me, Leonidas, *yiá sou!*'

She looks absurdly delighted as she shuffles along. He springs up and politely rushes over to save her the journey, kissing both her cheeks and clasping her hands. I brush the grass from my skirt as I stand, hoping my blushes aren't visible. I feel like I've been caught out, and I know my mother will never stop if she spies even the smallest inkling of an opportunity to pair me off. Especially given the revelation they were in touch after I left for America.

'Leonidas came to see my bees, *Mamá.*' I try to hold the gift from Leonidas behind my back, but my wily mother's eyes have already locked on it and makes a grab for it. She clumsily turns the wood over in her hands, her arthritic fingers caressing the carved honeybees. It is too heavy for her to hold, and I prise it from her grasp.

'This is wonderful, such craftsmanship. *Brávo*, Leonidas, *brávo*! But you encourage her to spend more time with the bees not people. Come to church with us this evening. I have been praying for you.'

One of her classic guilt trips, suggesting Leonidas is as bad as I for not attending services. I feel for him, but he pays no mind to the veiled suggestion. His late mother was much the same, I recall.

'Of course, I am honoured to accompany you.'

I feel a rising panic. I don't want to be seen with him in the village; it will only fuel the gossips into overdrive. I know my mother's tricks too well and I do not wish to be part of this scheme.

'I can't come. I have much to prepare for my classes,' I venture, knowing the torrent it will provoke from *Mamá*. Leonidas puts his hand on my arm. The feel of his touch sends a shock through my skin, and up my neck to Montana.

'Please, Maria, come to church tonight. We have much to give thanks for, if not only for your bees.'

He smiles with such warmth that I find myself nodding in concurrence. But I need to escape this weighted moment, before it plays out further in front of my mother. I begin to back away, still holding his gift, and hurriedly mumble, 'Thanks so much for this. I have to go. I'll mend the hive later.'

I race away to the safety of my kitchen where the homely smell of yeast from the *tsoureki* bread fills my nose. I feel the dull thud of fear reverberating through my body. I cannot trust anyone else with my heart. I lost my visions when my ex-husband rejected me. What more would the Fates take from me? What else would I lose, if I allowed such a thing to happen again?

# Chapter 12

## *Alessandra*

Richly perfumed incense floats in puffs of clouds around the cavernous building. Alessandra walks into church with Maria by her side, ahead of Eleni and Leonidas. Alessandra notices the distance Maria has deliberately put between the two parties.

Alessandra scans the pews for a space; the Thursday service is busy. The monotonous clang of the bells signal that proceedings are about to begin. There is room on the edge of a row for the two women, with enough of a gap for Eleni and Leonidas to sit together in the next pew. Leonidas looks quizzically at Maria as she takes her seat and indicates for them to do the same in the row in front. Alessandra senses churchgoers budging up away from Maria as a tiny but unmistakable rush of gossip ripples from the back of the congregation as heads turn to see the spectacle.

'It's very like the churches in Rome,' says Alessandra to Maria in hushed tones as she looks to the rafters, admiring the gilded archways and shrines along the sides. But Maria seems distracted by a woman across the aisle. Her eyes have locked on a mother and daughter, who both narrow their eyes at her. Maria shuffles uncomfortably in her seat and mutters to Alessandra about bearing the brunt of Leonidas and Eleni's scheme, plotting to force them into church together like some dysfunctional family. Alessandra observes the shift in energy and quickly deduces the main players in the sorry play.

'You have committed no crime, Maria. There is no need to feel guilty. He is a very beautiful man and could be yours to take if you wish,' she whispers.

'Shhhh!' hushes Maria, cringing. 'There will be no taking or wishing. It's nothing.'

Alessandra raises her pencilled eyebrow and says no more as the service starts. She thinks back to the rumble that travelled through the crowd at Maria's appearance in church. Speaking to locals and mentioning where she is staying, they automatically crossed themselves, as if harm would come to them by her proximity to Maria. Small-minded nonsense, she thinks, and feels grateful she lives within the anonymity of Rome to shield her from judgement. But it couldn't protect her from her daughter's.

She closes her eyes in prayer as the priest in his long black garb rattles off a stream of foreign holy words, but the sentiment is universal. As she opens them, she sees Maria's eyes are fixed on the back of Leonidas' head. His thick hair shines in the candlelight, caressing his nape in slight waves, revealing tantalising glimpses of his dark skin.

116

He is certainly very attractive, Alessandra thinks, akin to a matinée idol, and she considers him to be a good match for Maria. His neck pulse is visible as he turns his head and Maria unconsciously taps her fingers in time. Their heartbeats are synced. Alessandra smiles to herself, struck by romance of the moment they're both oblivious to. As if Maria becomes aware she is beating Leonidas' life-giving rhythm, she puts her hand to her scar instead.

A gasp draws Alessandra's attention as someone spots Maria's gesture. Maria had told her as they'd walked to church that people in the village thought she'd been marked by the devil, so a simple act of touching her neck would no doubt fuel such petty beliefs. Alessandra sees several people making the sign of the cross. It becomes contagious throughout one side of the congregation, and she feels outrage on Maria's behalf. Maria looks to the heavens for strength, but Alessandra fears her prayer will go unanswered and squeezes her hand in solidarity.

Father Kyriakidis chants a prayer and the crowd collectively murmurs along. Alessandra feels Maria's phone vibrate, the tremor travelling through the wooden pew. Maria discreetly glances at the screen on her lap. Alessandra peers at it too and sees the sender is called 'COWARD'. Curiosity gets the better of her and she reads the message over Maria's shoulder, but as soon as her eyes alight on the words, she wishes she hadn't seen them.

> **You don't belong here.
> You will burn in hell.**

\* \* \*

117

'*Kalo Pascha*, Leonidas,' says Father Kyriakidis as they all leave the church. 'It is good to have you returned to your home after all these years. Look at you and Maria – it is like we travel back in time!'

The elderly priest explains to Alessandra their age-old friendship as he glances at Maria, clearly amused to see the childhood friends reunited. Maria excuses herself and moves away to speak to Giorgos, the hardware merchant, and his wife. Alessandra stays beside Eleni and Leonidas, intrigued to uncover more about their shared past from the priest.

'I've been busy settling back into Petalidi these last few weeks, Father. Eleni insisted I come with her tonight, which, of course, is impossible to refuse.' Leonidas twinkles at Maria's mother, who giggles girlishly at him.

'Perhaps, Father, you can speak to Leonidas about the restoration plans? You need new pews. It was a very good service, but the seats are most uncomfortable and my back is killing me. I fear I cannot help Maria with all that must be done ahead of the weekend; she has so much to do. If only we had a man around the house.' She sighs for dramatic effect.

Father Kyriakidis beams. 'Well, of course, Leonidas, we must commission you to make pews for your village church.'

'You should see the carving he did for Maria, Father.' Alessandra can tell that Eleni is deliberately speaking loudly so those within earshot can spread the word. She suppresses a smile at the push and pull of small village politics yet cannot help but feel protective over Maria after witnessing that awful message earlier. Eleni continues to wax lyrical about Leonidas' gift.

118

'A beautiful depiction of her bees. A most thoughtful and generous present.'

As Eleni wishes, the news begins to spread in whispers through the crowd, and Leonidas is cajoled by Eleni into something Alessandra doesn't catch. She is too busy watching groups of villagers as they receive the gossip. Alessandra watches as Eleni's relayed words reach Maria, who strides over at once. As she nears, Leonidas says, 'But if your back is in so much pain, I would be only too happy to help Maria and accept your offer to dine with you all.'

Alessandra looks on as Maria's mouth drops open. Her expression indicates it's the first she's heard of her mother's ailment. A covert plan seems to be unfurling in front of Alessandra and, although she feels a surprising need to shield Maria from any pain, she is firmly on Eleni's side. Maria needs a small shove towards this wonderful man, which Alessandra is only too happy to help facilitate. Although the old woman seems to have it covered. It is settled: Leonidas will be coming to eat with them all during Easter.

Alessandra will ensure she and Kayla make themselves scarce. How receptive Kayla will be to such collaboration is yet to be determined. She is too aware of Kayla's continued unfriendliness. Aside from her animosity, it is clear she is caught in an invisible battle, aside from the end of her marriage, which prevents her from opening up. Alessandra is certain Maria holds the key to unlocking whatever problems Kayla has. Already she can feel a change within herself. Resisting an encounter with the musician marked the shift. All she can think about is a need to be with Phillipo, wishing he were here. It's contrary to their whole union and confuses her.

Being in Petalidi has encouraged her to reach down into her heart and discover what she wishes for her future. Now, in touch with her true desire, it shocks her how conventional her needs have become. Initially, it seems disappointing, in contrast to most of her existence. But the thrill of unearthing something unexpectedly new, no matter how traditional, charges through her. Maria's magic has cast light on an undiscovered dimension within herself. And it is deliciously surprising.

\* \* \*

Later, Alessandra steps forward through the olive trees and smiles as she observes Maria beside her bees. Maria kneels in front of the hive with Leonidas' new carving across the top, her fingers tracing its shape as if she were caressing a spine. Maria had told her that each day at sunset, she takes a glass of wine to sit with her bees and tell them about her day. The insects appear as irritable as Kayla in this relentless heat, but Maria's voice seems to calm them, their angry hum diminishing further as she speaks.

As serene as the tableau appears on the surface, there's an element of tragedy about it. A woman as loving and caring as Maria deserves the same and more in return than she gives to others. She'd concealed that terrible message, hardly reacting save for her trembling hand when she replaced the phone in her pocket. Maria doesn't warrant such dreadful treatment and Alessandra longs to seek out a way to bring some joy, if not love into her life. One unchangeable thing about Alessandra is her ability to seek out pleasure in whatever form it appears. To do that for Maria would be deeply gratifying. But how to orchestrate it . . . ?

A cluster of bees whips past her ear and heads for Maria. She catches cinnamon on the wind as they zip by – her favourite scent. The beginnings of an idea unfurl, filling Alessandra with a purpose. It is a welcome feeling, soothing away any fatigue. Her bones are heavy, although she has found solace in walking on the beach and bathing in the clear turquoise waters. But all other thoughts evaporate as her mind suddenly buzzes with excitement.

# Chapter 13

## Kayla

Kayla is trying to write, but her mind refuses to focus. The soporific drone of the church service through the speakers had echoed along the promenade, lulling her into an unproductive state. But the contents of her dream-like thoughts were the opposite of the intended religious content from the priest. Dimitris. Their silent, flirtatious exchange from last night conjures up inappropriate scenarios and her nerve endings feel raw, alert, poised for action – one she shouldn't indulge. It is as delightful as it is terrifying.

The placement of the patio chair and tables outside her villa afford glimpses of the sea through the foliage. It is peaceful and healing. Kayla feels as if she could lose herself amongst the jungle of flowers and herbs. She imagines herself as a bee, zooming around the plants and bountiful olive trees. The surroundings are hypnotic, distracting, invading every sense. Her eyes are constantly drawn back to Maria on the grass, speaking to the air.

Kayla places her fingers on the keyboard again and sighs, frustrated with her article. She managed to write a little while the others were at church, but she already knows she'll delete it tomorrow.

*I've never met anyone who'd holidayed on the Greek mainland before, forgoing the whitewashed buildings and blue domes of Santorini or Mykonos. But it is not to be discounted. As I headed off to the Ionian for a cooking experience at the famed Maria's Kitchen, I wondered how much more there could be to Greek cuisine outside of moussaka and tzatziki. How wrong I was. Not only did I uncover a whole world of recipes and flavour combinations, but Greece gave me more than I could have anticipated. The spectacular sea view in the little village of Petalidi eased me gently into each morning as the day braced to unveil a myriad of flavours: heavenly vanilla, cinnamon sweetness in a stuffed aubergine, fronds of dill adding syncopated fragrant notes to green beans in a rich tomato sauce, and crunchy pistachios garnishing the heavenly honeyed sweetness of sticky pastry.*

Deeply uninspiring . . . Her stomach rumbles and she ignores it. She'd hoped coming here would afford some perspective on how to move on after the end of her marriage. Yet all it has done is fill her head with questions and her body with an unexpected desire for another man.

What she does know is that she can't forgive Daniel; his adultery will always be lurking in the shadows like an invisible predator, ready to pounce on her insecurities. The blot he's put on their marriage is like a red wine stain on white silk: the faint outline will always be there even if most of it comes out in the wash.

She admits in her heart it is over, and if she were completely honest with herself, it has been for some time; she just didn't want to acknowledge defeat. Kayla wishes she could be more like Maria, accepting of her circumstances, truly fulfilled. *She* ought to be the famous role model, rather than Kayla, who wears the mantle so reluctantly. Although she loves her career, it is the fame part she cannot reconcile, a side effect she was unprepared for. It brings a fear of being unmasked and her secret revealed. She isn't the perfect example of domestic bliss the public believe her to be, she wasn't even before her marriage broke apart. And the ruin of her wedded not-so-full-of-bliss is only the half of it.

'*Ciao*, Kayla,' says Alessandra, and Kayla turns to see her walking wearily up the path. Although both women scurried away together when Leonidas arrived after lunch, resentment still loiters within Kayla at her Italian counterpart. She still feels embarrassed to have chosen to reveal Daniel's indiscretion to someone who wouldn't be appalled. It did her self-esteem no favours at all, and Kayla wishes she'd told Maria instead of the Italian who instead of offering tea and sympathy, encouraged her to step into an illicit encounter of her own. Kayla is deeply uncomfortable she's even entertaining the idea in the darkest crevices of her mind.

Although Alessandra is right: it wouldn't be adultery per se. Daniel's liaison with his fragrant friend has put a stopper in the bottle of their relationship. It's over and there's no turning back. Kayla feels utterly ungrounded by the prospect of starting again, with only herself to rely on to provide for Rosie. Is she enough, emotionally equipped to be the main caregiver? She has no idea.

'Oh, hi, Alessandra. I'm in the middle of working, so . . .' Kayla says hoping to avoid her company, but Alessandra stumbles on the pathway and falls.

Kayla springs up as Alessandra tumbles into a lavender bush, sending a chorus of angry bees up into the air. The contents of her bag scatters across the paving stones.

'Are you all right? You're bleeding!' Kayla asks helping Alessandra upright, seeing her arm has grazed on the gravel in the flowerbeds. 'Let me help you.'

As Kayla bends down to gather Alessandra's belongings, she sees several bottles of pills and vitamins, a book, sea glass and driftwood, then a bunch of leaflets. Picking up each item, she manages to piece together what was concealed before the bag spilt. As the last part of the jigsaw slots into place, Kayla looks up at Alessandra, shocked and surprised to find tears in her own eyes. The word on the piece of paper in her hand needs no translation.

Sarcoma.

Alessandra is more than just faint from the heat. She has cancer.

# Chapter 14

## *Maria*

'*Kalí Anastasi*, Happy Resurrection! It's what we say on Good Friday, but this will be a *great* Friday!' I exclaim as I spoon some honey onto my breakfast yoghurt.

I am trying desperately to be cheerful despite my overnight vigil having yielded nothing in my search for the person responsible for the nasty rubble beside my bees. It occurred to me when I abandoned my vigil at dawn that I'm not even sure it is just one individual I'm looking for. There could be one behind the texts and another behind the hive warnings. But they somehow feel linked, often arriving in tandem. In the warm morning air, it now feels like a tremendous waste of energy to have stayed up all night, and I regret even entertaining the notion I could solve a mystery that has lasted weeks with no sign of abating. I'm afraid it's something I may need to simply accept, and just pity who is behind it.

But I am uneasy, and the injustice hurts my heart. I've done nothing wrong.

Kayla and Alessandra are talking, heads bowed at the table outside my teaching kitchen as they take coffee. They're so engrossed in their conversation they don't hear me. Kayla is fussing over Alessandra, running off to refill her cup like she's mothering her. It's in total contrast to yesterday. They've unexpectedly bonded. It warms my heart, but I can't help but wonder, over what?

But as soon as the question enters my mind, I chill cold to the very marrow of my bones.

*Strange.*

'Morning, *buongiorno*, Maria, is another very hot day,' says Alessandra. I notice she is off colour, with dark smudges under her eyes. I look at Kayla, who seems unable to move away from Alessandra.

'Kayla, can I show you something at the hives for your article?' She stands reluctantly and links arms with me as we walk away from the house.

Unprompted, Kayla says, 'Do not react, as she wants to tell you later, but I found out Alessandra has cancer, a kind of sarcoma. I read up about it last night. Hers is rare and it's spread. The prognosis isn't good. Months at best.'

I swallow away my shock at the stream of terrible information and instead point to the bees in pretence to mask our real conversation. I feel the ice in my bones again, but the meaning behind the message remains a void, like receiving a blank postcard. Only the hint that something is wrong. I long for my gift to return; I need it more than ever. 'How did you find out? You haven't been the best of buddies so far.'

128

'She tripped and a bunch of pills fell out of her bag, as well as a book about living with cancer. She confessed, but in typical Alessandra fashion, she was very matter-of-fact about it.'

'Oh, God, that's awful,' I say, trying to process it all. 'Do you think she needs to see a doctor? She doesn't look well this morning.'

'I already suggested that, but she refused. I'm certain neither of us can change her mind,' says Kayla with a small laugh and I agree, having never met anyone more headstrong. Apart from my mother.

It seems timely that the church bells toll, one of the many times they will ring today, marking the solemnity of the crucifixion, the inevitability of death, which in this new knowledge is more acute than ever. We stand watching the bees whizzing about in the morning sunshine, wafts of oregano drifting on the wind as the bells continue to chime.

'Wow, what's this?' Kayla asks as she stoops to look at the piece of blue cloth. It has blown over on itself and I can't see what she means. She turns and holds up an evil eye, painted on the fabric with a skull in the middle. I snatch it from her.

'When did that arrive? It must have just happened . . .' I look around in panic, rushing to the seafront to see if I can spot anyone.

'Is something wrong, Maria?' Kayla asks. 'What does it mean?'

I look at the piece of cloth in my hands, so frustrated I've missed the culprit after sitting out all night, I could scream. Instead, I turn back to my guest.

'This? Oh, just silly Easter tricks,' I say dismissively. 'They do it all the time.'

I rub the chills that have risen on my arms at the sight of the skull. The messages and morning tributes seem to be growing in the severity of their meanings as well as their frequency, gaining pace, gathering momentum. Towards what, I don't like to think. I can tell Kayla is suspicious, but switches subjects.

'I was on the beach this morning and saw children picking flowers from the hedgerows. Is that for the procession this evening?'

'Yes, the Good Friday procession is amazing,' I reply. 'Emotional, too.'

'Such a tight-knit community, isn't it?' says Kayla wistfully and I see that the magic of Petalidi has woven itself around her. She is romanticising what so many holidaymakers see when they visit.

'Which is both good and bad.' I laugh. 'Helpful when there's a crisis, but hell for single women and suddenly everyone has a son, cousin, nephew, uncle, father who wants to go on a date.' Or if someone hates you, I add silently. 'Luckily, I don't have that problem.'

'I reckon you only have eyes for a certain someone.'

I look around at the house, the row of villas, the meticulously tended olive grove that was here when my dream cooking school was a germinating seed. 'There is no room for anything else other than me, Kayla. If you mean Leonidas, that is ancient history without a history. We're friends and that's all, always have been, always will be. I settled on flying solo in this next part of my life after my accident. Maybe it's self-preservation.' We begin to walk back to the house. 'I have my bees, my business and that's enough for me. So, let's get into that kitchen and fill our stomachs with the good stuff.'

Kayla looks unconvinced, but I don't need any more complications in my life. Nor do I need to explain the background with Athena, who tries to make my life tricky enough as it is. Imagine if something *were* to happen with Leonidas? There is no telling what she would do.

*   *   *

The shift in atmosphere amongst the three of us is pronounced. Tensions have dissolved as quickly as they arrived, like a storm grumbling high up in the Peloponnese mountains, tumbling down the sheer cliffs, and fading into nothing. We talk openly and honestly as we cook, and Alessandra confesses her illness to me as we prepare our simple luncheon: lightly pan-fried red mullet with a salad made from shredded cabbage, carrot and sundried tomatoes, dressed with a vinegar honey drizzle. One of the fishermen had a wonderful haul of the little red fish, *barbounia*, this morning and I bought a bagful straight off his boat. It won't take long to make, so we focus on the more complicated baklava dessert. Heavenly honey-soaked filo pastry with walnuts and a sprinkling of pistachios. I know they'll both respond to my bees' honey. It is a magical gateway to precious memories, providing a flavourful, luxurious comfort.

As we brush melted butter onto the sheets of pastry,

Alessandra explains about her diagnosis, which she received a year ago. She has a matter of months to live, and treatment would now make little difference. She halted any further rounds of chemotherapy or radiotherapy, not wishing to spend her final months in a bed. Brave, wise or foolish, I cannot decide which, but it is her life and her death, and I am glad she has some choice in it. So many do not.

'What about your daughter? Shouldn't she know you're dying?' asks Kayla.

Alessandra smiles sadly as she pours the spiced walnut mixture on a sheet of filo, nutty cinnamon scenting the air as she layers the dessert, building it delicately. 'I have tried to make contact, but I fear she would have no change in her heart whether I am alive or dead.'

'No!' shrieks Kayla suddenly, causing me and Alessandra to jump. 'She must – you need to give her the chance to say goodbye. You *have* to tell her.'

Alessandra and I share a glance, shocked at her outburst. Kayla is usually the epitome of control, but now she is bright red in the face. I move to her, wondering what on earth has upset her. She is gulping heavily, unable to form the words as Alessandra joins me and we both cradle our arms around her. We stand in the centre of the kitchen holding each other, the energy of sorrow and pain pulsing in the air, almost palpable. Eventually Kayla moves out of our embrace, wiping her face with a dishcloth.

'I'm sorry, I didn't mean to. I don't know what's come over me. Forget it. Sorry, it's none of my business.' Kayla winces suddenly. 'Ouch, God, my finger is killing me.'

She holds out her index finger, which is slightly swollen and red.

'What did you do to it?' I ask looking at it.

'I got stung by a bee on Wednesday night. I hope it's not one of yours because if so, I've killed it.' Tears start to pour down her face again. 'I can't believe I've murdered one of your bees.'

I lead her over to the sink as I take a clean cloth and pour cider vinegar over it and press it to her wound. 'It's the circle of life, Kayla, meant to happen. You couldn't have changed that bee's destiny.'

I urge her to understand. There's nothing we can do to alter Alessandra's situation, to shift the inevitable hand of fate.

'Sorry. I feel like everything's falling apart since I got here. I don't know what's going on. I can't write properly, my marriage is broken, I am devastated about her illness.' She turns to address Alessandra. 'I'm so sad you're ill, even though I fundamentally disagree with your lifestyle choices. Sorry, that was rude. God, what is happening to me?'

'You're being honest for once.' Alessandra gives an amused shrug. 'I like it.'

I take a teaspoon of honey and swiftly mix it into a paste with some baking soda. Cutting a small square of muslin, I soak it in a dose of apple vinegar before wrapping it carefully around her finger. 'It's slightly infected, but that will draw out anything that's stuck in there.'

'Thank you,' Kayla says, drying her eyes with her sleeve again.

If only I could apply such a simple remedy to Kayla

emotionally, but the honey will help. Besides, sometimes you need to take apart something that's broken in order to fix it properly, once and for all.

*   *   *

I set a table for lunch in the middle of the olive grove. The large branches provide a natural canopy to shelter us from the heat and I've hung flowers and hand-sewn bunting from the leafy boughs. Fairy lights wrapped around the trunks will illuminate at dusk, making it look like a magical fairy grotto. It's good to be outside; the atmosphere in the kitchen had become too intense following Kayla's outburst. She's gone to lie down, and Alessandra has gone for a swim. She wafted away in a beautiful green and orange kaftan. It wouldn't surprise me if she was naked underneath, she is so free. There's a healing in nature, and I am glad she finds peace in being here. My mother appears, shuffling through the tress.

'The table will be set for five today, just to remind you, Maria *mou*,' she states. *My Maria* . . . why is she being so nice?

'*Mamá*, come back here. What do you mean, five?' She turns around slowly, for dramatic effect and partly because it's the pace her frailty allows.

'I will be joining you, as will Leonidas, in case you'd forgotten, which I see you have. Please ensure there is enough for him. And remember, it is still Lent, I will have lentils, not fish.'

Instantly the wings of nervous butterflies twitch in the

pit of my stomach. 'Why, why are you doing this, *Mamá*? It will only cause problems for me and for him in the village.' I move over to her, trying to impress the importance of my point. 'You know someone comes to our home each day and makes a crucifix out of stones or a *mati* in front of my bees? I get messages on my phone warning me. This is serious – somebody hates me here and wants me gone. Why would you wish this trouble on Leonidas as well? Please, I beg you, don't meddle.'

Her mouth hardens into a thin line and she looks up at me with her beady black eyes. She is so small, yet so formidable. 'Because, Maria, there will be no other man for you. I prayed it would be him from when you were young. But no, you chase your silly dreams to America, encouraged by your father, and he is left here for another woman to snap up.' She clicks her fingers close to my face. 'And you marry another man, which, as I foretold, was a big mistake. Then you return, and Leonidas suddenly leaves the village for Thessaloniki, disappearing into air like a ghost for ten years. Is like you are both dancing across time, like two people in a cuckoo clock: in and out, in and out. Now is the moment for what should have happened over thirty years ago when you made the worst mistake of your life with Leonidas on that terrible day. If it is last thing I do on this earth, I will see you happy with a man.'

'But I'm happy *without* a man. And my dreams weren't silly; they gave us this life. Thank God *Babá* believed in me otherwise I'd have been stuck here at seventeen with no ambition, just a bored housewife. Surely you wouldn't have wished that on me?'

135

My mother shakes her head in fury. 'Stop! You may think I am old and stupid, but I see things very clearly. I am sick of this nonsense. You think you are the only one to have the gift of sight?' She laughs bitterly, looking around to ensure nobody is within earshot. '*I* had it, your *yiayiá* – my mother – had it and we passed it to you like some terrible disease. I keep this secret to myself all my life, yet you run around shouting about the spirits you see, and everyone thinks you're touched by the devil.' She crosses herself three times. 'I know in my heart you and Leonidas belong together and it's meant to be. I have seen it. I only wish to hurry it along, so I am still alive when it happens and not in my grave.'

One of my bees could knock me over. I cannot believe it. My mother has the same gift as I used to, but never in all the years when she had ample opportunity did she mention it. Instead, she chose to bow to convention, afraid of being different from what our community expects. My shock turns to fury and I cannot be near her. I storm off along the beach, my feet crunching on the shingle beside the tideline. She must've been horrified to have spawned such a fearless rebel. I'm unsure what smarts the most: her secret or what she foresees.

I stop walking and look across the bay, willing the past to leave me be. It is not possible for me to be with Leonidas; it's too late to revisit our history. Besides, he doesn't think that way about me anymore. Any love or deeper feelings are gone. You cannot force what isn't there, despite what *Mamá* reckons she has seen. It will never happen; it mustn't. I can feel the danger it will cause thudding in my bones even without my visions. It is the remnants of *my* gift and I cling on to my instinct. That and my bees are all I have to guide me.

# Chapter 15

## *Kayla*

'It's going well, thanks, busy. Is Rosie OK?' Kayla asks Daniel. Their conversation is stilted, strained with forced politeness.

'Yeah, she's doing great. Missing you, of course.' He pauses. 'Both of us are.'

His words hang in the distance between them, and Kayla stifles the sob rising from the ache in her chest.

'Are you?' she says in disbelief.

'You have no idea, Kay. I'm sorry, so sorry for hurting you. I still care about us. You know that.'

'But I don't know, Danny. How can you when you've done this to us? I can't even stand the thought of it, but I want to know all about it. Every time I close my eyes, I think of you with someone else and I vow to ask you the next time I speak to you, but I don't and instead I feel like throwing up.'

'Don't, Kay, please don't.'

'I can't help it. It's like it's finally dawned on me, it's real. We can't go back. It's all broken.'

'I know, and I'm sorry, but let's talk when you're home. Not like this.'

Kayla twiddles her hair around her finger as tears fill her eyes. Hearing his agreement that their marriage is done makes it true. It is agony, and she can't seem to take a deep breath. A tapping at the window draws her attention, but nobody is there. Then she sees a bee bashing against the windowpane, trapped inside the villa. She opens the sash to let it out. It sits on the sill, legs lifting one by one as if deciding what to do. It is perfect, beautiful. She imagines flattening it with the palm of her hand, just to endure another sting, to enjoy the beautiful sweetness of pain. The idea of wrecking something so alive and precious is both horrifying and appealing. A species that is intrinsically good and giving, not like humans, inflicting cruelty wherever they go. A life could be snuffed out by her will if she decided. The mere thought gives her a feeling of power, and it's enough to stop her from acting on it.

'Is it over, you and her?'

He hesitates just enough for Kayla to know the truth.

'. . . yes . . . it's . . . yes . . . let's not do this, Kay.'

She feels resentment rise at the obvious lie, a bitterness churning in the pit of her stomach, coiling around her gut and squeezing like a snake constricting its prey.

'Tell me it's not Eve Houseby – she's been ringing me nonstop. It would be the ultimate stalker's trophy to have gone to bed with *you*.'

140

'No, Kayla, it's not that stupid woman next door,' Daniel replies, wearily.

'Who is it, then? Why won't you tell me?'

'Kay, please . . . there's no point . . . not on the phone.'

She hangs up abruptly, unable to quell her tears. Throwing her mobile on the bed, she looks around her little villa, wondering if it was a huge mistake coming here.

The bee on the windowsill seems to turn its head to stare at Kayla before lifting off, soaring into the sky before flying into the olive grove. She watches it, thinking about her conversation with Daniel. She should have cancelled this trip but chose work instead of staying home and trying to fix what remained of her marriage. But it would already have been too late. What's the point of dwelling on what is irretrievable? That sentiment has been her undoing since her parents' deaths. She looks down at her immaculate manicure, the perfect gel extensions masking the torn, discoloured realities that live underneath. Her real nails hardly grow anymore, after years of continued damage, a side effect of her secret.

One by one she puts them in her mouth and rips them off, jagged edges, shards of nail and flakes of coral polish cover her clothes. Not allowing anything to be naturally nice about herself that she could admire or worse, someone else could. So, she covers it up with a fake coating, as she did with everything that mattered. It's what she always does.

Realisation slowly descends that she's been living in a bubble of her own creation and has chosen work over Daniel to the point it drove him to look for affection elsewhere. He shouldn't have, but men are sometimes that stupid, and certain women are so obvious, it makes it easy. *She* had made it easy for him. If only she was more like Alessandra, she'd brush off Daniel's encounter and maybe get her kicks from hearing about it. The only place anyone ever wants her is the kitchen, but that's work. She isn't sexy, she's approachable, homely, the perfect domestic goddess.

*If only they knew . . .*

One thing Kayla does know is she can't carry on like this. It has to end.

She walks into the bathroom and stares in the mirror. Her reflection repulses her, eyes gleaming emerald-green from crying, and her face is as red as her hair. Shaking her head in disgust, she fills a glass with water and swirls in one of her special sachets of powder as she begins to cry again. She thinks about her daughter Rosie, which makes her sob harder.

Kayla reaches into her washbag again, then kicks the bathroom door closed.

# Chapter 16

## *Maria*

I hastily dismantle the second of the morning's malicious offerings at the foot of the path leading to the beach. Two in one day is new, a cross made from driftwood and pebbles. At first glance, one could think it was a symbolic tribute to Good Friday, but I know otherwise. It's an additional taunt having sat up all night waiting for them, only to be outwitted twice in a day. The church bells are tolling once more, letting the village know the mid-morning service is about to start. My bees are busy, flitting in and out of their homes, zooming over the lawn to the botanical part of my garden. It's what gives their honey such a magical flavour, harvesting on the flowers and herbs.

A prickle on the back of my neck brings an awareness I am being watched. Hoping it's my mystery menace about to be caught in the act, I whip around to face the sea. Framed against the backdrop of aquamarine water is

Leonidas, smiling. I cannot prevent the broad grin that betrays my joy at seeing him. Whilst I wish my body would try to act in accordance with my mind, it's so good to have a familiar, friendly face on my side for a change.

'Are you spying on me, Leonidas? Happy Resurrection, by the way.'

He moves nearer. 'Happy Resurrection, Maria. Although we are probably the worst churchgoers in Petalidi, so why do we pretend?'

'Because even though the village believes I'm a witch, I still hold some traditions dear.'

He blanches at my words and shifts uncomfortably. 'Not the whole village. *I* would never think that. I always believed your visions. There were things you could not know by any other means. It was magical, like a mythical goddess with a strange power.'

I'm speechless at the alien comfort of a supportive friend, and I laugh out loud to hear that he considers me from a higher place. Our kinship and connection seem to slot into place whenever we are together, but beneath it all there's a tension building, neither of us mentioning *that* day on the beach. The memory bears down and suddenly I can hardly stand its weight.

As I look up at him, drinking in his appearance, a sadness cascades from my heart, and I find myself regretting the years we spent apart, estranged. When I heard from my *mamá* he'd married Athena, I decided he was my enemy as well. Then, as my own marriage and work consumed me in America, I pushed any thoughts of him firmly away. Although being in Petalidi again when I returned felt wrong without him beside me, like putting on shoes a size too small. But I was focused on looking after my father and rebuilding myself after New York. I didn't want him to see me scarred and spoilt. Then he left. Even when I knew he'd divorced Athena, he stayed away in Thessaloniki. But now I can't avoid him. At the rear of my mind, my mother's prediction lurks, trying to nudge itself forward, but I shove it as far back as I can once more.

'Well, that was all a long time ago, Leonidas. Much has changed since.' We walk amongst the olive trees.

'And yet very little changes . . .' responds Leonidas as we reach the table now set for five. 'I hope you don't mind me accepting your mother's invitation.'

I turn to him, the sun casting dappled shade across his body. He is wearing a navy linen shirt, which makes his skin gleam. It is a marvel how he retains his boyish charm in his grown man's body, his long lashes framing his twinkling hazel eyes, which always seem to indicate mischief is near. The ageing process in a man seems more effortless than in a woman.

'No, the more the merrier. You can meet my other guests. I love to entertain, you know me . . . well you don't . . . you did . . . Excuse me, I must cook the fish. Ah, Alessandra, you remember Leonidas. Could one of you pour the wine? I need to start cooking lunch.'

I scurry away into the kitchen, flustered, letting my flushed body cool in the air conditioning. Was it Leonidas, my hormones, or the weather? Being near him makes my temperature soar, and despite my attempted resistance, I know my feelings are growing for him again. But they mustn't. We could have remained as ghosts of each other's past without a present or a future, but I admit, I'm as

145

drawn to him as he seems to be to me, like magnets seeking the other out across the decades.

I feel a dart of resentment, though, believing the fantasy I'm entertaining is *Mamá*'s doing, planting a ridiculous idea in my head. The more I think about it, the less absurd it becomes in the same way that if you tell yourself a lie repeatedly, it eventually turns into truth. I determine once again to keep our friendship at arm's length. And besides, Leonidas is simply being polite and kind, as always. He feels nothing more and must've forgiven me for what I did, now seeking me out merely as a friend. Surely, he is repulsed by my scar and were he to harbour any feelings outside platonic affection, the map of the Americas burnt into my neck would quash them immediately.

I pick up the lightly floured fish and heat a pan on the stove. Through the windows, I can see Leonidas and Alessandra laughing. I watch as Alessandra touches his forearm in response to something amusing. From a distance they could be mistaken for lovers as Alessandra leans in, intimately whispering, her face becoming serious. Leonidas nods gravely in agreement, as if acquiescing to a plan, and smiles. They look like conspirators arranging a liaison. As they both look over at the kitchen window, I quickly avert my eyes as, despite all my resolutions, the sharp pang of jealousy stabs at my heart.

I place the mullet in the pan, which sizzles in response. Removing the baklava from the oven, I spoon the cooled honey and orange syrup over the top, watching as the sticky liquid oozes over the filo pastry.

'Please, protect me and bring us healing,' I incant as I tip the remaining syrup on the dessert.

'Who is it you are speaking to?' Leonidas says from behind me, making me jump.

'You're making quite a habit of creeping up on me!' I joke, my heart racing from the fright and from seeing him. 'It's one of my silly prayers I say when I make something with my honey.'

'Is it the rhyme you made up when we were kids? Let me try and remember . . . "Sweet honeybees, gather your spirit to fly . . ."'

I am stunned and touched at how he'd remember something so trivial from so many years ago.

Leonidas walks forward to the counter and takes the ladle from my hand, towering over me. 'Maria, I . . . I must tell you something.'

A drizzle of the honey trickles down the handle to his fingers, which he puts to his mouth and gently sucks the sticky sweetness away. My eyes are transfixed by his lips, like I'm being pulled into quicksand. A bee sits on a shelf, its buzz vibrating against a copper pan, and the sound draws my attention. Its presence encourages me back to my food, as if it is there to warn me. I pick up a fish slice and turn the mullet in its pan, as the bee knocks the light fixture and zooms out the door.

*Thank you for saving me, little friend,* I say in my head to the bee, before looking to Leonidas.

'We nearly lost our lunch then! What kind of teacher would I be if I served up burnt food to my guests? It'll be two minutes. Sorry, you were going to tell me something . . .'

'It doesn't matter,' Leonidas says quietly with a look of sudden disappointment. 'Shall I take these to the table?'

147

I indicate to a platter of salad and the basket of bread with a nod and he leaves. I rest my fists on the cool marble beside the stove, taking a series of calming deep breaths. I repeat my honey prayer over and over again . . .

*Please, protect me and bring us healing . . . please, protect me and bring us healing.*

But as I squeeze my eyes shut, wishing harder with each word, I feel tiny fragments of my heart leave my body and float towards the object of my affections.

Damn my mother for messing with my head. But I will my bees to help me ensure he never discovers what I've locked firmly inside.

# Chapter 17

## *Kayla*

A knock on the door brings Kayla's attention to the present. She is sitting on the bathroom floor, sniffling, clutching at her stomach as she waits for it to settle.

'Just a minute!' she shouts hoarsely as she springs up to wash her face.

As she steps into the lounge and opens the front door to her villa, she finds Maria, slightly flushed. Her demeanour shouts nerves, which is strange for someone usually so self-assured.

'We're having lunch, but you don't have to join us. I wanted to check if you're OK.'

'Yes, totally fine,' Kayla says too eagerly. 'I was just . . . not feeling that great. Maybe I'll sit with you, but I'm not hungry. I'll grab something later.'

As they join the others, the conversation is in full flow. Eleni grins broadly in her immaculate black dress, and

Leonidas is charming Alessandra and vice versa, so much so that Kayla wonders if Alessandra will invoke her open-marriage arrangement in Petalidi. She knows she never would, though.

Kayla pours a large tumbler of rosé and gulps it down thirstily, then hastily refills her glass. Her empty stomach protests at the alcohol, but she doesn't bother to heed its warning. Nobody is paying her any attention, and she is glad. Maria can't seem to tear her eyes from Leonidas, the unmistakable spark of affection, and perhaps something more, is obvious. Alessandra is engrossed in everything he is saying too and Maria's mother beams, also hanging on his every word. Even through bleary eyes, Kayla can see Leonidas has a compelling charm, making it impossible to ignore his presence. And he is devastatingly handsome.

Lunch is delicious and ends with satisfied noises by all but Kayla, who doesn't partake. Eleni passes on pudding, since she is still fasting, which means no indulgences or animal products aside from fish. She wishes to lie down before the church procession later on. Alessandra helps Maria to clear the table, taking plates to the kitchen. Kayla feels she ought to make the effort and wobbles unsteadily with an empty platter. Even though the scent of lunch had tempted her, Kayla had been resolute upon refusing food. Solid fuel, that is . . . she'd demolished the best part of a bottle of wine. She manages to carefully place the crockery on the kitchen counter before slumping into a corner chair facing out to sea. The other women pay her no mind as they continue chatting while Kayla watches them through her blurred vision.

150

Maria loads the dishwasher as Alessandra says, 'Thank you. For not treating me differently, after learning about my sickness.'

'Of course, it changes nothing, but kind of everything too. Yes, I'm worried about you, though it makes me more determined to give you an incredible experience. I may be able to help people with what I cook, but sadly some things are beyond even my healing powers.'

Kayla feels a wave of sadness, but Alessandra laughs in contrast. 'I'm not so sure. There is something about this place and you. I know this will be my last trip away from Rome and I'm happy I chose here . . . or perhaps it was chosen for me. Whichever it is, you've helped me, and you'll always be in what's left of my life.'

Maria puts down a stack of dishes and hugs Alessandra. It almost makes Kayla giggle, they are so physically different. Alessandra is dressed in a riot of colour, and it almost hurts Kayla's eyes to look at her. The patterns on her smock blur like a kaleidoscope.

'I will also rest before the procession. Thank you again, Maria.'

Alessandra deposits two kisses on Maria's cheeks.

Kayla follows Alessandra outside, wishing she could express her depth of sorrow. Instead, she watches the tall Italian glide through the herb garden, picking up a white flower as she goes, pressing it to her nostrils. A sadness circles around Kayla's heart and she cannot decide which is worse: knowing someone is going to die and being powerless to help them or being confronted by the shock of unexpected death. Both are hideous.

Kayla knows grief is a trigger for her and Alessandra

has provoked so many different feelings within her in the short time since they met. Kayla leans against an orange tree, resting her head against the hard bark of its trunk. She feels exhaustion crash through her body, as if she doesn't have the energy to face the tumult of emotions pinging around her mind. A tear escapes as she thinks about her dead parents. It was so desperately unfair. Why did they leave her all alone? Daniel too will leave and there will be no rock to ground her, nothing to tether her. She doesn't even know if she has the strength to give Rosie what she needs, because all of Kayla's compulsions that have plagued the years since her parents were killed are emerging like bamboo shoots breaking through a lawn, threatening and unstoppable.

Kayla decides she needs another drink, to blot out her feelings, an anaesthetic for her thoughts. She walks back to the table where Leonidas is sitting. Something Maria said echoes through her head: it is impossible to love someone else until you're able to love yourself. And therein lies the rub as it slowly dawns on her through her foggy mind. Kayla has absolutely no idea how to do that.

# Chapter 18

## *Maria*

'Would you like some baklava, Kayla? Or bread? I really think you should eat something,' I implore. Kayla is drunk, her hands waving wildly.

'Am fine,' she says slurring, her wine slopping out of her glass. 'Mmm fine. I'm not drunk . . . I'm great. Perfect in fact, just like I'm s'posed to be. I like you, Leonidas; I really, really like you. But here's the thing . . . you divorced your wife, didn't you?'

'Kayla, I'm not sure . . .' I start but Leonidas interrupts me.

'It's all right, Maria,' he says calmly. 'Yes, that is true. We are as amicable as we can be because of our daughter, Zoe.'

Kayla's face drops as she attempts to focus on the table setting. 'I'm probably getting a divorce. Failed at love . . .' She picks up a spoon and drops it with a clunk on the table. 'Men are all the same. Apart from you. You're lovely.'

'Maybe we should take you for a lie-down,' I suggest.

'Noooo, I don't want . . .' Kayla tries to stand up but falls back down into her seat, giggling. 'I think I might be drunk . . . My marriage's over. And my dead are parents. I mean, my parents are dead . . . I'm nearly forty and . . .' She dissolves into tears, resting her head on her forearms on the table. Leonidas and I look at each other with concern.

'Come on, let's get you to bed,' I say, taking one of Kayla's arms and hoisting it around my neck. Leonidas does the same on her other side and we coax her out of her seat. Walking unsteadily through the trees isn't an easy task. Kayla is muttering unintelligible nonsense and crying. I feel my back twinging in protest.

'Come, it'll be easier if I carry her. Kayla, do you mind if I pick you up?' he asks. She stops still for a moment, trying to focus on his face.

'You're asking my permission?' she says stunned and swaying, before starting to cry again. 'You . . . you are the kindest man I have ever met. You . . . you should marry Maria and live with her and make baby bees. A big buzzy, fuzzy happy family.'

Leonidas scoops her effortlessly into his arms. She must weigh next to nothing. Kayla looks like a small child, tiny in his large frame. Our progress is much faster and we quickly reach her villa. Leonidas places her gently onto the sofa.

'I'd better fetch a bucket, just in case,' I say, stepping outside to find one. As I return, I hear Kayla's voice. 'What scared you away? Was it Maria? 'Cause she came back, then you left but stayed away, got divorced and now you're back again. S'funny timing if you ask me. I notice things – I used to be a journalist.'

154

I stop still, frozen, waiting to hear his answer. I hadn't wished to pry about his circumstances. There are rumours he left for another woman, deciding not to return to Petalidi when he and Athena divorced, but I don't pay mind to idle gossip. I step as quietly as I can, craning my neck to hear his answer.

But there is silence. I start as Leonidas suddenly appears in the doorway. 'She's out for the count. I'll put this beside her.'

He takes the pail from my hands as my head swirls with the questions I'm desperate to ask. But they dry on my lips as I watch his care for Kayla, the kindness and tenderness he shows all who encounter him. His strong back and broad shoulders make me imagine being scooped up into his arms with the same care and attention . . . The first bell chimes, marking the start of the evening's lengthy solemnities, breaking my impure train of thought with a reminder of the sanctity of this day. It is almost time to gather at the church and it is perhaps a sign that I should banish such ideas from my head and heart once and for all. I was meant to be alone, and I don't need anyone else to look after me.

\*   \*   \*

The queue to enter the church to kiss the *epitafio*, the depiction of the body of Christ shrouded in flowers, stretches across the village green. Songs of lamentation are sung by Father Kyriakidis, amplified by the speakers attached to the pillars outside. The sound bounces off the buildings and drifts out to sea. Dignitaries have gathered, dressed in their finery. Robes and vestments catch the light, adorned with customary trinkets to denote their superiority and rank. There is no denying the poignancy of our Good Friday service. Father Kyriakidis jokes with me that I only do Easter for the fireworks and the barbecue. He's partly right, but when I lived in America, I longed to see Good Friday in Petalidi again.

My mother stands beside me, shielded by a parasol to ward off the late-afternoon sun. We wait patiently outside the church for our turn with the floral casket. It is the hottest day yet and there are reports of spontaneous forest fires breaking out in the eastern Peloponnese, not too near, but close enough. We know how fast they can spread, and the ground is bone-dry. There is the faintest tinge of burning in the air. It's hard to tell if there's a sea mist or if smoky fire vapour hangs in the bay, cloaking the view like a smear on a lens.

As we reach the altar, the *kouvouklion* on which Christ will be carried, is covered in wild white flowers and magenta orchids. It looks like a large floral tent, draping the figure of Jesus, which has been removed from the large crucifix adorning the wall. My eyes travel to the bare cross, naked and stark without its holy centrepiece. A crown of candles sits atop the shrine, and men from the village dutifully stand guard, ready to bear it around the streets and seafront. My mother leans in, under the canopy, and kisses the flowery tribute. I cross myself out of habit rather than devotion.

Hearing a tut beside me, I turn to see Athena looking at me with disgust, shaking her head. I have done her no harm nor mean her any, yet she cannot piously set aside spite for this magical occasion. A lengthy peal of bells rings out; they are so loud it is impossible to think, which is for the best.

I lead my mother back outside and we wait for the procession to form. I see Alessandra watching from the edge of the green. She strikes a solemn figure, respecting the traditions, which must be familiar to her coming from Rome. My mind reaches for Kayla, hoping she finds what she needs. She is so troubled. I only hope she has spirits walking alongside her, as I wonder who she looks to for help.

As the ceremony commences, the body of Christ is carried outside and held aloft. Bells clang intermittently during breaks in the liturgy, their sharp sound cuts through the evening. Another *epitafio* arrives and the crowd shuffles to accommodate the second shrine. Slowly, we walk in an elongated funeral march. Illuminated by crosses, garnished with candles, the floral tributes sway as the men find their step. The air becomes heavily fragranced from the incense Father Kyriakidis swings in an embellished silver container. Its smell hangs undispersed in the claggy atmosphere, blending with the scent of candle wax that engulfs our sombre religious party.

'What are you doing tomorrow, Maria?'

A voice at my shoulder startles me. Leonidas. He is unaware of the eyes that flick in our direction – or perhaps he doesn't care. I wish he wouldn't persist in speaking to me in public; I don't want to damage his reputation. My mother's head twitches as she pretends not to listen to our conversation, but she isn't subtle in her efforts. Thankfully, her deafness prevents her from catching most of it.

157

'I have my food to make for the feast on Sunday. I don't have class, but I have much to do.'

'Nonsense,' scoffs my mother, having heard enough to know what I'm trying to do. 'There is nothing that cannot wait.'

I sigh, aware we are in a crowd, unable to escape. Others listen to our words, and I feel a shame I don't deserve, but experience nonetheless.

'Then come with me . . . to Kalamaki.'

I balk at his suggestion. Of all the beaches we could visit, why that place? He continues despite my lack of response. 'We have so much to catch up on. Please. It is impossible to talk to you here with all these distractions.' He leans in, adding, 'And all these ears.'

I catch his scent, like sandalwood and salt with the smoky note of sawdust. It makes me dizzy.

'But I . . . I have to . . .' I search for a cause to avoid being alone with him, especially in Kalamaki where the memories will surely be too painful for us both.

Why would he wish to walk in our ancient footsteps? It would be like picking at a scab that never heals, reopening the wound. But as I meet his gaze, his full lips give a wry smile, as if he can read my mind. I have no reason to refuse his invitation, other than what people will think and my own worries about revisiting the past – and he knows it.

'Your bees can spare you for the day, Maria. Please.'

I smile at him as we shuffle forward within the crowd, unable to tear myself away from his stare. He is convincing in his plea, and I'm out of excuses to decline. I notice for the first time that his eyes have flecks of gold around his pupils. They were always the richest hazel colour, like dark wintry honey. The gold must have appeared after I left. We've missed so much of the other's life, although his physical changes are of course less dramatic than mine.

'*Endáxi*, OK,' I reply. 'Why you have to wait until we are surrounded by a thousand ears to ask me these things . . .' My voice is teasing, my meaning serious.

'Because here you can't run away to your kitchen. I have your undivided attention. It is settled: we go to Kalamaki tomorrow. I will collect you early.' He smiles and my heart leaps in my chest. I can't help it, like touching a pan you know is hot, but you want to test it, knowing you'll get burnt.

'*Babá*, why are you speaking to *her*? *Mamá* wishes to see you.' Leonidas' daughter, Zoe, tugs at his sleeve and he frowns at her rudeness.

'Hey, *zouzounaki*, this is no way to speak about Maria and in front of Eleni. Please, apologise.' He is stern as he addresses his daughter despite using his term of endearment, little bug. I do not wish to make a scene in front of the whole village.

'Leonidas, it's fine, please.' I touch his arm, willing him to leave it. Zoe's eyes travel to my fingers and I snatch my hand away.

'It is not fine. Zoe, say you are sorry to Maria.'

She lifts her chin in defiance, and manages to briefly meet my eyes, a little of her bravado evaporating. Her high cheekbones hint at the elegant face beginning to emerge from her puppy fat. She cannot help but look at my neck and her generous mouth curls in disgust. It is a similar shape to Leonidas', but, unlike her father, kindness isn't forthcoming from her lips.

'Sorry.' She smirks; she doesn't mean it. I don't blame her, though. It's not her fault. Her head is filled with irrational hatred absorbed from Athena. Leonidas turns to me and lowers his voice. 'I am sorry, Maria, for my daughter. I will see you tomorrow.'

He puts his arm around Zoe's shoulders and disappears into the crowd. Although he was firm, it is clear he adores her. I shudder as the word 'Kalamaki' echoes through my mind. A special place, almost a site of sacred pilgrimage, but not one I would dare to revisit and haven't since I returned home. Like a ruined archaeological dig never to be restored to its former glory, preserved to hang in destruction forever and forbidden by time to fulfil its promise. It became a mythical scene in my mind, a sort of echo from a movie I might have once seen.

'Do not say a word,' I hiss to my mother as she takes a breath to fire a thousand questions at me.

As we continue within the procession, I try to under-stand what Leonidas wants with me in Kalamaki. Perhaps he needs closure from that moment on our beach over thirty years ago. So much has happened since. But some-thing sits uneasily with me about tomorrow, like it will shift the sands of time irreparably. As if decades ago was a dress rehearsal, and tomorrow is the first performance.

If anyone should discover us, or the eavesdropping ears spread a version of our snatched conversation, it will only send waves of disapproval around the village. Of course, I don't care – I'm used to it – but I feel guilty in case Athena or Zoe should hear of it. I can't afford to make any more enemies. I already have one who is upping their quest to hurt me, and this may fuel their campaign. Against my will, there is a growing trepidation within me. I can't help but wonder and fear what they will do next.

# Chapter 19

## *Kayla*

Kayla wakes with a thumping headache, the pounding in her skull marked by the constant clanging of the early evening church bells, which pierce her eardrums even from this distance. She swears and groans as she puts a pillow over her head, cursing her lunchtime drinking session on an empty stomach. Her phone rings and she blindly answers from beneath the cushion, not wishing the sound to prolong the fresh wave of pain behind her eyes.

'Hello?' she croaks.

'Oh Kayla, so glad I caught you. It's Eve. Eve Houseby. I've been trying to get hold of you, neighbour!'

Kayla swears silently at the ceiling. How could she have picked up without checking who it was first!

'Hi, Eve,' she rasps. 'I can't talk right now.'

'I know how busy you are, but I really must speak with you,' she insists.

'What is it?' Kayla sighs and grinds her teeth, again regretting the day she invited her neighbours into her life.

'Oh, things are madly busy in Blighty. Milan has a boyfriend. He looks just like Prince William, haw haw!'

A wave of irritation rattles Kayla's frame. Surely Eve hasn't called to brag about some snotty little boy looking vaguely like royalty? As if the comparison made the Housebys more important by an imagined association.

'Sorry, Eve, I've got to go . . .'

'No wait, Kayla! I'm not really sure how to say this . . . but I thought you should know . . . Well, while you've been away, I've noticed that there's . . . It's hard to . . . Oh, I'm making a bit of a hash of this. I'd much prefer to do it in person.'

Kayla wouldn't put it past Eve to get on a plane and hunt her down in Greece. Kayla feels herself rapidly losing patience.

'Well, I'm away for another four days, so perhaps it can wait 'til I'm back, or speak to my assistant. I *know* you've got her contact details.' The poor girl had fielded a barrage of messages following each call of Eve's Kayla had declined.

'I'm not sure it can. I wanted to explain, everything really, from the start. The thing is, you seem so happy and have everything you could wish for. I suppose I thought if I could capture a bit of that, it would make *me* happier. To have what I haven't got. Stephen is very . . . difficult . . . specific in the way he likes things done. You've seen his cravat. Haw haw . . .' She laughs nervously.

Kayla rubs her eyes as a frown crosses her forehead, puzzled as to why Eve seems to be calling with this strange, unhappy confession. She makes a grand pretence of her perfect life to anyone who would listen, keeping up appearances at the school gates, overtly competitive about Milan's achievements and talents. But at Eve's admission she is having problems, Kayla finds herself reluctantly softening. She loathes hearing of anyone's unhappiness. At least they agree on one thing: Stephen's cravat is absolutely monstrous.

'I'm sorry if you're having a rough time, Eve.'

'That's just it. I wanted to emulate your life in order to cover over the cracks a bit. We're very similar. I mean we live in the same house, although next door, and it seems, unfortunately, we're married to the same man. The same type, at least. I'm so sorry.'

The pit of Kayla's empty stomach gives another lurch, and her throat constricts. 'Wh . . . what do you mean . . . married to the same man?'

'Stephen is . . . well, you know how he is, the way he leers at other women, says cringy things. The long and short of it is, he plays away, has bits on the side. I'm not an idiot; he thinks I don't know, but I *do* know. Sorry, I simply had to phone you and let you know.'

'Eve, I really don't know what you're trying to say,' says Kayla, although she suspects.

'It's Daniel. I don't mean to pry but there's been someone going in and out of your house, staying over . . . I assume Rosie is at her grandparents', but you've a regular house guest. I don't mean to poke my nose in, but thought you should know.'

The tears start to prick at Kayla's eyes as panic grips her heart. 'But you *are* poking your nose in. You don't know what you're talking about. You don't know anything about my marriage or my life. Mind your own bloody business and leave me alone!'

Kayla ends the call, her breath high and shallow at Daniel's continued deception. Apparently, in that sense, she and Eve share common ground, more than Kayla would like to admit. It confirms Daniel's additional lie and, as if she needed it, draws a deeper line in the sand marking the complete destruction of her marriage. It's time she stops hiding and faces the way things are.

\* \* \*

## Alessandra

Alessandra can see the long snake of people in the Good Friday procession through the approaching dusk. She's on the beach in solo solace to reflect. Her sometimes thrice daily walks and occasional swims give her a mental clarity, despite her body betraying life, gradually succumbing to disease. She watches as the men wade into the water to waist height, carefully navigating the slippery stones, holding the floral shrine high beyond the shallows with blessings from the priests on the shore.

The sea is like a mirror, glistening in the diminishing sunset colours as the candles glow brighter in the hands of the travelling congregation. It's truly magical. The haunting sound of foreign religious song is hypnotic. Alessandra lets the music sink into her bones and finds her body responding to the melancholy sound. She begins to dance. The pebbles under her feet clink with her movement, pouring all the sorrow from her heart into each extension of her arm, every step across the tideline. With no care for appearances, she allows the music to move her, leaping high and low, twirling around until Greece blurs in her vision, the holy soundtrack leading her body. The lowlight descends quickly. She's invisible to the procession, but dances on regardless, solely for herself, for all she has lost and will lose in the weeks to come. She is dancing for her life.

*　　*　　*

## Kayla

After her call from Eve, Kayla needed fresh air. She hoped to shed her horrible headache made of overindulgence and the news of Daniel's continued relationship with another woman. Kayla can just make out a figure in the dusk on the beach. Moving with such passion and energy, pain and anger, as if they'd extracted the insides of her mind and performed the inner torment solely for the sea to enjoy. Hundreds of twinkling candles coil up the hills of the village, spilling onto the far end of the beach. She can hear the religious incantations of the service, peppered with song, punctuated by bells.

As Kayla nears, she recognises the solo dancer as Alessandra. Kayla finds herself captivated by Alessandra's private performance and her troubles almost evaporate. She sits down on the stony beach, transfixed. She is moved by the emotion conveyed in the dance. Alessandra is like an elegant nymph in silhouette. Only the light refracted from the water allows her shape to be glimpsed. Kayla's lip begins to tremble, then tears stream down her face. The depth of feeling renders her as still as the sea, suspended in limbo at a crossroads in her life. She cries for all she has lost and is still perhaps yet to lose.

As she watches Alessandra crouch to the ground, her back heaving from effort, something inside Kayla stirs and her mind refills with her woes, but in a different order. So much has been taken away from her. She'd had no choice in her parents' deaths and therefore her broken childhood, which ended when she was fourteen the moment a drunk driver stole her mother and father away. Her hideous neighbour's call has confirmed there is no way back for her marriage. But she already knew that. It doesn't smart that Daniel has someone else; it hurts that he lied. But she is aware she is a liar in a worse way.

She has concealed part of her since she met Daniel and the time for untruths, surely, is over. Kayla knows what happens next is entirely down to her. Her life for the first time is firmly in her own hands. Not her agent's, the public's, nor her therapist's. Hers. It always has been, she realises, but it hadn't felt like it before. Maybe she should use the opportunity to be reckless, have a fling with that delicious waiter. As the thought flashes appealingly through her mind, she thinks instead of Alessandra and the difference she can make to her new friend. She wants to; she needs to.

Kayla has felt a growing connection to this woman, despite their rocky beginnings. She cannot halt the inevitability of Alessandra's fate, but there is something else she can do. As the pallbearers emerge from the sea, tentatively wading with their holy cargo, the beginnings of an idea form in Kayla's head. If she can prevent another's pain, halt the all-too-familiar regrets that presided over her teenage years, she may be able to heal her own old wounds and help someone else at the same time. She still might seek out Dimitris, but she will certainly search for something far more meaningful.

Kayla smiles at the inky sky as she sees a cluster of bees buzz merrily back home. She nods and settles on her decision. It is the most positive choice she has made for years.

*The bees watch the ancient ritual, hovering high above the crowds, drawn by the scent of flowers. One enters a cloud of perfumed incense then soars into the indigo sky. This drone is a new soul, waiting to be born into its earthly vessel.*

*'Rebirth and resurrection, we are the link to life,' the queen had said.*

*She is a wise spirit and has lived many times before. There is much to learn from her before his next beginning. It wouldn't be too much longer.*

# Chapter 20

## *Maria*

It is early, only just light, and there is nobody around. Sheer, blissful peace before the day unfurls and the church bells commence their relentless ringing. Even the fruit seller is yet to wake. His repetitive day-long song is like an alarm clock for Petalidi aside from the holy clanging, listing his wares from the loudspeaker in his van as he drives through the village:

'*Pepónia, achládia, karpoúzia, fréska froúta . . .*'

Melons, pears, watermelon, fresh fruit . . .

I bask in the all-encompassing silence, walking to my bees, my arms stretched high above my head to banish sleep knots.

I gasp as I near the seaward path. I'm too late again. A pile of sticks is in front of the hive that boasts Leonidas' carving. On top of the stack of twigs is a doll. Her face is marred by a clumsy red smear of paint that travels down to her neck. I begin to tremble; my legs shake uncontrollably and my breathing becomes ragged. It's an effigy of me – poised for burning.

I will my legs to move and rush to the promenade, looking left and right along the beach. But there is nothing save for the whisper of the lapping tide and hum from my bees. The cruelty of the miniature unlit bonfire shakes me against my will. It feels more significant than the other warnings. It means me mortal harm, communicates in no uncertain terms that this person wishes me injury . . . or death. I'm already a bundle of nerves ahead of my morning with Leonidas, and this seems like a weighted warning I shouldn't go.

I return to pick up the doll and stare at its inert face, the red smear transferring to my fingers. It appears to be lipstick. I frantically wipe it off, and my stained fingers taint my pristine apron like blood. I search my mind for an answer as to who would do such a thing. There are so many options in the village. Most residents are afraid of me, but surely their fear hasn't morphed into wishing me to be hurt. I may never find out, and perhaps now I don't wish to. It could be someone I know or trust.

I put the doll in my apron pocket and force my mind away from this toxicity. I let the soothing pulse from my bees calm me and gradually my thoughts return to my business of the morning. I fill a jar of honey to bake with later. The golden syrup oozes from the tap, trickling quickly to give me the amount I need. I thank the bees and say my prayer of gratitude. The hive vibrates as if acknowledging my sentiments.

I walk through the gardens to pick lemons for my cake and consider what food I should take to Kalamaki.

174

Even the sound of the place gives me a shiver of longing. It represents a day that could have changed the course of my life and Leonidas' if I'd had the courage to take a leap of faith. But my nerve failed. I have little inclination to revisit something that never was but could almost have been. Should have been, and will be, according to my mother.

Why does Leonidas wish to rehash our youth? He was so hurt and furious. Yet, I cannot help my curiosity, some morbid masochistic wish to torture myself with the parallel pattern of my life that resides firmly in 'what if'.

\* \* \*

'*Kaliméra*,' I say, greeting Alessandra and Kayla who are taking coffee together outside the row of villas. I had the idea to include thyme in my citrus honey syrup for the glaze on my Easter Sunday cake, so have been rooting about in the herb garden. Once again, I immediately pick up on their energies and find their friendship reverberating in the atmosphere. After five days of ups and downs, there is finally plain sailing between them. The dynamic between my cooking pupils has ebbed and flowed faster than the tide. Although I am yet to discover the exact cause of Kayla's drunken meltdown yesterday, her wine-infused ramblings cited her marriage breakdown and her parents' deaths. I hope Alessandra can be of some comfort to her, although sympathy doesn't seem to be her natural strong suit.

'Morning!' they both chorus, smiling knowingly, which makes me wonder what they are up to.

'And where are you off to today?' says Alessandra.

'Nowhere looking like this,' I say, noting my red-smeared apron and muddy fingers from pulling weeds in the herb bed.

'Aren't you going somewhere . . . ?' says Kayla, but how she remembers anything of the last twenty-four hours is beyond me and I certainly wouldn't have mentioned my trip with Leonidas to anyone.

'I am, but it's nothing important – just visiting an old friend,' I say vaguely as I catch Alessandra glance to Kayla with a raised eyebrow and they both exchange a meaningful look.

'Ah, well, old friends are very important. It is easy to let them go as we let new people into our lives, but they know us the best and are the ones we should cherish.'

What is Alessandra on about? I'm being paranoid, feeling guilty for stowing away with Leonidas when I have no reason to. I begin to consider small plates of food to take with me to the beach.

'Maria? Maria . . . ? Coo-eee . . . where did you disappear to?'

I am brought back to the present as I'd drifted off to my kitchen with the thought of the mezze.

'Sorry, I was cooking in my head.' I laugh. 'What did you say, Kayla?'

'I was wondering if I can sit down and interview you properly later, before the midnight celebrations, if you have time? And sorry about yesterday, had a bit too much to drink. I hope I didn't say anything inappropriate.' She cringes before continuing. 'We can chat later, or whenever.'

176

'Sure, I'll give you a shout when I'm around. You can watch me bake my Easter cake this afternoon.'

'Don't rush back!' calls Alessandra as I head for my teaching kitchen.

I stop still and turn to face them, opening my mouth to speak before thinking better of it. They don't know anything. They can't.

Instead, I say, 'Have a great day,' and leave them to their morning.

'You too!' trills Kayla.

*　*　*

My mother shuffles into my kitchen as I prepare snacks for Kalamaki. She says nothing, but the mere raising of her eyebrow is enough to indicate she thinks she knows what is going on. She looks irritatingly smug, but I don't rise to it; I have other topics to discuss with her.

'Why did you never tell me, *Mamá*?' I ask gently.

She leans forward in her chair at the small table in the corner. 'I cannot hear you. Speak up.'

A convenient loss of hearing. I stop slicing up the zucchinis I plan to grill in a moment and walk over to a chair beside her. The time for pretending is past. Perhaps it's the oppressive temperature or the wrought emotions of my guests over the last few days, but I can feel a charge in the air, like a storm is brewing.

'I said, why have you kept your gift from me all these years?'

She huffs out a loud sigh and shakes her head. 'I would have thought it obvious, *ángelé mou*. Look at the way people

177

react to you. I was afraid of my power and never really used it even as a child. I did not have your courage. Your *yiayiá*, God rest my mother's soul, told me I must practise, to develop the gift, otherwise it will never achieve its full potential. She tried to make me, but I was scared.' Her eyes widen as she speaks. 'I didn't want to see the dead, so I closed my eye to it, blocked it as best I could. And I kept it from you. I prayed you wouldn't inherit this curse. When my *mamá* died, my secret went with her, until I told you, to make you feel better. It's done the opposite, I see. I should have trusted my instinct and kept quiet. Nothing is to be gained by messing with spirits. It is ungodly.'

'But you could've made such a difference to me,' I say on behalf of my younger self. 'I might've felt less like an outcast. That tiny shred of reassurance was all I would have needed, just to tell me you had it too. I would have kept your counsel. But instead, you let me believe the way people treated me was my own fault, that there was something wrong with me.'

'I wished to shield you, yes, but also myself. I didn't want to embarrass your father; this village is so judgemental. I loved him, but I kept my abilities private, even though he was thrilled by what *you* could see. You made no attempt to conceal your talent, but I hid mine from you both. Don't you understand? I was afraid. My gift went away the day he died when his love left my heart, so what is the point of this discussion? I won't be chastised for wanting your happiness. I see love coming for you even without the spirits. Why can you not embrace it?'

'Why do you refuse to see me as I am?' I shout suddenly. 'I *don't* see it. Not with Leonidas, not with anyone. Your

178

endeavours are pointless. He thinks of me only as a friend, and I him. I know my heart and I will not risk it. It's already happened once and I will not permit that to be repeated. How can I give it to another who may reject me for this?'

I pull my scarf down to expose the worst of the clumped, mottled skin of my scar, my fingers point along the Mississippi River. My mother shrinks at the sight, her eyes betraying her horror as they linger around the Caribbean Sea, and she crosses herself from habit.

'You see?' I continue, more quietly. 'You're supposed to love me most on this earth and you cannot even look at it. Expecting another to want me is a ridiculous idea. Now *you* know this: I will not be forced into love by you or anyone.'

'But you go with Leonidas to Kalamaki this morning, yes?' she says doggedly.

'Thanks to your meddling, I'm stuck with it. But it's nothing more than old friends catching up away from prying eyes like yours. I beg of you, let me be, *Mamá*. To live my life as I choose.'

She eases herself out of the chair and straightens up as much as she can. 'Well, you should be careful what you wish for, Maria. One day sooner than you think, you will have a very long break from me, which will last forever. Then you may find you are sorry. Or not. Perhaps you will be too busy with your bees to notice I am gone.'

She moves slowly, reaching the door as a timely handful of bees enters the kitchen. She raises her hand to the air in their direction. 'You see . . . here they are to drive me away, your little winged minions. All right, all right, I will leave you, I am going,' she says to the insects rather than me.

'*Mamá*, don't be like that. Please, just accept me as I am.'

Whether she doesn't hear or chooses not to, she trundles out of the kitchen. I begin to cook again to reset my feelings, but I cannot forgive her for keeping this from me. The relief from isolation I could've had, knowing I wasn't the only one with my power. Yet she chose to permit small-minded opinions to grow, inadvertently encouraged the bullies who ostracised me from their friendship groups because I was different. I find myself resenting her for it.

I continue slicing zucchinis, and say a prayer to the food, the bees and to everyone listening I can no longer see.

'Please let me be accepted for who I am by those I love. And by everyone, I beg you.'

# Chapter 21

## Kayla

### My Easter Greek Odyssey by Kayla Moss

*I've not been truthful to you over the years. I have a secret; something I've tried to hide from those I love, from you and, in a way, from myself.*

Kayla holds down the delete key the moment she finishes typing the sentence. She daren't write this; it would mark her ruin. She tries to analyse her thoughts, gripping the armrest of the comfy chair in her villa, to work out why she would want to sabotage her career in this way. Aside from Rosie, it is the measure of her own success, forging a profession from her desolate beginnings. Yet, she's considering committing professional suicide at the start of an article that's supposed to be about Greek food and Maria's Kitchen. In a way it is

– she is changed by this trip, but she isn't ready to share quite how yet.

As she looks out to the gardens, inhaling the salty air, she wonders if there really is a kind of magic here. The fruit trees, honeybees and tempting morsels scenting the wind, as the breeze creates a natural percussion, dancing through the olive grove. Greece is truly a sensual delight. It smells inescapably of food and something else she cannot quite place. It makes her feel reckless, free from her self-imposed binds, hence why she was about to write some hideous confessional. Kayla closes the document and pulls up a previous version. Much safer to stick with what is expected of her, to continue to follow the recipe in a measured and predictable fashion. That way nobody can guess what she's hiding.

But inspiration is far from her grasp this morning as she wrestles with her work. Daniel's treachery hurts more than the fact he has chosen another woman. It pairs with her own deceit, having concealed a secret for so long, as if they were two strangers existing in a marriage of pretence. She feels betrayed by him but most of all by herself.

Kayla is riddled with a nagging urge to rip everything about herself apart and start again. Except Rosie. She is her shining light and even though she loves her with the fiercest part of her heart, Kayla knows she has on occasion chosen work over being at home with her beloved daughter. The mummy guilt is sometimes too much to cope with, a battle she knows she isn't alone in. The pressure to be superwoman, to be all things to everyone has tipped her life out of kilter, and her marriage beyond repair.

She holds her head in her hands and tries to concentrate. Taking her laptop to sit outside, Kayla switches her attention to something more worthwhile. She sends friend requests to Maria and Alessandra on social media.

Alessandra's profile has no security; it is laid bare for everyone to see, her world of hedonistic jollity. Alessandra has uploaded old photos stretching back to the 1960s when she was in a dance company in New York. A scanned polaroid of Studio 54 reveals a gateway to a fabled, iconic time consigned to footnotes or films. She's unwittingly on holiday with one of the original party girls who must be brimming with the most extravagant tales. Stories Kayla wants to hear about, not Alessandra's tawdry antics.

Kayla returns to the brilliant idea she had on the beach yesterday evening and immerses herself in the role of amateur detective. She claps her hands with glee when she discovers her first lead. Ten minutes of targeted searching and she pieces together some options to make contact, starting with an exhibition of contemporary paintings in Naples. Alessandra's daughter, Arianna, appears to be a relatively successful artist. Feeling excitement building as adrenaline starts to pump around her body, Kayla smiles, sensing her mark is close. You can take the girl out of the newsroom . . .

'Come, let us walk,' Alessandra says to Kayla, suddenly appearing from the villa next door. 'The beach calls, then it will be time for lunch.'

Kayla slams her laptop lid shut, looking guilty.

'Am I disturbing you watching something you shouldn't?' asks Alessandra mischievously.

183

'No! I was just . . . work stuff. No biggie.' Kayla is a terrible liar, for the most part – unlike Daniel.

'I have this wonderful site I watch if you wish to see something beautiful, very tasteful . . . sexually intriguing—'

'La, la, la,' Kayla sings, covering her ears. 'Please spare me the gruesome details.'

Kayla stands, taking her computer into her villa and retrieving her shoulder bag.

'Maybe if the spark has gone from your marriage, you could consider . . .'

'Alessandra, with the greatest of respect, I might not take marriage advice from you. Yours isn't like anything I've experienced, nor aspire to, so forgive me if I ask you to stop with the counselling. Let's talk about something else. For instance, a little birdie told me you were a bit of a girl about town back in the day in New York.'

As they walk, Alessandra regales Kayla with exploits from her youth, which Kayla laps up, losing herself in her new-found friend's freeing experiences.

When she was twenty-one, Alessandra had secured a job to perform with Martha Graham's Dance Company straight out of college. Her family asked her to be decent, to do the right thing by marrying before she took the job, which she and Phillipo dutifully did in Rome before setting off for New York City. Phillipo was working as a freelance photographer at the time with no tether other than where his new wife was.

They revelled in the creativity of the disco revolution, discovering a playground of wonder for the freaks and the fabulous, and they thrived within it. Drinking martinis with icons who held court nightly at the infamous Studio 54.

But the greatest thing about that scene had been the freedom to be queer and explore the many versions of love on offer. Alessandra and her colleagues in the dance company could be their true selves and they gave themselves permission to enjoy pleasure in any way they wished.

'And *mio Dio*, did we ever,' Alessandra recalls. 'It is hard for you to comprehend the way our relationship works, but my heart always belonged to Phillipo. It still does. It is simply how we are.'

'Do you think about what will happen to him . . . after . . . in the future . . . when . . . you know.'

'After I'm dead?'

Kayla winces at Alessandra's abruptness. It isn't only her choice of language, she is unafraid and unapologetic, never skirting around any issue.

'Yes,' Kayla replies softly.

'I tell him to live his life and not to mourn me. We've had a wonderful marriage and he's been the greatest companion I could've wished for. My friend, my adventurer . . . but as things end, you must let them go. To die is to wake to life in many ways. Like Maria says, it is exhausting to carry the burden of sadness and grief with you. It's like you have a backpack filled with rocks. The only way to make it lighter is to set it down and take out the stones one by one.'

Kayla falls into contemplative silence as they walk along the beach. Small stones crunch underfoot, the sound of the tide, cicadas in the seagrass.

'Do I make any sense at all?' Alessandra laughs.

'I was digesting what you said.'

'Interesting . . .'

Kayla quickly says, 'I was thinking how wise you and Maria are. I feel like a child. Emotionally I mean. I know I'm not exactly a teenager, but I still have a lot of growing up to do, apparently.'

Alessandra stops and catches Kayla's arm. 'It makes sense. You have put the brakes on your emotions because of your parents being killed. You're in your thirties, yes? But inside you're stuck being that teenager who receives terrible news. So, you never learn how to cope with death nor with life. Is very simple psychology – I watch many online seminars on it. I see you trying to be in charge of everything around you. I expect you are like this at home and at work. For a job it is good to be this way, in the marriage . . . not so much. In the bedroom, however . . .'

Kayla laughs, despite never having felt more vulnerable. Both Maria and Alessandra see her more clearly than she is able to see herself. She thought she was better at hiding her pain. Apparently, she's as transparent as a pane of glass.

Alessandra puts an arm around Kayla's slightly sunburnt shoulders. 'Don't feel bad – everything can be fixed, if you wish it. Come, let's eat. And as your first experience of not being in charge, I am ordering lunch for us both.'

Kayla tries not to become rigid under Alessandra's half embrace, but her heart begins to pound at the thought. Relinquishing control over anything would be a struggle, but why did Alessandra have to test her like this?

# Chapter 22

## *Maria*

Leonidas seems intent on transporting us back in time with this trip, beginning with his music choice. As we wind up the coastal road, the Mani Peninsula across the water sparkles as if it were coming alive to the sound of Leonard Cohen's gravelly voice, which fills the car.

We used to listen to his albums over and over when it wasn't cool to do so, but we thought it was the most meaningful poetry we'd ever heard. I smile as the music prompts anecdotes from our schooldays and we laugh, singing together, harmonising badly. My mind flashes back to our times after class, lying in the grassy meadows shrouded by wild flowers. In my father's fields, the bleating sounds from the goats replaced the melody of this very album playing on a battered cassette player. We knew we were listening to something profound, even if we didn't fully understand it, and it had heightened my growing muddled feelings for him. We would stare at each other for hours, our innocence slowly diminishing. That's as far as it went. Then.

The car roof is down, and I lean my head back in the seat, reaching my hands up to let the air caress my fingertips. My straw fedora squishes against the headrest as I look up at the endless sky, tracing the path of jet streams from aircraft as they streak over the blue expanse, as though someone has doodled with a piece of chalk. Plumes of smoke from the forest fires are visible across the water in the Taygetus mountain range, and I feel a twinge of unease, but Greece immediately wields her sensory power to distract me. As we ascend a steep incline, the sheer drop to the side of the road gives a clear view of the ravine below, crammed with foliage.

I so rarely venture outside Petalidi, I'd forgotten how beautiful my motherland is. The cypress trees grow tall and straight in contrast to the twisted, gnarled bark of ancient olive trees. The glimmering sea peeps between hillsides, then disappears behind the mountain vista. Greece is breathtaking as I see it through the eyes of a tourist.

The air fills with the scent of pine as we begin our final twisting and turning, bound for the little cove of Kalamaki. It would've been a more direct route to drive along the coast than take the inland scenic mountain drive, but Leonidas wanted to enjoy the landscape. Passing through the main street of the nearest town, we see that it is busy with families making their final preparations for the feast tomorrow. A charge of excitement runs the length of the village. It is a beautiful place, remaining unspoilt by tourism, with the majority of holidaymakers heading for the resorts at Koroni and more famous parts of the mainland.

We turn off the highway, along the makeshift concrete track above *Chelonariá*, or Turtle Beach. I begin to feel the beating of apprehension in my tummy, thankful for the music filling my mind, but it makes the anticipation of any meaningful conversation greater. I am a tangle of emotions, guilt, fear, remorse – and they're the ones I can pinpoint. The rest churn about like they're in a whirlpool within.

Leonidas finds shade for the car, and I collect the cool box from the back seat. Even though it is early morning, the sun is blasting the sheltered cove, and the acrid taste of burning hangs in the air from the far-off fires.

We find a spot with an overhanging tree, and I spread a blanket on the ground, kick off my shoes and sit. We catch the other's eye, smile but say nothing. It feels significant yet is effortless; ordinary but special.

The thumping rhythm of a helicopter makes me start as I shield my eyes to watch it. It hovers beyond the craggy perimeter of the cove and lowers its filling pipe to take up water.

'The fires must be getting bad if they've deployed the helicopters,' I say loudly over the noise, watching the skilful pilot manoeuvre the craft up into the air like a mechanical bee.

'This heat has been insane. Goodness knows what the summer will be like if it continues. Greece will be alight again, like it was before. Terrible.'

I recall the past television reports of what looked like an apocalyptic inferno on the island of Evia, near Athens.

189

Forests and homes irreparably destroyed; livelihoods extinguished in a moment; generations of bees snuffed out in an instant. That area of Greece hosts many of our country's hives; the damage will be long-lasting. As I think about it, a foreboding shiver cascades down my neck and my scar seems to protest. I shake it off and unpack some food, which makes Leonidas laugh.

'You were always destined to cook, Maria. Even after school at the farm, you would somehow produce a home-made snack from your bag. Your mother was proud she taught you so well.'

I huff. 'Oh of course, she would take credit for my cooking. My father was actually the one who encouraged me to explore flavours. The goat's cheese he made was the best. I remember experimenting with different foods and when I discovered that honey went perfectly with cheese . . . it was like unearthing the greatest magic trick. But no, I couldn't possibly have a natural gift of my own, it was all down to her.' I laugh, still brewing resentment towards my mother for concealing her own abilities from both my father and me.

'Speaking of gifts . . . you do not mention your spirits anymore.'

I look out to sea, the crystal-clear water shimmering brighter than before as the powerful sun beats down. I can smell how clean the ocean is with cool ozone refreshing the air, despite the faintest tinge of burning. I take a breath and look at him sitting beside me. His knee bends and brushes my thigh. I'm afraid to move.

'I cannot see them anymore. They're gone,' I state, and his brow furrows in surprise. 'It was strange the way it happened. It was the day my ex-husband left me, like he took his love away and the spirits decided to leave at that moment, removing what made me special along with what was in my heart. Gone forever.'

Leonidas looks deep into my eyes and I feel the warmth of his soul, his affection surely nothing more than friendship, despite what my mother claims. I cannot keep my gaze pointed at him; it is too powerful. My eyes travel down his neck, his perfect skin that glows in this crisp morning light. I pull at the ends of my silk scarf to hide what I can of my scar.

'Your gift was not what made you special, Maria. That was only a small element of how extraordinary you were . . . are. No, your heart is what's special, your kindness. *Your* spirit, not the other kind.'

My breath catches. I cannot speak.

The pounding of the returning helicopter breaks the moment, swallowing up tension in its all-consuming sound, and I feel a swoop of relief. A flashback to the last time we were on this beach begins to play in my head, the familiar feelings of guilt and regret resurface pulsing around my veins in time with the rotary blades. I stand abruptly and walk along the shore, unable to be close to him a moment longer. His compliments make me uneasy; I cannot read his intentions. I need to put physical distance between us, as my mind reaches back into our own distant past.

We had arrived for a blissful day at Kalamaki to bid summer, each other and the beach goodbye. We were both seventeen, almost eighteen, having finished school, and our futures stretched out before us like a pristine white sandy beach. I'd secured an apprenticeship in a Greek restaurant

191

in New York, owned by a distant relative of someone in the village. I was filled with such excitement about leaving Petalidi, it was my escape route out of the small-minded place where I'd never truly belonged. I was consumed with my grand plan, the new life I'd carve out in America and was glad Leonidas would get to travel for his national service before returning to work for a local carpenter. It was healthy for us both to leave home, have adventures elsewhere, our suitcases packed with hopes and dreams. I was excited about who we would both become away from Petalidi.

On that last day, Leonidas and I had lunched and laughed in the sunshine, swum in the refreshing water, seeking out sand-coloured fish and searching for deep-sea treasures. Greece gave us the perfect backdrop to say farewell to our childhoods. It was as casual and affectionate as it had always been between us and seemed like the perfect way to say goodbye, not knowing when or how our paths would cross again. But it wasn't sad, it was jubilant, and the day smelt of sponge cake and pebbles.

Then, as we were clearing up the picnic I'd made, he suddenly took my hand and pulled me to him. I recall the sunburn on my skin tingling as I became alert and alive to every sensation in my body as my heart began to hammer loudly.

'I can't let you go,' he said in a low, insistent voice.

I was blindsided with no idea where this emanated from. The day was sliced open, like a steel blade cutting through the softest butter. I couldn't respond, inert beneath the glare of the sun and within the intensity of his stare. Until that moment, it had been light and fun with no grand gestures; simply old friends easing themselves into

192

their next chapter. I couldn't comprehend what he wanted from me. But he wasn't finished. 'How can you bear to be apart, Maria? We've always been together. I can't lose you, I mustn't.' He'd almost shouted the final couple of words, but my innocent mind remained oblivious as to what he meant. The frenzy of energy within his declarations had summoned the spirits of our relatives, causing them to swirl around us, making my head spin.

'We can stay in touch; nothing has to change,' I had replied gently, prising my hands away.

He stepped in closer to me, his hands reaching for my shoulders. I felt vulnerable in my bathing suit, his naked torso in front of my eyes. I could see traces of salt clinging to the hairs on his chest from our earlier swims, a dusting of white coating his tantalising suntan. My shoulders felt scratchy under his touch as the sand on his palms seared my love for him into my skin. An innocent excitement began to grow within me, as if I could taste him, a flavour laced with sweat and sun lotion, sea and sunshine.

'But nothing will be the same unless you stay. Be with me, Maria, marry me. We can build our life together in Petalidi.'

'No!' I shouted suddenly, shocked and appalled, stepping back away from him in horror. No spirit or instinct had indicated this was a wish he'd harboured before.

Regardless of my feelings, the way this was happening seemed desperate, for all the wrong reasons, as if he wished to prevent change when I was hellbent on it. He didn't want to let me go and pursue my dreams. But after the endless battles with my mother about my leaving, the affectionate conflict between her and *Babá* who'd supported my voyage to America, I'd already vowed that nothing would chain me to Petalidi and it couldn't be Leonidas. Despite this, in that moment, as his eyes flashed with the darkness of betrayal, I wished I could retract the word 'no' that hurt him so. I then tried clumsily to make it better.

'I . . . I mean, no, because I'm going to America. I have to leave, follow what I've always wanted. I can't . . . I won't stay here. Not even for you.'

He hung his head and angrily exhaled all the breath from his body, his hands clenched in tense fists by his sides after he dropped them away from my shoulders.

'I thought you felt . . .' His face snapped up, his eyes blackening further. 'My mistake, I got it wrong. Very wrong, and you let it happen. Go to America, find your happiness. Good luck to you.'

'Leonidas, please, don't be like that. You're the most important person to me.' Tears started to burn my eyes. 'I'm sorry, I didn't realise . . . I didn't know.'

Even though I had silently given my heart to him so many years before, I'd become used to the idea my love was unrequited. Nobody accepted me for who I was and despite his friendship, I didn't ever entertain the thought that he could want me. His apparent change of feelings was so unexpected, I rejected it out of unfamiliarity, bewildered from shock. I should have said 'thank you' instead of 'no'. But it was too late to take it back. I was too young to settle, too ambitious to stop my life before it had started.

He instantly became cold and distant, and our beautiful goodbye had dissolved into a petulant, awkward standoff on both our parts. His pride was dented, his ego crushed. I now know I foolishly confused his declaration with what

194

the village had represented for me: somewhere I needed to escape from, and I'd lumped him in with what I wished to flee. But he asked me to give up on my dream and it wasn't fair of him. If he didn't know it at the time, he certainly knows it now.

Doesn't he?

I shake off the terrible memory and will the shame of hurting him to leave my body as I watch the fire-fighting aircraft as it hovers low again, in the harsh sunlight. I spot a piece of rare amethyst sea glass and bend to retrieve it. Once my eyes are attuned to the coloured gems nestled within the pebbles, they glint and I find a more common piece of green, then white and brown. I reminisce about the hours Leonidas and I would scavenge on the beach, seeking out the precious jewel-like pieces for him to transform into one of his creations.

I suddenly stiffen, chilled to my bones as a thought occurs. The handmade daily ornaments beside my hives aren't dissimilar to his childlike beach-foraged projects . . . My phone suddenly begins vibrating in my bag slung across my body, and I reach for it. The sickeningly familiar name appears on the screen.

> You haven't listened to my warnings.
> You will be sorry.

I whirl around, as if the person responsible for the message is nearby. I see Leonidas is holding his phone. A fraction of a second later, he meets my eye from across the beach. My pulse accelerates as I consider the coincidence. I attempt to summon rational thought to replace

195

the pieces of this puzzle I am assembling, arriving at this horrifying solution. Where is my gift when I need it? Spirits, help me! I am surely going mad for even thinking it. Leonidas wouldn't frighten me or hurt me in this way. But I injured his pride badly here on this very beach, and perhaps he still resents me for it all these years later. And he is wielding a punishment.

As he smiles over at me, any misgivings melt away. I laugh to myself, dismissing the ridiculous idea. I'm letting the perpetrator win by suspecting those I cherish. No, he would never do this to me. His platitudes are making my mind jittery; I can't think straight.

I walk back over to him, unable to reconcile the fanciful idea he seems to have of me. He suggested I am like a goddess and told me how special I am. It's too much. I sit back down beside him, adjusting my scarf and removing my hat. I run my fingers through my hair, freeing it from its ponytail as I search his face for any disdain. 'Why did you want to come here, Leonidas?' I ask, yearning for closure.

'Because I want to know you again, who you are now, Maria.'

He reaches for my hand as he speaks. I look down as he clasps my fingers. My hand looks tiny in his, yet it fits. Our skin is so different; his is a richer, darker colour than mine, like varying hues of honey.

'But why? You already know me of old – there is not much more to discover. I fear you will be disappointed, my friend.'

I try to make light of it, wishing I'd never asked why we came here. I could have said anything instead of leading this grown-up, loaded conversation.

I drop his hand and open a plastic tub of home-made *tiropitákia*, delicious mini cheese pies. I offer him a slice and he takes one. Flakes of filo drop onto his lap. Eventually he speaks.

'We missed out on so much of each other's lives. In the years you were away in America, I thought of you. Even in Athens in the army. You know, one time, my friends and I stole up to the top of the Acropolis and hid behind a column until the guards had gone. We camped out over-night, but I could not sleep. I only thought of you, wishing you were beside me, looking down over our capital city as it slept under the ruins of the gods. You couldn't do that now! When I was back in Petalidi in the early years when you were gone, I would walk in the meadows between our houses watching your father tend the animals. It was strange to be there, but it was like you were all around in the flowers and the bees. I like to think some of those bees from that time live on with you now.'

'Perhaps they do,' I say enjoying him speaking of my insects with such affection. 'Sometimes, I wish we could go back to when life seemed so simple. But it wasn't. Not for me. Petalidi brews cruelty at its core.' I hesitate, consid-ering how to address the unspoken subject between us. 'You know that I associated you with the village in my mind. It is why I had to refuse your proposal. You do understand that, don't you? I was so young . . .'

He visibly tenses and I can tell that his pride is still damaged. My fear is realised. Then he drops his head in shame. 'I must have hurt you. Kids are stupid and unkind. I watched how everyone treated you and I should have stood up to them more. But in our time together away from everyone, it felt like we could be ourselves. I tried to hide how I felt about you. Maria, you were my best friend, my light in every new day. More than that, as it turned out. I'm sorry I put you in that position with my question. Your reaction hurt me, I admit, for a long time. Maybe it still does.'

'Oh, Leonidas, it was all a different me, another "us" ago. I was so lonely as a child, but you gave me glimpses of a normal life.' I shake my head, wishing to cast away the past to the tideline, sad that he remains wounded at my hand. 'But does any of it really still matter?'

'Are you lonely, Maria?'

'No. I am alone. That's the difference. I choose to be without another. That way, I cannot be hurt again. It is the way things are and it will not change.'

He takes a bite of pastry raising his eyebrows. He leans back on his arm and gazes out to sea. As the helicopter's engine becomes a distant note, the waves the downforce created on the once-still water crash noisily against the beach. The shoreline scrapes and clunks, as shingle is pulled backwards before grinding once again against the shore. Eroding land and time. Eventually, it becomes calm again.

'I am sorry if I ever hurt you, Maria, that your thoughts of me were tarnished by the cruelty you endured. It was the most important part of my day when we would be together. I could tell you anything and everything. When we sat on this beach thirty-five years ago and said goodbye, yes, we were set on our different paths, but my heart longed for you to stay. Yet you rejected me—'

'Leonidas, please,' I interrupt him. 'You have to let go

of the past. I spend all my time encouraging my students to do so. It only weighs you down and you forget to exist. My mother walks amongst what has gone before, and she is so drained. She looks forward to nothing other than dying and doesn't remember to live. I hurt you, and I'm sorry, I really am. And you've had your fair share of pain, too. But at this point in our life, isn't it a waste to live in what may have been? I am truly sad about you and Athena. It is the biggest disappointment to have failed at love – believe me, I know. But why return to a time that only gives you sadness? For me, now, I try not to think of my failings.'

His eyes darken briefly, the anger from that day resurfacing as I'd feared it would, before subsiding as quickly as it arrived. I think I hear him mutter 'lucky you', but it is indistinguishable as another aircraft returns to the bay. Although he attempts to mask his discomfort, I saw the flash of feeling and it concerns me he isn't over our past at all. After a considerable silence, despite the helicopter, he eventually speaks.

'I wasn't true to Athena, and she knew it, from the very beginning. It was over before it began, and I stayed with her longer than I should. When I took the job in Thessaloniki, I thought it would make me appreciate the family I had, but it only highlighted what was missing. She wasn't prepared to make the effort and come to Thessaloniki, and in a way, I was glad. We to-ed and fro-ed, but it wasn't enough. Yes, we have Zoe, and she is wonderful. But I was a fool convincing myself Athena was for me when I knew she was not. I had to find my own happiness, which is why I needed to leave and seek it elsewhere. It was unfair for us both and it became a terrible mess. I broke her heart. I will regret that forever.'

So, the gossip must be true: he had another woman. I don't judge him for it. On the contrary, it pleases me he once found a kind of love, however long it lasted.

'Well, that's why I only wish to help other people and cook. It is all I need to be happy. It is liberating not to have that pressure to hunt for love. It's too exhausting at our time of life.'

'But what about helping yourself?' he asks.

'Now, you sound exactly like my mother,' I tease, thrusting a plate of grilled zucchinis at him. 'I insist you eat and stop dwelling in sadness. Look where we are. There is nobody around, we are the only two in the world. Let's enjoy here. It's beautiful.'

He smiles reluctantly, but says in a whisper, 'You are beautiful, Maria.'

My pulse quickens as he directs his piercing eyes my way, hinting at something I cannot entertain. It is difficult to reconcile this adult version of him when his eyes and features represent my childhood. He has aged but is still as handsome as he always was, and my teenage heartbeat resurfaces, beating loudly with the purest desire, but my thoughts do not match the innocence. I don't comprehend how he can say such things when I look as I do. As if he has solidified some sanctified version of me in his mind from the past, he is unable to see who is in front of him today.

'Leonidas, please, I can't hear it.'

'But you should, you are.'

'Enough!' I shout. 'Don't you get it? You're clinging on

to an idea from your childhood. I don't know what you want from me, but whatever it is, I can't give it to you. Please, I need you as my friend. That's all I ask.'

He takes a deep breath and sighs, managing a small smile. 'Fine. If that is all you ask of me, then, yes, I will only be your friend.'

But his sentiment doesn't reach his honeyed eyes. I don't believe him, but I'm unwilling to wound him further.

He replaces the lids on my boxes of food, signalling the morning is over. He fishes into his trousers for the car keys, emptying out the contents. It's like a schoolboy's pocket, save for his mobile phone: a piece of driftwood, string, and chunks of dark blue sea glass.

Just as I'm about to show him my rare amethyst find on the beach, I stop. The blue sea glass was on the evil eye cloth left for me to find. It matches in its unique hue, a deep royal blue – not the azure, turquoise or aqua. This is specific. The doubts I dismissed moments ago resurface. I stare at him, probing for clues. I suddenly feel unsafe and can't deny my suspicions any longer. He isn't over my rejection, feels humiliated by my refusal all those years ago. I didn't realise how angry he still is, but he is unable to hide it. Today has made that much clear to me.

I know him too well.

Or I used to.

Could he really be the one who has been threatening me?

# Chapter 23

## Maria

I arrive home to striking silence, a weighted stillness lingers in the air. It feels odd, unworldly, no birds are singing, the clang of bells is absent, and I feel cold in spite of the humidity.

The return journey from Kalamaki was tense, the easiness between me and Leonidas melted away. My heart ached like a muscle being exercised for the first time in years, and yet, I remain riddled with suspicion.

There's no sign of the others or my mother, so I assume they have all gone into town. As I stand on the lawn, I notice even my bees' sound is dulled. I suddenly feel horribly alone.

A strong breeze buffets me, and I brace against it. I close my eyes and whisps of shadows flit across my blackened vision, goose bumps rippling across my skin as spirits almost come but withhold their insight at the last moment.

I think to my pressing task of creating my surprise honey cake for the Easter Sunday revellers tomorrow. Taking deep breaths, I permit ingredients to float through my mind and assemble in a set order, allowing my innate knowledge of food and flavours to guide me.

In my kitchen, as if in a trance, I lay out flour, baking powder, cinnamon, salt and sugar. There is no need to weigh ingredients; I instinctively know what to add. I zest lemon and the smell illuminates the room with a citrus tang. The April wind swirls in circles around the counters, in and out of cupboards like a naughty sprite. I make a honey syrup, which combats the sour fruit, permeating the room with heavenly sweetness. A bee enters the kitchen and I smile, thanking it for its assistance.

A knock on the door returns me to my surroundings and I see Kayla, nervously wringing her hands.

'Hey, Kayla,' I say warmly. 'Come on in.'

'I'm not disturbing you, am I?' she asks, looking terribly uncomfortable. It seems to be a never-ending roller coaster with Kayla. The bee circles over her head, like a guardian angel, fanning a hint of vanilla in its wake.

'No, just making my magnificent Easter Sunday cake. I reckon I can get three sponges out of this. Did you want to talk, interview me . . . both?'

Kayla sits at the kitchen island and watches as I deftly cream butter and sugar together. She inhales the natural sucrose, which seems to calm her in preparation for what she came to discuss. I permit the silence to drift, knowing she is searching for courage to speak.

'I think I did a bad thing,' Kayla begins, her voice high and tense. 'I've contacted Alessandra's daughter.'

I don't react. Somehow, I knew this would happen, and quietly prompt her to continue. 'And . . . ?'

'Well, nothing, yet. But I feel terrible. What if I've opened a hornets' nest and it sets a terrible chain of events in motion?'

I raise my eyebrows and chop up a handful of walnuts to add to the cake mix, offering her one, which she refuses. 'Surely that's up to fate, Kayla. There's a reason you've been compelled to intervene. I wouldn't think too much of it. If Alessandra's daughter hasn't spoken to her for twenty years, it's unlikely she'll pick up the phone just because you sent her a message.'

Kayla reluctantly nods her head and I offer her a spoonful of cake batter. She hesitates as the bee hovers above her head, before plunging the spoon into the golden liquid, scooping some into her mouth. She pauses, savouring the raw taste of the creamy flavours, the sharp notes of lemon. The sweetness will remind her of vanilla – which I am convinced will access her true feelings. Then I hear her crunch on the earthy nuttiness of a chunk of walnut. I watch as the ingredients weave their spell, having learnt over the years that flavours invoke moments in time, which rise to the surface like a bubble in a pan of water as it begins to boil. One by one, recollections can spring up out of nowhere. Some are wanted and joyful, others painful; there is no controlling what taste or smell can inspire from your precious memory store. My bee dances above her, and I can tell that the magic is working.

Kayla licks the spoon clean, ensuring she hasn't missed a drop. Her gaze becomes distant, as if she is watching a far-off scene playing in her mind.

'What are you thinking about?' I ask softly.

'Baking with my mother.' Kayla's voice cracks. 'When I was little, perhaps nine years old. She was obsessed with walnuts and vanilla. All her cakes had one of them, sometimes both.' Tears fill her eyes, and she looks down at her hands still holding the teaspoon. She grips it hard, as if she's clinging to the key that will unlock a forgotten happiness.

'Tell me more about her,' I nudge tenderly.

Kayla's lips lift in a sad smile. 'She was beautiful. And funny. I mean, ridiculously funny and silly. She was so childlike and made everything fun. Even when I was grumpy, she would make me laugh. We had the same red hair – Rosie has it too. And she made up nicknames for everything. Even the car had a name . . .' She breaks off and runs her hand through her glossy titian mane.

I see as pain registers amongst joy on Kayla's face as I ask, 'And what did she call the car?'

Kayla's head shoots up, about to protest or wriggle out of discussing it, but the breeze brings the safe scent of honeyed syrup from the stove and it convinces Kayla to continue.

'Freddie . . . Freddie the Ford.' She laughs bitterly. 'I loved that car. She made up a voice for it and we'd have whole conversations, me and Freddie – her pretending to be him. So stupid when you think about it.'

'No, that was the magic she wove through your childhood.'

'I wish I'd had her and Dad for longer. It's so unfair they were both taken from me . . . killed. I was only a baby, just fourteen. And I said some awful things, Maria. I feel sick even thinking about it. My last words to them were hateful, horrible. I can never get past that. I loved them so much. How do I let them know what they meant to me?'

Kayla crumples in her chair and sobs as if the accident has only just happened. I wrap my arms around the poor girl, longing to be able to see spirits again if only to reassure her.

'I'm sorry,' cries Kayla, her face contorted in grief. 'I've done nothing but cry and cause drama since I got here. I'm supposed to be interviewing you; this is incredibly unprofessional and embarrassing. What must you think of me? I'm a wreck.'

'Hey, I've seen worse, believe me. This is obviously what you needed to do: let it all out. You can't keep it all locked inside forever, Kayla. You need to forgive yourself first, and them for being taken from you. Stop fighting. It'll eat you alive.'

I mop Kayla's tears away with a piece of kitchen paper as she looks up at me. An understanding passes between us.

'You know, don't you? What you just said . . . what I'm hiding . . . my secret. You see it.'

I feel such sympathy for her and nod sadly. She can't say it out loud. Yet.

'What am I going to do, Maria?'

'That's over to you, but you need to get help. Whatever you do, you need to be authentic and true to yourself. It's way more time-consuming to pretend to be who you're not, concealing what's underneath. You need to be brave, but here's the great news in all this – you already are.'

Kayla shakes her head in protest, but I continue. 'You may not think it, but against all the odds, you've succeeded in so many ways. You have the courage to go on national television, write beautiful words millions of people follow, and you've changed the way people cook. And you're a mother, with a little girl who I instinctively know idolises you, the way you did your own. Even though you may not feel very lucky, you must try to seek out the blessings and be thankful. I believe in you, Kayla.'

Kayla takes a moment to allow my words to sink in. They would be sentiments she'd long to hear from her mother, but I know in my heart, she is here watching over her daughter. I can feel the shift in energy and if I could see spirits, I'd see her arms wrapped around Kayla. Several more bees enter the kitchen and as if in validation, Kayla rubs her arms with a shiver.

'Thank you,' she says, wiping away the remains of her tears. 'You know exactly the right thing to say. So does Alessandra, in her own strange way. What I'm thankful for in this moment is for whatever brought you both into my life. I find it very hard to trust people and I don't have any real friends, not outside of who I work with, but that's all surface; it's showbiz fakeness. This is genuine and it's helped me try to find who I am.' Kayla manages to pull herself together and flicks into work mode. 'Now, what about that interview?'

I laugh and move back to the work surface to finish my cakes as Kayla blows her nose, then switches her phone to record. As we talk freely with the surprising ease of old friends, we make plans for supper together later that evening along with Alessandra. I notice all but one of the group of bees leave the kitchen.

*The remaining bee watches heartbreaking grief shift to the solace of friendship. It sees the dead woman with red hair embrace her daughter with similar colouring and the daughter feels it with a shiver. A man stands over Maria's shoulder. Tall, dressed in a formal suit, his jet-black hair is glossy, lit by a golden glow. He towers over both women, but only watches Maria, beaming with pride, as she cooks. His head turns to see the bee and they hold each other's gaze. Satisfied he will play his part, the insect returns to its hive.*

# Chapter 24

## *Alessandra*

'Is Leonidas not joining us?' Alessandra asks with a wry smile as she tucks into supper.

Maria sends her a warning look, although she knows there is no malice behind the question. 'No, he's with his daughter, I think. I don't know. He'll be at the fireworks later, I suppose.'

Kayla looks up from her plate of food and exchanges a glance with Alessandra.

'Is that at midnight?' asks Alessandra.

'It's the breaking of the fast and welcoming in Easter. You'll hear everyone shouting *Christos Anesti*, Christ is risen, and to celebrate it, fireworks are let off to make as much noise as possible. We Greeks are very good at making a celebration as loud as we can. Then everyone goes to the tavernas to crack red eggs and eat a lamb offal soup and then even more lamb from the barbecue. I tend not to eat that late, and I don't fast anyway, so I just go for the spectacle. And there's more grilling tomorrow.' Maria takes another bite of her food. 'Thank you for cooking tonight – I love this.'

Alessandra and Kayla had insisted they preside over supper duties this evening, making a blissfully simple squash ravioli with a fresh sage and butter sauce, all the herbs and vegetables picked from the garden.

'It's a very straightforward recipe and Kayla makes incredible pasta, much better than mine. It was fun to cook in your beautiful kitchen and watch the big TV star work her magic,' she jokes affectionately, and Kayla blushes. 'I don't have the energy much at home these days, but here . . . I know we only have three days left, but I feel like I could stay forever.' Alessandra sighs contentedly.

As she says the words, she realises she really does want to be here longer. Perhaps she and Phillipo can take a house to rent. It doesn't matter anymore where they are in terms of geography; since Arianna is out of her life, they have no remaining ties to Rome.

A beep on Maria's phone interrupts her thoughts, and Alessandra scrutinises her reaction closely. She reads the message and rapidly turns her phone face down on the dinner table. Alessandra catches the flicker of fear cloud Maria's features. She longs to ask about the message she saw in church yesterday and deduces this one is in a similar vein. She feels a flash of fury that anyone could be so unkind to her gracious hostess. She is an exceptional woman and Alessandra has encountered many in her varied lifetime, but nobody is like Maria.

Alessandra feels a sudden, overwhelming urge to help her,

212

to repay in gratitude how much Maria has changed her. Only she doesn't know exactly how yet. But when an idea occurs to Alessandra, there is absolutely nothing that can sway her from her fixed course.

*   *   *

## Kayla

Kayla is struggling to focus on dinner, which she enjoyed cooking, but the thrill quickly evaporated. She's allowed herself to be unpicked by these two fabulous women with whom she shares a table; voluntarily pulled apart. Maria has somehow seen her darkest secret, which has been her daily battle since her parents died, the only way she could wrestle control back in her world. But it has taken charge of her, she finally admits.

Her nerve has also deserted her thus far in seeking out that gorgeous waiter. She hasn't felt brave enough to enter any kind of physical encounter with a stranger. Yet by accepting her marriage is over, she is free to make such a decision that is entirely about her own pleasure. Although a therapist would probably say it is another way for her to be destructive and reckless, the idea of doing something so out of character is nagging away at her. It could be the gateway to unveiling something she is yet to unearth on this voyage of self-discovery, and she admits the concept is tantalising.

In her life, she's scrutinised and critiqued by everyone. She has no choice but to plough on, too afraid to jump off the relentless conveyor belt of fame in case she finds

213

herself alone. Who is she if she's not famous? She recognises now she's lost sight of that person. What is left of Kayla aside from the labels of mother, wife, chef, writer and darling redhead of British cuisine? If she stripped them away, dare she unfurl who remains? Wife can be struck from the list, and she's terrified to cast away more of those titles in case she loses too much and is disappointed by what is left.

However, with two pairs of extremely wise eyes fixed upon her, there is nowhere to hide. As freeing as being unburdened feels, it is utterly terrifying, and, she knows, it about to become even more frightening.

# Chapter 25

## *Maria*

Walking along the village promenade, I have a sense of looming anticipation. At least the weather has improved and is less claggy, although this breeze is stronger than those taking part in the Saturday procession would like; their candles will struggle to stay alight.

Our pace is slow, and I strain to make my mother hear me above the crashing sea, which thumps on the shore. The air whistles like a kettle boiling on a stove as it whirs around the cove but the gusts are like inhaling desert air.

*Mamá* is carrying my Easter bread in a basket, the red eggs are lustrous within the glazed bake. Father Kyriakidis will bless it according to tradition and we will feast on it for Easter Sunday breakfast tomorrow. It's a favourite moment I share with my mother, and one I cherish. We will competitively take a red egg and smash it against each other's. The aim of the game called *tsougrisma* is to keep your shell as undamaged as possible. Whoever receives the fewest cracks will have the most luck in the coming year – a superstition *Mamá* firmly believes in.

My stomach gives a lurch as I remember that she has invited Leonidas to Sunday lunch. As I think of him, a group of bees swarm past. Are they here to warn or comfort me? I feel uneasy about seeing him again after this morning in Kalamaki. It already feels like a lifetime ago, but I'm haunted by it. An image of Leonidas holding his phone when I received a hateful message flits through my mind. He does have a reason to hurt me – in his mind, anyway, though I had every right to refuse his proposal. I was so taken aback in the moment, I lost touch with my heart. He is still angry by his own admission, but I never had him marked as the vengeful type. He is too caring and kind. Or was.

I hear Kayla and Alessandra chattering behind me. I'm so glad they have found a place of calm after such a difficult beginning. I will keep Kayla's counsel about her attempt to find Alessandra's daughter. I only hope her interference doesn't cause problems. I know the tribulations caused by over-involvement in another's business first-hand by my mother's relentless quest to find me a man.

As we reach the village green there's a carnival atmosphere. Unlit votives and tapers are clutched in readiness to receive the holy light during the service. Children run around, clambering on benches, risking their pristine outfits with grass smears and stains, overly excited to be up so late. This is far more thrilling than Christmas.

I park my mother with her friends on a seat near the

216

church entrance. Most are widowed. They look like an aged girl-gang, dressed in their black mourning weeds, clucking and tutting as the younger generations dash about. They smile as I deposit *Mamá*, quashing their superstition temporarily for her sake, resisting the urge to cross themselves.

My eye is drawn along the top of the green, across the chairs and crowded tables of tavernas nestled under the trees, to the row of stores. And I see him. Leonidas' head turns as if he senses my stare, and he smiles, raising his hand. I return his wave, but his arm is tugged downwards by Zoe. I watch their heated exchange and she storms off in a teenage huff. I return to Kayla and Alessandra, and we wait for the service to begin.

'Won't you come and light a candle with us, Maria?' asks Kayla.

'You got bit by the religious bug, then.' I laugh, nudging her with my elbow. 'I knew we'd get you!'

'Ha! I wanted the three of us to light a candle together. Resurrection and beginnings . . . I thought we could mark it. Friendships, a new-found courage and all that.'

She hands me a small white candle, blushing in the lowlight, and I accept. It's a beautiful sentiment and in the spirit of the festivities, even if I don't wholly sign up to the religious element, I'd like to partake.

There's an infectious magic about tradition, which is hard to resist, and I understand Kayla's captivation. As the bishop and priests light candles from the holy flame, the scent of molten wax floods across the green, and more lights are ignited. A hush descends as villagers share flames with their neighbour and the distinct smell of wild oregano

217

swirls from the rushes strewn across the ground. Laurel leaves make up an archway to frame the holy men on a platform as they continue the lengthy service. Their dedicated fervour is contagious.

Afterwards, the congregation spills over the main square, holding their precious candles. The atmosphere shifts to celebratory, the shackles of mourning cast aside. I'm lost in the crowd, unable to see *Mamá*, Alessandra or Kayla. Pushed from side to side, I struggle to move in the opposite direction to the flow of people. I turn to see Athena looking my way with disgust. Others make the sign of the cross, some sneer as they unwittingly find themselves before me. Children shriek in mock fright, swishing sprigs of oregano like talismans, as if I were the local bogeyman, a fabled monster sent to scare them. My chest constricts in claustrophobia as I look frantically around, wondering if somewhere in this crowd is the person who means me harm.

I jump as I feel a hand on my shoulder and turn to see Leonidas. In the chaos, it's as if the noise melts away for a moment. There is only us. His hand is warm, imprinting my skin as it did on that day in Kalamaki. I look into his soft hazel eyes and feel our connection, friendship, a crackle of something else whispered on the wind. But my nerves brim with fear and suspicion. I try to squash it but like the ripples of a wave meeting the pebbled beach, it returns, lapping again and again, heightening my darkest thoughts. I see my bees swirl over his head.

*What is it, my little friends?* I ask in my mind.

But of course, there is no answer.

'Come,' he shouts above the din. 'Your mother is over here.'

Despite my lingering suspicions, I am grateful he appeared when I needed him. I hadn't realised how affected I've been by the increased warnings and messages these last few days. He guides me to the edge of the green where my mother is fanning herself with an order of service.

She gestures in the heat, complaining. 'This weather – there is no air! Even the wind brings no relief. Maria, I will go home. Ah, Leonidas. *Christos Anesti*.'

'*Alithos Anesti*, Eleni,' Leonidas responds with the correct religious response for the time after resurrection. Although not quite midnight, I'm sure he will be forgiven. I smile as I watch him converse with my mother. Her eyes twinkle with something approaching flirtation, even though she does not want him for herself. She wishes him for me. But he inspires such a reaction in everyone he speaks to. I am not alone in that sense.

Alessandra's shoulders are a little rounded and her elegant posture seems strained as if each movement is an extreme labour. She says, 'I will take your mother home, Maria. I am worn out and cannot wait until midnight for the fireworks. I will see them from the villa if I'm awake that long.'

'Are you sure? I'll go with you.'

'No, you stay here. Kayla, are you coming?' Alessandra nods at Leonidas and I see something pass between them. I try to stymie my lurch of jealousy rushing up from deep within. I turn my head to Kayla, who is slightly subdued since the service.

'I'm going to hang around for a bit. Research for my article,' Kayla says sheepishly and I inherently know she isn't being truthful. I catch Alessandra's eye and wink as Kayla reddens, visible even in the darkness.

'I won't be too late,' I say kissing my mother on the cheek, bidding her goodnight.

I watch my mother amble away on the short walk home along the promenade with Alessandra attentively by her side. She is almost double my mother's height, and they look a comical pair. Their difference in size isn't dissimilar to mine and Leonidas'. My mother cradles the now-blessed Easter bread, and I cannot wait to tuck into that in the morning. I must resist the temptation of my honey cake, too. I did have enough for three sponges in the end, and I thought it fitting to represent the Father, Son and Holy Spirit, even if my attempt at religious symbolism may be lost on everyone else. The collection of bees chase after *Mamá* and Alessandra. I'm glad they're returning home to watch over them both.

It is still thirty minutes until midnight, when the cacophony of noise will become deafening. The crowd is already roaring in celebration, excited about what is yet to come. Musicians strike up; people sing and dance, anticipating the official start of Easter. The bells strike in regular clanging peals every few minutes. Cats mew in protest at the racket and rush to find shelter in the under-growth.

I watch Kayla wander off towards the far end of the beach away from the village. I am glad if something has spiritually moved her, affording strength to journey into her next chapter, whatever that may hold. Although, she seems to be headed for the grill house. Wherever her destination, she will need all the reserve she has to be brave and face her past in order to get to the future. She ought to take a risk and see where it leads her.

Leonidas has gone in search of wine from one of the tavernas surrounding the square. I still feel the eyes of the village upon me, watching my interactions with him. I shift uncomfortably, feeling more observed than I have for years. I've avoided exposing myself to more scrutiny than necessary, but here I am in the thick of it, thrust into the lion's den. And I feel afraid. The prickle of a message steals along my spine and the candle I'm holding flickers violently. A foreboding knowledge penetrates my blood and resonates within the marrow of my bones. Tonight will be significant for us all, somehow. I know it. I feel it. I just don't know how.

# Chapter 26

*Kayla*

Kayla senses a profound shift, like she's stepped into a different body and despite the poignant religious service, her thoughts are far from holy. The acceptance in her heart to meaningly move on from her marriage and her past has transported her to a mental state she's only dreamt of. A freeing excitement is rising, as if she is a twenty-something at university, enjoying the liberty to explore her version of life and love. Instead of the one she had: consigned to her dormitory room, keeping a food diary and worrying if she'd ever make friends. But now, this is bold Kayla, making decisions and finding herself again.

As she reaches the grill house at the end of the beach, she stops within the shadows with a start as she spots Dimitris. He is sitting at a table with a cigarette, which sends plumes of smoke into the air. Kayla watches the wind buffet the vapour as Dimitris drinks his glass of wine. The

223

taverna is deserted, as all the village residents are congregated in the square, awaiting the celebrations.

Kayla gathers herself, allowing her eyes to enjoy Dimitris. She feels like a voyeur, watching something forbidden, and it heightens her excitement. A gentle wind lifts the edges of her skirt, and she breathes it in, exhaling who she was before this moment, embarking on the first step to what comes next. This is exclusively about her – owning her sexuality and femininity, who she is underneath. What lurks below the masks of layers born of responsibility and adulting? Not mother, nor career woman, simply Kayla.

Unable to contain her growing lust, she boldly walks across the stone floor. As he notices her, he smiles. Breath is high in her chest, as the thudding against her ribcage increases. Dimitris stands as he abandons his cigarette with a flick onto the sand. He takes a slow sip of his drink, a smile creeping seductively over his features. He is about to put his glass down on the table, but Kayla takes it from his grasp and drains it, searching for chemical courage to take the next step. The tang of the sharp white wine warms her insides, which pound from a further rush of desire.

She steps closer. The warmth from his body makes her tremble in anticipation of his touch. He takes the glass and puts it on the table. With his index finger under her chin, he gently tilts her face upwards. They stare at each other for what feels like an eternity. His pupils are enlarged, matching her need. Dimitris slowly leans down to meet his lips with hers. The softest of touches at first, teasing her mouth. Her breath catches as their kisses deepen. She stretches her hands around his neck, enjoying the pleasing graze on her fingers from his shaved neck, pulling him as close as possible. But she wants more.

Running her hands across his strong shoulders to his waist, she reaches underneath his T-shirt and finds soft skin coating hard muscle. She shudders with excitement at touching another man's body, Daniel being the only one she has ever known until this moment. She is desperate to feel Dimitris' skin against hers, wanton and assured. She has no care for the confines of her career nor her broken marriage. She is truly living in the moment, throwing caution to the hot wind and pleasing only herself for once. Like stepping into a fantasy of her choosing, she permits herself to lean fully into the moment.

Dimitris lifts her onto a table set for supper and she wraps her legs around his waist. Glasses topple and cutlery drops to the floor. Neither hears the shouts and cries from the crowd in the village square as the countdown to Easter builds, they are too immersed in their own ascending pleasure. As he kisses her neck, Kayla is aware they are on the sand for all to see. Although she has cast her restraint aside, she isn't foolish enough to continue what she plans to do in the open air.

'Not here,' she manages, her voice husky, barely a croak.

Dimitris' face is buried in her hair as his hand slips underneath her skirt. His fingers travel to the place she longs for them to go.

'I live not far . . .' he mutters.

'Where?' Kayla says desperately with a sharp intake of breath as he finds his mark, thrilled by the danger of following him home. Her eyes are closed, focused on her building pleasure and she doesn't see where he indicates.

'Moments. Above the taverna,' he says as he expertly circles his thumb, coaxing a gasp from Kayla's lips, which he stifles with a kiss. She throws her head back, clutching on to his neck, trying to silence her cries, knowing she needs more, yearning to feel his naked body against hers like her existence depends upon it. As her legs begin to quiver in the aftermath of the exquisite sensations pinging around her body, she pushes him backwards and smooths her skirt down.

'Let's go,' she says, and he takes her hand, leading her along the frontage of the taverna and up a flight of stone steps at the far corner. He unlocks the door and as they cross the threshold, Kayla pushes him against the wall in the hallway. She has never felt so empowered. Putting herself in this deliberately vulnerable situation makes her feel more alive than she can ever remember feeling. She pulls off his top to reveal the athletic torso she's fantasised about from when she first arrived in Petalidi. Exotic tattoos snake down his ribcage and a sleeve of inking coats one arm. He is so free, the opposite to her carefully controlled world and she allows herself to revel in the thrill of the difference. Her eyes travel down his body, appreciating his contours of sinew and muscle, what is on display and what is yet to be revealed. She feels in charge, making a conscious choice to enjoy this man and all he is offering her, and she bathes in the freedom of her decision.

Dimitris presses against her, whispering words in his language, none of which she understands, but the sentiment is universal. She finds it deeply erotic to hear him speak in his mother tongue, and another layer of arousal floods through her veins. She is transported to another place, but it is a world of her making and she basks in the sensation. There is no doubt in her mind: he wants her as much as she desires him. He drops to his knees and his mouth takes up the place his hands explored earlier. Kayla has no need to hide her cries this time, although the occasional firework outside masks her moans for any latecomers to the festivities walking along the beach outside.

Her legs turn to jelly, unable to endure more, her sensitive nerve endings alive, satisfied and yet craving more. It still isn't enough. He lifts her once again and carries her across a room she did not notice earlier. She can taste herself on his lips and a further flood of longing cascades through her body. He places her gently on his bed and stands above her as he unbuckles his jeans. Her eyes follow the movement of his hands; she has never been so hungry for someone's touch. She sits up to speed him along, not wishing to be teased further. She needs him to possess her body, to fill the vacant space within. As they move together, frantic and passion-fuelled, any other thoughts and troubles dissolve into the night air. This signals the start of her freedom, a rebirth, reminding her she can make her own choices about her life. And in this second, she chooses to give herself to this beautiful Greek man, permitting him to totally cleanse all that she was and propel her to who she is yet to become.

\* \* \*

'I must go to work soon,' says Dimitris as he holds Kayla close to his chest, wrapped in his bedsheets. 'But stay if you wish.'

227

Kayla searches herself for any hint of shame or guilt and is surprised there's none. She checks every corner of her body and mind that has been consumed by Dimitris for the last few hours and is pleased to find only languid satisfaction. An emotional and physical zen-like state. The only disappointment she finds is the thought of him leaving the bed and being deprived of his body.

'How long will you be?' she asks, hoping to lure him back beneath the covers.

'All night,' he replies as he rolls her onto her back, staring into her eyes. He leans down and kisses her once more. 'You are making it very hard to go.'

Her hand travels downwards as he smiles. She experiences the thrill of being so wanted at the hands of this beautiful stranger. She gently guides him inside once more and he groans with faux reluctance as he moves within the softest part of her. Kayla loops her legs around him and raises her hips to allow him the deepest access. At the precise time when shards of her carefully crafted world are shattering and she ought to be more wary of out-of-character decisions, she's chosen to do the opposite. It is the most exhilarating thing to happen to her for years.

As she watches him dress, zipping his fly, her eyelids feel heavy. She is completely spent, basking in the afterglow. She barely remembers him kissing her forehead as he left for work, sinking into the deepest slumber she's had for longer than she can remember. Tonight, there is no car-crash dream, no faces merging with other cast members in her nightmares, only black, the sheer bliss of sated darkness.

For the first time since she was fourteen, Kayla rests truly contented in her own skin. Such peace isn't the product of a man's desire; it's a result of her independent choices and a determination to decide who she is and who she wants to be. Not the fragments of a broken teenager, nor defined by celebrity but the authentic, real Kayla Moss. That is who she celebrates as she yields to the anaesthesia of sleep.

# Chapter 27

## Maria

I scan the crowd for Leonidas and spot him emerging on the village green holding a jug of wine and two tumblers. He's been gone for over half an hour, and I'd begun to doubt he would ever return.

As he pours our drinks, he says slightly out of breath, 'Sorry I was so long. *Yiá mas!* To Easter, and to you, Maria.'

I take a glass from him and clink it to his to join his cheers. 'I will drink to Easter and . . . to new beginnings. *Yiá mas.*'

A silence descends between us, which seems implausible amongst the noisy villagers. He glows in the glimmering candlelight from the one in my hand and those around us. We receive Easter greetings in passing, but we don't look away from each other. We can't.

'So . . .' I start nervously.

'I need to speak with you,' he says urgently.

'Again?' I ask in apprehension. 'You had all morning with me, and we will have lunch together tomorrow. What can you still have to say?'

'Please, can we go to the beach and find a little quiet?'

I reluctantly agree, dreading the tremor of gossip that may travel through the village. I only hope it doesn't prompt my mystery messenger into action. Assuming it's not Leonidas himself, of course. But I am drawn to him, so I follow against my better judgement. Once more, the tingling on the nape of my neck begins. Whether it is a warning or encouragement, I have no way of interpreting. I catch the smell of woodsmoke. It must be from a barbecue, ignited in anticipation of grilling the midnight lamb, but it seems strange and out of place, like I imagined it. Perhaps it's the distant fires across the bay.

The short walk to the beach is crowded. Family groups converse, teenage lovers steal kisses in the shadows. We laugh at the youngsters taking advantage of the euphoria of the evening and the fact their parents are distracted from policing bad behaviour. The waves are growing in ferocity with the increasing wind, but we sit on the stones and look out at the water. Lights twinkle across the bay as the Easter celebrations are marked throughout the land. Church bells continue to ring, tolling the quarter before midnight when holy bedlam will let loose.

I sip my cold, fresh wine, which soothes my nerves. I set my candle down in front of us. Again, my neck prickles as I am transfixed by the flame.

'I need to explain something to you, Maria.'

I turn my head to him, and he raises his hand to stroke my cheek. I flinch at the unexpected, intimate contact, but his fingers remain on my skin.

'When I was younger, it wasn't possible to feel complicated emotions that I know now, but even then, my heart felt heavy, like it could burst. I did not understand what love was, what it was supposed to feel like, but I didn't want it to stop. It was an alien feeling here, in my stomach, so strong, like a torture but I wanted more. A drug of sorts, it consumed all my thoughts.'

He drops his hand and takes a sip of his wine as he looks back out to sea. I have to lean my head closer to him to hear what he is saying over the ocean and the bells. I realise I've been holding my breath as he presses on with what he is attempting to impart.

'When you left to follow your dreams in America, you left me with a broken heart. It was like a punishment, and I was afraid I wouldn't find someone to love me. You didn't know how I felt back then, I realise now. But I wanted to be married, to have a family with the woman I loved.'

'But Leonidas, you did all of those things, you had a family with the woman you loved and then went to Thessaloniki to be with another. I don't understand why you're talking of punishment and fear.'

He puts his wine glass on the pebbles and cups my face in both his hands.

'You misunderstand what I am saying. I am talking of you, of us. I have loved you, Maria, for as long as I can remember. But you went to America, and you made it

233

clear when you said no to my proposal you did not feel the same. I can no longer hide. There was no other; there was only you. I am too old to play games or waste any more time away from you.'

I go to interrupt him, but he insists on continuing. 'Please, let me finish or I may never say this. When you returned to Petalidi, I was afraid to see you again. I couldn't face another rejection. It confirmed what was inside of me: I never stopped loving you and I knew my marriage was a lie. I decided to do the right thing and leave Athena and my Zoe. I had to get away from the village, from you and what was in my heart. It is why I took a job in Thessaloniki, thinking my love would lessen. This place, Petalidi, I blamed it. Your bad memories of this village are the reason you refused me and why I left. I couldn't be here and exist without you and it would have been wrong of me to break my vows by telling you how I felt when you returned.

'I thought my feelings would diminish if I went away. But as the years passed, my love became stronger. You were all I could think about. I read in the newspapers of your cooking school, and I was so proud. You did everything you set out to do. Then Athena and I couldn't make it work and so we divorced. Although I still stayed away, my love for you strengthened. I was looking for you in everyone I met. I wanted to tell you for myself, and I've eventually found my courage. It took a while. It's why I came home. Home is where you are, Maria. I cannot hide any longer. I know in my heart you feel the same and I long to hear it. I am yours. I love you. It's always been you, Maria.'

234

The screech of a rocket and the sudden persistent clanging of church bells makes me jump out of my skin. I stand up with my hand on my heart, feeling it swell with the love I've suppressed for so long. It is like opening a dam. The barriers are being beaten down, dismantled by his words.

Leonidas rises to face me. His head is framed by multi-coloured exploding lights in the sky, which cascade downwards like a golden weeping willow. He looks beautiful. Shouts of 'Christos Anesti' reverberate around the village, along with bangs of firecrackers thrown into the air by youngsters. Dogs begin to bark.

Tears fill my eyes. I don't know what to tell him. It is as if my body has been split in two; half wishing to melt into his arms acceding his claim to my heart and the other half filled with absolute terror, knowing I could never survive being hurt by him. In addition, my earlier suspicion remains and I'm racked with indecision and confusion.

'Maria, please, say something,' he shouts, trying to make himself heard above the din. 'Please, I love you. I know you feel the same. I feel it.'

He takes my hand and pushes it against his heart. I feel its rhythm. It's perfectly in sync with mine.

But I can barely hear him. I'm trying to process what he's told me; the end of his marriage was my fault, unbeknown to me, giving Athena ample grounds to despise me, more so in recent years than from our youth. But I don't understand how he can love me when I look like this. I am not the woman he says he fell in love with before I left for America. I'm marked and maimed. I'm not the same.

235

He puts his hands either side of my face and kisses me on the cheek, so tenderly it feels my heart could crack with longing. I feel a tear run down my face, pausing at the tip of my scar below my chin, pooling in a pockmark near New Hampshire. The feel of his lips I've yearned for since I was a teenager, the scent of his skin is like coming home. I can feel the heat from his body, except . . . my blood slowly begins to ice with cold. Starting at the small of my back it creeps along, freezing my bones until I am shivering violently, convulsing so much so that Leonidas pulls back.

'Maria, what is it, what is wrong?'

I must unburden myself of suspicion. He has to know.

'I need to tell you. Someone here hates me. They leave me warnings by my beehives. Home-made things, of sea glass, skulls, the *mati* . . .'

His eyes widen. 'Who would do such a thing, Maria? That's horrible.'

I raise my chin defiantly and it wavers. Tremors continue to rob my muscles of strength. 'You tell me, Leonidas.'

My eyes accuse him even though the words fail me. I am shivering so hard.

'Let me fetch you a blanket,' says Leonidas, running off in search of warmth.

My neck is being pricked with a thousand pins and my vision starts to swirl. My scar pulses with something between pain and excitement. I haven't felt this since . . . New York . . . on the day my husband left me.

I don't know what is happening. I look to where Leonidas was standing, and my breathing becomes laboured. I feel a surge of energy. Otherworldly forces charge through my whole being. Goose bumps resurface on my arms as a figure slowly forms in front of me. Vapours at first, like a gently whirring sea mist, then a solid outline of a man emerges. I know him.

It is my father.

My gift has returned.

He looks like he did as a young man, tall, his shiny black hair gleaming under the night sky. I am afraid at first; it is such a shock to see a spirit again. Then I feel his love flood over me. '*Babá?*' I say, but his expression is grave as he lifts his arm to point beyond my shoulder. I frown at the apparition. He is urging me to turn around with his eyes. My phone vibrates and he shakes his head as if begging me not to look at the message. But I am too stubborn to listen to the living, let alone the dead. I reach for my phone and read what's been sent, instantly wishing I hadn't.

> **You are finished. Die.**

Leonidas appears holding a blanket that he thrusts around my shoulders.

'Maria, what is it?' he asks, and I look back at him, my eyes narrowing in suspicion. Yet another message has appeared when he was near but not within eyeshot. I was unable to see if he sent it or not.

I turn around slowly in the direction of where my father is pointing, back along the promenade. An ungodly scream peals from my lungs. I throw off the newly placed wrap from my shoulders and run as fast as I can down the beach, kicking my candle over in the process, the holy light extinguished in an instant.

Flames are leaping into the air, bright oranges violently

237

dancing against the pitch night sky mimicking the colours of the fireworks. But this is no celebration.

My house and my precious beehives are on fire.

# Chapter 28

## *Maria*

I cover my mouth in horror as I approach from the seaward side. The wind is fanning the blaze. Most of the lawn has caught, bone-dry from the arid weather. Two of my hives are burning brightly as silhouettes of swarming bees fly for their lives. The flames are slinking towards the main house, moments from licking the door to my mother's annexe, already blocking a safe route.

'*Mamá!*' I scream, but I can't make myself heard above the roaring fire and the sea. The elements conspire to silence me.

Leonidas appears, panting, from the pathway. 'I have called the fire brigade. Do you have a hose we can link to your kitchen? We need buckets, anything!'

The horrifying sight of my home stuns me into inertia. Leonidas grabs my shoulders. 'Maria, we need to do something. Come on.'

He urges me into action as he covers his mouth with his sleeve and tries to approach the house. The heat from this side is too much to stand.

'Leonidas, no! Go through the other door. Please, save my mother. Be careful!' I shout as he heads for the far part of the house. I manage to run around the worst of the fire, which burns brightly on the grass to my tool shed. The power of the flames seems unreal; the intense heat makes me wince. I drag a hose through the orchard to my cooking kitchen and connect it to the tap.

The blaze hasn't reached the guest accommodation, so Alessandra must be safe, but I haven't seen Kayla since before midnight, although she was headed in the opposite direction. I pray she is elsewhere. When the fire service arrives, and I know my mother is safe, I will look for them both, but in this moment my mother and now Leonidas are in peril.

'Please save them,' I cry. 'Protect them all.' I turn on the tap and water spills across the floor of the kitchen. Jars of golden honey harvested from my hives glimmer in the reflected burning light, a heartbreaking taunt, like a perverse celebration of the destruction of my bees. But I can't think of them now. I am focused on my mother and Leonidas.

\* \* \*

## Leonidas

Leonidas enters from the roadside door of the building, snaking his way through Maria's part of the house. Smoke has filled the rooms, masking any distinguishing shapes since all the lights are out. He bangs into chairs, heavy

240

pieces of furniture. Ornaments smash to the floor, but he forges onwards, shouting for Eleni. He is disorientated, unable to see, imagining the layout from the outside. He comes up against a locked door. Forcing his weight against it, he hopes it is the entry to Eleni's annexe. Through the windows he can see the lawn is ablaze, burning furiously as the fire spreads in the wind. Flames are mocking him with their manic movement and sweat pours down his body.

'Eleni!' he shouts but there is no response.

He feels the wood give against his shoulder, hears the crack of the surround splintering. The room is black, and burnt air pours over him, the light from the fire outside highlighting the volume of thick smoke.

'Eleni!' he shouts again. The pollution catches in his throat, and he begins to choke, unable to draw a clean breath. He drops to the floor and crawls along on his forearms, searching for purer air. He has no way of seeing where he is, blindly moving across the carpet, his elbows chafing. He doesn't feel the sting. His eyes stream although they are little use to him in this moment. He hears a faint cough close by, but cannot make out any shapes.

'I'm here, óla endáxi, Eleni.' He reassures her all is all right, but doubts she can hear him; his voice is a thin rasp.

Butting his head against what must be the bedframe, the thump sends painful darts through his skull, but he is undeterred. Feeling his way along, he finds Eleni. He shakes her gently, not wishing to startle her, but she doesn't wake. Only a weak groan confirms she is barely conscious. There is no time to waste. They will both suffocate if they spend a moment longer in the thickening dense smoke.

He scoops her up like a tiny, weightless bundle and attempts to retrace his steps. But he has completely lost his bearings. Kicking out his feet in front of him, his chest burns with the effort, the oxygen supply insufficient to fuel his movement.

He comes up against an unfamiliar door. It makes no sense. He has no idea where he is. This isn't what he had planned for tonight. All he imagined it could have been has turned on its heel and become a disaster. His strategy failed and now he is in grave danger. Closing his eyes in frustration, charcoal tears spill down his face. This may prove to be a fatal mistake. He has gone the wrong way, further into the annexe rather than out of it. Eleni feels limp in his arms as he turns in the opposite direction. He feels faint but, mustering his remaining strength, he fights forwards.

The siren of the emergency services signals which way he should travel, knowing now he must head for the flames, towards mortal danger to be able to see or be seen. The sound of glass shattering brings his drifting mind back to the peril of the moment. His spirit concedes there is no point; it is over. His energy drains rapidly in the claustrophobic, toxic atmosphere. His muscles scream at him, urging escape.

Leonidas says a silent prayer. He pictures Maria's face and smiles. His heart is saturated with love as his body begins to fail. Any fear of what is happening slowly dissolves as he succumbs to his fate. Sinking to the ground, he sets Eleni down carefully, making the sign of the cross over her. Leonidas searches for comfort in his final moments of consciousness. Maria knows he loves her.

His eyes flood further with tears of soot. If only they'd had more time, he would know how she felt about him. There was no chance for her to respond; the timing of the fire worked against them. He will never hear her answer. His plan for tonight has played out of order. It wasn't supposed to go like this, and now it is too late.

# Chapter 29

## *Maria*

'Please, help,' I shout desperately to the fireman who appears at the side of the house. 'My mother and my . . . my friend are in there.'

I point to my mother's annexe. The fire has spread so rapidly, it's encroaching on the main structure. Tears are coursing down my face at the thought of losing my mother. It is too much to bear – not like this. My paltry efforts have had no bearing on the flames. The temperature is sweltering, but it is hard to tell if it's the weather or fire heating the air. It's so humid, but the wind is howling, nudging flames forwards.

'Please, you have to save them!' I scream frantically to the firefighters and to the heavens, dropping the hose to the ground. The water seeps into my shoes, but I barely notice. There is nothing more I can do but wait and pray.

'Maria, what has happened? I heard the sirens,' Alessandra shouts as she appears through the orchard, rushing to my side. I feel her pull me backwards, away from the burning building. Crowds from the village have spilled along the promenade to witness the spectacle. I hear questions being directed at me, but I cannot look away from my home, searching the blaze for signs of life.

'My mother . . . and Leonidas are in there.'

'Oh, God! But where is Kayla?' Alessandra asks.

'I don't know,' I sob. 'Please, she can't be in there too.'

As the firemen continue to douse the flames, it seems hopeless. Black smoke billows from the building, though it doesn't appear to have spread much beyond one part of the house. But that's where *Mamá* is and now where Leonidas might be.

'I can't stand it any longer; I have to do something,' I cry as I lurch towards the house in frustration. I can't stay here, watching and waiting, not knowing if they're alive or dead.

'There's nothing you can do. They will find them,' Alessandra tries to reassure me, but it is little comfort. She holds her arms around me to withhold my urge to run at the fire. I start to shiver in shock.

The *pip pip* of an ambulance sounds along the road and paramedics appear, waiting to see if their services are needed. As the minutes pass, it is increasingly likely they will be required. I continue to search the flames, repeating prayers over and over in my head, begging my father to protect them. The moment I have the thought, I glance upwards in desperation. As my head tips back-wards, seeking answers from above, a crack of thunder booms out to sea and forked lightning illuminates the night sky. It is as if the world pauses in silence, the sinister crackle from the furnace dulls, and the sea flattens to sheet glass.

Then, the heavens suddenly open as if the gods have flicked a switch and the most torrential downpour descends, soaking the spectators to their skin in an instant. The water feels warm and the raindrops so large they almost hurt, landing on the heads of those watching the unfurling drama. The lawn hisses as the tropical deluge begins to quench the fire. Steam rises from the grass and the smoke funnels away into the night.

'Thank you,' I whisper as stars previously hidden from view are slowly revealed. My knees almost give way with relief, but the danger has not yet passed.

The shape of a fireman emerges from the smoke, which undulates in ripples, curling up into the air like a shape-shifting storm cloud. My mother is cradled in his arms. The medics spring into action, placing her on a stretcher, fitting an oxygen mask over her mouth. I shake off Alessandra's grip and run across the lawn, slipping and sliding on the sodden grass. Mud coats my dress, which clings to my legs. The material is saturated from the miracle rain shower.

'Is she alive? Tell me, is she alive?' I shout.

'She has a very weak pulse; we need to take her to hospital immediately.'

*Mamá*'s breath is barely misting the plastic mask on her face.

'Did they find the other person in the house? Leonidas?' I sob.

'We have to go. You cannot ride in the ambulance, miss. Do you have someone who can take you to the hospital? You shouldn't drive.'

'I don't know,' I start to cry harder, feeling terribly alone.

'I will take you,' says Alessandra. 'We go in my hire car.'

I feel a hand at my elbow urging me forward. My feet splash in filthy puddles, freezing my toes further. I numbly climb into the passenger seat.

'I am here for you, Maria. Anything you need,' says Alessandra as she starts the engine.

But what I need is for my mother and Leonidas to survive. There is nobody on earth who can grant such a wish. I look around for my father's apparition, but he is gone. Everyone, it seems, has left me.

*The swarm shifts in shape, billowing and folding in protection, hovering above the havoc below. The queen saw who did this. The striking of the match woke her from her slumber. Now, she can only watch on helplessly as her colony is destroyed, her family murdered in the name of a careless cruelty. The perpetrator didn't expect this consequence, but it is too late, and judgement will come. As some of her minions succumb to the smoke, they drop from the air, landing upon the burning ground to complete the circle of life, becoming one with the earth once more.*

# Chapter 30

## *Maria*

I hate waiting as much as I loathe the smell of hospitals. I spent so much time in them after my accident, they only remind me of bad news. I'm not alone in that feeling, I'm sure. Alessandra must be enduring her own private torment; this must be the last place she wishes to spend her night, given her illness.

Hospitals make me think of the end of life, of heartbreak, long, sad walks through lengthy corridors, holding in your pain until you find a way to release it. But all we have been through makes us what we are now, moulding how we evolve. Which, for me, depends on the news that arrives through a door I cannot tear my eyes away from. It encloses me in this torturous prison.

The waiting room off the emergency unit is deathly quiet, save for a clock proudly marking the seconds. Each tick reverberates throughout my body. A doctor hasn't updated us for so long, but I have no concept of time, despite the hands beating my pulse from the wall.

'No word from Kayla?' I ask as Alessandra looks at her phone. She shakes her head.

'I will get us coffee,' she says. 'It's the middle of the night – we need all the help we can get.'

'Isn't that the truth,' I mutter. I try to move my legs, but they feel too heavy to lift. My adrenaline has faded, and I long to curl up and sleep, exhausted by the events of the evening. But I am nevertheless alert, dreading what may yet come.

I check my own phone for any messages. Not even my 'COWARD' is sending their special brand of hatred. Perhaps their work is done, potentially destroying what I've tried to build here, the life I've made. They did this. I know it wasn't an accident. I am consumed by my thoughts and fears for *Mamá* and Leonidas. I step outside and watch the bustle of accident and emergency, the back and forth of medics, tearful and concerned relatives streaming down corridors.

'Please, my mother,' I begin as I catch the arm of a nurse. 'Eleni Leventi – is there any news?'

She consults her chart and looks to the wall, where multicoloured illegible scrawls populate a whiteboard.

'*Ochi*, no, someone will come to you soon,' she says, but I grab her arm again.

'And Leonidas Balafoutis? Can you tell me how he is? If he is here?'

She sighs. 'Are you his wife?'

I blanch and stutter, 'No . . . I . . . I'm a friend.'

'Then I'm afraid I cannot discuss him with anyone

outside of his family. Sorry, I have to go.' She rushes away. I try again with someone else, but the result is identical. I return to the little holding cell defeated and more anxious than ever.

The door opens and my heart lurches. It is only Alessandra clutching two paper cups of steaming liquid.

'Anything?' she asks.

I shake my head as I add sugar to the murky brown coffee. Alessandra hands me a chocolate bar, which I accept, saying, 'Alessandra, you don't have to stay. Please go back to your villa.'

'Don't you even think about anyone else. I am here for you, and I know Kayla is, should she ever turn up. We already both decided to stay in Petalidi a while longer, even before the fire. But now we can be here to help you.'

I exhale with relief at having reinforcements with me, unsure of what news each hour will bring, let alone the coming days. 'You're welcome, of course, to stay, but don't you have things to sort out at home in Italy?'

'Not really. Phillipo and I can be anywhere we choose and now, the most important thing is you, Eleni and Leonidas.'

I smile at her as she clasps my hand.

Leonidas.

I feel utterly wretched.

'They are the most important people in my world, but they don't need to be in yours. Don't use this as an excuse to hide from reconciling with your daughter,' I say gently.

She looks down at her lap, knowing what I've said is true. It's easy to find reasons to avoid confronting what you must. Although I'd be grateful of the company, my

253

tragic circumstances mustn't be the cause of her neglecting her own troubles.

'I fear it is too late for us both to find satisfaction. And that, as you say, is my plate to stop spinning.' She meets my eyes sadly. 'Do you think we should be worried about Kayla? She was not in her villa when the fire started. I told as many people as I could to look for her.'

I try to phone Kayla, but it goes straight to answer machine.

'I'm certain she's just having fun . . . more than us, that's for sure.' I manage to find a smile at the thought.

'Ahhh, that waiter! Yes . . . he is good for her. She needs excitement,' she says in approval. 'Good sex is an ideal way to address any problems.'

I can't help but laugh, even within the dire circumstances. 'You are the best worst therapist I've ever met.'

'One very wise woman told me we have to have hope, even when all seems lost.'

She indicates me with her eyes, and I accept her compliment. Alessandra is quite extraordinary. Even within her own hopeless situation, she makes the best of it in her inimitable fashion. I feel the tinge of sadness that someone so incredible has entered my life, armed with such an unjust expiry date. But isn't that the case with everyone we come to love? There is always loss paired with love. Life exists side by side with death. As if we cannot comprehend one without the other, a painful measuring stick, a definite line in the sand. The world doesn't permit us mortals to have one in isolation. And I am yet to hear which side of the line my mother has found herself on.

\* \* \*

254

'Please, Ms Leventi, come with me.'

I follow the doctor, who walks with urgency into a private room. The shock at having to suddenly move makes my legs feel like jelly. My mother's breathing is being forced by a ventilator. The sound is akin to being underwater or like the tide labouring towards the shore, pebbles resisting the rhythm of nature. She looks terribly frail, cocooned in hospital bedsheets tucked tightly around her. There is hardly anything to her physically, but I know the ferocity that lurks within and I long to be on the receiving end of the sharpness of her tongue once more. Her hand is icy as I clutch it, like a bird's foot, a miniature collection of fragile bones.

I hate to see her like this. It seems deeply undignified to have tubes providing life, lying passive, being given breath. I wish Leonidas was here. I push away the thought, even though the tears streaming down my face betray my feelings. But I must focus on my mother. The doctors still won't talk to me about what happened to him; I am not his next of kin. I don't know what I am.

Like a terrible nightmare, at the backs of my eyes I see the roaring flames consuming my beehives, Leonidas disappearing into the blaze . . . The dreadful scene plays continuously on a loop. It hurts me to think of it all. My heart feels bruised, aching with a sorrow and a tumult of emotions from what Leonidas had said to me moments before the fire. And to think I blamed him for the messages. This is like a punishment for being unable to accept love.

My father is in the chair beside my mother's bed. He doesn't take his eyes from her, as if I am not here.

Perhaps I am not, maybe I am the one who is dead. I rest my head on my forearm, still holding my mother's hand, and fall asleep.

\* \* \*

I come to as the sounds of church bells mark Easter morning. A day to celebrate new life, but I am somewhere between an ending and a beginning, each as terrifying as the other. A nurse brings me a cup of coffee, the good stuff, she says. She knows of me from the write-ups in the regional papers and her sister has apparently taken one of my courses. The nurse reassures me my mother is strong and is doing well. But the continued presence of my father leads me to believe otherwise. I smile at her gratefully as the caffeine hits my bloodstream. I should get home and freshen up; I am still covered in mud from the soggy lawn.

I sigh as my head replays Leonidas' words on the beach. He shouldn't have told me what he felt. I feel angry my mother has become an unwitting victim of someone's vendetta against me, possibly fuelled by the time I've been spending with Leonidas. The fire could have been an accident – it's perfectly possible – but innately I know it wasn't. This feels like revenge against me for my very existence. Especially given the message I received moments before I saw the flames eating my bees alive.

My bees.

A lump lodges in my throat. I stand to stretch and walk over to the window in the little room. It is a beautiful day once more, hot again I expect, but the hospital remains

256

cold and clinical, temperature-controlled. Any traces of last night's rainstorm are gone, swallowed up by sunshine. The torrent of water appeared at precisely the right time like a blessing from the heavens, helping to dampen the fire, preventing it from taking more of the house. I shudder to think of the damage.

I watch birds flying across the sky and I massage my aching neck. I can smell the acrid scent of burning on my clothes. My nails are black, dirt and soot embedded underneath them. I sent Alessandra home in the early hours, since there was nothing to be gained by her sitting with me – and she needed to rest. I decide to call her and ask if she could collect me, and to see if she's heard from Kayla yet. I can return to the hospital after I drop my cakes and biscuits to Father Kyriakidis for the Easter feast. Perhaps he can say prayers for us all.

On my way out, I stop at the desk and see a different face, the morning shift having replaced the tireless overnight team, and decide to try just one more time.

'Please, can you help me? I'm here with my mother, Eleni Leventi. She was in a fire and my . . . someone else was with her, Leonidas Balafoutis. Can you tell me how he is? He was brought in late last night, I think.'

I watch as the girl rummages through papers and taps on her computer. She barely looks old enough to be in charge of delivering the post, let alone potentially life-changing news.

'And you are . . . ?' she asks.

'A friend, an old friend. Please just tell me if he is alive.'

She shakes her head. 'I'm sorry, I can't tell you anything. Only next of kin.'

There's no point begging. I say a silent prayer for Leonidas, hoping I haven't used all of them up on my mother.

\* \* \*

I cannot look at the ruined hives, blackened shells on the lawn. To see the devastation up close would break my heart; years of nurture burnt to a cinder. My dream, which rose from the wreckage of my marriage, has now been ruined, as tarnished as my skin. In the clear afternoon sunshine, the damaged wing of the house is dark against the pristine technicolour surroundings. It looks out of place; it doesn't fit. Is that how people see *me*? A blot on the landscape, something that doesn't belong? I haven't heard a peep from the 'COWARD'. Their work is complete. I half expected to receive a gloating sentence or two, but the silence is as frustrating as it is to be on the end of their hate. The police wish to speak to me about the fire, but they can find me later. I already know what happened. This is the culmination of someone's vendetta against me.

I walk over to the entrance of my mother's annexe. Drips plop into pools on the floor, where the carpet is a sodden charcoal sludge. The fire didn't make it very far into the house thanks to Mother Nature, but the smoke damage and water marks look as bad as if it had.

The remains of my mother's gilded religious postcard glints in the sunlight that streams through the windows and doors. Its edges have curled up in protest against the heat. The glass is broken on my father's photograph, lying smashed on the floor, the shards mask his image. I pick it up, brushing the sharp slivers from the picture. He appeared on the beach to warn me of the fire. I invoked his help and the rain began, but since then, he has sat in vigil beside my mother in her hospital room, not interacting with me. I see no sign of other spirits, only him. Maybe there is nothing more to tell, no further messages to impart.

As I move around surveying the damage, I see that my part of the house is unblemished, save for the smell of smoke. I am able to shower and wash away the fragrance of last night. Someone has kindly opened the windows to clear the stench, but burning still lingers in the atmosphere.

In my mother's rooms, I find several buckets of disinfectant, which tinge the air with chemicals, sponges floating in the dissolving bubbles. I don't know who has started to clean up, but I am thankful. Tears prick at my eyes as I wonder how I can make this right again. Anger stabs my chest at all I could have lost, but also at what is gone forever.

I stand outside on the terrace looking out to sea. From this vantage point it is as if all is as it should be. That is, if I can manage to ignore the scorched lawn and burnt wooden coffins that house the bodies of my beloved dead insects. The sea sparkles as always. The sun has risen on this most holy of days and the sky seems bluer than ever. I can smell the scent of lamb being cooked from the village, carried towards me on the lightest of breezes.

I remember my cakes in my teaching kitchen. There is no fire damage there, as if it never happened. The recipe I was so confident would be a triumph of the Easter revelry now feels like a pointless endeavour. What is my food for? To heal strangers who flock to my cooking school when I cannot heal myself. My mother is right, as was Leonidas. I spend so much time looking out for others that I neglect my own needs, convincing my heart I am fine. I believed my own lie; I'd said it so many times. But when I teetered on the brink of casting all cares aside, lured by Leonidas' words of love, my life's work of my bees was being destroyed. And my mother's life threatened. I close my eyes and inhale the fragrances from the flowers, olive trees and herbs. Then a flash of my mother being laid onto a stretcher darts across my mind.

My cakes are baked, wrapped in paper tied with string, ready for delivery to church. I know the feast will be in full swing by now. I am isolated in my sadness, another reason to feel separate from this village. I try not to permit resentment to flood my veins, but this, I know, is the work of someone's hatred.

A piece of paper on the work surface catches my eye: a note from Alessandra. She baked my Easter cookies while I was showering, kindly remembering they were meant for today. She's packed them up and already taken them to the village on my behalf. I'm not used to others being so thoughtful and a lump forms in my throat.

I pick up my sponges. The waft of honey and citrus invades my senses. It is as if the contents of my cakes vibrate from within, charged with an energy. I hope the villagers enjoy them – if anybody dares to try a slice.

I march with a purpose along the promenade, reversing my frantic dash from last night. I will be swift and only wish to speak with Father Kyriakidis. As I near the part of the beach where I stood with Leonidas, the sudden pang of regret stops me in my tracks as I hear his words to me. He loves me. But how can I return his affection when destruction is the consequence of our meetings? No, I will heed the warnings. He will never hear my response to his declaration. It is too late.

# Chapter 31

## *Kayla*

Kayla's eyes flutter open. Her long, tinted lashes brush her cheeks as the sunlight pours through the windows, making her squint. She hears music and shouting. It is Easter Sunday and the feasting sounds to Kayla like a carnival. She listens to the tinkling guitar and cries of encouragement to what she assumes must be dancers.

She stretches like a cat and enjoys the sensation in her satisfied muscles. A thought suddenly occurs to her. How will she get out of here unseen? There seems to be a full-blown party happening in the taverna downstairs and she will have to perform her very own walk of shame through the middle of it. If someone saw her, they could sell a story, filling the gossip columns with invented details. She shakes off any thoughts of concern and tries to celebrate her choice. It was a heavenly night.

She turns on her phone and leaves it on the cotton

coverlet as she gets up from Dimitris' bed to retrieve her clothes. There's no sign of him, and she assumes he's at work. Her body tingles with the memory of last night. He was just what she'd needed. Someone to unleash her pent-up frustration upon in the most spectacular way. When he'd returned to bed in the early hours, he'd wanted to tell her about some drama in the village, but she hadn't been interested, only wanting his body, not his mind. So, they'd continued in the same vein as earlier in the evening, drinking ouzo and indulging in their passions until the dawn chorus had signalled the new day's arrival.

But something weighs her heart down. She knows this act of wild abandon is the end of a chapter in her life. She's retaliated against Daniel's infidelity with her own version, pretending she could emulate Alessandra's attitude to sex by giving herself to another so freely, like playing a role in a sordid little play. Kayla refuses to shame herself but is unable to prevent the smallest clang of self-judgement tolling in time with the church bells outside. But, despite this, she manages to find a small smile. She is free. It sends a wave of giddiness around her body, making the first step towards the new her. She didn't need a man to send her on that journey; it was merely a nudge. And if the prompt came in the form of a divine waiter, then so be it.

As she picks up her discarded underwear, she surveys the simple apartment. What was dark and mysterious last night looks tatty in the stark morning-after sunlight. Her phone suddenly springs into life. Multiple pings cause a panic to run through her body. What has happened? Not Rosie, please not Rosie. She rushes over to her mobile nestled within the bedclothes, just as she was moments ago, blissfully unaware of the real world.

PING

> Kayla, it's Alessandra.
> Where are you? Please call me.

PING – BBC news alert
*Home-Grown Chef Missing in Greek Inferno*
What?

PING – Sky Breaking News
*Celebrity Chef Missing in Fire Abroad*

Oh no. No, no, no, no . . .

PING – Mail Online Breaking
*Has Greek Easter Blaze Claimed Our Kayla?*

Holy shit. And what fire?

She must call Daniel. She sees several missed calls from him and frantic text messages. But where was this fire? Her head is reeling from too much passion and too much ouzo. As their call connects, he launches into a furious rant.

'Where the *hell* have you been? You're front-page fucking news, and why was your phone off? I've called every hospital in Greece and spoken to every police contact I could find, and nobody knew anything. Jesus, Kayla, where on earth were you? I've been out of my mind with worry. The press were preparing your obituary, according to your publicist. Do you know what I've been through all night?

And not to mention keeping Rosie off school in case she found out her mammy could be dead.'

The flush of humiliation consumes her, knowing she was indulging in the best sex of her entire life whilst letting her family think she was in danger or worse.

'Daniel . . . I . . . I don't know . . . I'm fine. What fire . . . where?'

'What fire?! The cooking school you're staying at was almost burnt to the ground according to the press and apparently you were missing. I don't know why this is news to you. Unless you're somewhere else . . .'

'I . . . what? Oh my God, is Maria OK? Alessandra? I have to find them.'

'Who are you talking about? Christ, Kayla. It sounds like you're not where you say you are.'

The slight inference ignites her resentment. 'You have absolutely no right to interrogate me. Save that for your day job. You messed up our marriage so you can keep your questions to yourself.'

Daniel laughs bitterly. '*I've* messed up our marriage? That's rich coming from you. You treat me like a fool. You don't think I know what goes on with you, what you're hiding? I'd be the worst detective in the world if I hadn't figured that one out. But I let you get on with it, scared of rocking the boat, just wanting you to be OK. Well, I'm done with it, Kayla. I'm done with you. Carry on with whatever or *whoever* you were doing and when you're home, we need to sort this out. I'll be filing for divorce and custody. I'm doing what's best for our family for a change, not just what's best for you.'

'Wait! You can't . . . you can't take Rosie . . .'

But Daniel has hung up. She sits down, winded, her hands shaking uncontrollably. Daniel has threatened to take away her ray of sunshine, Rosie, the one thing that motivates her to keep going, striving to provide everything for her daughter she'd missed out on growing up.

She calls her assistant, then her publicist to reassure them she is fine, not divulging that during the fire she had been safely pinned under Dimitris' muscular body. A statement will be released correcting all the tabloid histrionics. But she somehow needs to get out of this apartment, without even a pair of sunglasses to hide behind.

She finds a baseball cap on a chair and tucks up her distinctive red hair as far as she can. She takes a deep breath, searching for the bravado that brought her here last night. She must find Maria and Alessandra, to find out what happened, hoping nobody was hurt. As she looks at herself in the mirror, tears prick the backs of her eyes and the familiar feelings of disgust surface. This had been a pointless, ridiculous escapade that's landed her in trouble and possibly a custody battle.

What on earth had she been thinking?

# Chapter 32

*Maria*

The village green is alive with people, swarming like ants as they dance to the music, chinking their glasses and feasting with indulgence. There's hardly any room on the grass nor the benches as scores of people shout and sing in celebration. As I pass by, all the taverna chairs under the trees are taken, not a spare table in sight. Yet for all the jollity, the revelling appears subdued. Last night's fire was not the ideal start to Easter. To some it will feel darkly symbolic. There are those who may suspect it is the work of the devil; others will feel terribly sad about the accident and for my poor mother, Leonidas and maybe even me. I am certain Father Kyriakidis will have held us in his prayers at this morning's service. But someone knows exactly what happened and, more importantly, why. I hope they are racked with guilt.

Three lambs are roasting on a spit beside the church as men gather around the fires, summoning their primal instincts to guard the charring meat. Women fuss around the long tables of salads and sides, ensuring their home-made plate has prime position.

As I near, I feel somewhat sickened. There is nothing to celebrate, not whilst my mother lies in a hospital bed, lingering somewhere between life and the next one. And Leonidas . . . I cannot bear to think of him.

A sudden hush descends as I near the church. The musicians put down their instruments, cutlery clatters onto plates and whispers ripple across the square. The people part, unable to meet my eye, a corridor made of their shame gives way to make a passage for me.

Father Kyriakidis strides over as quickly as his age permits and accepts my special cakes from my hands. He places them on one of the many trestle tables piled high with food then folds his arms around me. As he pulls back and looks into my eyes, I see his are shining with tears. He makes the sign of the cross over me and whispers, 'I am so sorry, Maria.'

'Thank you, Father. Please remember my mother and Leonidas in your prayers.'

He nods gloomily, his long beard twitching as he does so. 'And you made food for us, Maria.'

'The cookies arrived earlier, but I made a special cake recipe, my invention. For what it's worth.' I give a sad smile.

More people arrive from the tavernas along the beach to investigate the sudden pause in the festivities. Father Kyriakidis unwraps one of the parcels on the table. The hushed crowd crane their necks to see. Immediately the lemon zest and honey fill his nostrils and he inhales deeply. He holds a cake aloft.

'A reminder that on this Easter Sunday so filled with joy, the blessing of the resurrection, a second chance at life for Jesus, it must also be a time of reflection for us all. The solemnity of Good Friday, the days of fasting, are meant to encourage us to look inwards and learn to be better people, guided by the hand of God.'

One of my mother's friends stands beside Father Kyriakidis and unwraps the second cake, followed by the third. The wafts of rich flavours are taken up by the wind, growing in intensity as he continues.

'This offering from Maria is symbolic of our commemorations. The lemon reminds us of a sourness that can fester in our hearts. The sweetness of our faith is the honey, purity spun from nature, which can be overpowered by the bitterness. Yet, if they join forces, they are perfectly harmonised. Like Maria's honeybees, we are not born with a sting. It is an armour of defence that develops against those who would threaten us. On this special day, we must remember those less fortunate. Despite the tribulations Christ endured, He forgave those who wronged Him, accepted the flaws of His enemies. He offered love instead of hate. If we are truly to mark the resurrection, we must hold these sentiments in our hearts. Eleni and Leonidas remain in our prayers with Maria. We give thanks for all she has given our village and for bringing us her beautiful food when her own heavy heart is filled with sadness.'

I am overcome by his words in his impromptu sermon and I cross myself, as the majority of the spectators do. Father Kyriakidis lifts a knife from the table and slices the cake into tiny, bite-size slivers. He moves to the next sponge and repeats the action like a ritual of communion.

271

When he completes his task, he holds his hands above the cakes and blesses them. He looks up to me and a smile spreads over his face. I feel his love and affection for me travel across the space between us, along with his gratitude for my food. It is the best I could hope for, and I leave them to their feast.

\* \* \*

Father Kyriakidis lifts a square of sponge to his lips, breathing in the aroma once more, and takes a bite. His eyes close as he savours the taste that dances around his palate. The sticky honey elegantly combatting the citrus zestiness makes him think of his mother and father when he was a child, playing on the beach together on a family holiday on the island of Sifnos. The salty seaweed and shining stones, cold water swirling around his hot ankles, wading up to his chest and somersaulting beneath the waves.

An aged woman follows the priest's lead. As she bites into the sticky crumb, the glaze trickles down her fingers. She giggles girlishly as she remembers her late husband kissing her for the first time. Her stomach flips with butterflies at the memory. She recalls the red ribbon in her hair tickling at her neck in the sea breeze as they danced together in the deserted village square beneath the moon's silver beams.

Giorgos, the hardware merchant, steps forward and takes a slice for himself. His mind transports him to a summer's day in Albania, long ago in the war. During a moment of respite in the fighting, he and his comrades had swapped tales of their families back home as they had all longed for the touch of the women they loved. The scent of the heady pine forests provided shelter from the heat as leather and sweat had infused the air, the sun having beat them into a shady retreat.

One by one, people step forward to sample the magical cake.

The solitary female queen bee flits down away from an angry swarm above and watches the villagers, enjoying Maria's alchemy, the contents of the cakes contain honey from her dead family. She knows whose hands are responsible for the destruction of generations. All gone with a deliberate flame.

She hovers above, considering what comes next. There has been enough sacrifice, it is time to rebuild. Soaring back up into the honey-sweetened air, she follows Maria along the seafront to seek out a new home. What remains of her swarm trails obediently behind.

# Chapter 33

## *Maria*

In the few hours I've been away from hospital, nothing has changed. My mother is passively allowing breath into her lungs. My mind keeps returning to Leonidas. I am still unable to discover any information, no matter how desperately I plead with the nurses and doctors.

I have brought some of the Easter biscuits with me, hoping the aroma can rouse my mother from her sleep, but even my food fails me; the one thing I can always rely on. Before the fire, I had become used to the unkind jibes. Whispered remarks rebounded from my soul. But now, everything feels different, like my self-belief that rooted me has been rocked. The threatening messages from 'COWARD', which began to terrify me against my wishes, manifested into mortal danger for my mother and perhaps Leonidas. That person behind the texts is responsible for the warnings beside my hives and the fire. I know it.

Leonidas could be dead, and it would be my fault. I didn't see Athena or Zoe at the Easter festivities. They could be in mourning for his loss, but if he is dead someone would surely have told me. Poor Zoe. Nobody should lose a parent so young, and I pray that isn't the case. Kayla is living proof of the wound that never seems to mend from a premature death.

I look at my mother, clinging on to life. She's so ferocious in spirit. I'm certain she's working as hard as she can to stay with me. But she's longed for the day she is reunited with *Babá*. Perhaps it's her time, although it arrived in the cruellest way. The thought of being without her, my nemesis and battle friend, moves me to tears. It is because someone detests me that she is lying here, hovering between life and death. My tears are guilty droplets. As much as our relationship is fraught and fractious, I know her unkind remarks are born of love, obscured by her barbs, only wanting the very best for me. Or what she thinks is best.

'Please, *Mamá*, stay, for me. You wanted to see me happy and in love; your work is not yet done. I still need you.'

I speak through my tears, wishing hard to summon a response. Although I have no yearning to settle down simply to appease her, I have a churning inside the pit of my stomach when I think of Leonidas. He may have been taken from me, but was he ever mine to begin with?

I hear the sound of the door opening and I turn. It is as if the air is knocked from my lungs, and I cannot catch my breath. The subject of my thoughts has manifested upon request. Leonidas is in the doorway, dressed in charred clothes, his dark hair singed and wild. Patches of it are burnt off, but I pay no mind to his appearance.

'Leonidas!' I cry and run to his arms. 'I thought you were . . . They wouldn't tell me . . .'

'Shhhh,' he says comforting me, his bandaged hand cupping my head. 'It will take more than a fire to stop me.'

His voice is harsh and rasping from smoke inhalation, and I hear a deep-set wheeze from his chest. I look up into his face, where his beautiful honey-coloured eyes glow warmly. I reach up to touch his cheek. I have no words; I cannot say what is within me. Phrases dry on my lips as my heart protests, desperate to spill its contents. Having guarded my feelings for too many years, I am afraid to tell him what's inside me. His fingers leave my hair and gently move downwards, tracing the start of my scar beneath my jaw, asking permission with his eyes as he touches my neck. I suck my breath in. Nobody has ever touched me there. It is virgin skin. It feels as if my heart could stop.

And my mother's heart stops.

The piercing scream of the flatline jolts me back to reality and I run to her bedside as the room fills with responders who briskly hustle us both out of the room. I wriggle under their grasp, but they hold me steady until I am out of sight of *Mamá*. Then, they go to work behind closed doors.

In the hallway outside her room, I crumple to the floor, leaning my head against the cold wall. The acute weight of guilt bears down on me. I should have been with her last night when the fire started, but instead I was with Leonidas on the beach, and she was in peril, alone. Then just moments ago, as I had turned my attention away from her and towards him, beginning to give in to my feelings, her heart forgot how to beat. What more signs do I need that this is wrong and cannot be between us? These warning shots from the universe already tried to take my mother once and failed. This time, if it succeeds, it is entirely my mistake for choosing my happiness over others. Here is my instant karma wielding its ruthless sword. A steely resolve begins to ice my veins and I know what I must do. I stand up and look at Leonidas with as much detachment as I can summon. His head turns to me with trepidation as he feels the shift in the atmosphere.

'I think you should go, Leonidas,' I say coldly. 'I need to be here for my mother, to care for her if she needs me. If she dies, then I want to be here on my own.'

'Maria . . .' he begins shaking his head. 'You are in shock, please let me help you.'

'No! Don't you see? *We* are the cause of all of this. I abandoned her last night and look what happened. And just now . . . I . . .'

'You what? Allowed me to touch you, to try and love you?'

'But at my mother's bedside in a hospital, as she is unconscious and unable to breathe on her own. I have shown such disrespect, and this is the consequence. Go, Leonidas, please. I don't want you with me. I should never have gone with you to the beach last night and I will always regret it. It's pointless you being here. I need to be with my mother. Alone.'

The look on his face is agony to watch, as if I have

punched him hard in the stomach. It is the same hurt expression as on the beach in Kalamaki all those years ago. I have injured him again with my words, struggling to protect myself by lashing out in penance for my mother's life being risked. She could already be dead for all I know.

But I am resolute. His love will not be returned; there is no hope for us.

'You have made yourself clear, Maria. Of course, I will leave you,' he says with a gentle kindness I do not deserve. 'At least let me know how your mother is. My phone was lost in the fire, but get a message to me, please. I will send you another way to reach me. You are both in my thoughts and in my heart.'

I nod, then I have to turn my back on him, in every sense. I can't watch him leave; I don't want him to see me cry. The cause of my tears is my heart breaking into a thousand pieces; for him, for me, and for my mother.

\* \* \*

The hours tick by painfully, as if someone is slowly drawing out a knife from my chest, sending excruciating waves through my body. Eventually one of the medics comes out of her room. I scrabble to stand, but he bends down to my place of vigil on the hard floor.

'She is stable, Ms Leventi, for now. But she is still not out of danger.'

I nod gravely at the news, tears betraying any semblance of composure. I manage to thank the doctors for their care and attention. Even though the nurses try to reassure me with 'she is strong' and 'she's a fighter' it's hard to

281

believe them when her shell is so still. The moment her heart gave up still echoes in my ears, ringing like a horrible alarm clock, but it signalled the opposite of waking. I have resented her endless stream of opinions, but now I want to hear her voice more than anything, telling me what I should and shouldn't do.

Yet the one thing she longs for, I cannot give her. She is right about Leonidas' feelings for me, but we will not be together. The signs of danger and threats to the lives of those I care for puts paid to her fantasy. I am resigned to my role of village spinster, mocked and tormented for being Maria the bee woman. *Mélissa*.

An intense sorrow crushes me as I think of my beautiful insects destroyed by a flickering flame. My companions and my constants, they didn't judge me, but gave unconditionally, yielding their harvests freely and in return I loved them so. I honoured their exquisite produce with my food. Who am I without my flying friends? My unpleasant nickname doesn't apply anymore, the root of it burnt to a cinder, engulfed in smoke, suffocated in a smouldering wreckage. I cannot bear to think of thousands of tiny furry bodies turned into dust. Perhaps I could impose on Alessandra to dismantle the remains of my hives. Or Kayla, if she appears. Goodness, I haven't asked Alessandra if she found her. I curse my selfishness and send her a message through my blurred vision.

I am allowed back into my mother's room and I sit holding her hand. I sob for all that has been taken from me. Not just by fire but by the path my life has taken. I cry for my broken marriage, my ruined skin, the beautiful life I created in Petalidi against all the odds. All of it is now as tarnished as my neck, my map of the Americas has infected everything around me. I permit myself to grieve what has been stolen away in the most brutal circumstances. Here is another tragedy in my life that changes its path forever. But this may be the cruellest twist from the Fates.

*       *       *

I arrive home for the evening, my stomach growling with hunger, but I have no appetite to appease my pangs, unable to summon the energy to cook. It seems my love for food has deserted me too. I am weary and my bones ache with sadness. I'm not used to this feeling, having always found the glimmer of light within the darkest of moments before. But I cannot seem to muster a single positive thought. I'm the bitter, angry woman at the end of the village with the burnt bees.

The idea of sleeping in the house, knowing the empty scorched corner of my mother's wing is downstairs, gives me shivers. Although the structure has been deemed safe, I don't want to be there. I go to one of the guest villas instead. The doctor suggested I leave my mother's bedside to rest, assuring me he would call should her condition change. I hate the idea of not being there if she dies, although she wouldn't know any different and would likely resent me for seeing her so unalive as she is now, let alone to see her dead. She was too dignified to permit such a thing.

Is.

I chide myself for thinking of her in the past tense.

I turn on the shower, desperate to wash the hospital smell from my skin. The faint smell of burning still lingers, but perhaps it is in my mind's eye rather than on my body. I strip off my clothes and stand in front of the full-length mirror and my eyes trace my own contours. Sun-tan lines and stretch marks, rich honeycomb skin and then the dark permanent mottled patch from my chest to my jaw, snaking down my neck. The ever-present reminder of both my survival and my failures. I'd always insisted it's a badge of honour, but it's also an unwanted emblem of my disappointments. Who did I think I was, doling out wisdom as easily as I dished out *kleftiko* stew? Using my terrible scar and accident as a reason for being able to give such sage advice like some battle-hardened warrior. And people listened as I spouted my useful nonsense.

I know deep down I've helped so many, been hailed as a kind of food guru, but the truth is, I am out of insight. The spinning plates have all crashed to the ground, smashed to ruin. My strength of spirit was the root of my success, able to make others happy, nursing them through their own pain and sadness with my food, wishing for nothing in return. Just as a honeybee generously pollinates a flower and gives life to the world. But my spirit is broken.

I lift my phone from my bag and notice that it is out of battery. I plug it in to charge and turn it on. Alessandra has messaged, confirming she has located Kayla, having hunted Dimitris down. I exhale with relief. One problem solved, but still a million more to deal with. I tell Alessandra we will cook as planned tomorrow for our final day of class. I can telephone the hospital first thing and then go to my mother for visiting hours in the afternoon.

A slow shiver descends on my skin as I open the final message.

> **Please let me know how your mother is. You are in my thoughts, always. With love, Leonidas xx**

But this number is already in my phone.

My mother warned me to beware of what I ask for, and she is right. The mystery I yearned to uncover, I regret ever wishing for it. To think, I almost gave him my heart, but he has proved himself to be cruellest of all in this village. This is why I could not read him before, mistaking complete honesty for the monstrous secret he hid. His resentment for my refusal when he asked for my hand in marriage has manifested in revenge, a wish to torture me for managing to exist without him. I'd searched for the warning prickles but was powerless to interpret them. He is adept at concealing his truth, tricking me all along, to mock me and break my strength as punishment.

As I reread the message, the disgusting thread floats above it, reading like a novel of vitriol.

But now, the missives are claimed. I change the contact name in my mobile phone book, feeling nausea swell as I do so. My hidden feelings that lingered silently on my lips and in my childhood dreams, nestled within my heart for so many years, are shattered. A grave mistake has been made and my perpetrator is unmasked, accidentally returning to the scene of his crime, claiming ownership of the anonymous hate.

In my contacts I slowly delete the word 'COWARD' and replace it with 'Leonidas'.

# Chapter 34

## *Kayla*

Kayla managed to scurry out of Dimitris' apartment unseen. When Maria arrived at the village green, the crowds flocked to gawp and, with their attention focused elsewhere, Kayla had been able to sneak back to her accommodation. Her stomach flutters with the thrill of her illicit liaison but Daniel's threat to challenge for custody outweighs any ideas of liberation.

As she nears Maria's home, she covers her mouth with her hand at what she sees. The once perfectly manicured lawns are black, and the unmistakable silhouette of flames coils up the side of the house like filthy spectres. She feels the prick of tears in her eyes as she sees Alessandra appear on the terrace, wringing out a cloth, black liquid depositing itself in a pool on the patio.

'Kayla! We thought you'd gone missing, but I ran into your divine waiter who told me you were OK.' She looks into Kayla's teary eyes. 'Though you don't seem it.'

Kayla throws her arms around Alessandra, ignoring her mention of Dimitris. 'Sorry if you were worried. I should've called but my phone was off, and I didn't know anything about this until this morning. What happened?'

'You can see for yourself. Poor Maria. Eleni and Leonidas are in hospital. He went in to save her. That's all I know,' replies Alessandra, squeezing out her cloth once more.

'Was it the heatwave that caused it?' asks Kayla surveying the sad scene, her brow creased in horror at what's transpired.

Alessandra shakes her head. 'Sadly, I think not. Maria gets messages threatening her. I've seen her receive them and I read one when we were in church. She was not surprised by it, so I suggest it is not the first of its kind.'

Kayla gasps, horrified. 'Why would anyone want to hurt her? I can't believe someone would do this.'

'I know, and those things beside the beehives, I think it's all connected. I've been trying to clear up to feel useful. I'm sure the police will work out what happened.'

'It's awful,' says Kayla. 'I don't understand why.'

'I suspect her spending time with Leonidas has caused this, and I feel responsible. When I told you they were going to the beach together, well . . . what I didn't say was I encouraged him to go somewhere special with her. We planned it at lunch on Good Friday. It is clear for all to see he loves her, but she will not open her heart.'

Kayla considers whether now is the time to tell Alessandra she's tried to contact her daughter. Since Alessandra has interfered with Maria's relationship, she thinks, perhaps she won't feel too angry with Kayla for doing the same. But there is nothing to tell; Arianna hasn't responded. If she does, Kayla decides, only then she will share what she has done. Nonetheless, it sits as an uneasy knot within her stomach. If Alessandra putting Leonidas and Maria together has set off a chain of events resulting in the fire, what will happen if Arianna replies to her message? Kayla hopes she can broker a reunion. Her own daughter could be snatched from her if Daniel follows through on his threat, and she can't imagine being without Rosie. Kayla wants Alessandra to have that magical mother-daughter bond again, even at this twilight stage of her life.

'Do you want to talk about last night?' Alessandra says, breaking into Kayla's thoughts, a smile spreading across her lips.

'Nope,' replies Kayla.

'Did you have fun at least?'

Kayla can't help but grin at the memories that flash through her mind. 'As a matter of fact, I did. Although not so much this morning.'

'Why? You've done nothing wrong.'

'I know. Do you mind if we don't talk about it? I'll freshen up, then help you.'

Alessandra continues to wash down the walls and Kayla eventually joins to assist. Their doubled efforts make faster progress, and the surroundings are vastly improved working together.

'Do you want to go into the village to eat? We've been cleaning for hours. Maria won't be back from the hospital until later. We should keep our strength up. I'm sure even you have worked up an appetite.'

Alessandra prises a dirt-soaked cloth from Kayla's reluctant hands and the two women stand to survey their work. They've made headway, but the stench of burning still loiters. Even though the damage isn't as extensive as it could've been, it is enough. The windows will have to stay open for days. But superficial damage can be covered up, painted over and polished away. The residual emotional damage will be much harder to erase.

\* \* \*

The dusk is lengthening, gradually extending the days. In the short time Kayla has been in Petalidi, she has noticed shadows growing as the sunsets stretch for an extra few minutes each evening. The glorious promise of summer. The romance of the history and traditions of Petalidi has worked its way into her veins, the dry heat each day and the herb-scented air. She realises she has a rose-tinted holiday perspective, but it's a lesson in the simplicity of life, when hers has become so complicated. She isn't anonymous here, or anywhere, so there's no point trying to run away from herself. She's reminded who she is everywhere she goes.

Kayla sighs. She needs to speak to Daniel.

The ringing tone sounds for what seems like an age as she waits for him to pick up her call. She curls up on the small sofa in her villa, tucking her feet underneath her. He isn't going to like what she has to say, but he will surely be reasonable about Rosie. He has to be. Her heart beats high in her chest with nerves, begging her courage not to fail.

'Hi. It's me,' she begins as if she doesn't know how to speak to her husband of ten years, like they are strangers.

'The funny thing about mobile phones, Kay, is your name flashes up to let me know you're calling.'

'Right . . . Look, we need to talk.' She's all business, wanting to get the words out. 'I'm sorry I worried you, I really am, but I'm not coming back on Tuesday. I've changed my flight and I'll be out here another week. Maybe more.'

'What?' he exclaims. 'You can't just ditch life back here. What about Rosie? My parents can't just pick up where you've left off. What's going on?'

'Don't start. Maybe you could be a parent for a change, rather than just turning up for bath time and the fun stuff. See how you like it trying to hold down a full-time job as well. Give you a little flavour of how much I actually do since you think you can manage it all by trying to take her away from me.'

'It's too short notice. You've got responsibilities here, Kay.'

'Oh, I'm well aware of them. You're the one who conveniently forgot your own responsibilities when you were playing away. Have a taste of your own medicine for a change.'

'What do you mean?' Daniel asks.

Kayla stands up from her seat and begins to pace the tiled floor of the lounge.

'I mean for once in forever, I'm going to please myself. Do what I want and be where I want. And right now, I want to be here, far away from you. If I could take Rosie out of school, I'd fly her here too. But I can't. I know it's over, Danny; it just took me a while to realise it.' Kayla exhales with relief at her own assertiveness, having said what's on her mind for the first time in a long while.

'So, you've given up, then.'

Kayla laughs in astonishment. '*Me* giving up? No, Danny. That was you, the moment you got into bed with someone else months ago. You made a choice. Now *I* get to decide what happens next.'

'Our whole relationship was on your terms. The problem is, you didn't realise until it was too late, Kay.' He is pouring fuel on Kayla's fire, leading her to stored ammunition.

'Don't waste your breath blaming me. I accept my part in it all but at least I was faithful to you. Until last night.' She pauses and hears a sharp intake of breath at the end of the line. 'Stings, doesn't it? I'm exhausted trying to please everyone. It's time for me and if you don't like it, then tough. You ended our marriage, so this is me beginning my life without you.'

'Kayla, please don't be like this.'

'How do you expect me to be? I'm hurt. I can't believe you lied to me for so long. And you're still doing it. Don't gaslight me by making this all my fault. If you want a divorce and a custody battle, you've got one,' she adds before hanging up the phone, breathing heavily with anger and heartache.

After a moment, she regrets her harshness. He doesn't deserve her spite. Though, if Daniel had contained his urges they wouldn't be in this predicament. As soon as she thinks it, she knows it's not true. Slumping back down onto the couch, she holds her head in her hands. They'd been living under the curtain of pretence for so long.

Within her new-found enlightenment, thanks to Maria, she admits she has played an equal part in the breakdown of their marriage and is as guilty as Daniel.

She's been battling depression and struggling with her secret as long as she can remember. It must have been more than challenging for Daniel to helplessly watch like a tragic bystander. She feels the tug of sympathy for her soon-to-be ex-husband. Although his affair cuts deeply into her insecurities, she understands it. She is partly at fault for where they've ended up. The fame added additional pressure to their increasingly fragile foundation and in the end, it wrenched them asunder. It's a reason, not an excuse, and it's time they both admit responsibility for their failings instead of apportioning blame. The waiter was a temporary respite from the truth. Kayla concedes what is long overdue: she needs to fix herself before she can entertain what her future looks like.

There's one thing she's sure about, though: there is absolutely no way she will let Rosie go.

# Chapter 35

## *Alessandra*

Alessandra walks towards the village, the beach shingle crunching pleasingly underfoot. She's on her way to look at a house to rent, hoping it will be the perfect place in which to spend her remaining weeks or months with Phillipo, their final adventure together.

It strikes her as odd that despite having such an alternative life all these years, she has chosen the most traditional of places to bid it goodbye. She is detecting a curious enjoyment in shedding the wild trappings of the arrangement upon which her marriage thrived, finally finding contentment within a more conventional union. To simply be husband and wife, only for each other. Alessandra feels a frisson of excitement when she thinks about her future, no matter how limited it is. Seeing the heartache around her has taught her how lucky she is and makes her more determined to cling on to what she has while she still can.

A simple one-storey house sits above the beach. Its green window shutters are closed, and their position makes the building look like a dormant, sleeping face. It is vacant, being so early in the season. A small terrace with a wooden overhang for shade looks over a gravelled garden, planted with luscious succulents and palms. Although there is a sadness deep within her that she will never see Rome again, she has wrung the city dry for all its thrills and attractions. It is time for peace, despite the lack of resolution with Arianna.

But dwelling upon the situation with her daughter is a waste of her remaining energy. Although a large part of her heart wishes they could find a way back to each other, it is time to say goodbye to that dream. But as much as she tries to push away her sorrow at their estrangement, it's as if her mind wishes to replay their last confrontation, like a final exorcism.

Alessandra was being watched by all in the nightclub, but she never minded eyes upon her. The performer she used to be still lurked strongly within, and she had confidence and a grace on the dance floor that commanded attention. The DJ had been playing Latin music and Alessandra had previously taken tango classes on a whim and had become proficient. The man whose company she'd been enjoying that night was coincidentally from Argentina and he'd whirled Alessandra effortlessly around the room, creating a sensual and captivating spectacle. As the music reached its crescendo, he had lifted her up on his hip and spun her around, her back leg splayed behind her with a beautifully pointed toe, displaying her dancer's instep to perfection. She'd landed faultlessly and allowed him to bend her backwards, her supple spine curving beyond normal ability.

As they'd enjoyed the rapturous applause, he had kissed her, and she wrapped her arms tightly around his neck, savouring the taste of Campari on his lips. When they broke apart, she'd smoothed her hair down and turned, coming face to face with familiar eyes. Arianna. Her daughter was staring stock-still in absolute horror, her eyes filled with tears of betrayal, and she'd bolted out of the club. With Alessandra in pursuit, they reached a deserted piazza and Arianna had suddenly rounded on her. She spat viciously at her mother's feet.

'How could you behave like a common *puttana* in public. And to do that to *Papà*? You are disgusting to me.'

'Please, Arianna, it is not what you think.'

'It is exactly what I think. There is no other explanation. I hate you for this.'

'Listen. Your father and I have an arrangement. It is what we do. I have shielded you from it until I thought you would be able to understand but there was never the right time to tell you. We didn't want you to find out this way.'

Arianna's face had become ashen under the glow of the lanterns around the little square. The overhead lighting cast elongated shadows over her daughter's nose, highlighting her cheekbones and the smears under her eyes – evidence of a long weekend of decadence, as usual. Her jaw had dropped as she realised what her mother was telling her.

'You mean you and *Papà* . . . with other people!? What kind of marriage is that? It's a farce . . . a lie . . . It's horrible.' She had begun to cry, and Alessandra instinctively stepped towards her.

'No!' Arianna had shouted. 'Don't you dare come near me again. You are nothing but a filthy low-life. You will never see me again. As far as I am concerned, I have no mother. You are dead to me.'

As Alessandra steps up to the little Greek house, she steadies her breathing, trying to dismiss the old ache of judgement from Arianna. She takes some photographs and sends them to Phillipo, ensuring the water is in the background. It will entice him. They are so used to travelling on impulse, nomads with no true roots anywhere, he will jump at the idea. The owners are probably busy with their Easter celebrations, but she will meet with them tomorrow, she hopes, having sent an email of enquiry.

Looking at the sea lapping in the concluding sunset, she closes her eyes, allowing the rhythm of the tide into her bones. There is something in the air, the echoes of history in the rocks out at sea, the ghosts of love stories past and present. This magical place has changed her, Maria has changed her, and Alessandra didn't think it possible she could ever be altered. She's always been so doggedly steadfast and certain of her convictions, travelling through life led by her passions, side by side with Phillipo.

But now, she feels different. She knows with complete assurance that this enchanting part of Greece is where she will take her last breath.

# Chapter 36

## *Maria*

I feel nausea in every cell of my body. My insides hurt and my skin flushes with hot and cold as if I were guilty of some heinous act. But I'm not. Leonidas is. I sit on the terrace of one of the guest villas with a small, assorted mezze and a glass of rosé. I raided the fridges of my teaching kitchen and managed to create a small plate. But I am only vaguely aware of flavours – tangy Kalamata olives, creamy, salty feta and the heat from the spiced sausage the Mani Peninsula is famed for – and they don't connect with my heart.

I am still reeling from the knowledge that Leonidas is behind the threats, though it makes a horrible sense. Part of me had suspected, but I hadn't trusted my usual razor-sharp instinct because I didn't want to believe it. The handmade tributes in front of my hives are certainly down to him as well. When we were children, he would scavenge the beaches for driftwood and sea glass and create minia-ture people or objects from his spoils. But why do all that and pursue me at the same time? So that he could swoop in and rescue me from the mystery menace, be the big man saving the poor frightened woman, make me vulnerable so that he could strike? I have never needed rescuing and I'm not about to start now. To think, I almost fell for his charms, within a millimetre of returning his affection after all these years . . . I will never entertain the idea again.

In that moment, I recall my father's words to me as I'd been indulging my love of cooking when I was little. He had said, 'Maria, you must promise me something.' He had checked to see *Mamá* was unable to overhear us, then put his hands on my shoulders. 'Never settle for the simple life here in this village. There is a whole world that can be yours. You are different, special. Do not compromise who you are for your mother, for me or for anyone who tries to steal your heart. Follow your dreams and you will have no regrets. Your talent is your ticket out of Petalidi.'

*Babá* inherited the farm nestled in an olive grove from his own father and he from his before him. It was an inherited certainty that the descending men would be goat farmers. Consigned to an existence of barns, animals and village life, regardless of any creative flair. The genetic inevitability had quashed my father's ability with food and produce and instead, he'd made cheese only for a hobby. I know he could've been so much more, but the ambition was squeezed out of him by an invisible pressure to conform to tradition. Now, more than ever, I must protect myself; there is nobody else I can depend on. My mother being in hospital highlights how alone I am.

As I look around at the beautiful sanctuary I created, my dream rising from the end of our family's male line, I realise my father's farm became more than he could've imagined. The repurposed outbuildings transformed into the holiday villas where I sit, the seeds we had sown together to propagate the kitchen gardens that fuelled my bees' nectar. I am thankful he lived to see the birth of my business and I raise a toast with my glass to the heavens in his honour. Isn't the farmer's prayer to leave the land better than you found it? I'd hoped I'd done that in his honour, but now, I can't help but wonder what it's all for. There is nobody to pass it on to. When I am gone, it will be sold, redeveloped, likely turned into holiday lets or second homes and all traces of me and my family will be lost, bulldozed down and returned to the earth, becoming dust once more, joining my dead bees.

As I raise my glass to my lips again, it is a quiet toast of a different kind: a promise. I have a God-given purpose and a unique gift, and I refuse to waste it wallowing in self-pity and misery. I will continue my mission and vow to be better than ever: to heal with my magical food and flavours.

# Chapter 37

## *Maria*

I replace the telephone receiver and breathe a huge sigh of relief. The consultant says *Mamá* is stable once more and breathing unaided, although not yet awake. I whisper another prayer of thanks. Father Kyriakidis would be proud. I've not prayed this much in my whole lifetime as I have these last two days. Perhaps *Mamá* has surprised herself with how much she wishes to live on, if she has such conscious thoughts. I will visit her this afternoon.

I sent a message to Kayla and Alessandra insisting we gather this morning for the last official day of their course. It feels like an age since we last stood in my kitchen and cooked together. The storm at midnight on Saturday has done its work and cleared the air. This morning has a sunny crispness more akin to usual April weather. The sea is calm, only disturbed by swallows as they dart around, swooping low above the water, dipping their feet to break the surface. The ripples they cause spread out then disappear, as if they were never there. A mist hangs around the cliffs and across the bay. Clouds cling to the tops of the Taygetus mountains as if protecting the peaks.

It's hard to believe such a beautiful place is harbouring someone who would be so destructive towards me. A friend, someone I cared deeply for, and trusted. The police believe it to be an accident, maybe a careless cigarette end and the case is closed. For them. The dry grass and wooden hives would have needed no accelerant to ignite.

Having discovered the perpetrator is Leonidas, I don't wish to dish out vengeance by informing the authorities about the messages and my evidence. The universe will find its own way to deliver justice and I trust in that. I just want him out of my life and wish for nothing further to do with him. He destroyed my hives, as if he wanted to break me apart after hoodwinking me. Then, it seems, his plan was to play the knight in shining armour by rescuing my mother from the flames. Perhaps he didn't expect the house to be damaged and her life threatened, or his as it turned out. He only wanted to kill my bees, to take away my identity. But he hasn't; I won't allow it. Even though they're gone.

I turn my eyes away from my ruined hives. A dark carpet of dust coats the grass like an unwanted cemetery on my front lawn. I am curious as to why my gift returned in that moment before the fire, but it seems only to apply to *Babá*. I have seen nobody else. Perhaps I am out of practice and have closed off that part of me, blocked it like a disused chimney.

In the house, I make coffee and add a teaspoon of honey to it. The jars from previous harvests are even more precious now. I am inclined to use them sparingly, but it would be wrong to hoard the honey for the sake of sentimentality. It is meant to be shared in my food and I'd do my bees a disservice if I withheld their bounty.

My mind begins to race as I consider what we will cook this morning. Our lunch will be the perfect Greek taverna style spread; *kolokithokeftédes* (zucchini balls), *tzatziki* dip, meatballs, grilled shrimp, *gigantes* (giant beans in a tomato sauce) and a classic Greek salad. We will also make one of my favourite lemon cakes, *lemonopita*, and use my honey for the sticky syrupy glaze. In response to my mental list, my appetite wakes and the bubble of excitement about being creative fills every cell of my being. My outlet during good times and bad has always been food, feeding away sorrow and sadness, celebrating joy with flavour elation. It will be my route away from this unexpected tragic turn of events.

I banish any remaining thoughts of Leonidas from my mind and my heart. All I intended for my life in Petalidi when I left America was to be fulfilled with my long-held dream of a cooking school and to keep bees. One of those is gone, and in the future I may replace them, but it won't be the same. The colony I watched over are descendants of my original cluster. In the meantime, teaching will be my entire focus from now on and nothing, nobody will sway my attention. I won't make that error again.

\* \* \*

305

It reassures me to see Alessandra and Kayla in their usual huddle over coffee. Considering the challenging start we had with Kayla's disapproval of Alessandra's lifestyle. But that was Kayla's projection of her own challenges, which she's come to realise. As she works through what she's dealing with, I'm glad she found an unexpected friendship to sustain her. This week has been unlike any other, even aside from the fire and drama. I've formed an attachment to these women. A lifelong bond. Of course, I become fond of all those who come to my cooking school – emotions unlock during the simple act of cooking, naturally joining us. Whether it brings up a difficult memory, an undealt-with trauma or a way to unpick a current set of problems, there's always a part of them that remains with me. But these two are extra special.

'*Kaliméra*, morning,' I say as I reach them.

Alessandra jumps up to hug me and Kayla follows suit.

'How's your mum doing?' asks Kayla.

'Stronger, surviving, but still having the biggest sleep.' I'm still unable to entertain the notion that this could be my mother's time. The overwhelming urge to mount a bedside vigil nags at me and it divides my heart, having responsibilities here. But I abide by the visiting hours and I know she wouldn't thank me for seeing her so helpless, the opposite of how she is. She'd said so in the past:

'*Promise me you will not sit and watch me fade away, Maria. I do not want you clutching my hand and weeping while I die. Remember me how I was and make sure a priest is with me. But you must stay away.*'

Brutal, as usual, but her wisdom now makes sense.

There would be nothing worse than having my final memories undermine who she was in life. But it's going against my instincts to save and rescue. For once I am doing as I am told. *Mamá* would be thrilled.

As we move into my kitchen, Alessandra says, 'I found a house to stay in, along the beach, and Phillipo is joining me soon. I cannot wait for you to meet him.'

I smile broadly, glad that Alessandra is staying out here. It suits her, she's found a connection to nature and to herself, the ultimate healing balm. I instruct them to begin shredding the filo pastry for the lemon cake and fall into a natural rhythm of teacher and pupil. The dynamic is well established – I only need signal with my hand, and they carry out my instructions with enthusiastic chatter.

'What about your daughter?' Kayla says to Alessandra. 'She won't be able to find you if she . . . well, decided to get in touch.'

I feel the unease growing in my stomach at Kayla's attempted interference, but Alessandra shrugs. 'She has many ways to contact Phillipo or me. If she truly wanted to find me, she could. But she won't, and I accept that.'

Kayla looks at me and I see the panic cross her face. I distract her by teaching her how to make honey syrup for the top of the cake.

'And how about you?' I ask Kayla as she measures out sugar and zests a lemon. 'Alessandra mentioned you also may stay longer.'

She puts down the grater and turns to face me. 'I wanted to talk to you about that. Would it be a terrible imposition for me to stay another week? I'll help with the clear-up after the fire. I can always find somewhere else. I'm just

307

not ready to go home yet. And with all the drama in the press thinking I was missing in the fire, it's better for Rosie and for me if I lie low here.'

I clasp her hand in understanding. 'Of course you can stay. My season starts properly in the middle of May, so there's nobody else to disturb your peace.'

She exhales with relief. If she needs the extra time to consider her troubles, then I couldn't think of a more ideal setting for her. She's much more relaxed in our Greek seaside haven, affording space to find herself again.

I've become used to having these two around, especially since I don't know what tomorrow holds for my mother, let alone today. I'm glad they'll be here for moral support, although goodness knows they both have enough to deal with. They were sent to be here to live through an extraordinary chapter in all our lives. It's like it is meant to be.

\* \* \*

As I drive along the coast road again towards Kalamata hospital, my thoughts drift off, replaying recent events like a strange compilation of someone else's life, another world, but it's mine. I try to avoid thinking of Leonidas, but it's a struggle. I promised myself I wouldn't entertain a single thought of him and I share my mother's obstinate nature in that sense. I shove him firmly from my mind.

I reach the nurse's station on my mother's ward and enquire after her.

The nurse laughs in disbelief. 'She opened her eyes very briefly and managed to speak before falling asleep again.'

'She woke up? What did she say?' I ask as my conscience screams in protest that I wasn't here.

'Well, she said your father was dressed in a terrible suit, so she's a little confused as I understand she is widowed. The medication will make her drowsy.'

I smile to myself. The first words out of her mouth are criticism and directed at poor *Babá*, whom I assume she can also see. It seems her gift too has returned. Strange that he has appeared to us both. But the fact she is giving the apparition of my father a hard time leads me to believe the old girl isn't finished with life yet.

Opening the door as quietly as I can, I see she is resting peacefully, a half-smile on her lips. I feel the rush of affection towards her, grateful beyond words that she is still here. Even though we push each other's buttons, she is my mother, and I am not ready to let her go. I resolve to make the most of her being here. It's never too late to make amends – although that doesn't apply to Leonidas, of course.

I creep carefully over to the stool beside her bed. As if she senses my presence, her hooded eyes blink heavier and manage to open. She coughs a little and I hand her a glass of water. She finishes drinking, breathing heavy with the effort of carrying out the smallest task.

'So, you came,' she croaks.

'Of course, *Mamá*, I was here yesterday as long as I could be and visiting hours only just started.' Tears fill my eyes – I can't help them. 'It's so good to hear your voice.'

'Well, your father is dressed terribly. Wait until I get to those gates and tell him to change his clothes. And what are *you* wearing? Is like you have been dragged along the beach by a horse and cart.'

I swallow a sharp retort, looking down at my olive-green skirt, smoothing the wrinkles away. I smile as sweetly as I can. 'I think he looks very smart.'

Her eyes widen as she understands that I too can see him.

'It seems we can both see spirit again,' I say.

She doesn't respond with words, just a harrumph.

'A great deal has been going on, *Mamá*. I still have my pupils and there is a lot to do to clean up the house.'

'You see, still you work, work, work, Maria.' Her eyes close and I can tell that she is quickly running out of strength. 'And yet when your heart fills with love, you see spirits once more. This is why it returns and why I can see your father again; you have love in your heart, you are complete, but still, you fight and resist. I heard what Leonidas said to you in this very room and knew I could leave. But no. I am back again. Because you . . . cannot . . . accept . . . love.'

Her last word is a whisper as she slips once more into sleep.

In life's continuous cycle of regeneration, we evolve. A slate wiped clean to begin again from scratch. The onward route may be troubled, consigning pain to what has gone before. But upon reflection, just as a phoenix rises from the ashes, its feathers bigger and brighter than before, so can be said of the surviving bee. The time to create a new colony is near. To mourn what is lost, those who have passed and the promise of what is yet to appear. Regardless of what the day brings, the moon will rise and set, pulling the tide towards the shore with an invisible thread, allowing it, at the perfect moment, to subside.

# Chapter 38

## *Kayla*

'I couldn't eat another thing,' says Kayla, holding her flat stomach.

Alessandra raises an eyebrow at her as she reaches for another meatball to dip into the rich tomato sauce of the giant white beans, *gigantes*. Their lunch has spanned the afternoon hours. There is no rush, nowhere to be apart from languishing in conversation and friendship. Maria will be back from the hospital later, having promised to enjoy the cake together.

'I feel like we should do something special to thank Maria for this week. But I'm not sure any gesture is enough. I feel transformed, but I can't work out if it's this village, Greece or Maria who's the most magical,' Kayla says sipping her wine.

'Maybe it's all of them,' replies Alessandra. 'I agree, let's think on it. We have time since we're both staying for longer. Even with all Maria is going through, she wants to take us out this evening for dinner.'

Alessandra shakes her head, and they both sit quietly marvelling at their exceptional hostess. Although Kayla has no delusions about the disease ravishing Alessandra's bones, it's as if there has been a detectable healing quality to this past week. Perhaps not physically, but spiritually she feels the shift. As Kayla looks at the unchanged landscape, she absorbs the thousands of years of history pulsing throughout the peninsula – the vibration of battles and heartache, lovers and myths. It is the most life-changing experience she could wish for, particularly at this point in time.

Both women sit in silence contemplating the past few days, particularly those before the fire. They'd begun in enmity – although really that was only on Kayla's part – and now have evolved to a place of love, an unswerving connection, which will outlive Alessandra's remaining time. Kayla knows it isn't solely Maria who has shifted her outlook. This eccentric Italian has profoundly affected her, stripped away her prudish notions and replaced them with acceptance; of herself and of others. The time for falsehoods is gone.

Alessandra breaks the quiet. 'You know, Maria shows her love of people through cooking. Food is her language to show she cares. What breaks my heart is why she cannot allow someone to do that for her. She won't permit someone to love her. Leonidas does; it is clear to see.'

'I'm not sure we should pry. Yes, he obviously adores her, but she has her reasons, I'm sure. We can't just assume things about her because she's so open. They have history we don't know about, and maybe she doesn't want to live in the past. I don't. It's too exhausting,' Kayla says.

Alessandra claps her hands together in amusement. 'My, she *has* changed you. I like this Kayla better than the one I first met. You're opening up. If only you were brave enough to say your innermost thoughts out loud, then I'd be really excited.'

'Has anyone told you how pushy you are?' Kayla laughs, amazed she isn't bristling from the criticism. Alessandra has unearthed her secret too it seems.

'Yes, everyone I meet, but does it bother me? No. You care too much what others think.'

'But I have to,' Kayla replies.

'Says who?' Alessandra takes another bite of meatball, dipping the remaining half in the smoky sauce. 'How pointless it is to live pleasing everyone else. On social media, all this blathering about a perfect life, pretending to be something that's a lie. You only end up miserable. Yes, I may be an extreme example, but for your own sake, Kayla, learn to exist in your own skin and be happy. You might be surprised and quite enjoy it and inspire others along the way. Stop going to battle with yourself, because nobody wins that war. Ask what it is you really want and then go ahead and get it.'

Alessandra heads off for another walk on the beach, and Kayla goes to her villa bathroom as would have been her usual ritual after a meal. Except this time, she takes the sachets of powder she has come to rely on for so many years and pours them away. It feels momentous, like the beginning of a recovery she never thought she would find. She flushes away one of the tools that fuel her secret and moves into the lounge, considering both Maria's and Alessandra's suggestions about being brave. Could she really help other people by confessing what she has hidden for her entire teenage and adult life? Or would it be the end of her career? The irony could be too much for the public; they may never trust her again.

Her thoughts are interrupted by the shrill sound of her phone ringing, and the screen shows a number from Rome, Italy. Kayla's heart immediately begins to race.

'Hello?' she answers.

'Yes, hello, this is Kayla Moss?' asks a husky female voice with a thick accent.

'Yes, it is. Arianna?'

Kayla hears a lighter clicking at the end of the phone.

'Yes, but I don't understand why you have contacted me. I am no cook or food person.' She gives a throaty laugh, and Kayla hears her inhale her cigarette deeply. 'So, it is strange to have this famous person in my emails asking I call as a matter of urgency.'

Kayla hesitates, unsure how to say what she needs to, cursing that she hasn't taken the time to think this through.

'It's not about cooking, no. It's about . . . your mother.'

'What? What has she done?' Arianna speaks in a series of staccato questions, heavily accented, like firing bullets. 'I have nothing to do with her. She means nothing to me.'

'Wait! I need to explain. Sorry, I know it's difficult between you.'

Arianna snorts. 'It is not difficult; it's simple. I do not wish for her in my life.'

'You might feel differently when I tell you this. I'm in Greece at a cooking school with her. Believe me, I wasn't

316

such a fan at the beginning. But the thing is, she isn't very well.'

'And?'

'And . . . I'm really sorry to tell you this on the phone, but she doesn't have long to live. Your father is travelling to see her and they're going to move her here, to Petalidi, until . . . well, until the end.'

Kayla hears a long exhalation again and forces herself to fall silent. It is an impossible situation, but this is the only way. Kayla crosses her fingers, hoping Arianna can mellow towards her mother, knowing how she may punish herself in the future if she doesn't.

'And she has asked to see me?'

'Yes!' Kayla regrets the half-truth as it fades into the air. She can't take it back. 'She said she'd love to see you, but I wanted to make it a surprise. I'll pay for your flight. My assistant can make the arrangements. I know I don't know you, Arianna, but it's really important you come.'

Arianna laughs. 'I've never been to Greece . . . maybe . . . I will think about it. May I let you know?'

'Of course. I would say no rush, but there is a bit of a time factor here.'

'*Sì*, I will tell you tomorrow if I will come. Or not. It has been many years since I last saw her. I suppose she has not changed.'

'I wouldn't know – that's for you two to work out. But she's really helped me and been such an amazing friend. I want to do something for her, while I still can.'

After they hang up, Kayla does her best to push away her disquiet at going behind her new friend's back. And of late, she knows all too well the sting of betrayal. But this

317

is for the very best of reasons, she thinks, to try and protect Arianna and Alessandra from a world of additional agony. She only hopes it works out the way she intends. If it goes horribly wrong, she'll have risked a genuine friendship and caused Alessandra heartache in her final stretch of life. Kayla holds her hands together almost in prayer, fervently wishing her plan to work.

She emails her assistant to alert her she may have to book a flight from Rome to Kalamata at short notice, hoping that by putting it in writing, she will conjure it into reality. She moves to her laptop and begins to type, emboldened by the force of friendship and a surging independence filling her bloodstream with courage. She suppresses the urge to return to the bathroom, to fill a pint glass with saltwater and gulp it down, to engage in the destructive habit that sustains her, when truthfully it has been doing quite the opposite. She mustn't. This is make-or-break time and she wishes with all of her heart it isn't the latter.

*I can be brave, I will be brave, I am brave,* she repeats over and over in her mind.

# Chapter 39

## *Maria*

It has been another long afternoon at the hospital and I am glad to arrive home. My mother is speedily recovering her spirit, bossing the poor doctors and nurses around, suggesting their time is wasted on her and they should concentrate on the old people. I laugh as she may be allowed out sooner than the medics would have normally permitted, because *Mamá* is clearly driving them potty.

But there is so much to do to ensure her surroundings are comfortable when she does come home. Everywhere downstairs needs to be repainted and the carpet replaced, although the walls have now been washed clean by my fantastic new friends. It's a beginning. There are fleeting moments when I wish there was a man around the house to carry out the practical tasks: moving the furniture, clearing out the rubbish, rebuilding my hives, but I refuse to give in to the stereotype. I'm more than capable, and I have Kayla and Alessandra to help. Sisterhood and friendship – there's nothing more powerful than women uplifting other women and joining forces to make something happen.

After parking the car, I look up at my home, my parents' house that is now mine in name, but where *Mamá* still rules the roost.

*For as long as I still have her,* I think solemnly.

After *Babá* died, I became cruelly aware that my mother was not invincible, despite her relentless energy, but over the years it was as if I'd somehow forgotten about the frailty of life. As much as I feel a simmering anger towards Leonidas, I can't help but feel defeated. He tried to manipulate me, led me to believe he had feelings for me, isolated me from those around me further with cruel anonymous taunts, making me emotionally vulnerable. Then, he dared to extend an invitation to his heart, hoping that I would be in a delicate enough state to accept it gratefully.

It is desperately cruel. His plan of revenge for my rejection of his proposal all those years ago nearly worked. But even if it didn't play out the way he'd anticipated, the damage is done. Our friendship is over; I'd never entertain someone who could propagate such innate vindictiveness, no matter how forgiving my nature. This is beyond reparation.

As the sun sinks lower in the sky, the sharp sadness dwelling in the pit of my stomach begins to ache, pulling and contorting my insides. In the golden light, the silence where my bees would fill the air is marked and the burden of their absence bears down. It lodges a cry in my throat, like a lump I cannot swallow away until I feel like I'm being suffocated. I cannot keep it in. All the turmoil since Leonidas came back into my life, leading up to the fire and all I've discovered since, rises up and explodes outwards in pure, base emotion and primitive rage.

I sob, falling to my knees, clawing at the earth, tearing the remains of the hives apart with my hands. I grieve for my dead insects and my broken friendship with Leonidas, despite what he has inflicted. I weep angrily for the pain he has caused me. My skin quickly becomes blackened by the burnt wood, splinters catch and snag in my fingers, but I continue, scooping up piles of ash as if I am clearing up after an unwanted cremation. Tears stream down my face, and my crying becomes hysterical as I bid farewell to my beautiful bees.

Through my tears, I desperately peer closely at the dust, searching for signs, a wing, a fractured leg, but there is nothing distinguishable. They are returned to the earth, as we all are destined to become. I rake at the ground until my nails ache, digging up clumps of their remains, breaking apart charred wood, which disintegrates. My body is racked with misery and pain as I scream my nickname into the air at the top of my lungs in a feral cry: '*Mélissa!*' Consigning the unpleasant moniker to the heavens is like an anger-fuelled eulogy to myself, filled with hatred. My hands sink into the soil as my teardrops mix with what is left of the bees.

Balling my fists, flashes of New York ricochet through my mind. Me, lifting a skillet of scalding oil from the heat, shouting to my team to mind their backs. The unseen slick of grease on the floor, my dead grandmother's warning arriving too late in my mind. Hissing liquid lifting into the air, descending towards my body like a slow-motion nightmare. The sizzle and stench as it landed on my chest and neck, like a searing steel sheet of burning agony.

As my tears subside along with the brutal memory, my breath still hitches in my throat. I stand and dry my face with a handkerchief, wiping away the dust and dirt as best I can. I walk down the path leading to the sea and wash my filthy hands in the tide. The saltwater stings the lacerations on my fingers from the splintered wood. I rinse my face like a baptism, shedding the past and consigning it to the ocean.

I calm my breath and look along the walkway to the village. I spot Giorgos, the hardware merchant, and his wife. Behind them streams of people process along the promenade, marching with unknown purpose. I search my brain for the custom they are taking part in, but I can't find it. My brain feels foggy. What tradition is this after Easter? But I cannot alight on one. Children dance alongside their parents, who carry bottles of wine, streamers attached to baskets of fruit flap like a gymnast's ribbon. I hear song, excited chatter and the sound of my name carries on the wind. Not my nickname, my real one: Maria.

Giorgos looks solemn as we meet on the path below the lawn, and his wife's expression is identical. Behind him, the crowd surges towards my home, and I feel as though I'm in the midst of a dream. I track bobbing heads as far back as it's possible to see, like a swarm of ants, the setting sun tinging their heads pink. I can't quite believe what is happening and suddenly feel afraid. The entire village appears to be heading in my direction.

# Chapter 40

## *Maria*

Giorgos' wife, Emilia, is holding a plate in her hands, which she thrusts into mine.

'Please, this is for you. It may not be as wonderful as *your* food, Maria, but we wish to help. Know that you and your mother are in our prayers.'

Giorgos squeezes my arm and nods as they move to the side. I am holding a moussaka in my hands; Emilia's dish is still warm and the homely smell engulfs me. The next villager steps forward and offers a platter of tomato fritters. I am bewildered, unable to understand what is happening. I continue to be astounded as two by two people place their dishes at my feet as I've run out of hands to hold their offerings. Like a religious statue at a festival, I stand in the middle of an impromptu buffet, unable to speak, moved by the generosity of the community.

Giorgos summons a group of men from the rear of the

325

crowd, which includes Dimitris. They step forward, holding a huge roll of carpet, buckets of paint and brushes, ready for work.

'We are here for you, Maria. We will help restore your home.' He smiles warmly at me.

Kayla appears at the top of the hedge to see what the commotion is and gasps, then hurries around to me and begins picking up platters of food from the ground.

'Maria! This is amazing . . .' She breaks off as she sees Dimitris step forward. His white vest displays his caramel skin and muscular arms to perfection. She turns beetroot, managing an embarrassed 'Hi.' Her gaze drops and she pretends to be distracted from his biceps by the plates of food. I notice the exchange with amusement, and it brings me out of my shocked state.

'I see you're acquainted with the local dish of the day,' I tease Kayla in hushed tones.

'You could say that,' admits Kayla, her voice just as low.

'Alessandra suspected as much. You deserve some harmless fun.'

Kayla stoops to the ground and lifts up more of the platters, which are still coming thick and fast from the crowds lining the seafront.

'Let's get these into the kitchen and see what we can freeze. You won't need to cook for a year, Maria!' she says, altering the subject swiftly.

'This is Greek hospitality on steroids. All those negative things I said to you before about a small community – well, this is the incredible part. I just never expected to be on the receiving end of it,' I say as I laugh for the first time in what feels like an age.

'I'm not sure you realise how special you are.' Kayla smiles. 'You've had an impact on so many people – in fact, everyone you meet. This is their way of repaying your generosity. Do you not see that? You've helped them, so now it's time they help you.'

Alessandra strides across the lawn and also starts to scoop up the food, forming a sort of production line, passing plates and platters along until they reach me, now in my kitchen at the head of the human conveyor belt.

As the final plate is placed on the countertop, the three of us stand and gawp at the volume of dishes. The kitchen is rich with a thousand beautiful assaults on our taste buds. I am unable to believe that the villagers would do this and emotion grasps me, making my eyes water. They are my people of course, but very few have ever acted like it. But now, I'm enveloped in a giant food hug. It is my love language. They want to care for me, to let me know I'm prayed for and appreciated. It is unexpected and unsettling. I've longed for such acceptance but could never have anticipated how it would happen. The village has pushed aside superstition and gossip and finally, after a whole lifetime, has acknowledged me for who I am.

Kayla looks at her phone and gives a small gleeful yelp as a smile spreads across her features, followed briefly by panic.

'Is everything all right?' I ask.

She nods her head too eagerly and looks incredibly guilty. Probably Dimitris, I conclude as she beams.

'So, now what?' asks Alessandra. 'We have food, your mother is doing well, the house is being repaired. What is left?'

She sends me an impenetrable, inescapable look, and I immediately know what she is alluding to.

'If you mean Leonidas, you can forget it.' I take a deep breath as I boil the small *briki* pan on the stove to make Greek coffee. 'For weeks I've received the most awful messages. You've both seen those strange bundles by my hives. They're warnings. And Leonidas is behind them. The messages, the beehive nastiness and unfortunately the fire. It fits.'

'What?' shouts Kayla. 'You must've got it wrong. He wouldn't; I've seen the way he looks at you. He loves you. He would never send you a horrible thought, let alone set fire to your bees.'

'I agree with our emotional friend,' chimes Alessandra, placing a hand on Kayla's arm to settle her. 'Impossible he is responsible for this. I don't believe it.'

'Well, think what you like, but it was him. Here, look!' I open my phone and explain the change of Leonidas' number. His mistake was thinking I wouldn't make the connection, that I wouldn't have kept all the spiteful messages. I also explain my rejection of his proposal before I left for America, outlining my theory he's harbouring sufficient resentment to make him wish me harm.

'So, I suggest you forget any romantic notions you have about Leonidas riding in on a horse and carrying me off into the sunset. He says he loves me, but how can he? His pride is mortally wounded, and my mother nearly died because of his need for revenge.'

Alessandra and Kayla look at each other, horrified. I know they disbelieve Leonidas would do such a thing. But the facts are indisputable, and I am, sadly, certain.

Something else about Leonidas occurs to me, which makes me believe my dreadful theory further. He wasn't with me the moment my hives were set alight, he'd disappeared for a long time, supposedly in search of wine, so had ample opportunity to ignite the lawn.

I shake the toxic thoughts away, unable to bear to think of it anymore. His betrayal is like a rug has been pulled from underneath me and I can't help but doubt our entire history. And I wonder whether he ever meant a single kind word he said.

# Chapter 41

*Maria*

The following few days pass in a blur of activity: painting, sanding, washing and defrosting.

I've been gifted so much wonderful food that, although grateful, I find myself missing cooking.

I've watched Kayla flirting with Dimitris as he flexed his muscles in between shifts at the grill house, working hard to restore my mother's part of the house. He's like a peacock, preening and posturing for her benefit. His motives in helping out may not have been entirely altruistic, as I suspected a certain redhead was the real inspiration behind his dedication. Nevertheless, Kayla has become unmistakably lighter for it. From the usual tranquil rhythm of my life, so much seems to be happening at once. Alessandra is moving into her rental this afternoon, Phillipo arrives from Rome this evening and I am about to collect my mother from hospital. The doctors are keen to discharge her, and there is plenty of hustle and bustle to prepare. Kayla, Alessandra and I make final touches to the house. Nobody wishes to risk the wrath of Eleni if anything is out of place. I am relieved she's still around to dispense her fury and I mentally brace myself to listen to her diatribe of displeasure, which warms my insides. I am lucky to still have her.

This morning, Kayla is being coy and secretive, asking me to reserve another one of the villas for this evening. She won't say any more, but I wonder if it involves Dimitris. It's her money, and if she wants a second villa to cast her binds to the wind, it's none of my business. I cannot help but worry about her though. She is so fragile, but seeing her carefree and a little reckless is surely harmless. Alessandra has had a greater influence on her than Kayla could ever have predicted.

Tomorrow, I am throwing a party for the village and to celebrate my mother's return home. She can come and go from the house as she pleases, resting as per doctor's orders. As if she will follow them. I chuckle. I have twelve large moussakas, six *pastitsios* and countless other dishes that need to be eaten up. I need to empty out my freezer; otherwise it will all go to waste. I must cook again – it's my soul's sustenance. The gathering tomorrow will be like clearing the decks, although there is no telling if the spirit of empathy has already evaporated into the sea air. But if the industry of the volunteers was anything to go by, there's been a marked shift towards me, and although it feels strange, it is welcome. Another reason to celebrate, although part of me still grieves for my bees. Even the thought of replacing them seems cruel, ungrateful for all the generations I loved and nurtured and all they gave me.

*　*　*

Kayla and Alessandra stand in front of the house to welcome my mother home, lining up with flowers in hand like a receiving line to greet royalty. She is beaming, although quite unsteady on her feet and using a walking stick. We make gentle and slow progress towards them, and I make to clutch my mother's arm tighter, but she shrugs me off.

'*Endáxi*, OK, I can do it, Maria. I am not done for yet!'

I smile and bite my tongue, hovering close should she stumble. She stops and looks at the women. 'You are still here. What about your husband and family?' she says to Kayla. 'And you, where is your husband?'

Back to form, I see. Alessandra steps forward and gives her a kiss on the cheek. 'Don't you worry about our menfolk, just get well. Here.' She hands my mother a bunch of beautiful wild flowers, which my mother accepts in her free hand.

'Oh, how kind to think of me. But do not abandon your men. Keep hold of them; otherwise you will be alone.'

My mother indicates her head to me, and I cannot help but laugh. I squeeze Kayla's arm to let her know my mother doesn't mean it. 'Let's get you to bed, *Mamá*. The doctors wish you to rest.'

'I know what they say, but I know myself better. I will sit in the garden after I inspect the damage to my home.'

Alessandra takes up the mantle and escorts my mother

into the house, telling her about all the new things she's bought for her rental, while Kayla and I remain on the lawn.

'She's back to normal then.' Kayla grins.

'Yup, you wouldn't think she'd had a cardiac episode. But she recovered as fast as she declined. Between you and me, the doctors are glad to have her off their hands, although they took such good care of her. So, what's new with you?' I ask.

Kayla puts her hands into her pockets and shrugs. 'Not much, but I feel great. I've never had this amount of time just for myself and it's a relief not to have to be anywhere, look after anyone, or fulfil work obligations. I know it's not real life, and I miss Rosie like mad, but it's good to take a break from it all for a while.'

'Whatever gets you through. Have a fling, don't get too attached and then prepare to face the music.'

'Something like that. Sorry I've been distracted, but . . .' She checks that Alessandra hasn't re-emerged. 'I made contact with Arianna, Alessandra's daughter. And that's what I need the other villa for. She's coming in tonight from Rome.'

'You're kidding?! But Phillipo's arriving tonight too . . . landing at half six. Oh Kayla, I don't know, I have a bad feeling about this.'

'What's the worst that can happen?' Despite her apparent nonchalance, she looks terribly unsure. She clearly needs reassurance, but I can't offer it to her.

'Do you want me to answer that?'

'No! I'm having a complete panic about it and I feel terrible. I never thought she'd respond, but she's arriving at . . .' she checks her email on her phone and sighs '. . . six thirty this evening. The same flight as Phillipo.

Oh God, Maria, what if it all goes wrong? I told Arianna her mother has asked to see her.'

I put my arm around her and lead her towards the water, away from Alessandra possibly overhearing. 'That is out of your hands, now, and your control. If it works, amazing; if not, knowing Alessandra, she'll be upset but incredibly practical about it. Try not to worry, please.'

We start to walk along the beach, both engrossed in our own thoughts and fears, until Kayla eventually breaks the quiet.

'I've been thinking about how to take charge of my future. Since Daniel wants a divorce and a custody battle, I'm going to get ahead of it and jointly announce our separation.' Kayla's face is serious but underneath her expression, I see a relief in her eyes. 'I'll draft a statement, ask for privacy, blah, blah, blah . . . It's long overdue. I can't hide anymore, can I?'

I fold my arm around her shoulder. 'No, Kayla, you can't. I'm so proud of you and although it will hurt, it'll set you free. I know it.'

I feel a tingle of confirmation down my spine, and although no spirit comes, I immediately know she's taking the right steps towards her own healing. My stomach bubbles with concern, though. She may be making important strides in her own world, yet she may have set off a time bomb in someone else's: Alessandra's. I'd hoped we could find some drama-free time after the fire, my mother's illness and Kayla's many ups and downs. But it seems there may be more headed our way.

\*    \*    \*

Alessandra and I sit on the terrace each with a glass of ouzo with a light lunch of mezze. My mother finally relented and took to her bed for rest. I am holding my hands tightly in my lap, so nervous about Arianna's arrival that I keep fiddling with random objects and it's a struggle to resist the urge to pace up and down. Kayla has gone to speak to Daniel and have their big conversation. If my bees were here, I'd ask them to protect her and also Alessandra for what she may be about to endure. Instead, all I can do is appeal to the invisible spirits to guard them.

'I must confess, Maria,' begins Alessandra, 'I feel a little responsible in all that's happened. You see, I encouraged Leonidas to take you to that beach: Kalamaki. I came up with the idea about you two being alone, away from the village, and we cooked it up together on Good Friday. It is so clear how he feels about you and you him, but you prevent it from happening. I'm sorry, I cannot believe what you say – he wouldn't hurt you like this.'

She indicates to the lawn where my bees would be with her elegant hand. Her words linger in the warm air and, despite the initial pang of irritation, I know it would be hypocritical of me to reprimand her. I instinctively know I shouldn't warn her about Arianna; I want no part of Kayla's scheme. Although she inserted herself in my business and it does sting a little. Especially because my scenario is beyond repair.

'The facts are there, Alessandra: it was him behind the messages and the warnings in front of the bees. He cannot be in my life anymore. He's shown how wounded he still is and clearly holds a grudge against me. Please respect that. I'm sorry it won't be the grand love affair you and Kayla wish for.'

'Perhaps not, but I've learnt a little wisdom in my time: that one should never write off something with potential. Love comes in many forms and arrives in unexpected places. Do not close you heart to possibility.'

'I hear you, and I've always said it's the plate I will keep spinning, but it's not him, believe me,' I say trying to appease her, and swiftly change the subject. 'Anyway, I need to see Father Kyriakidis about my mother's party tomorrow. It'll be wonderful to have Phillipo here with you. I cannot wait to meet him and . . .' I stop myself, almost giving the game away, poised to say Arianna. 'And . . . and we can all celebrate together.' I add 'hopefully' to the end of the sentence in my head.

She nods and I stand to check on my mother before walking into the village. Alessandra's first evening in her new place might not be exactly as she planned. I let out a deep breath. I'm no good at keeping secrets nor hiding things. I'm too much of a straight shooter for any skulduggery. At least tonight when Phillipo and Arianna arrive, there will be nothing left to hide.

\*　\*　\*

My walk to the village is bewildering and takes twice as long. I'm stopped along the way by everyone I encounter. Kind enquiries after my mother and me, offers of help and more food. It's an efficient way for me to spread the word about the party, and a further inkling that finally, after ten years back home, I'm being accepted for who I

337

am. It's what I've longed for from those around me. My mother's warning echoes . . . be careful what you wish for . . . but it is coming true. Aside from my mother finding her own peace with who I am and my choices, but I know *that* time will never arrive.

I walk on in search of Father Kyriakidis, who'll be able to announce the party in his morning service, when I see Athena in the middle of the green staring up at the church tower. She cuts a lonely figure without her followers, and I cannot help but feel sorry for her. She must be desperately unhappy: her husband, Leonidas, left her because he supposedly loved another – me – and she is yet to find a suitable replacement. Maybe she still loves him and for that I feel pity.

I walk towards her, and she turns her head. Her eyes narrow in their usual way, but she stands firm.

'*Yiá sou*, Athena, *ti káneis*?' I ask how she is, not expecting much of a response.

'*Kalá*, thank you, Maria,' she replies, saying she is well, as my eyebrows rise in surprise at her unusual politeness. 'I am very sorry to hear of your mother, and well . . . I am just sorry, I truly am, for it all.'

She looks at me, then hangs her head. A sprig of oregano could have toppled me. Before I can say anything else, she turns and scurries across the green. Well, that was unexpected. And a pleasant outcome from all the horror of the last week.

With a spring in my step, I walk into the dimly lit church and see Father Kyriakidis rearranging candles in front of a shrine.

'Hey, Father,' I say. 'I think hell just froze over!'

He turns and his moustache twitches with his customary amusement at my crossing the fine line from godliness to near blasphemy. 'Dare I ask why, Maria?'

'Well, things are looking up. First, I must thank you for whatever you said on Easter Sunday, because the whole village is changed. Even Athena. She apologised to me. For what I'm unclear, but it's a start, right?'

'I'm happy for you. As with all things, they begin with hello and in the middle there must be time for sorry in order to be able to say goodbye with a clean soul.'

His words almost always make me tear up, his advice and wisdom so bountiful. 'You know, you could've had a great career as a motivational speaker. You're wasted in this village.'

'I'm not so sure. The greatest reward I have is watching the toing and froing of life and love. If people listen to anything I have to say, I am glad. But what gives me the greatest joy is when good prevails. You've given great things to this community and finally the rewards are yours. I had nothing to do with it; it was all you. Cherish this moment – you worked hard for it.'

I feel heat rush to my cheeks and I drop my eyes. I never expected any plaudits for my work – the sole satisfaction I crave is for my food to be appreciated. I tell him about my plans to hold an open house party tomorrow to use up all the donated Easter food in my freezer and he gladly accepts my request to deliver the message during his service in the morning.

As I leave the church, it feels like a new chapter in my life is beginning. My mother is getting well again. She's safe and loves me, in her own way. I've made lifelong friends in Alessandra and Kayla and Leonidas is gone from my life. No longer a friend – it's not possible. Although what did Father Kyriakidis just say about an apology? It may come from him, but it won't be enough. The alternative way this could've played out is too devastating to entertain and is almost blood on his skilled woodworker's hands. There's not enough forgiveness in me for this one. I can skip to the end of Father Kyriakidis' sentiment and say goodbye to Leonidas with my heart. There is no space for him there. Although letting go of such long-held affection will take time, I am firm about his part in my future. He doesn't have a role to play. My mind fleetingly returns for the final time to the beach before the fire. I briefly think about what my reply would have been to him.

But it is now too late and I will never say those words – nor think about them again.

# Chapter 42

## *Kayla*

Kayla hangs up the phone and stares at it in her hand.

It is really happening; she's set the wheels in motion and called time on her marriage, officially. She'd had such high hopes for this trip to Greece, wondering if it would give her the perspective to forgive Daniel. It certainly transported them both to a place of decision, beginning with the public announcement of their split. There's also been a collision of both fortunate and unfortunate timing. Although Kayla had already decided to announce their separation, a tabloid had received a grainy photo of her and Dimitris walking on the beach together. Her publicist managed to trade off against them running it in return for an exclusive on her marriage break-up statement. Another loose end yet to be tied up, if only Dimitris wasn't so deliciously addictive, but it's the one habit Kayla knows she can easily break.

Her secret, which she is yet to reveal, will lead people

to believe she's having a breakdown, treating her with kid gloves like a fragile, broken child. The truth is, she's never felt stronger. As frightening as it will be, she notices the tickle of excitement within her. Barely detectable, but there. If Daniel could share Rosie with her, then they could all find resolution. She's the main breadwinner and is likely to be granted full custody. Kayla doesn't have the appetite for a spat in a courtroom, and surely Daniel can find a way to be reasonable. She doesn't wish to hurt him in that way and isn't bitter about their ending, despite how much it hurts inside.

Her publicist has made some amendments to her statement, impressing on the editor, who is already salivating in anticipation, that it is an amicable split. Kayla is relieved she made the decision to stay in Petalidi rather than in London. Although the press knows she's out here after the fire debacle, it's better she's in Greece than at home where she'd be swarmed by photographers.

Her conversation with Daniel had been strained at first when she informed him of her plan, but he hadn't mentioned battling for custody of Rosie again. Officially separating was a belated discussion they should have had months ago before either of them invited another into their bed. It had been surprisingly liberating for them both to speak so openly. He had said as much, and they apologised to each other for being cruel and for concealing their own truth. Kayla appreciates his honesty and is proud of her own. Though it is a bereavement of sorts, it marks one more step towards Kayla's ultimate confessional.

*   *   *

It is a beautiful evening, the sun performing one of its most spectacular displays casting a fiery orange triangle as it kisses the sea, making it shimmer like satin. Kayla sees Dimitris skimming stones on the water. They bounce on the mirrored surface of the sea. He cuts a heavenly silhouette in the golden light, and her nerve begins to fail as desire grips at her insides.

'Hey,' she says as he turns to her.

'Hey yourself.' He smiles and her resolve melts further.

'Look, can we talk?'

If she says what she needs to as quickly as possible, she won't be tempted to return to his apartment. They move to sit, and she takes his hands.

'I just wanted to say, that . . . the thing is . . .'

Dimitris puts his hand to her cheek and rubs his thumb across her lips. 'Shhh, I know what you are about to say, and it is OK.'

'You do?' Kayla asks, despite the erotic gesture.

'Yes, you are about to say, "This was fun, but you are going home soon." Am I right? To your husband, your famous life . . .'

Kayla exhales in relief although can't ignore the jolt of panic that he knows who she is and probably has the whole time.

'Sort of. My life is – well, it's complicated and I'm leaving on Sunday, so . . .'

'So . . . we have two days to enjoy each other. If you want.'

Mustering all the self-control she can summon, Kayla sighs. 'I do want, but I need to focus on me. I've a lot going on and I just need to sort out what I want right now. At this very moment, yes, it is you, but it can't be. I'm sorry.'

Dimitris shrugs and seems content to accept her decision. Kayla finds herself feeling slightly wounded he isn't devastated, but after a moment, she realises this probably isn't his first holiday-fling rodeo, and she scolds her silly ego. They stand as the darkness spreads over the bay. Lights begin to ping on across the water, flickering like hundreds of stars.

Kayla stands. 'Thank you, Dimitris.'

He wraps his arms around her and gently kisses her, brushing his lips with a featherlight touch against hers. If she doesn't leave now, she'll cave.

'Goodbye,' he says.

\* \* \*

Back in her villa, Kayla sits at her laptop and takes a deep breath. There is one last thing to do and it's perhaps the hardest. Maria has put fresh flowers on the coffee table and beside them sits a plate of biscuits. Kayla reaches for one, daring herself to choose the largest. She stares at it, examining the crumbs for so long, she could have counted the tiny cracks in the surface. Pressing the biscuit to her nose, she deeply inhales. Vanilla and honey travel through her nostrils and into her body. She returns to her cherished memory of being with her mother, baking in the kitchen. Allowing herself to celebrate the recollection, rather than mourn it, she takes a tentative bite.

Chewing slowly, she walks through the happiest times of her childhood in her mind, permitting reminiscences to spring forward in multicolour and replace those that are filled with heartache, consigning them to grey wash, pushing them into retreat. She takes another bite, followed by a third and closes her eyes, inviting enjoyment, which eventually comes as she marries up each mouthful with happiness.

As she brushes off any fragments from her lap, Kayla smiles. Another step forward. She glances at the bathroom out of habit, then turns back to her computer screen. And begins to type.

# Chapter 43

*Alessandra*

Alessandra is making her rental as homely as possible. It was already fully furnished, but she'd bought some beautiful bed linen in Kalamata along with new white muslin drapes to match the simple beach-chic interior. The open patio doors reveal the now familiar stunning seascape that shifts in colour and texture throughout the day; even at dusk it is mesmerising.

She places a vase of wild flowers on the patio table she'd picked from the hedgerows earlier and waits for the sound of the taxi delivering Phillipo to her. Her tummy flips like a teenager awaiting a first date. This will be their elongated final encounter, but she doesn't dwell in the sadness. Instead, she's prepared some of the honey-roasted feta learnt from Maria along with a Greek salad and marinated octopus, which Phillipo loves. She longs for her husband's touch, more than she's ever craved a stranger's.

She can't wait to feel his strong arms around her, rocking her to sleep in the well-established embrace she's known and loved for decades.

As she stares out at the hypnotic sea gently yielding to darkness, she inhales the clean, salty air. She feels healthier in Petalidi than she has since her terminal diagnosis. Not that she is under any illusion she's been miraculously healed. But there is something on the wind, in the food and from the energy Maria gifts through her cooking that nourishes her bloodstream. It wills her to grasp the remaining part of her life and wring it dry for all it can offer her and Phillipo. Together.

The sound of a car engine snaps her awareness from the water and she glides back through the simple villa, checking her reflection in the mirror as she passes. Her cheeks have a glow as if she is radiating something special from within, rather than sickness. Her skin is tanned, and she knows she looks her best – or the best version of what is possible at this moment.

She opens the door and sees the cab with its boot open. From behind the tailgate emerges Phillipo, his jet-black hair streaked with a track of silver that shines even in the lowlight, the sun having completed its slow bow beyond the headland. She always joked affectionately he was her badger, his shock of grey reminiscent of the creature.

Phillipo's face breaks into a smile as Alessandra runs to him, covering his face in kisses.

'It is like we have been apart for a month rather than ten days, *caro mio*, my darling. I am so happy you are here.'

She pulls back to scrutinise his face and features, drinking them in. He looks strained and tired – probably the journey, she thinks, although it is only a short flight. She brushes it off, putting it down to his worry about her.

'You look beautiful, *stella mia*.' Although he calls her by his pet name, my star, he looks grave. He doesn't seem as happy to see her as she him.

'*Caro*, what is wrong?'

Alessandra's gaze travels to the taxi driver who rounds the open trunk, depositing another bag on the driveway paving slabs. Phillipo turns to pay him, not responding to Alessandra's question. As the driver returns to close the boot, the source of Phillipo's worry is revealed. Alessandra starts. Her hand covers her mouth in shock. Her emotions jostle for prominence: relief, delight, fear. She feels ambushed, unprepared. Her time in Petalidi with Phillipo is supposed to be tranquil and precious, but now it threatens to be everything but.

As she looks into the eyes identical to her own, she sees the same tumult of feelings reflected back. Alessandra steps forward hesitantly, then thinks better of it, utterly unsure of herself and the reaction she may prompt. She is afraid of the expression returning her stare: unrepentant, arrogant . . . That crushing judgement remains apparent. There is no warmth to be found there.

'*Ciao, Madre*,' Arianna says, her voice dripping with disdain as she uses the formal term for mother.

Alessandra steels herself to respond. '*Ciao*, Arianna. Wh . . . why . . . how . . .'

As she searches for the words, Alessandra feels her energy fizzing away, like an effervescent tablet dissolving in liquid. Black spots prick at her vision as the foliage on the driveway begins to blur and her knees buckle. The last things she sees is Phillipo dropping his bag, rushing to catch her. But the world turns to black, and she doesn't know if he reaches her or not.

\* \* \*

Alessandra's eyes blink open. At first, she thinks it was a nightmare, before reality slowly fuses with her mind. She carefully swings her legs out of bed, momentarily unclear how she came to be there. Then, remembering Phillipo is here, she hurries to stand up. She is still slightly dizzy and stretches tentatively as if checking her limbs can function. In the bathroom, she splashes her face with water. The absurd aspect of her fainting is she'd felt so well before it. The shock of seeing Arianna ignited Alessandra's suppressed emotions about their estrangement, material-ising as a physical attack upon herself. As it did the first day of cooking class with Maria.

Opening the bedroom door, she finds the living room is deserted. Then, she sees her daughter and husband on the terrace, candlelight casting shadows across their faces. She silently slinks closer, like a cat stalking its prey.

'I don't know if I can forgive her . . . she won't be different. She doesn't care enough about me.'

'Your memories may be inaccurate, Arianna,' Phillipo says. 'And why you are able to speak to me with no anger, but she sparks such fury within you, I do not understand. Neither of us do. But you're our daughter, and we love you. Please, just talk to her.'

Arianna's gaze darkens as it falls on Alessandra beside

350

the patio doors. Phillipo stands and says, 'I will leave you both and cook some supper.'

As he goes, the tension between the two women is palpable. Arianna drains her wine glass and reaches for the bottle to refill it. Alessandra bites her tongue, knowing how irrational her daughter can be after too many drinks, unable to be persuaded down from whatever wild imaginings she's conjured up. But now is not the time to address that issue.

'It is a shock to see you. But a good surprise, Arianna.' Alessandra manages a feeble smile, which fails to mask her trepidation, unsure what her daughter may say next.

'It looks like you've recovered from earlier.' Arianna lights a cigarette and exhales the smoke with a hiss. The vapour lingers above the table. 'I thought long and hard about coming here, but I hear you are ill. *Papà* wouldn't say much, he says it's your news to tell. Well?'

Alessandra sits and pours herself a small glass of red wine from the depleted bottle. She takes a fortifying sip. 'I don't know how long I have. I am dying, Arianna, of cancer. I'm sorry it's come to this.'

Arianna cannot seem to help but look concerned, and her brow creases with worry. 'But what do the doctors say and what treatment are you having?'

'There is no more treatment. I've stopped it. Nothing will change, so why should I make myself feel terrible for as long as I have?'

Arianna's eyes flash. 'That's so typical you, so selfish, thinking only of yourself.' Arianna becomes angry as tears prick at her eyes. 'What about *Papà*? And me? Don't you want to be around for as long as you can?'

'Of course I do. I'm not prepared to get into the details. It's all very stressful.'

'Well, I've been stressed too, I have a lot of exhibitions coming up.'

Alessandra snorts with laughter. 'Because that's the same thing! It's like comparing an ear infection with cancer, not at all alike.'

Arianna's eyes cloud with irritation. 'I can't believe you're not taking the doctor's advice. What does *Papà* say?'

'It is because of your father I don't want to be an invalid in bed for my final months, with him nursing me. Don't you see? That will happen at some stage, but why do it now? It's my body, my sickness, my choice! I can wait to be confined to a bed.'

The colour rises in Arianna's cheeks from both wine and anger. 'Well, it's always been your favourite place, hasn't it, in your disgusting example of a relationship? I'm surprised you don't want to spend *all* your time lying on your back – it's what you're good at.'

'Please, Arianna.' Alessandra knows which way this conversation is headed, and no joy will come of it. 'Try to calm down.'

'No! This was a mistake. I will call your friend who made me come here to send me back home. I don't want to see you again.'

'What friend?' asks Alessandra in confusion.

'Your fancy famous friend – Kayla. She orchestrated all this, but it's pointless. You haven't changed. I'll leave you to sleep with all the poor villagers until you take your last gasp. *I* won't be here to see it.'

White-hot anger floods Alessandra's body. Kayla? How

dare she thrust herself into a situation she knows nothing of. Alessandra stands abruptly, her chair screeching against the patio floor.

'Do what you wish, Arianna. You like to judge me from your high horse, but the facts are, the apple doesn't fall far from the tree. You waste your life enjoying the more decadent side of life; your passions and impulses control you. You're much more like me than you care to admit. Go on, please yourself – you always have. But answer me this: who will you judge when I am dead? Your father? I doubt it. He is a willing part of our arrangement. You seem able to forgive him, yet *I* infuriate you. That is because when you look at me, you see yourself. A reflection you cannot escape. When I die, I will still be there in the mirror looking back at you and you'll hate yourself as much as you hate me now. You'll find no satisfaction from it, I promise you.'

Alessandra storms off towards the beach, trembling with rage. She never loses control. It isn't in her nature to be provoked into fury about anything, even at the hands of her own flesh and blood. She's usually able to brush off confrontation and see it for the pointless endeavour it is. But this new sensation is maddening, and her anger is directed at Kayla for thrusting her into this scenario. She's probably writhing underneath that waiter, but when Alessandra finds her, she plans to unleash her wrath on that girl.

As she stomps down the promenade into town, she spots a small bar and orders one of those brandies Maria gave her when she felt unwell: *Metaxa*. As she takes her drink to a table, she sees Leonidas sitting alone. He lifts his head and smiles warmly at her, indicating to a chair.

'*Kalispéra*, Alessandra, please, join me.'

'It's not a good time, Leonidas. Families . . . relationships, why is it all so complex?'

As she takes a seat, she feels the edge of her temper soften in the presence of his calming energy. As she sips her strong drink, she looks at Leonidas, refusing to believe he is behind those awful messages Maria received – or the fire. Since interfering appears to be the order of the day, Alessandra tells Leonidas the whole story, about the warning tributes and finally the text messages that came from his phone, linking him to the fire.

His eyes widen and his jaw sets. 'I have to go.'

He stands abruptly as his chair falls backwards onto the floor with a clunk. Throwing some coins on the table, he rushes away.

'Leonidas, wait!' she shouts after him, but he doesn't look back. Although she wants to believe the best of him, this looks very much like the actions of a man who has been caught out.

Alessandra feels a weight descend on her heart. What has she done? She is as guilty as Kayla, with all her meddling – well meaning as they both were. The problem with her and Kayla's actions is they have absolutely no control of how it plays out.

# Chapter 44

*Maria*

I prise off a few yellowed leaves from my fruit trees, ensuring they continue to yield their harvest for as long as possible this season. I notice the villa Kayla had reserved has the blinds closed. So, Arianna must have arrived last night.

My bones cool at the thought of Alessandra being confronted with her daughter. I'm not sure how she will react, but innately I know it won't be good. As indifferent as she likes to appear, Alessandra's life is entirely on her own terms and any deviation from that could rock her. The same could be said of Kayla; they are more alike than either would like to admit.

I pick some fruit to make my mother a hot fresh lemon tea and select an orange for her breakfast yoghurt. Today will be a special moment for both of us. A party in her honour, but a celebration of our community. I sense *Mamá* is quietly glad my bees are gone, the only good to come out of the fire for her. My nickname '*Mélissa*' no longer applies, but she hasn't seen the new thaw in relations with the villagers. Maybe their change in attitude will encourage her to also see me in a new light. I laugh as soon as I think it. That would be an Easter miracle, but we've already had one of those when the heavens opened to douse the fire.

My teaching kitchen looks like it is braced to feed the five thousand: foil squares, porcelain platters and plates of food piled high ready to be roasted, broiled and baked. Goodness knows whose crockery is whose, but I'm sure they'll be claimed one way or another. I take a tray of *bougatsa* out of the oven; a crispy Greek pastry filled with a velvety smooth vanilla custard. I sprinkle a light cloud of icing sugar on top and grate the zest of one of my freshly picked lemons. I brew some coffee and inhale the flavours of my decadent breakfast dish. I want to take some to Alessandra and to welcome Phillipo before the party. It smells divine and the aroma is enough to draw the newest arrival I am yet to meet from their villa.

I see a tall, strikingly beautiful dark-haired woman outside the guest villas. Her skin is pale and I see bruises of exhaustion underneath her eyes. Although her features are unlike Alessandra's, her physique is identical. The same willowy limbs and enviable height. She is sniffing the air like a bloodhound before following the scent and reaches the doorway.

'Hi, you must be Arianna. I'm Maria. Welcome to my kitchen!'

I fear last night's reunion didn't go well at all by the look on her face, but she manages a broad smile. 'What is that incredible smell? Sorry, forgive my manners – thank you so much for having me here.'

'Don't you worry, *bougatsa* has the same effect on me. Here, try some.'

She nods with enthusiasm, and I add a further grating of zest, certain it will ignite her subconscious and invoke the resolution she seeks. I sense lemons are her gateway flavour to unlock healing. She almost rolls her eyes in ecstasy as the flavours get to work.

'You have to give me this recipe. I was reading about your school on the plane in the airline magazine. Great article and it was right, you seriously can cook!'

'Thank you,' I say, graciously. 'Maybe we can make something together one evening, with your father and mother.'

Her face becomes steely. 'I'm not sure that's going to happen. We had a huge fight last night and I said awful things to her, as usual. And she was pretty spiteful in return. We're at an impasse. When we get to that point, I run. So, I'll head back to Rome, maybe tonight.'

'Don't,' I say, reaching for her hand. 'Give it a chance. It might be your last one.'

She takes another bite, and her expression lightens.

'Perhaps. It's been a long time since I saw her, and it brings back all the frustration I felt years ago when I saw her with that man. I take it you know about their arrangement?'

She shakes her head, her expression now suggesting disappointment rather than judgement. 'It undid the romantic illusion I had of my parents, and I blame her for it. She doesn't understand my feelings.'

'But equally, you don't understand her . . .' I suggest gently.

Arianna smiles with irony. 'She said we are similar. I couldn't think of anything worse than being like her.'

'Could it be that you responded with anger because you know deep down she may be right?'

Arianna laughs. 'I didn't realise I was such an open book.'

'You're not.' I return her warmth. 'I've seen it all in this kitchen. Nobody comes just to cook. They tend to be looking for something, escaping a situation or hoping for an answer. We are all hiding from something, Arianna. Most people find what they seek in their own way, but each path is different. I'm being overfamiliar, but I sense time is an issue – not just with your mother, but with your decision to stay. Imagine yourself at a crossroads with choices in front of you. You go left with no recon-ciliation, and you risk regretting it for the rest of your life. Or you turn right, make amends, and accept Alessandra and yourself. Then you get peace.'

She considers my words with a wry smile, leaning both elbows on the countertop finishing her piece of *bougatsa*.

'What if I go forwards or backwards instead?'

'The outcomes don't change . . . to move forwards is the same as turning right – you get closure – and if it's backwards you choose, you'll be going left, and nothing will change.'

She laughs with a husky smoker's rasp. 'Wow, this is some serious wisdom you're dishing out over breakfast. I'm not ready for this before coffee.'

I move to the stove to make her the drink she craves, adding a little cinnamon to further caress her palate. If she is as like her mother as I suspect she is, she'll respond to the spice like Alessandra does. Coupled with the lemon flavour, it could be the momentum she needs to move forwards. I can only hope for her and Alessandra's sake she chooses the right direction of travel.

\* \* \*

My mother sits like an emperor on a bench set into the remains of the grass. She asks people not to make a fuss, but I can tell that she's relishing every second. Her friends surround her, clicking their teeth as she retells the story of the fire and recounts Leonidas' bravery. They shout scorn at the wind, gesturing wildly with their fists, reacting in fury at the elements for having caused this. They accept the official police report that cited it as an accident caused by the sweltering weather and praise Leonidas for his heroic acts.

I wince at the mention of his name. *Mamá* is unaware her hero rescuer has been behind the torment I've endured these last weeks and is responsible for the furnace that almost claimed her life. I bite my tongue so she may enjoy her moment in the sun. I dismiss my pang of grief for his injurious acts, irritated I permitted him to enter my mind for a moment. Instead, I focus on the point of today, which is to celebrate my mother, and to distribute the food mountain kindly donated by the villagers. This is about moving onwards. To what, I know not, but it is my own future to make.

Trestle tables are laden with food and the chairs that cover the blackened remains of the lawn are borrowed from every neighbour in walking distance. They screen the indented earth where my beehives sat for ten years. Like a crime scene outline of a murdered body, the squares where the hives once were torment me with their barrenness.

Several people have brought instruments with them, and Giorgos begins a *zeibekiko*: a slow, measured but energetic dance requiring dexterity and stamina. Despite his advanced years, he moves beautifully with an unmistakable Greek swagger. Others join him, and it's the celebration I hoped it would be. My mother beams from her vantage point and I spot Kayla hovering by the never-ending buffet.

'I'd recommend everything,' I say as she turns to look at me, 'but the *talagani* cheese *saganaki* is heaven.'

She takes a helping of my fried cheese salad, scattered with pine nuts and mint and says, 'It's strange to think about going home tomorrow. I feel safe here. With you.'

I put my arm around her as I lead her to a chair and we sit down. 'You are welcome anytime, Kayla. We're friends. You always have a seat at my table; you just have to promise me to eat when you get there.'

Laughing, Kayla takes a forkful of the crispy fried cheese cubes to prove a point. 'Oh, for crying out loud. This is heaven!'

I watch her enjoy the food and consider the long journey she has been on since she came to Petalidi. She swallows and says, 'The announcement about the end of my marriage is out in the media and my phone is blowing up, so I've hidden it under the bedsheet. I know Daniel and I are doing the right thing, but it's all so public, having your personal life picked over by strangers, making up their own minds about who's at fault and why. We're going to explain it to Rosie when I'm home – together. He's kept her out of school until I'm back. She's so young but I don't want her to be disturbed by this.' Tears flood her eyes when she mentions her daughter.

I try to comfort her as best I can. 'You both love her, and she'll understand your truth; that's the most important thing. It's the start of your new what's next. Terrifying, but kind of exciting, right?'

'I suppose so. I keep wavering between bravery and despair. It's not great timing as I'm supposed to be filming my show next week and the Greek food article will come out just before that. I've written it . . . my review . . . It's not about food, but it is. I'll send it to you when I get home. My publicist will go mad at what I've written but I feel completely cleansed. Like an emancipation – see, that religious bug must've bitten me! It was so cathartic writing it that I almost don't care what happens, because for the first time I'm not hiding. Unlike my phone under the duvet.'

'I'm so proud of you.' My eyes swim with emotion as she leans into me.

'You, Maria, have changed me forever. I never expected any of this when I took the assignment to come here. Writing an article about your cooking has become so much more.'

'If you were told before you came to Petalidi that you'd gorge on fabulous food, have wild sex with a waiter, announce the end of your marriage and be honest about your demons, you would've run for the mountains.'

'A hundred percent. But as painful as it's all going to be, it's for the best – I know that, thanks to you. Although, be warned I'll be calling for a pep talk when I doubt myself – brace for your phone to ring . . . a lot.'

'Always. I'm here for you.'

'Right, now stop talking, you're keeping me from my lunch!' She giggles.

Alessandra and Phillipo enter the garden and I spring up to greet them. I introduce myself, having missed my chance to meet him before now, because of my interlude with Arianna. He didn't get to try my *bougatsa*, but he can eat everything else that's on offer in my garden, which today looks like the ultimate Greek taverna. He's as warm and charming as I imagined and they make an elegant couple, both so tall. I catch Alessandra shooting Kayla a burning look and assume she discovered who's behind her unexpected family reunion with Arianna. I take Alessandra to one side, wishing for no further upset. Not today.

'I met your daughter this morning.'

'Lucky you,' Alessandra snaps before saying, 'I don't know what to make of this, Maria. She is here but shows no sign of wanting to make amends. I don't need such trouble in my life.'

The emotional upheaval is evident on her face, which is very unlike her.

'Maybe it's worth another go,' I suggest. 'One last chance and then if it comes to nothing, at least you tried.'

She fixes me with teary eyes. 'I don't know if I have the energy. But as usual you are very convincing. Later, perhaps.'

I sense a reluctance but am determined to help them make a memory that will endure in the heartbreaking times to come. That I can give them, if nothing else.

362

Alessandra returns to Phillipo's side, and I smile as I watch them interact. The evidence of their decades together is revealed in the insignificant gestures: her hand at the small of his back, his fingers brushing tendrils of hair from her forehead, the way they look at each other with a mutual understanding. It's like their own private dance, towards the end of love. We are all navigating our way to that inevitable destination. To traverse the peaks and troughs with innate, unconditional affection is the dream. Their version of love, no matter how unconventional, is one to be admired. Such a goal is, now, far from my reach, those imaginings are crushed beyond repair.

As the party finds its full swing, it unfurls into the longest lunch, merging into early afternoon with the promise of beyond as the sun reaches its highest point. The sea is illuminated with a thousand specks of white flickering across the water. I inhale the dense air – my herbs and aromatic fruit trees mixed with crisp salt – but the missing link is the sweetness from my honeybees.

I shake myself out of the sadness and absorb the music and chatter, observing the revellers in my garden. I check on my mother, who dismisses me for fussing. She has plenty of people around her ensuring she is eating and has all she could want. But I know deep down what she truly wishes for. I cannot give it to her. She won't live to see me find love, and I suspect she may have resigned herself to that; her predictions being false about Leonidas and me, despite what she heard in the hospital. She doesn't know what he is capable of.

I watch as the dancing continues and Alessandra joins, taking the floor as those around her kneel, yielding the spotlight to this accomplished stranger. She twirls and despite dancing steps that are unfamiliar to us in Petalidi, her interpretation of the traditional Greek music renders it impossible to look away. Her natural grace and elegance are magical as she unfolds her leg high in front of her, holding it aloft as she bends backwards, defying gravity and a mortal understanding of balance. Her orange hareem trousers billow with the movement and her muscles flex and tense.

I stand with Phillipo, transfixed, as the entire party appears to freeze to absorb the spectacle. Nobody here has ever seen anything like this exceptional display.

Emerging unseen by the rest of the attendees, I see Arianna creeping through the orchard, her face slowly revealed from the shadows of the fruit trees as she steps cautiously into the sunshine. Her eyes don't move from Alessandra and as the sunlight bounces off her tears, I feel her emotion across the lawn; she is moved by her mother. We all are. Alessandra is so vulnerable, in contrast to her strong and free natural demeanour; her own cheeks are wet from performing her story. As if she were dancing her last dance, pouring all she feels into each extension of an arm or foot. Even my mother wipes a tear away as Alessandra finishes and a rapturous applause breaks out. The roar from the spectators takes Alessandra by surprise as if she were in a trance, jolted from it by cheering and clapping.

Arianna slinks backwards into the shelter of the lemon trees, then spins around and runs back to her villa, wishing to remain unnoticed.

I allow myself to feel hope as I whisper a prayer to my

father. 'Please let there be reconciliation and comfort for those who seek it, *Babá*.'

The crowds gather around Alessandra to congratulate her, and I find myself alone on the sidelines, where I am used to being. A sudden movement catches my eye beside the edge of the lawn, and as I look over, my pulse begins to race.

It is Leonidas, and he is walking towards me.

# Chapter 45

## *Maria*

I immediately tense at the sight of him. Emotions ricochet throughout my body, the dominant one, anger. I don't want to make a scene on such a happy occasion, but he is not welcome in my home, not after the damage he's caused.

He reaches me, and I register anxiety on his face, which briefly causes my resentment to subside. I regret the automatic swell of affection in my heart and urge it away as hard as I can, although it is unable to be erased with a thought. But he cannot know how deep my feelings run. He doesn't deserve them.

'*Yiá sou*, Maria. Your mother looks well.'

I wince at the formality of his tone, then I remember the havoc he has wreaked. His audacity at showing up here forces my body to flush with fury.

'She is, no thanks to you. I don't know how you have the gall to show your face. You're not invited, Leonidas.

Of all the people in Petalidi, when I thought you were my only friend, it seems everyone else except *you* deserves to be here.'

I turn to leave, but he puts his hand on my arm. 'Wait! Please. You must listen to me.'

'After what's happened, how can I ever trust anything you say again? Leave me alone. Haven't you done enough?'

I snatch my arm free and march away, but Leonidas follows. I move quickly, speeding into the sanctuary of my teaching kitchen away from the crowds. Leonidas' long legs cover the same ground with one stride to my two and catches up quickly.

We reach the confines of my kitchen, my place of comfort, and I round on him, unleashing my pent-up rage. 'How *dare* you, Leonidas. How could you play with my heart, torment me with your messages, yet all the while act like my protector? You said you loved me, but it was a lie. You've made me a joke, more so than anyone else in this wretched village. How could you?!'

Tears stream out of my eyes, and I curse them for revealing the pain I'm in. Leonidas steps nearer, but I back away, raising my voice. 'Don't come any closer. I'm warning you.'

Leonidas holds up his hands. 'Maria, please, listen to me. I did not send you those messages. I only knew about them recently and I understand how hurt you must be. I was furious when I found out. But you have to believe, it wasn't me. I had nothing to do with any of it. Why would I do that to the woman I love? It makes no sense.'

His words make me falter. 'But . . . I know it's you. It *does* make sense. It was your phone the messages came from. The piles beside my beehives – you used to make such things when we were children. And all because I wouldn't marry you over thirty years ago. For Christ's sake, is your ego so inflated you still can't take that rejection? You murdered my bees and almost killed my mother!'

He is visibly pained, as if my words cause him physical wounds, but he has earnt my harsh words. He has marred me more than my accident did.

'Please, wait here . . .'

He leaves the kitchen, and I place my hands on the cold countertop, willing my gift to point me in the right direction, searching the spirit realm for a clue. But nothing is forthcoming, not even my father. I stand in the beautiful workspace I created and look around. The setting for so much love and healing has become like a cold and empty shell. There is no warmth. My honey stock depletes daily, like a drawn-out hangman's torture, chipping away until there is nothing to show for my legacy. Leonidas will find no pity or mercy in me.

As I stare at the glowing golden hues of the honey on the shelf, a queen bee darts into the kitchen and lands on top of the jars. It sits on the highest container, too far to reach. I gasp at the sight, but I have no home to offer her.

'Please, sweet queen, find a place to live. I don't have anywhere here. I've failed you. I'm sorry – forgive me,' I plead.

The queen turns her head and we survey each other for a moment. A prickle snakes its way along my spine, reaching my neck and embracing my scar, filling the Americas with her love.

I know her.

As the bee lifts upwards and out of the door, I smile. A

Greek superstition of leaving the way you came seems fitting for the cycle of a bee's life, and for what has happened to her colony. They are returned to dust from whence they rose, and she will either settle elsewhere to create another family or give up on life and die. She is a survivor, protected by an unseen force, poised to shape her own destiny.

That is who I am and what I will do.

My determination musters, weaving a spell around my heart, garnered by the power from the bee. In my mind, I cleanse the kitchen of any lingering sorrow, like I'm holding a bundle of smoking sage, sending it into each corner, extracting bad energy from the atmosphere.

As I spin back around, I see Leonidas standing in the doorway. My mental sage failed to remove him. I fix him with a steely look even though my heart sinks. I fold my arms, wishing to convey strength. But we know each other of old, I cannot conceal my heart from him. He sees me. But now, I see the real him.

'Maria, I ask for your open mind, I beg you. There is someone who wishes to speak with you. She is not perfect, but she is not her mistake.'

He steps aside and his daughter, Zoe, is revealed from her hiding place behind him. Shrunken in her teenage body, visibly quivering, her face fills with shame, her eyes cast low. I am frozen to the spot, hardly daring to breathe. Why is she here?

Leonidas nudges his daughter, who finally lifts her green eyes, filled with tears, to mine as her cheeks darken beneath her honey skin.

'I . . .' she begins, then looks to her father for reassurance and he nods his encouragement.

370

'I . . . I'm sorry, Maria.' She seems relieved as if the words had been burning a hole in her throat.

A question mark forms on my forehead.

'Go on, Zoe . . .' says Leonidas.

'I didn't mean it, but I thought I could make it better. For my *Mamá* and *Babá*. But I couldn't stop it when it started. The wind did it; it was too late.'

Fat tears plop onto the collar of her blouse, yet still I'm unclear what she is saying. Leonidas places a hand on Zoe's shoulder, which makes her start.

'Go from the beginning, *agápi mou*, my love, please, speak plainly.'

She looks up to her father, her terror obvious to see. I cannot help but feel sorry for the child and wish to ease her fears.

'Zoe, whatever it is you have to say, don't be frightened. Please, sit with me.'

She shakes her head and cowers behind her father. 'Here, perhaps some baklava will help.'

The young girl's eyes light up with temptation, but she checks herself and refuses once more. 'No thank you,' she says in a whisper.

Leonidas ushers her to a chair, his patience running out. 'Come on, be brave, Zoe, we cannot be here all day. Maria has Eleni to care for.'

At the mention of my mother, Zoe busts into noisy sobs. 'I didn't mean it. I didn't mean to hurt her as well. It all happened so quickly.' She gulps for air and I fetch her a glass of water. As I'm about to set it down, she blurts, 'I'm the one who set fire to your beehives.'

I hover the glass above the table, unable to move. I want

371

to squeeze the fragile vessel in my hands until it shatters, wanting delicate shards to pierce my skin.

'I'm sorry, I'm sorry, please don't hate me or send me to prison. I didn't mean it to happen like that. It went wrong.'

'And the rest, Zoe *mou* . . .' Leonidas says gently patting her arm.

'I sent you the messages from my old phone and made horrible things to scare you and put them in your garden. I heard my mother arguing with my father about you and she said it was your fault he left us. And then I saw you together all the time since he came back a few weeks ago, in the hardware store, on the village green, at your house. I was afraid he would leave me forever, because you'd cast a spell on him. They say in the village you're a witch.' Zoe holds her head in shame once more. 'I was scared he wouldn't want me anymore if he chose you. I thought he returned from Thessaloniki to be with us. But it was about you . . . the whole time. It was always about you.'

I stare at the plate of baklava on the table, unable to meet anyone's gaze. The silence in the kitchen hangs as heavy as a storm cloud in the mountains. I notice Zoe's fingers quivering as she pulls at the cuffs on her shirt, tugging them downwards. Leonidas reaches for his daughter's hand and squeezes it. A thousand thoughts race through my mind, but the prevailing emotion is one of pity for Zoe. The adults around her have failed, unpacking their baggage without a thought for her. Influenced by gossip and the frenzy of nonsense that filled her head had led her towards drastic action. I feel my heart pang with sorrow at how badly this child has been let down.

I set down my glass and push the plate of treats forward. She tentatively picks one up, asking permission with her eyes and I nod. As she takes a small bite, I say, 'Thank you for telling me, Zoe. That was very brave. But you know what you did was horrible. You could've killed my mother *and* your father in the fire—'

'I know, I'm sorry,' she interrupts, as if she can't stand to think of it.

'Let me finish.' I say and Zoe shrinks into silence. She closes her mouth and chews with effort, eventually managing to swallow her mouthful.

'I understand how frightening it must've seemed. Grown-ups sometimes forget about others when they think about how they are feeling, and I'm sorry you thought your *babá* didn't want you.' I lean forward and reach for Zoe's hand. 'He loves you very, very much, and would never choose anyone over you. I can promise you that.'

Zoe manages a half smile, but it disappears as she says, 'I'm so sorry about your bees. Are they all gone?'

I nod sadly. 'Yes. Although I loved them a great deal, people cannot be replaced. You are lucky it wasn't worse. But you must understand how frightened you made me with those messages, and what you left by my hives. I felt bullied, that everyone hated me. Can you imagine what it's like hearing over and over again that someone wishes you gone, or dead?'

Zoe's eyes once more fill with tears. She shakes her head again, looking pitiful, but I forge on. 'You know, when I was little and people were mean to me, the only way I felt like myself, like I could matter, was when I cooked. When

373

I moved to New York, food let me travel in time back to the few happy memories I had of home. It gave me self-worth because nobody else could do that for me. I was very lonely when I was growing up, and it's been the same since I came back to Petalidi. I've tried not to be sad or let it affect me, but to know it was a child who meant me harm almost makes it worse. You must find a way to be able to talk to people about how you feel, Zoe. If you keep it all locked up inside, that's when it comes out in bad ways.'

'I know, but my mother is so angry with my father . . . with you both. And he . . .' She looks up at Leonidas. '*Babá* seems only happy when he is with you, Maria. I don't want either of my parents to be miserable or alone. But I want them to be together, with me.'

I feel unlimited compassion for this poor girl, who starts to whimper again. She's been driven to extreme measures for attention and revenge, trying to cling on to her broken family. I clasp both her hands to distract the child's attention from her misery.

'Zoe, if you can imagine a recipe for the most delicious cake, but you forget to put any sweetness in . . .' I move to a shelf and take down a jar of honey '. . . what does it taste like?'

Zoe thinks for a moment. 'Not like a cake – it would be weird. Like bread.'

I nod. 'Right, you realise there's a missing ingredient. So, you make it again, but this time you forget the flour and baking powder, what happens then?'

She puzzles on my question before saying, 'Maybe it stays flat when it's cooked. That would be annoying.'

'Exactly. So, you make it again, but you forget something

else and then again and again. What I'm trying to say is, if there aren't all the right elements combined in the correct way, you don't get a cake, you get something nobody wants and not what you hoped for. If your parents lived together, it would be like baking with the wrong ingredients. It wouldn't work, and everyone would be unhappy. Does that make sense?'

'I think so. But . . .' Zoe looks once more to her father, who has been watching our exchange closely. 'What does that mean for me? I want you to be happy, *Babá*.'

Leonidas glances at me then back at his daughter as he says, 'Then you must accept your mother and I are better apart. But *you* are the most important person in our world. That will never change. And if, one day, I find another who will love me, you remain the centre of my universe. It is not Maria's fault I left; it is mine. She is blameless in all of this, yet she has been punished the most. I am as responsible as you, Zoe, although I am so disappointed you would be so cruel.'

'I am sorry I have let you down, *Babá*.'

'No, *I* let you down, and myself. But what you did was terrible, although I think you know that.' Leonidas says, 'Thank Maria for being so understanding.'

Zoe looks at me properly for the first time in her life without pretending to be scared, running away or for fear of catching my scar like it's a contagious disease. Her eyes travel down my neck through the Florida Keys to Hawaii. But she doesn't recoil – she sees me as I am. Not a fabled goblin or a fairy-tale monster, but as a person who never deserved unkindness or to be made to feel less than. She whispers a barely audible thank you.

'Zoe, I forgive you. There is no need to worry about the police. They think it was an accident, and we will leave it at that. But promise me one thing?'

'Anything,' Zoe replies, clearly consumed with remorse.

'Please, please be kind, as much as you can to everyone. In everything you do. And never allow yourself to feel unheard. If you're worried about something, there's always something there for you: the wind, the sea or even an insect. I used to talk to my bees about my troubles, and they listened. It made me feel better, less alone. Or I cook – that's when I feel the most alive.'

Zoe manages a small laugh. 'I'm not very good at cooking.' She looks at me beneath her fringe, which catches on her long eyelashes. 'Would you . . . could you . . . maybe . . . help me learn?'

It's like my heart could burst, affection replacing the heartbreaking sadness I'd previously felt for this poor misplaced girl.

'I would like nothing more. But only if it is agreeable to your mother. I do not want to cause any more upset in your home. Now, go, be with your friends. And please eat something before you leave!'

I push the jar of honey over to her and she takes it, hugging it closely, nodding her thanks. She leaves the kitchen with relief, almost skipping out the door to join in with the feasting on the front lawn.

Leonidas and I remain at the small table, the plate of baklava filling the air with the sweetness of honey from my dead bees. I feel their presence like tiny, winged ghosts soaring in the sucrose air. Their spirit gives me comfort. But I don't know where Leonidas and I go from here.

Whether we can climb an emotional mountain higher than the Taygetus peaks, I don't know. This summit seems insurmountable.

# Chapter 46

## *Maria*

Leonidas and I sit for what seems like an hour, yet can be only a handful of minutes, at an emotional impasse, a stalemate of the soul. Finally, he takes a deep breath, and begins to speak.

'The phone I sent you the message from, about your mother, is Zoe's. Mine was lost in the fire, as you know, so I asked Athena if she had a spare while I waited for a replacement to be delivered. She gave me one she found in Zoe's bedroom. It wasn't the glitzy everyday phone Zoe uses, so we assumed I could use it for a few days as it was wiped blank.' He hangs his head and shakes it, the shameful responsibility clearly weighing heavily upon his shoulders. 'As soon as I heard about these messages, and they'd come from that number, I suspected Athena as the culprit, but never, ever thought my child would do such a thing. Athena is horrified. Devastated. She found out the day before

I did. Zoe confessed in her journal about the fire, the messages, everything, and Athena found it.'

I allow the final piece of the terrible jigsaw to slot into place. It does explain Athena's out-of-the-blue apology to me on the village green. I am consumed with too many emotions, mainly guilt that I suspected him. I cannot believe I entertained such thoughts. Eventually, I excuse myself for fear I'll blurt out the contents of my heart. It is pounding so much it's almost causing me pain. I wish I could rip it out and stop its tyranny. I can sense he wants to talk more, but I need time to consider all that has transpired; there is too much to unpick. I stand and walk away and, knowing that I need space to process everything, he lets me go.

\* \* \*

Later that afternoon, as the final few stragglers make their way unsteadily over the lawn, we try to restore order to my garden. Alessandra and Kayla are clearing empty platters and piling them high. Phillipo is folding up tables and stacking them neatly for collection by whomever owns them another time. I didn't see Leonidas leave the party, but it's for the best. I have nothing else to say to him.

As I lift a stack of plates to take to my teaching kitchen, I overhear Kayla and Alessandra exchanging words.

'You should know better than to interfere, Kayla. Phillipo was blindsided seeing our daughter on the plane and he is very troubled by it. I am. We have enough to deal with, but now we have my volatile and unpredictable daughter in our Greek paradise. I don't know whether to thank you or throttle you.'

380

Although Alessandra's words are harsh, I sense underneath she is grateful for a final chance to try to make amends. Although so far, it isn't progressing well.

'Look, I'm sorry, but I'm not. I did it more for her than for you. I didn't get to say goodbye to my parents. Yes, the circumstances are different; they were killed in an accident. But the fact is, she now knows you're not going to be around for long and can either take the opportunity to make up or not. But at least she gets the chance. You wouldn't want to wish a lifetime of regret and guilt on her, would you?'

Alessandra sighs and turns to me. 'I like this Kayla better. She's irritating but wilful. I blame you and your food, Maria. You've transformed us all!'

I laugh at her and Kayla grins as well.

'Me?!' I say in mock outrage. 'I only showed you how to cook a few Greek things – that's all.'

'Ooh, that reminds me. I need to give you your cookbooks back,' says Kayla running off to her villa, and I take the plates into my kitchen to wash up. Alessandra follows me.

My kitchen looks like an end-of-the-night post-dinner party. Empty glasses litter the countertops and bin bags bulge with their contents. Except this has been a meal for several hundred people. Both dishwashers are on, humming away under the counter and the sink is full of soapy water, poised to make a further dent in the dirty crockery.

'Did Leonidas speak with you?' asks Alessandra.

I look up from the soap suds and hand her a wine glass to dry, eyeing her suspiciously.

'He did. Was that your doing? Again? You can't reprimand Kayla if you're guilty of the same. Twice over!'

'I know, I know,' she admits. 'I'm a hypocrite, but I wanted him to redeem himself and discover why you'd shut him out. But then he ran off. Did he explain what happened?'

I think for a moment, deciding whether to tell her, but I need to speak to someone about it. 'It was his daughter Zoe.' Alessandra looks shocked as I continue. 'The poor girl, I actually feel sorry for her, despite the fact she could've killed my mother and has destroyed my bees. I thought I'd be furious. But a child? I only feel pity. For her and for Athena. They directed their frustration at Leonidas leaving towards me. Although I'm blameless, I am to blame. He left because he loved me and has done, so he says, all this time. Since we were seventeen. Athena has always come second to me, even when I was away in America. It must have felt impossible. When I said no to his proposal, she made herself available, to lure him in. But he should never have married her. It's sad Zoe wasn't protected from her parents' battles. No child should be exposed to the ins and outs of the breakdown of a marriage.'

Alessandra puts her hands on her hips and looks at me after setting the dry glass down. 'You are the most extraordinary person I've ever met. Someone destroys part of your home and all of your bees; your mother nearly dies and you forgive them. Not only that, you feel empathy. You're a saint, Maria, quite incredible.'

'I second that!' says Kayla entering the kitchen with the pile of her cookbooks she promised to sign for me when she arrived.

I shake my head at their attempts to canonise me. 'No, I'm merely aware of the frailty of human nature. Very few people are inherently bad. There are reasons for all our actions and choices, whether they're conscious or not. Every single person who's come to my kitchen was reaching for something out of their grasp. If my food helps them come to terms with their problems or urges them to face them, I'm merely a conduit to help them on their way. It's happened with you two, but the big difference is you've both helped *me*. And I didn't know I needed help! My mother should be thanking you both. She'll be delighted to know I'm reassessing my life and what comes next – what I want and what I need . . . which aren't the same, by the way.'

Kayla and Alessandra look at each other excitedly, and Kayla jumps up and down on the spot. 'You mean you're going to tell Leonidas how you feel?'

Despite myself, I grin. 'I don't think that's what I said. But I am open to where my heart may . . . or may not lead me. And that's the last I'm going to say on the subject.'

Kayla hands me the signed books and again makes me promise not to look at them until after she leaves early tomorrow morning.

*     *     *

We charge our glasses and toast each other at the table. As the sun sets, the shadows on the lawn almost cover the dark imprints where my hives sat. I've sowed grass seed in the hope that nature will cover up the evidence of what once was there. I can't imagine being here without bees. I know I'll have more, but not yet.

I fetch some more mezze since Kayla, Alessandra and Phillipo have devoured the dishes of *spanakopita* – small

383

filo spinach and feta tartlets – marinated anchovies and gleaming purple Kalamata olives. It is heartening to see Kayla enjoying food with more pleasure.

Phillipo offers to help me in the kitchen as I decant treats into bowls, replenishing their contents. He is quiet and considered, his energy very different to Alessandra's infectious bohemian nature.

'I want to say, Maria, how grateful I am. This place, it's beautiful. We never would have found it if it weren't for you and your cooking school.' He pauses and I see the apparent emotion in his face.

'It feels like the perfect place for Alessandra to end her days. The light is magical, and there is something in the air that soothes my heart.'

His voice breaks and I reach for his hand. 'I am here for you, for both of you. You're only minutes along the seafront. If you need me, I'm there. She . . . well, you already know how special she is. I've never met anyone quite like her before.'

He chuckles a rich deep laugh. 'I know. She is unique. She is irreplaceable. For me.'

His eyes suddenly water, and a solitary tear journeys down his cheek. I cannot imagine how painful the long goodbye must be, especially since they've been together for so long. Regardless of the amount of time, love is love and it is gut-wrenching to watch the person you've chosen every day of your life be taken away, dissolving moment to moment before you.

'I'm so sorry, Phillipo. I only hope Arianna can find forgiveness in her heart, to give you the time you need as a family to come to terms with this.'

384

'I think I can,' says a husky voice from the doorway.

We both turn and see Arianna standing there, her face stained with tears.

'You can?' asks Phillipo tentatively.

She nods and walks slowly towards him. When she reaches him, she throws her arms around her father. I feel like a trespasser in my own kitchen; I shouldn't be here for this private moment. I make to move away and through the windows I see Alessandra and Kayla heading for the kitchen, holding an empty wine bottle. This will go one of two ways and I brace myself for what will unfurl.

'Oh!' both women say simultaneously as they see Arianna in her father's arms.

'Kayla, let's leave them to it.' I take her arm and start to lead her back outside.

'No, please stay,' says Arianna in her throaty rasp. 'I am grateful to you, Kayla, for bringing me here. It is a long overdue reconciliation if that's what this is. Without you, I wouldn't have this time with my parents. And Maria, you have brought us all together.'

Kayla blushes, as uncomfortable as I to be thrust in the middle of this complicated family dynamic.

Arianna turns to Alessandra and faces her head on. '*Máma*, today, I watched you dance. I haven't seen it since I was a little girl. It was funny, like there were ghosts in the air that took me back in time. The smell of lemons as I stood in Maria's orchard made me recall the parties you and *Papà* had. I would drink home-made lemonade and you and your crazy friends would dance in the garden. But today, knowing I was watching what could be your last dance, I realised what a waste of time these years have been. We missed out on so much because I was stubborn. I don't agree with what you and *Papà* do in your marriage, but you are still my mother. I've been so angry with you and with the world, it was easier to forget I had parents. I tried, but now . . . I realise, I don't want to lose you again. Not like this.'

Her voice breaks as she tries to stem her tears, but they breach her dam. Alessandra steps forward, tentatively at first, but her pent-up emotions soon rise to the surface, and she embraces her daughter for the first time in decades, perhaps longer. As they break apart, Alessandra holds Arianna's face, wiping tears away with her thumbs.

'You don't have to give another thought to our marriage. At this point in my life, it is now time for only us. Who would've thought it would take cancer for me to want something more traditional?'

Typical Alessandra, making inappropriate, factual remarks but in this moment absolutely right. It appears to be the reassurance Arianna needs. Although it will be a long way back to any semblance of a mother-daughter relationship, they have a mortal ticking clock to race against, which may accelerate their progress. I'm relieved they've begun to put aside their past and differences. Life is too short to wallow in anger and regret.

Kayla and I give them privacy and return to the garden; she can say her goodbyes later. We sit in silence, watching the navy-blue sky swallow up the burnished light of sunset, the residual colours caressing the sea. I sense Kayla doesn't wish to leave Petalidi. Not because she's afraid of what she must face at home, which has been splashed across the press online, but because for the first time in her life, she's experienced self-acceptance. Nothing gives me a greater pleasure, and although I will be sad to see her go, she needs to set off on her own journey of healing that she began here in my kitchen. Her task is to take that spirit from Greece onwards. I know she's saying goodbye in her mind; it's almost as if I can hear it. We are transfixed by the sound of the tide, the hypnotic rhythm as it gently sloshes against the shore, engrossed in our own thoughts.

Alessandra appears, her eyes bleary with tears. The three of us stand and hold hands on the lawn, a circle of friendship, the continuous shape of love, an unbreakable bond.

Kayla turns her head to me. Her emotional, freckled face looks like a porcelain doll's. 'I want to thank you both . . . for everything. I've never felt braver, like I've met myself for the first time. I didn't enjoy it at first, stripping away all the layers I'd papered over the cracks with, but it's new and exciting and I'm not afraid anymore. I've found myself and it's kind of OK being me. Finally, I think I'm growing up and leaving that poor, broken teenager behind me. I can't believe all it took was travelling to a cooking school in a tiny corner of Greece run by the most magnificent woman I have ever met. Thank you, Maria.'

She turns to look at Alessandra. 'And you . . . I know I'm a writer by trade, but I don't think there's a word for you. Exceptional, maddening, spectacular . . . I love you, my fabulous friend.'

We laugh and move to hold each other as the wind whirls around, weaving an invisible thread of magic that will bind us together forever.

I am moved by Kayla's words. It is more than I could've wished or hoped for her. She's a fearless warrior and already was but needed to discover it for herself. Now she has, my heart is overflowing with pride on her behalf.

I break our embrace, smiling with elation at how far Kayla has travelled within herself. 'Watch out, world, and get ready, the real Kayla Moss is coming!'

# Chapter 47

*Maria*

When my mother and I next go into the village, the journey is decidedly different to those we've taken together in the past. My mother insisted on walking to church, refusing to be treated like an invalid. Her sharp tongue hasn't dulled in her illness, though she has a slightly gentler air about her.

Usually, politeness prevailed for *Mamá*'s sake, people eyeing me with quiet suspicion or performing covert crossing of their chests out of view, but this morning, various enquiries interrupt our walk:

'You must give me the recipe for your Easter cake, Maria. It is unlike anything I've tasted.'

'My brother wishes to learn to cook. Now his wife has left him, he is bereft. Perhaps he can enrol in your school. He may even be a good match for you . . .'

'I cannot seem to get my filo pastry right and my husband will regret marrying me if I cannot make him the perfect *kreatópita*, meat pie . . . please help me, Maria, you're my only hope.'

*Goodness, how people change*, I think to myself.

Father Kyriakidis' sermon is about renewed beginnings, riffing on his post-Easter theme about new life, second chances and fresh starts. When he gives thanks for my mother, he shouts 'Eleni' triumphantly and wild applause breaks out, much to my mother's delight. The usual reserve of the village is gone, eroded by some invisible force.

Across the pews, I catch Zoe's eye and nod with a smile. Athena looks terrified, but I send warmth over to her and all those in the church. I am trying not to judge, since I'm already in the house of ultimate judgement. The knowledge of what Zoe has done is warning enough to Leonidas and Athena to be kinder to one another and put their daughter first.

As our reliable priest says:

'We are not our pasts, nor our mistakes, but who we prove ourselves to be in the eyes of God.'

*She is not her mistake.*

The words Leonidas uttered pre-empting Zoe's confession return to me, as he revealed his daughter as the culprit. He had begged with his kind honey-coloured eyes for my forgiveness, and he has it. His expression in that moment haunts me. I wish I had been braver and spoken my truth. But I missed my chance with him, again, like history repeating itself. Because I admit I am afraid. I can give love, but I'm terrified to accept it, petrified of what could happen if I am rejected once more. My heart was brimming with such agony as I faced Leonidas in the kitchen. Like a barrier braced against a fierce-flowing torrent of water, pressurising the blockade to yield. But I mustn't let it burst through. I won't. Today is about healing. I have always belonged in Petalidi, but now, for the first time, I am accepted.

After the service, I stand patiently with *Mamá*, who chatters away to her captive audience. The sea calls to me and I deposit her on a bench and move to the water's edge. This beach marks another moment I could have chosen Leonidas and shifted the sands of time. But instead, his daughter's plan prevented it. Zoe's scheme did work in one way. I never had the chance to reveal how I feel and now never will.

I watch a fishing boat head for the harbour. The village cats know there will be juicy fresh morsels for them, and they creep forwards, furry necks craning to see the catch on deck. As the fisherman guts his spoils for customers, he throws the innards to the feline spectators, who hiss and fiercely guard their easily procured lunch. I walk over to buy prawns for shrimp *saganaki*. I'll also make a beetroot and feta salad, my mother's favourite.

As I return to the village green, I catch the end of *Mamá*'s conversation with her friends.

'She is such a good girl, looking after me as she does. And I am glad others have come around to the same view. My daughter has cared for this village for so many years. I am glad people are finally realising what she gives us all.'

I stop still, unable to move, shocked at my mother's public praise. Her friends all nod and enthusiastically agree, claiming always to have admired my food. The words my mother has been unable to say directly to me, the validation I'd always hoped to hear from her are being sown on the village green like cornflower seeds.

Father Kyriakidis is correct, having shared his reliable wisdom in his sermon.

*'Out of tragedy there is a new beginning, better than one could ever have imagined before; from the darkness there will always be light.'*

\* \* \*

I make lunch in the main kitchen of the house, not in my cooking school. All traces of the fire are gone from inside, cleaned away and covered over. It has that fresh-paint, new-house smell, save for the delicious flavours wafting around from the stove. It's almost as if the fire never happened. But it did. I am reminded of the damage every evening at sunset when I used to speak with my bees, but now cannot. I find myself whispering to their spirits on the wind, as if they still surround me, and they do; in the earth and hovering invisibly in the sky. I only wish I had their company. I miss them horribly.

Despite the turnaround in the village, I still feel isolated, but perhaps it is partly my own doing, having had to fend for myself over the years, carving out a solo path. Forgoing friendships because none were forthcoming, the offer wasn't there. Now, there is potential, and I surprise myself by wishing for companionship. The void my bees left needs to be filled with a meaningful connection.

I serve our simple lunch in earthenware bowls, and the scent of ouzo-rich tomato *saganaki* sauce hosting the freshly caught shrimp lures my mother to the terrace table. All of that praying and chattering in church has worked up a considerable appetite for us both. I notice

392

the beginnings of grapes forming on the vine beside the pergola. Only one of the vines survived the fire. The leafy overhang that was covered by the plants is now exposed and the wooden surround looks strange. I'd been so used to seeing their bright foliage. Yet another natural bounty destroyed. I used the leaves for stuffing with flavoured rice, making *dolmades*, and the grapes were bountiful to make wine. Now there would be barely enough for a glassful – and besides, the smoke would've ruined the fruit, so there is no point trying. But the rudely formed nubs will ripen again. Another reminder of the passing of time and how nature unrepentantly continues.

'This is very good, *ángelé mou*,' says *Mamá*. Her voice remains a little hoarse from smoke inhalation, and the fact that she has been talking constantly since leaving hospital. Compliments are so rare from my mother that I accidentally drop my fork in a clatter on the table.

'Thank you, *Mamá*. The shrimps are straight from the boat this morning.'

'I saw you buy them . . .'

It's clear she has something to say and I tense in anticipation, imagining what it could be. How the sauce could be improved, my hair ought to be shorter or perhaps Leonidas . . . I watch my mother from beneath my eyelashes, waiting. Eventually, Mother speaks.

'When your father came to me in the hospital and sat by my bedside . . .'

I nod, holding my breath.

'He told me I was not ready, there was still a part of life outstanding that I must return to oversee.'

My heart sinks. She is going to start about me finding

393

a man. It's what she longs for, lives for, to see me settled and in love. I grip my fork to prevent it falling again, willing my frustration not to appear in a temper.

'*Mamá*, I . . .' I begin, wishing to see off the pending subject.

'No, Maria, you must listen. Your *babá* told me I must speak with you, to resolve our problem.'

'There is no problem, *Mamá*. All is well, I assure you.'

'It is *my* problem, Maria *mou*. I must say to you what I've been unable to. All that occurred this Easter time has taught even me a lesson. One is never too old to change. So, I must say to you I am sorry. I am sorry for keeping my gift from you, I am sorry for always being critical of you, when I am so proud, incredibly proud at how brave you are – fearless, in fact. You didn't care what people thought of you and you were always true to yourself.

'I could never be that strong. I am ashamed to be swayed by what everyone may think, scared of them judging me. But you, my bold little daughter, were free from the moment you were born. I saw it in your eyes. I was even frightened by your will. I envied it, because that strength evaded me; it always has. So, I masked my own fears by criticising you. Your father recognised your spirit, though, and embraced it. He encouraged you to chase your dreams, to never be stuck in a small village. Yes, I loved him deeply, but I was angry with him. You see, I wished to protect you against everyone, and I could only do that if you were near. But you were such an old soul, you knew in your heart if you were true to yourself, all would become right eventually. I wish I had even a teaspoon of your courage.'

I gently place my cutlery down with shaking hands, unable to believe what I'm hearing as my mother takes a sip of wine before speaking again.

'I owe you a great debt for how you cared for me over the years, and what you do for those you teach and for this village. Without you there would be no visitors here. If you hadn't returned to Petalidi there would be only terrible food at all the feasts. If you weren't here . . . I would be alone.' She reaches for my hand and looks me in the eye. 'I am sorry. Know that I love you and I am proud of you. My beautiful, brilliant daughter, Maria. I'm just sorry it has taken me my whole life to say it.'

If a gust of wind had travelled down the mountains in that moment, it would've scooped me up and dropped me out at sea. My mother has never told me such things, let alone apologised for her jibes. To hear her say I am beautiful isn't about vain validation, it is about acceptance. My prayers have finally been answered. All the incantations to my bees, the blessings I whispered over the food I made with their honey have been heard. Relief washes my body clean of the feeling that I was never good enough for her. I return the squeeze on my mother's hand, managing to quell the catch in my throat.

'*Mamá*, all I ever wish for is to make you proud and do the right thing. I am glad *Babá* sent you back. I was not ready to let you go.'

*Mamá* sniffs and returns to her food. 'It would have been a very sorry way to exit this world. All those flames and drama. I would've walked the earth for a thousand years, angry about it. I am grateful to you and to Leonidas for saving me.'

My happiness subsides at the mention of his name. 'Neither of us did that, *Mamá*. You saved yourself.'

'Well, we will see. I may have been wrong about him for you. Perhaps I've become confused in my old age about how to interpret the signs. You see! I can say I'm wrong . . . It must be the medicine the doctors gave me.'

Her eyes twinkle with mischief and we laugh, returning to our food to dine with unbridled joy. It has never tasted so good.

# Chapter 48

## *Maria*

Dearest Maria,

   How are you? I miss you and Alessandra so much already. Attached is my article in all its monstrous glory . . . What have I done?! Things at home are the best version of good, Daniel has moved out but is still close by and the great news is we've agreed to share custody. Rosie is happy and enjoying the novelty of separate sleepovers so far . . . Also, our annoying neighbours, Eve and Stephen Houseby, I told you about, are moving away, which is a great relief. They'll begin anew somewhere else and continue to lie to each other and the world, pretending everything is perfect.

   That's not for me anymore. I feel like I've got my life back and it's thanks to you and Alessandra. Please send her my love, and I'll be out to see you soon, I promise. By the way, I'm planning on pitching a

cooking series on YOU! More to come, speak soon.
KM xx

*   *   *

*Attachment*: A Grecian Odyssey by Kayla Moss

*We all have secrets we hide from each other and from ourselves. But there comes a time when the strength to carry a heavy suitcase laden with demons fails. And I cannot bear its load anymore. It is time for me to unpack my suitcase.*

*When I travelled to a cooking school in Petalidi, little did I know how I would change. The place, culture and a spectacular woman called Maria Leventi worked their magic and transformed me. Maria cooks like a goddess and dispenses wisdom as freely as she dishes out the most incredible Greek food. My trip which began as a work assignment became an unexpected journey of self-discovery. I will never be the same and I will be eternally grateful.*

*I have bulimia and anorexia. I've gone to battle with food since I was a teenager and have hurt myself and those I love in the process. You may ask how I can have such a disordered relationship with food, yet make it a career. But that's the somewhat misguided point. I thought if I could control food, it couldn't possibly be my enemy. But it was and still is. The irony is, I adore cooking and I crave trying new foods. Home-Grown Chef isn't my job, it's my passion. Such is the contrary nature of having an eating disorder. I cannot explain it away; it makes no sense, but it's poisoned every aspect of my life, and it's time for me to confront it. Part one is to say it out loud. I can no longer hide. Here I am, for the first time saying to you all: this is me.*

*There are over a million people with an eating disorder in the UK, which means there are millions of parents, wives, husbands, friends and siblings watching helplessly as someone they love dismantles themselves. It isn't vanity, it's not about being skinny and it isn't just women; it's a way to try and alter the way you feel about yourself from within. Mine began in reaction to both my parents being killed when I was fourteen. I was plagued with guilt. The only thing I could control was what I ate. When everything around me was overwhelming and out of my hands, I could decide what I put – or didn't put – into my body each day. I've spent years abusing laxatives, my precious powders I carried everywhere, purging what I ate, making myself sick or starving for days.*

*The most freeing part of writing this confession is knowing my pain might help someone. If it helps shine a light or bring some comfort, then it is worth it. To expose myself to ridicule and more scrutiny seems like another way to invite harm, but I need to force a change in my life.*

*Maria's Kitchen in Petalidi taught me how to welcome food into my heart. Maria is by no means running a treatment centre, but, as you may have* read, there was a terrible fire during the Greek Easter period in which she almost lost her mother, and I learnt the most valuable lessons from her. She continued to care for everyone she encountered during those darkest days. She is inspirational, the most gifted cook and one of the most exceptional human beings to walk this planet. She taught me the value of selfless kindness, forgiveness and the preciousness of second chances. Everyone deserves another attempt at life if they get it wrong on the first go. As we cooked together, my mask slowly disintegrated, until I could no longer conceal what I was hiding. In some ways I didn't want to; I longed to be found out, to be held accountable for my illness. Maria gave me the strength to take the reins of what comes next for me, which begins with telling you my truth. I also met another extraordinary woman in Greece, Alessandra. From her I learnt the importance of not judging others, because you never know what goes on behind closed doors, what pain people carry with them out of sight. I have made two friends whose love saw me through the first part of my metamorphosis, and I know their friendship will encourage me onwards.

I urge anyone with a love of food to discover Maria's Kitchen, if not for the glorious Grecian seaside haven, then for the honey-roasted feta or vanilla biscuits Maria makes. Your taste buds will never be the same again! She is a magician with food, and instinctively knows how to open your mind with flavour. It is an otherworldly gift, and she's changed *thousands of people's lives in the ten years she's run her cooking school. Mine is altered forever.*

*I'm sorry if I've misled you about who I really am, but I intend to do better. I love food so much; only how I make sense of the world when nobody is looking will lead you towards the opposite conclusion. But I assure you, it's not. I won't be appearing on the new season of Home-Grown Chef, but I will be back in the future. For now, I need to be a present mother and co-parent my daughter with Daniel as we navigate an unexpected path. But we're committed to making our separation seamless for Rosie. To do that, I have to get well.*

*I hope you understand and can forgive me, as I am trying to understand and forgive myself.*

\*　\*　\*

'Wow!' says Alessandra as she puts my phone down, having finished reading Kayla's article, which will be published tomorrow. Both Alessandra's and my eyes water at the bravery and honesty of Kayla's confession. Not only for the compliments, but the fact she's taken charge, making the time to focus on herself and her family.

'I know,' I reply. 'She astounds me. That uptight little redhead who pitched up here ended up fiercer than any of the Greek gods. We did good, right?'

'*Certo*, certainly,' says Alessandra. 'I'm glad we all met. It's like I can't remember a time without you both. I hope she comes back soon . . . I want to see her again before . . .'

I take her hand. 'I know.'

'I have much to thank Kayla for. Arianna is here and, although it's not straightforward, I have my daughter back. She gave me that and so much more.'

I smile, remembering how hostile Kayla was towards Alessandra initially. 'And you gave her your own gifts. You encouraged her out of her shell, to be bold and she navigated a small-minded judgement that can plague us all.'

Alessandra shrugs, dismissing the compliment, changing the subject. 'Will you cook with us this evening, Maria? I want Arianna and Phillipo to make a meal together.'

'I couldn't think of anything I want more. Why don't you all come here? I don't want to leave my mother on her own for too long,' I reply knowing how it will bring the family together on neutral ground.

Alessandra nods and our plan is settled. I begin to dream up a magical menu to create with them. My neck prickles with a hundred ideas as recipes and ingredients collide in my mind before settling and deciding. It is perfect, a celebration for us all. We have much to be thankful for.

*　　*　　*

The lamb chops are marinating in the fridge, coated with lemon zest, mustard, olive oil and oregano. I watch Arianna, Alessandra and Phillipo tentatively shift as their emotions dance between their difficult past and their unexpected now. Awkward silences transform into heartfelt recollections, years of news, people, and places. I remain quiet save for dishing out cooking instructions, quietly observing this family piecing itself back together. Phillipo and Arianna have much in common, his daughter having dabbled with photography before turning her hand to painting. They make plans for her return trip to photograph some of the ancient relics at the Palace of Nestor, discuss a visit to Epidaurus to see the world-famous amphitheatre.

I watch as they make our food. Alessandra vigorously grates cucumber for *tzatziki*, Arianna diligently trims the succulent green beans to sit in a tomato and potato sauce for *fasolakia*, and Phillipo seems at home in a kitchen, overseeing the tenderising of the octopus, which is headed for the barbecue. It is boiling in a spiced mix with water and vinegar, the smell of bay leaves and thyme float around the kitchen. I see Phillipo and Arianna exchange looks as they giggle at Alessandra's expansive gestures, reminiscent of my *babá* and me in their dynamic. His badger stripe through his jet-black hair catches the setting sunshine streaming through the windows. Alessandra and her daughter share shy smiles and recall tender moments from Arianna's childhood.

Whatever stars aligned to bring this family back together feels like it is meant to be. Yes, Kayla intervened and hurried along the reunion, but it could've gone horribly wrong. The fact it happened in Petalidi, away from their painful memories has permitted them to reconnect in a special space; to correct mistakes, begin to heal their wounds ahead of the ultimate injury of death, which is inevitably heading their way. I commit the moment to memory almost on their behalf.

Kayla generously offered to fund Arianna's toing and froing from Rome so she could spend as much time with her mother as possible. It is a touching gesture and part of her own healing, although Alessandra refused her money. It's a reminder of how far they have come on their journey to reach friendship. I spoke to Kayla earlier and even though she sounded wobbly ahead of her article coming out tomorrow, I'm relieved she and Daniel are forgoing any legal wrangling over Rosie. It's one more obstacle out of her way as she travels onwards towards her peace. The Kayla Moss recipe books are back on the shelf in my kitchen with her hand-signed words sitting within the pages. She wrote:

> My magical honeybee goddess, Maria, the original Home-Grown Chef. I am transformed because of your gifted cooking and your immense talent. You are a flavour alchemist, weaving spices and herbs in the most elegant way. And you are changing lives through your food. You have helped me to heal, and I will treasure your friendship, always. My sweet bee woman, Mélissa, I adore you.
> Kayla xx

I cried when I saw the inscription and wished I could have read it to my bees, to hear their hum of appreciation. She used the Greek translation of honeybee: *Mélissa* and made it beautiful, not knowing what I used to be called in the village. I wish I still had bees to take ownership of that name and exist within its power.

My magical insects helped me heal people, their golden

nectar conjured up memories to comfort hearts and yield strength to unveil what was sought. My limited supply of jars is diminishing. With each pot of honey I use, I am closer to the moment when I'll have nothing to show for them. I know it sounds ridiculous, but they were mine, like the children I never got to have. I watched them hatch from eggs, loved and cared for every single one. And now they're gone.

Phillipo heads outside to light the barbecue as the octopus cools in its cooking liquid before being soaked in a balsamic, caper and garlic marinade ready for charring on the grill. Arianna goes with him, and I hear their laughing through the windows. Alessandra, despite her joy, looks tired, wrung dry by the recent upheaval following Arianna's arrival. I pour her a glass of wine, which she gratefully accepts.

'How does it feel having her here?' I ask.

Alessandra thinks about my question taking a swig of her wine.

'Hard and wonderful. We still have cross words and I suspect always will, but then it's replaced by a happiness as we learn to love each other again. I hope it's enough for her and for me when it's time to say goodbye.'

Her voice snags, so unlike the unemotional woman from Rome who arrived here. Arianna's appearance along with Phillipo's is a reminder of her finite time. *I* don't want to lose her having only just found her, so cannot imagine how her family feel. But it's the best version of the end I could envisage for Alessandra; to have two people who love her instinctively holding her hand until it is over. I clink my glass to hers. There's no need for words. It is tragic for a terminal illness to be the reason for such a vital reminder; to ensure those you love know how you feel. An urgent sadness wraps itself around my heart and the back of my neck tingles as Alessandra's husband appears.

'Maria, could you come outside for a moment?' asks Phillipo.

I nod and put my wine glass on the counter as Alessandra puts her arms around Phillipo's neck and nuzzles him with such affection, like she is making every kiss count.

Outside Arianna is raking the flaming coals on the grill and nods towards the grass, grinning. I frown and turn my head to see Leonidas standing in the middle of my lawn. Nerves instantly appear as butterfly wings, beating around my stomach. I'm unable to move for a moment. He looks so beautiful against the backdrop of the sea. The lush vibrant colours of the undamaged foliage heighten his skin and frame him like a painting. He's holding a large box in front of him, which piques my interest.

'*Yiá sou*, Leonidas, *ti káneis?*' I don't know what to say to him other than hello and ask if he's well. My pulse is drumming so hard, I am sure he can hear it.

'*Nai*, yes, Maria, *kalá*, I am very well,' he replies formally. I know he wants to say more, but I'm not sure I can hear it.

'What's that?' I ask, looking at the box, seeking any distraction outside of my swirling mind.

I feel my scar tickle around Cape Cod to Vermont. I wish I'd worn a scarf, but perhaps it's time to stop hiding, to follow my own sage advice I'd given Kayla. What am

I ashamed of? My scar is part of me and unchangeable and I should show the pride I have in my battle wound; it represents my achievements, my failings and how far I've come since my accident. And it inspires me onwards to where I will go next.

'This is something for you. Zoe helped me in my workshop. It is not much, but it was her idea, to help make amends.'

He kneels on the grass, and I crouch down beside him. We look into each other's eyes. The gold flecks around his pupils sparkle with mischief and something else that I am too afraid to acknowledge.

'Here,' he says.

He pushes the box towards me and, with a questioning look, I begin to unwrap it. As I tear a strip from the top, I see a sliver of a mahogany varnish, then as I rip the rest, a flat piece of wood glints in the sunshine. A piece of protective plastic is wrapped around something protruding from the middle and I unpeel it, winding circles of the synthetic material until the sight of what it masked makes me gasp. The most perfect oversized honeybee is sitting on a large flower, both carved in the same wood, to be used as a handle. It is stunning in its detail, tapered legs, veined wings, looking as if it had just landed to take a rest before suckling pollen.

'Leonidas . . . I . . . it's beautiful . . .'

'There is more,' he says, grinning broadly, and I continue to dismantle the package at his encouragement. The cardboard comes off in clumsy pieces and I'm making frustratingly slow progress, although I'm enjoying the tantalising glimpses of what it might be.

I sit back on my heels and look at what is before me. A perfect upright rectangle, a line of carved dancing honeybees forming a chain underneath the overhanging lip. One of the four sides is Perspex to be able to observe what I hope and pray will eventually take up residence inside, filling the honeycomb-shaped plastic hexagons with heavenly syrup. He has fixed a tap mechanism to it, so a simple turn of the faucet will yield honey without disturbing the insects, should they arrive. The other three sides are covered in exquisite depictions of flowers and more bees in relief and some engraved into the wood.

Leonidas has made me a beehive.

'I don't know what to say . . . Leonidas, it is the most beautiful thing I've ever seen.' I run my hands over the smoothness, which he has made with such craft and care. I want to hug it to my heart. I turn to face him. 'Thank you. I'm speechless . . .'

He lifts the lid and says, 'One last surprise, look.'

Inside the lid is carved handwriting:

*'Glykiá mélissa, me olo sou to einai na petaxeis'*

I burst into tears as I run my finger over the inscription.

'Sweet honeybee, gather your spirit to fly . . . it's my poem! Leonidas, this is the most incredible thing anyone has ever done for me.'

I push the hive across the lawn to nestle in one of the blackened patches where an old one once stood. I throw my arms around his neck to embrace him, standing on tiptoes, suddenly aware of how small I am in his arms and how close my lips are to his skin. It feels like the only place on earth I wish to be and I inhale his familiar smell

408

of sandalwood, salt and sawdust. I suddenly realise, it is the scent and the flavour of love.

I pull away, embarrassed, wiping away droplets of tears. 'Please thank Zoe for me. It's a lovely gesture,' I manage.

'It is the least you deserve for all you give this village and for what my family has done to you.'

His eyes cloud with shame, and I reach for his hand to reassure him of my forgiveness. I look down at his callused workman's fingers, tracing his palm. I turn his large hand over and see his knuckles are covered in terrible burns from when he tried to save my mother in the fire. Barely faded blisters, the light pink skin is still raw, glowing brightly against his dark colouring.

'Maria,' he begins, and I look up at him, 'all of us have our scars; some are invisible to the outside world. Mine live mostly in my heart. Yet these remind me of how helpless I felt, unable to find my way out of the flames with your mother. I thought I would never see your sweet face again. But if I had died in that moment, I was glad you knew I loved you.'

He lifts his scarred hand to my cheek, grazing the bumpy skin against my smooth face, gently tracing his damaged knuckles down to my chin, his gaze not leaving mine for a moment as he reaches my neck. He continues downwards with his caress and as his scars meet mine, our wounds intertwine like an exquisite trail of jasmine wrapping itself around a willow archway. His hand rests on my collarbone as he stares at me and I daren't breathe.

'Maria, you are beautiful despite your scars and because of them. I cannot imagine my life without you.'

I turn to look at the hive, as he drops his hand away

from my skin. The transparent window is perfectly clear, and I rest my palm on the lid as I would if the hives were full, asking for guidance and reassurance, seeking inspiration. But this one is empty and I long to hear the comforting hum of the colony. I close my eyes and search the spirit realm for help. There is little point looking to my heart for answers; I already know its most secret wish and yet still my head overrules it, reluctant to concede to its truth.

As my eyes open and focus on the smooth, gleaming wood, a small bee suddenly lands on top of the hive. And in that moment, I know. The wind gusts and I almost hear the whispers of spirits on the wind. I don't need them to help me decide. The bee is the reassurance I seek, the sign I need.

'Leonidas,' I say breathlessly, nodding at the insect. 'It's a scout bee. It must be from a swarm searching for a place to settle. It could be some of *my* bees.'

I'm overwhelmed at the thought of having my beloved winged children return home; the prospect is thrilling.

'But it's only one, Maria – it isn't enough.'

I slowly turn to look at him. As I do so, the feelings I've held within for so many years, so tightly wound, tentatively begin to unravel.

'But it's a start, isn't it? A new one, at least.'

He smiles at me with such warmth that I long to fold into his body, for him to wrap me in his beautiful bear hug of ultimate safety. Our faces are so close I can see my reflection in his eyes and for the first time in forever, I permit my soul to see myself as he sees me.

Exactly as I am. Flawed, but beautiful; marked, but perfect.

410

I take a breath and look towards the house and feel the pang of history. The meadows that once were here, all that has gone before and all that is yet to come. I see the figure of my father walking through the olive grove and towards the annexe. He beams at me as he goes, a big, broad grin, and my heart fills with joy that he sees me.

'*I did it, Babá!*' I say in my mind's eye, and I hear him say in reply, '*You did, and you were always going to, my brave Maria.*'

He's still wearing the same suit and the courage of his conviction, risking my mother's wrath, amuses me. I feel the love from him float upon the breeze towards me and the swell of feeling from Leonidas begins to invade my body, taking it over like an ethereal being. I nod at my *babá* and say goodbye once more with my heart and mind. I won't see him again – it is time for him to rest – but I know he will always be with me. He may be the last spirit I ever see, but I trust in my instinct and in my heart, what it holds.

As Leonidas and I stand in the ashes of what remains, it is time for me to finally share my response to his declaration on the beach before the fire.

I smile as the door to my heart slowly opens, never to be closed again.

I allow Leonidas, my childhood friend, to step across the threshold and inhabit the space that is and always was destined to be his.

*The old queen bee watches the incumbent take up her new position as the bees swarm towards the lawn. The next ruler was already prepared in anticipation of the fire and she relinquishes her crown to her daughter. The former queen is an old soul and had lived a thousand times before; she'd foreseen what would come.*

*Now it's time for the next generation.*

*The old lady at the window watches her daughter permit her heart's truth to sail outwards onto the wind, opening like a lotus flower. She sees Maria reach for Leonidas' hands, feeling the swell of an ancient, destined love across the distance. Eleni smiles and nods to herself, knowing Maria's heart can and will receive love. Her prediction was correct. She walks to the sideboard to collect the photograph of her dead husband, as the bee watches. Eleni stands still, considering his image for a while before saying, 'It is done.'*

*The old queen bee uses her last reserves of energy to follow the old lady into the bedroom, landing silently and unseen on the side table. They have both nurtured and loved, preparing the way for what will continue, the inevitable circle of life.*

*Eleni climbs onto her bed and lies down, holding her husband's picture to her heart, smiling, as his figure takes his place beside her, and their hands join.*

*The old queen and the mother both close their eyes,*

*yielding their hearts and minds to succession. Their families will go forth and flourish; their work on earth is complete.*

*The moment of finality is welcome as the ultimate peace descends.*

*All is well now. Gather your spirit to fly . . . It is time for them both to go.*

# Acknowledgements

Firstly, I want to thank YOU so much for reading my book. Stepping into this new world of authordom has been nerve-wracking and it simply wouldn't be possible without the incredible readers and book bloggers. The messages I received about my first novel, *One Last Letter from Greece*, spurred me onwards while I was writing this one and I am grateful beyond measure. I spent most of 2022 weeping tears of gratitude and joy.

This story is about love, self-acceptance, and survival but most of all is about sisterhood and friendship. I feel incredibly blessed to have found precisely that within the online writing community. Established authors have reached out with words of wisdom, and championed my writing and offered quotes. It is generous, selfless and inspiring to discover a world where women truly do support other women. Thank you to Santa Montefiore, Liz Kessler, Fern Britton, Helen Fields, Jo Thomas, Sue Moorcroft, Phillipa Ashley, Rosanna Ley, Caroline Corcoran,

Laura Jane Williams, Tessa Harris, Jeffrey Archer (an honorary sister!), Melanie Hewitt, Caroline Khoury to name a splendid handful. And Adriana Trigiani, your writing inspired me decades ago and your friendship gives me the love to carry on in this endeavour. Your support and shrimp sauce are both incomparable. And to my coffee/grilled cheese sandwich buddy, Liz Fenwick . . . you are the epitome of paying it forward and have made me feel less alone and marginally less crackers throughout this process! The RNA has created a world of support where we are all in this together.

The HarperCollins, Avon team – you are exceptional! My editor, Thorne Ryan, you are fabulous, having expertly guided me through my second novel, assuaging my anxiety with such love for my storytelling, even at 2 a.m. on email. Go to sleep, and I will miss you! Thank you, Sammy, Maddie, Ella, Gaby, Helen Huthwaite and every single person at Avon, your passion lives within every page.

Kate Burke, my agent . . . for goodness' sake, where do I begin? You truly are my spirit animal, you make me laugh more than should be permissible and you believe in me. Your friendship and professional guidance and karaoke song advice are more than I could wish for. Thank you to all at Blake Friedmann, especially James Pusey for brilliantly flogging my books overseas.

My version of Greece is a love letter and tribute to the culture and country that occupies a precious part of my heart. I may have tinkered with the geography but every corner of Greece – imagined or otherwise – is filled with my deepest affection. My Greek experience is all the richer for the special friends and immensely talented cooks I've met over the years. Thank you to Vasilis Balafoutis for allowing me to borrow your surname; Sophia who runs Vergos, the greatest grill house in the world; Christina, Yiula, Honey, Athena, everyone at Kafenion Akti for the greatest chicken souvlaki known to mankind; Kochili, for introducing me to portokalopita; and Wendy on Hydra, representing Croydon on that magical outcrop along with Zeus and Fiona – the fabulous gang at the Pirate Bar. I will set a book on Hydra in the future, which means I'm coming back, but Greek Easter on the island was like nothing I've ever seen and inspired me to write it into this one. Thank you so much to my fabulous reader, Jenny Kyriakidi, for brilliantly and kindly Greek-checking the book for me!

My friends and family are unswervingly supportive, and I love you all so much, I could burst. Impossible to name you all, but last year was a lot and would have been darker without you all. Alex Burnell and Erika Farwell, you are the richest sources of inspiration, fearless fabulous warrior women who give unlimited love and friendship and I adore you both more than I could ever say or write.

Alessandra's journey became too close to home to write as I navigated my husband's cancer diagnosis while I was already in the thick of this novel. It was devastating, but we thankfully got through it. And as Maria discovers in this book, when the chips are down, your own community rallies. The messages of support gave us strength to forge onwards. So . . . Thank you to Brittany, Leonidas, Nikos & Benny; Nick Burnell – we miss you, our dear dancing chum; Dani Southwood, Ads, Ollie the owl and Lady Sibs; the Mosses Kay, Alan, Jamie, Soph & Lee, Attie & Abe

Grumett; Emma Barton, my sister from another – goodnight! Jane & Len, my most excellent cousins and their thousands of wondrous grown-up babies; Louis Walsh; Jossy, Lucy & Phoenix; Kasia and Patch, and Indy Eleanora – team Methoni forever! Mickey Spaghetti Dalton; my fabulous and highly amusing Daddy Bear Lloyd for always believing in me; my less amusing brother in law Nicholas; Katie, Georgia and my Slinky Blanket band mate Harrison – the first album will come eventually! Paddy, Tiffany & my love bugs Tristan and Patrick; Chantelle and Juno, and the Lewis fam for being exceptional neighbours; Claire and Tony Hawke; the Liasi Family for my first experience of Greek hospitaity; Marie and John; Barbara 'Baba' Hutton and all the Webbers; Graham Rebak and Adam Disney Prince Wilkie; Sarah Gorrell; Uhtred son of Uhtred Lord Neil of Wigan & David Ridgeroo and ten wasps on the bed; Sarah and Dick Stephens and my sweet Nancy Noodle; Papoushka Gerald Cowell, my angel fur baby; Lewis Coles; Matt and Bambi; Liz and Laura; dearest Simon, Lauren and Eric; John & Alex; June; Luke, Claudia and the babies; David, Jenny, Dylan and Darcy. My dearest Mum, I miss you, but you're part of every word I write. Huge thanks to Nick Garner and Lucy for helping to offset my consumption of Greek cake, rosé and gyros.

And the most special thank you to Nicholas Munro for being an exceptional and straight-talking consultant, guiding us along a terrifying path. For enjoying our double act during chemotherapy and, above all, for saving my husband's life.

Which finally brings me to my Tony. You are my rock, anchor and biggest cheerleader, encouraging me to write

– and occasionally plot! Absolutely none of this would be happening without you and your belief in me. Thank you for making me laugh and dance, for letting me win at Backgammon and for holding my hand and heart so tightly regardless of what life throws at us. Your edits are (annoyingly) spot on, our plot walks invaluable, but most of all, I feel your love in every moment we share. Through our dreams, our hopes and our challenges, we are an incredible team. I am beyond lucky, and I love you, TC.

Will walking in her mother's footsteps help Sophie
discover who she was meant to be all along . . . ?

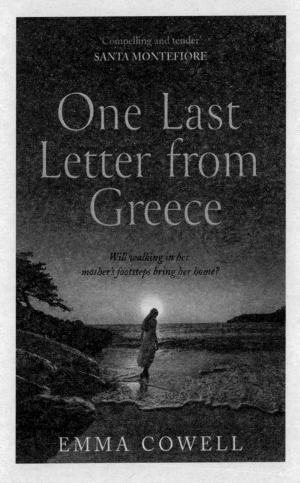

'Compelling and tender'
SANTA MONTEFIORE

One Last
Letter from
Greece

*Will walking in her
mother's footsteps bring her home?*

EMMA COWELL

The breathtaking, escapist debut novel from Emma Cowell.

Fern Britton Picks

Exclusively for TESCO

**EXCLUSIVE ADDITIONAL CONTENT**

Includes exclusive author content and details
of how to get involved in *Fern's Picks*

**Dear lovely readers,**

I'm delighted to introduce you to our next book club pick, *The House in the Olive Grove*, this summer's breathtaking, escapist read!

Set by the sapphire water and golden sands of the Grecian village of Petalidi, we get to know food journalist Kayla and jewellery-maker Alessandra as they visit the village to attend chef Maria's successful cooking school at her house in the olive grove. But it soon becomes clear that all three women have painful secrets from their past and their present that they are trying to run from. Will they find the strength to face these?

*The House in the Olive Grove* is a gorgeous, tender story of the power of female friendship and self-discovery. I can't wait to hear what you think!

with love
Femp x

Fern
Britton
Picks
Exclusively for
TESCO

Look out for more books, coming soon!

For more information on the book club,
exclusive author content and reading
group questions, visit Fern's website
**www.fern-britton.com/fernspicks**

We'd love you to join in the conversation,
so don't forget to share your thoughts using
**#FernsPicks**

# Emma Cowell's
# Greek Travel Guide

It was love at first sight! The moment I stepped onto the mainland of Greece, I knew my life would change, but I had no idea just how that would manifest. Fourteen years ago, we were invited by our dearest friends to join their annual Greek holiday. I can't put my finger on why I adore the place so much. I immediately felt a heightened sense of connection to the country, the landscape, food and culture. Whether it was my childhood obsession with the myths and legends of Ancient Greece, there was something almost tangible in the air that resonated with me . . . an echo from a life lived before, perhaps. I felt like I was meant to be there at that precise moment in time, like it was destiny.

Many people immediately think of the islands when it comes to Greece, but the mainland is just as rich in spectacular scenery. Stunning Instagram-worthy sandy beaches, simple shoreline tavernas and cooler mountain microclimates mean you don't have to board a ferry or hop to an outcrop to soak up authentic Greek life.

In 2013, the summer after my mother died, I found an incredible peace and healing, a spiritual alignment by being there, finding the space to process what life looked like without her. Greece gave me what I needed when I needed it, even before I knew what I was looking for. When I came to write my debut novel, *One Last Letter from Greece* – pouring my grief into a love story celebrating the mother-daughter bond – I set it in the place that had captured my heart in the southern Peloponnese: Methoni. It's around an hour's drive from Kalamata airport over hilltops and through olive groves, navigating sheer ravines which reveal tantalising glimpses of the sea. It's a beautiful place, guarded by a castle built by the Venetians in 1209 which hugs the bay with its ancient arms. Due to the protection around the ruined ramparts, there isn't much more that can be built, and it retains a charming authenticity. In my first novel, I admit I tinkered with the geography – sorry! – but the places featured are real. The bustling harbour town of Pylos with its giant trees creating a natural leafy canopy in the square is the perfect people-watching idyll as locals go about their business. I have whiled away countless hours nursing an ice cold frappé, watching the scurrying to and from the bakeries to secure the last slice of *spanakopita* – a life-changing spinach and cheese pie. There are several bakeries that coexist there and I've sampled delights from them all, returning for more each time I visit. Pylos is also a working port where you can observe the fishermen tending and mending their nets as hopeful cats pray for a scrap to be thrown their way.

One of the most spectacular features of the Peloponnese is the varied archaeological digs. The Palace of Nestor – around eleven miles from Pylos – was a key site in *Mycenaean* times and is one of the best-preserved palaces in Greece. It is mentioned in Homer's *Odyssey*, no less! The last time I visited, archaeologists were busy excavating, and it was fascinating to watch their painstaking efforts armed only with a toothbrush and scalpel. Over several decades, expert teams have uncovered artifacts dating back to 1200BC and early examples of drainage and sewerage systems have been revealed along with an extensive clay jar system for storing and preserving olive oil – the prized nectar of the gods!

But the ultimate place to walk in the footsteps of the past is Ancient Messene or Messinae. It is an almost complete city with a full-sized stadium, gymnasium, agora and temples. But the jewel in the crown is the breath-taking amphitheatre. Concealed initially behind the brow of a hill, you cannot quite believe it is real as each step forward reveals its beauty. The magical part of this site is you can touch the cool stone columns, sit on a marble throne in the theatre and trace the mosaics with your fingers. It was founded in approximately 370BC and is the most precious gift to immerse yourself in history. It's approximately half an hour from Kalamata airport and is always uncrowded, with the majority of tourists heading for the famed Olympia or other places of note. It is an undiscovered gem in the Peloponnese and even if a coach load of people arrive, it is so vast, you won't see another soul. My tip is to go early in the morning with a good litre bottle of water with you. There's a fountain to refill but if it's hot and you're determined to cover the several miles to see all the wonders, you'll need to replenish your fluids to brace for the walk back up the hill.

*The House in the Olive Grove* is set in Petalidi which is another village-cum-town, around twenty minutes from Kalamata airport. It tends to be a thoroughfare for tourists heading to Koroni along the coast, but it's definitely worth a visit, if only for lunch. There are fabulous tavernas around the sleepy main square where the church stands sentinel. But along the promenade, you will find a couple of fantastic fish tavernas. A chance stop and discovery of one of those eateries became my inspiration and ultimately the setting for Maria's Kitchen. I was in Kardamyli on the Mani peninsula (another beautiful part of the mainland) and met a wonderful Polish lady called Monica who had two chihuahuas who were available for constant cuddles! She told me about Petalidi and recommended where to stay. I spent a couple of days there and it certainly made an impact. The stony beaches and the buoyant salty water yielded yet another version of Greece to inspire me.

I couldn't imagine writing about somewhere without being immersed in the scents and smells of a place. Greece, for me, is the ultimate sensual experience. Earthy oregano floats on the wind, ensuring food is never far from your mind. I feel incredibly lucky to have been able to write in Greece. When I'm there, I feel a deeper connection to the scenery in front of me, recreating a moment experienced or overheard on the page. It feels as if the country becomes another character in my novels. Sense of place is what I often connect to in the books I read, so, I've tried to write a love letter to a country which has given me so much and has truly changed my life in countless ways.

And then there's the food . . . a theme for sure in this book and my first book – it's impossible to avoid in Greece! Being able to relive my own personal discovery of the delicious Greek cuisine through my characters has been a way to pay homage to the scores of talented home-cooks I've met over the years – the fiercest experts in their own kitchens. If you want to create authentic Greek cooking at home, I heartily recommend the Greek chef Akis Petretzikis, or try a Cypriot twist with the lovely Theo Michaels, or my wonderful friend from Crete, Irini Tzortzoglou. If you've read my first book, you'll know that I'm in a full-time relationship with the Greek orange cake, *Portokalopita*. I've tried so many versions but in Irini's book, *Under the Olive Tree*, she does a killer citrus version and it's heaven! Her recipe for the Greek Easter cookies mentioned in this novel is fabulous too. I will also be sharing some of my recipes on my website or on social media, so keep your eyes peeled and your tastebuds poised for a slice of Greek deliciousness!

A sneak preview for you . . . despite having waxed lyrical about the mainland of Greece which I will continue to visit and adore, for my third novel, I am off to a very special island. I hope you can join me for my next Grecian adventure.

# Questions for your Book Club

- What three words would you use to describe *The House in the Olive Grove*, and why?

- This book is set in a beautiful seaside village in Greece called Petalidi. Is Greece familiar to you? Did you learn anything new about Greek culture, food or traditions?

- Which of the point of view characters – Maria, Kayla and Alessandra – did you relate to the most, and why?

- The monogamy versus polygamy argument is a key element in *The House in the Olive Grove*. Do you agree with Alessandra that 'love comes in different guises and is not the same for everyone'?

- Maria receives anonymous threats throughout the story. Did your suspicions shift to and from different characters? Did you ever believe that Leonidas was behind this?

- Why do you think the author chose to include the bee extracts? What do you think these add to the narrative?

- Cooking and food are at the heart of the novel – it is what the three women bond over, and it helps Maria to reconnect with the rest of the village. Do you agree that food has the power to heal?

- Maria, Kayla and Alessandra are all on their own journeys towards self-acceptance. Do you think they achieve this by the end? And what role did they play in each other's journeys?

Fern's
Picks

**An exclusive extract from Fern's new novel**

# *The* Good Servant

*March 1932*

Marion Crawford was not able to sleep on the train, or to eat the carefully packed sandwiches her mother had insisted on giving her. Anxiety, and a sudden bout of homesickness, prohibited both.

What on earth was she doing? Leaving Scotland, leaving everything she knew? And all on the whim of the Duchess of York, who had decided that her two girls needed a governess exactly like Miss Crawford.

Marion couldn't quite remember how or when she had agreed to the sudden change. Before she knew it, it was all arranged. The Duchess of York was hardly a woman you said no to.

Once her mother came round to the idea, she was in a state of high excitement and condemnation. 'Why would they want *you?*' she had asked, 'A girl from a good, working class family? What do you know about how these people live?' She had stared at Marion, almost in reverence. 'Working for the royal family . . . They must have seen something in you. My daughter.'

On arrival at King's Cross, Marion took the underground to Paddington. She found the right platform for the Windsor train and, as she had a little time to wait, ordered a cup of tea, a scone and a magazine from the station café.

She tried to imagine what her mother and stepfather were doing right now. They'd have eaten their tea and have the wireless on, tuned to news most likely. Her mother would have her mending basket by her side, telling her husband all about Marion's send off. She imagined her mother rambling on as the fire in the grate hissed and burned.

The train was rather full, but Marion found a seat and settled down to flick through her magazine. Her mind couldn't settle. Through the dusk she watched the alien landscape and houses spool out beside her. Dear God, what was she doing here, so far away from family and home? What was she walking into?

When the conductor walked through the carriage announcing that Windsor would be the next stop, she began to breathe deeply and calmly, as she had been taught to do before her exams. She took from her bag, for the umpteenth time, the letter from her new employers. The instructions were clear: she was to leave the station and look for a uniformed driver with a dark car.

She gazed out of the window as the train began to slow.

# Available now!

Fern's Picks

*The No.1 Sunday Times bestselling author returns*

### 1932. Dunfermline, Scotland.
Marion Crawford, a bright, ambitious young teacher, is ready to make her mark on the world. Until a twist of fate changes the course of her life forever…

### 1936. Windsor Castle.
At first this ordinary woman is in a new world, working as the governess to two young princesses, in a household she calls home but where everyone is at a distance. As the course of history changes, she finds herself companion to the future Queen, and indispensable to the crown. And slowly their needs become her needs. Their lives become hers.

It's then she meets George, and falls in love for the first time. Now Marion faces an impossible choice: her sense of duty or the love of her life.

### Available now!